BLIND
FAITH

A NOVEL

Alicia Beckman

CROOKED
LANE

NEW YORK

Published in the United States by Crooked Lane Books, an imprint of The Quick Brown Fox & Company LLC.

Crooked Lane Books and its logo are trademarks of The Quick Brown Fox & Company LLC.

Library of Congress Catalog-in-Publication data available upon request.

ISBN (hardcover): 978-1-63910-178-8
ISBN (ebook): 978-1-63910-179-5

Cover design by Nicole Lecht

Photos by Geran de Klerk, Unsplash

Printed in the United States.

www.crookedlanebooks.com

Crooked Lane Books
34 West 27th St., 10th Floor
New York, NY 10001

First Edition: October 2022

10 9 8 7 6 5 4 3 2 1

For Debbie Burke

*How lucky I've been to find such a terrific
critique partner and friend.*

Remembrance may be the ally of justice,
but it is no reliable friend to peace.

—David Rieff

MONDAY
February 29, 2016
Billings, Montana

Sometimes change happens where you least expect it.

Lindsay Keller scanned the deed to the Rainbow Bar, the longest continuously operating bar in Billings, one more time. The redbrick building had anchored the Montana Avenue business district almost since the city's founding, and it had been an anchor of her life, too. On summer Sundays when she was a kid, her parents had dragged her along when they stopped for a beer after fishing on the Yellowstone, and old Pete Stenerud had made her a Green River or a cherry Coke.

She'd sat at the Rainbow's gleaming mahogany bar for her first legal drink, home from college on spring break and brandishing her driver's license with the magic date as though it were an Academy Award. When the boy she was with had one too many, she'd called her dad to come get her. Not something a girl did back then. Not something she would have done, before the accident.

The intercom buzzed: Carla with a call from the city attorney on another matter, another old building with a checkered past, this one a theater. Finally, she was working with an investor who had the experience to match his vision, if the city could pony up a little money. They went back and forth, the legal details clicking into place. Yes, she would write up the deal. Next on her list.

If people would stop interrupting her.

She hung up the phone and picked up the deed again.

Ole Stenerud, long since gone, had signed the 1935 contract for purchase from the Hamm Brewing Company, though everybody knew both the beer hall and the hotel upstairs were his mother's domain. In those days, Montana law required a man's name on the documents, and even the old lady couldn't fight that. The law was the law. Ole had left the place to his son, Pete, ignoring his daughter, Rose. Hadn't been hard to tell being passed over still galled Rose, but she was getting the last word. By week's end, the Rainbow would belong to her, her son, and her grandson.

There was a certain sweetness to helping make that happen, wasn't there?

"*Hamm's, the beer refreshing.*" The jingle began to play in Lindsay's head, not for the first time.

She heard the outer office door open and heavy footsteps squeak across the old pine floor. She wasn't expecting anyone. Let Carla handle it.

She reached for the next document in the file, the property tax calculations. Not just a spreadsheet; to her, the rows of figures were men on bar stools. Bottles of whiskey lined up just so. Glasses old Pete polished till they shone. Would young Thomas, soon to be the face of the new Rainbow, uphold the same standards? You never knew what might happen, did you, when one generation gave way to the next.

You never knew about your kids. She pushed that thought aside.

"*From the land of sky-blue waters,*" the jingle continued. In law school, everyone was a plaintiff's lawyer or a criminal lawyer in the making—on the side of right and justice. And she had worked as a prosecutor for a few years, in the courthouse only a few blocks away.

But that door was closed.

The liquor license transfer had finally made it past the eagle-eyed bureaucrats of the Liquor Control Board, but where was the file? She pushed back her chair. Carla would know.

"I'm sorry, Ms. Keller is on a deadline," she heard her secretary say. "If you'd like to make an appointment—"

Both Carla and the visitor turned their heads at her approach. Lindsay took in the man's worn brown Carhartts flecked with drywall mud, the hammer loop stretched from use, the dusty tan work boots. *"A man who worked an honest day,"* her father would have said. But what was his name?

She stepped forward, the name bubbling up as she held out her hand. "Trevor. Nice to see you. What can I do for you?"

"You remember that house we bought on a tax sale—you put all the details together," the man said. "The one we moved to a vacant lot over on North 24th."

They were made for the home and garden channel, Trevor Morris and his business partner. Two young, hunky guys who bought up houses sinking halfway into the earth and turned them into charmers. She nodded and he went on.

"A bunch of old wooden crates were stashed in the basement. We hauled them to our shop, but one got mixed in with our stuff. Cracked it open the other day and found this." He reached into a pocket and pulled out a black leather wallet. "It's got a guy's ID and a photo, some cash, and a couple of cards."

"Cash? That's strange. Just drop it off at the police station."

"I meant to, but we're racing the bank's clock on this job, so when I drove by your office and a parking spot opened up, I figured you'd know how to handle it."

"Sure," Lindsay said. "Carla can drop it off. No charge."

He handed her the wallet and she thumbed it open, the dust coating her fingers. From behind the plastic window, next to a gold medal the size of a nickel, a face stared at her. Stared through the clouded film, through the years, and right into her gut.

"We've got our eyes on an old warehouse down on Second," Morris was saying. "Any luck, we'll make an offer in a week or so, soon as we get the specs on the structural steel. I'll call you about the contracts."

"Good. Yes. Do that," she replied. He closed the heavy oak door behind him, satisfied with himself, his problem solved.

She could feel Carla watching her as she studied the face of a man she had admired, even loved. The man who had set her drive for justice in gear, whose disappearance and presumed murder still cast a shadow over the Magic City.

Her fingers wrapped around the dry leather and snapped the wallet shut.

TUESDAY
September 19, 1972
western Montana

The only sound in the car was Tony's heartbeat. No radio signal could penetrate these mountains, the woods so thick the road appeared to be carved through the trees.

Tony liked the silence.

He glanced at his watch, the large white face with its metallic green glow reflecting the last of the daylight. Any minute now.

A semi sped north, its trailer painted with the red and green "Consolidated Freightways" logo. Cornflake. A few minutes later, the light blue Ford station wagon came into view, southbound, a man at the wheel. Alone.

Tony eased his old brown Plymouth onto the highway. *Be careful.* At dusk, suicidal deer could leap onto the road in the blink of an eye and ruin everyone's plans. If he did this right, that's what the highway patrol would think.

He caught up with the station wagon exactly where he'd intended, hanging back so the driver didn't get suspicious. He confirmed the number three on the plates. Yellowstone County.

All just as he'd been told.

He followed the vehicle, letting the driver get nervous. Waiting for the right moment.

Now. He pulled close, too close, riding the man's bumper. The driver glanced in his mirror, eased up on the gas, slid toward the narrow shoulder in the universal signal to pass. But that wasn't Tony's plan. He bumped the wagon, then fell back. Took a few breaths. Sped up and bumped it again. By this point, the driver would be good and nervous, ready to react to anything. The driver had a family, too, hundreds of miles away in Billings. And Tony knew what a man would do to protect his family.

But he couldn't think about that. He had made his bargain with the devil, and he intended to keep it. Even though he was only adding to his guilt. He could never undo what had happened all those years ago at another mountain lake, never make up for the pain it had caused. Never break free.

They reached the open spot high above the lake, where nothing would stop a car from plunging down the steep shale slope into the water. Deadly cold, even on a sunny day. One more hard shove. He gritted his teeth and punched the gas, forcing his body to do what it didn't want to do, what it recoiled from doing. The sound of metal on metal scraped his ears as his bumper hit the rear of the wagon. Down it went.

Down, down, down. Even through his closed windows, Tony could hear the wagon crashing over the rocks and through the brush, the blare of the horn breaking the silence.

Or maybe those sounds were all in his head.

He let out a breath and sped on by. Tucked the Plymouth deep in the woods at the next turnoff. Picked his way through the pines, steadying himself against the trunks of the lodge poles and ponderosas, his thick, sweat-stained leather gloves catching on the rough bark. *For Chrissake, Woijowski, don't twist an ankle here, of all godforsaken places.* The forest duff gave off a dark, musky smell, the smell of fallen logs and small animals decomposing.

Ahead, he found the wagon. It had dived straight down the incline, the front end underwater, the engine steaming, the driver's door crumpled. Acid welled in Tony's mouth. He crouched on his haunches, aware of the weight of the pistol in the pocket of his leather jacket.

He watched. And waited.

The wagon rocked as the driver struggled to open the door.

It had been meant to look like an accident, an injured man drowning in a mountain lake. Call it payback, or fate. What goes around comes around. Figured, Tony thought. Fuckup that he was, he couldn't even manage that.

After a long moment, he pushed himself up, sidestepped down the hill, and plunged into the lake. When the driver saw Tony, waist-deep in the frigid water, he pressed his bloodied face against the spidered window and hope flashed in his eyes. Tony fought back the urge to rescue. He had never done anything like this before, and God help him, he never would again.

But this wasn't about him. It had never been about either of them.

There was no hope. But Tony wouldn't let a wounded deer suffer—he could do no less for this man, a clueless fool dying for other men's sins. He reached into his pocket, the plan be damned.

MONDAY
February 29, 2016
Billings

"How can I live with myself?" the woman asked, her voice high and thin. "I take karate class for exercise. Not to actually hurt people." She ran her hands through her short brown hair, fingers interlocking on top of her head.

"Honey, there's no telling what he would have done to you," her husband said. "He had a knife." He sat across from her, one forearm resting on the scarred tabletop in the Billings Police Department interview room.

Hands cradling her skull, as if to keep all the colliding images and emotions inside, the woman shook her head, her skin pale, her breath shallow, though the attack in the parking garage had been hours ago. Her husband meant well, but he didn't know what she was going through.

Detective Brian Donovan knew.

"You'd be surprised what you can live with," Donovan said, and her red-rimmed eyes met his. She lowered her hands.

"I don't get why you came downtown anyway," the husband said.

"It was for work. I told you," the woman replied.

"You work at the mall," he answered, as if she didn't know that. She let out an exasperated breath and turned her head.

"No reason to think he won't recover," Donovan said, banking on the odds. "We'll know more when the scumbag's out of surgery." He'd seen it before, a husband snapping at his crime-victim wife out of his own fear, or maybe his inability to protect her. Comfort wasn't Donovan's job, but kindness didn't cost him anything. He laid his fingertips on her arm. "Your quick thinking and your training kept you alive. Who knows how many other women you saved."

"You think he did this before?" Her voice trembled.

"He wasn't on our radar," Donovan admitted. "Colorado driver's license, key to a cheap motel—probably new in town. Until we get his record, we can only guess he was after more than your purse. But guys like that come with history."

And this guy's history had taken a swing for the worse when a small, fortyish woman in a puffy pink coat had kicked him where it counted. He'd stumbled backward, fallen, and smacked his head on the concrete in a downtown parking garage, his blood spattering the woman, the floor, and a white Honda. The knife had gone flying, but they'd found it wedged under the rear tire of a pickup two stalls away.

When he got home tonight, Donovan intended to dig out the brochure his daughter had brought home for the mother–daughter martial arts class at the Y. Beth, his wife, hadn't been interested—they didn't have time; nothing would happen in Billings; what could they learn in six weeks?

Plenty, he thought. *They could learn plenty.*

"You should call that therapist you used to see," the husband said. The woman pressed her lips together. The evidence techs had taken her torn, bloody coat, and she pulled the lightweight blanket the EMTs had draped around her shoulders a little tighter.

"Talk to your sensei," Donovan told her. "He's a good man. He'll know how you feel."

Donovan walked the couple to the entrance, held the glass door, and promised to be in touch. Watched them head up North 27th, the man reaching out his hand, the woman not taking it.

She had stayed calm at the scene and in the interview room, but the nightmares would come. Terror she couldn't explain, and that her husband couldn't forgive.

All while the scumbag enjoyed top-notch medical care and future room and board at taxpayer expense.

Inside, Donovan crossed the lobby to the stairwell and punched in his code. The buzzer sounded and the latch on the steel door opened. It banged shut behind him.

He took the stairs two at a time.

The detectives' second-floor office was empty. Donovan tossed his notepad on his desk and dropped into his chair. It squeaked in protest.

God, it was good to have their man in custody, but he hated to miss the chase. Not that he would ever say so, but there was something satisfying about turning the hunter into prey and snaring him.

He clicked open the case file, so new all it contained was the dispatcher's report and the statement from the eyewitness, a man who had left a package in his car and jogged back for it just in time to see the split-second confrontation.

Donovan logged into the interstate exchange system so he could request a criminal records search. Not that prior bad acts, as the law called them, were admissible, but they could give you clues, tell you what to look for, who you were looking at. You needed those details if you wanted to build a case that would stick.

"Vengeance is mine," the God of the Old Testament had said. But the human heart wants justice in this world.

The screen blurred. All he could see was the knife, a six-inch steel blade and a bone handle, lying on the concrete floor before the evidence techs packed it up.

Where'd this low-rent creep get a bone-handled knife anyway?

Without thinking, Donovan ran his left hand up his right arm, fingers tracing the scar put there five years ago. Five and a half, now. South Boston. *His* scumbag had come ripping toward him, a knife with a plain plastic grip in hand, intent to kill clear on the face Donovan still saw every night. He'd already stabbed two civilians. Donovan had taken aim and fired, hit the man square in the chest, but he'd had the drug-fueled strength to lunge forward, and his blade sliced into Donovan's arm at the exact instant that Donovan's second shot hit home.

He'd been lucky, everyone had said. Deaf as a haddock for hours, from the gunshots, but lucky.

Shitty kind of luck, that you had to kill a man to survive.

But he understood, in vivid flashes, that cops and criminals had more in common than prowling on opposite sides of the law.

Goddamnit. God*damn*it. Why did he have to have a knife?

Donovan exhaled. The fan on the wall heater kicked on, and for a moment, he thought it was his own breath, hot and noisy.

At least the woman in the pink coat would not have a reminder of the worst thing she'd ever done etched on her skin.

Caffeine. He needed it, like a junkie or an alcoholic in withdrawal, craving a jolt to steady the pulses and clear the vision.

He trotted down the stairs to the basement. He was turning thirty-five this year, and Beth had insisted it was time to start eating better. No way would he stop taking cream and two sugars in his coffee, like it was meant to be drunk, but giving up soda had been easy. What everyone out here called pop.

But right now, nothing else would do. He fed a dollar bill into the machine and drank half the can. He was starting up the second flight of stairs when the lobby door opened and the desk sergeant stuck her head in.

"You hiding from me, Donovan? You got a visitor." She held the door and he jogged back down the stairs.

His shoulders relaxed when he saw the slender brunette in the lobby, her black coat hanging open over a white blouse and a black-and-white-striped skirt, a bag over her shoulder. She slapped something against the palm of her hand, once, then twice, and jumped when he spoke, her hand closing around the object.

"Ms. Keller. What a surprise. What can I do for you?" He held out his hand.

"I need to talk to you. In private." Her voice was brusque, anxious, without the warmth and easy small talk he'd observed the few times they'd met. "And it's Lindsay, please."

He gestured toward the interview room, followed her in, and closed the door. She didn't sit. Neither did he.

Finally, when she still hadn't spoken, he said softly, "Lindsay, what's this about? Scott? The girls? A client?"

"A dead man," she said, and dropped the object she held, a black leather wallet, onto the table. She raised her dark eyes to his. "Twenty years dead."

* * *

Somewhere, some manufacturer of three-ring binders had turned a profit because of the Leary case.

Donovan slapped the dust off his hands. Boxes and boxes of binders. It had taken him and a patrol officer three trips to haul them up from storage.

Cops liked to say that ninety percent of the time, in a cold case, the killer's name or a critical clue was in the file. Cops liked to say a lot of things. In his experience—and Billings didn't have a lot of unsolved murders, but he'd helped clear two—this saying was true.

Twelve boxes. There better be a needle in all that hay.

For now, it was wait-and-see in the case of the parking garage asshole. Waiting on the forensics and return calls from detectives in other states. Waiting for the guy to regain consciousness. Waiting to see what charges the prosecutor would file.

Donovan had thought he might catch a breather, get home at a decent hour for a change.

And then Lindsay Keller had shown up with that dusty old wallet.

In 1995, when Father Mike Leary disappeared, Brian Donovan had been a smart-ass teenager heading down the wrong road in a rundown neighborhood in Boston. But he'd heard about Father Leary his first month on the job in Billings. Everyone on the force knew the case. Christ, everybody wanted to solve it.

They'd never had a decent suspect. Nothing but boxes crammed with reports, transcripts, and photographs that should have told them everything, but didn't. All just trivia, an unfinished story, waiting for the ending.

Now, the wallet.

Jesus.

He rolled a chair to the end of the conference table. Cold cases haunted police departments. This one was complicated. Used to be, you couldn't think why anyone would kill a priest. But now . . . When Donovan was in Catholic high school, everybody knew stuff had happened, that there were some priests you didn't want to be alone with. The big scandal in Boston didn't break until after he'd graduated, when the newspaper exposed the Church for paying hush money and moving priests around without telling parishioners they were perverts, but you knew.

Turned out that had happened all across the country. Not so much now, thank God, or his kids wouldn't go within a mile of a church, let alone go to Catholic school.

Roy Small, the original detective on this case, hadn't been afraid to ask questions about Leary. Came up with zip, but he'd asked. They might have to ask again.

Or maybe this killing had nothing to do with sex.

Donovan popped open a fresh Coke and leaned back, the 1995 incident report in hand. Start at the beginning, work his way through. Soon as he got the chance, he'd quiz the contractor who gave Lindsay Keller the wallet—the first piece of evidence to surface in years—though the story sounded plausible. Maybe they'd get lucky with the forensic analysis.

But how the hell had a dead priest's wallet gotten into a long-forgotten box of crap in a run-down rental?

And why was Lindsay Keller so shook up? Seemed unlike the woman he'd first met when Beth got hired at the college. Her husband, Scott Breck, had been on the search committee, and they'd hosted a welcome reception for the art department faculty and staff in their backyard. But Breck had left teaching to focus on his sculpture. When had Donovan last seen Lindsay? Some gallery opening, no doubt. Donovan racked his brain for the word that summed her up. More than calm or relaxed. Stylish and—what?

Poised, that was it. Lindsay Keller had poise.

Not this morning, she didn't. Donovan put her at about fifty, though still good-looking. Keller sounded German. You never knew with Germans—they could be Jewish, Lutheran, or Catholic. You couldn't tell much by a name anymore. She'd said Father Leary was one of her favorite teachers. Her jaw had quivered when she'd said it, and he'd wondered, but she'd seen the question coming and said no, he was never inappropriate—a vague, all-purpose word. He hadn't pushed her; his radar said she was telling the truth. What she knew of it. She'd known Leary years before the man's disappearance. Who knew what had happened in the meantime?

Donovan settled in for a long read.

Two Cokes and two hours later, he reached for the phone.

THURSDAY
September 21, 1972

The Billings Gazette—The Missoula County sheriff has identified the man whose body was found Tuesday evening in a remote lake in the Swan Valley of western Montana as Robert Ziegler, 33, of Billings. Ziegler, a married father of four, was found dead in his car, a light blue 1967 Ford station wagon. He had been shot.

The vehicle was found partially submerged in icy lake waters, its front end heavily damaged. The sheriff refused to comment on possible explanations, saying it would be speculation at this point.

Ziegler was reportedly returning home from a trip to inspect farm equipment for sale near Kalispell. A fourth-generation farmer west of Billings, Ziegler was an outspoken opponent of growth that he believed would result in the destruction of valuable farmland. "The houses of Billings will have beautiful lawns," he wrote in a letter to the editor earlier this year, "but the people will have no wheat or corn. We must preserve our land, as both our heritage and our future."

The vehicle was discovered by a passing trucker, who made an anonymous call to the sheriff from a service station

15

in Seeley Lake. Sheriff's deputies were able to locate the vehicle and body Tuesday night, but due to darkness, were unable to retrieve either until Wednesday morning, with assistance from a towing company and an underwater diver.

A coroner's investigation is pending. Funeral arrangements for Ziegler have not yet been announced. Anyone with additional information is asked to contact the Missoula County sheriff or local law enforcement.

FRIDAY
September 18, 1981

"Remember, O most gracious Virgin Mary, never was it known that anyone who fled to thy protection, implored thy help, or sought thy intercession was left unaided."

In the back row, Carrie West pressed her hands together and mouthed the words as the other girls sprinted through the prayer at a speed they would never reach while actually running. Though she was careful not to fidget, a girl in the front row tugged at the clingy green bottom of her gym uniform while another mimed rude noises, the girls around them trying not to snort. At the front of the gym, Sister Claire gazed reverently at the small bronze crucifix mounted on the wall, next to the clock in its black wire cage.

"Inspired by this confidence, I fly unto thee, O Virgin of virgins, my mother; to thee I come, before thee I stand, sinful and sorrowful."

Three weeks into senior year at the Catholic high school in Billings and acutely aware that she was still "the new girl," Carrie had already learned that Sister Claire viewed fidgeting as evidence of an idle mind, redeemable only by running up and down the metal bleachers that stretched along one side of the gym for the rest of the period. Sister loved sentencing wayward girls to run the bleachers.

"O Mother of the Word Incarnate, despise not my petitions, but in thy mercy hear and answer me. *A-MEN.*" The girls punched out the final word. The girl in front of Carrie, Mary Ellen Simonich, jabbed her right elbow into Lindsay Keller's side, knocking the shorter, dark-haired girl out of formation just as Sister Claire pivoted to face them. Her short black veil flared, mirroring the swoosh on her Nikes.

"Miss Keller!" Sister bellowed, the last name coming out "Kellah" in the New York accent Carrie only recognized because of the movies. "Can you not stand still to honor the Mother of God for one blessed minute?"

Carrie stiffened, heard the girls around her suck in their breath.

"I'm sorry, Sister," Lindsay said, her voice steady, straddling the line between penitence and defiance. Out of Sister's line of sight, Mary Ellen, a tiny smirk on her broad face, exchanged eyerolls with the girl on her left. Jana something—light brown hair, good in business math and terrible at PE.

Sister continued to glare at Lindsay, fingers white against her clipboard. But Lindsay didn't buckle, and after a silence so long Carrie wasn't sure she could stand still another half second, Sister spun away. She gripped the clipboard to her side with her elbow, grabbed the handles of two racks filled with sports balls, and shoved them forward. One rack glided smoothly across the gym's wood floor, but the other lurched sideways like a balky grocery cart. It began to tip and Carrie dashed forward to steady it. No telling how long they'd have to run the bleachers if the balls spilled across the floor.

Two volleyball nets stretched across the gym.

"We will work on our serve today." Sister said, making a rhyme of "WUHkk" and "SUHvv." Her Spanish and history teachers were part of a group of nuns from Ireland, and Carrie loved their kindness and the soft rolling lilt of their voices. But those blessings had escaped Sister Claire.

"No, no, no, Miss Stenerud." The nun stalked past the other girls and grabbed Jana's wrist as the girl swung her fist up toward the black and white ball. "We do not serve underhand. We serve like this." Sister snatched the ball, tossed it in the air with her left hand, and smashed it with her right fist. The ball arced over the net, right at Lindsay Keller, the designated retriever. Sister grabbed another ball off the rolling rack and thrust it at Jana.

Ball in hand, Jana extended her left arm. Her eyes flicked toward Sister, then she raised her right arm and crooked her elbow, fist hovering above her shoulder. Her left hand jerked up and down, but the ball stayed glued to her palm. A thin line of sweat ran down her temple.

Jana repositioned herself and tried again. This time, she managed to toss the ball weakly into the air and fling her right arm forward. Her fist glanced off the side of the ball, and it squirted toward Carrie, who caught it easily.

"Relax your left arm," she said in a low voice as she gave Jana the ball. "Don't hold it so stiff. Pop the ball up with your fingers, and keep your eye on the ball, not your hand."

Jana nodded once and shuffled her feet. By this time, the girls at the other end of the gym had stopped their practice to watch. Jana's jaw quivered as she raised the ball and prepared to swing.

Slowly, slowly, Carrie said to herself, eyes on her terrified classmate, mouthing the words as she had the morning prayer. *Softly, softly.*

On the fifth try, the ball hit the top of the net and tumbled into Lindsay's arms. All the girls cheered. Even Sister seemed relieved when Jana stepped aside, a shaky smile on her pale face, and Carrie stepped up. Three tries, three perfect—"PUH-feckt"—serves. Sister went through the motions of adjusting Carrie's stance, but it was clear she recognized that Carrie needed little instruction.

For the next twenty-five minutes, Carrie chased balls, volleyed with the other girls, and tried to forget she wasn't one of them. Not yet. Soon, maybe. These girls had spent every day together since freshman year, some since first grade. When they'd lived in a town with Catholic schools, that's where Carrie and Ginger, her little sister, had gone. Public or Catholic, though, the response had always been the same. The other kids regarded her with curiosity at first, giving her a verbal jab or two, exchanging quizzical looks or whispers. But it didn't take long for them to forget she was new, especially when they saw that she was a natural athlete.

No, it was she who held herself apart. She who knew they wouldn't stay long. They'd followed her dad's work in trucking and construction, until he went in the Army. Then he'd been killed when she was nine, in far-off Vietnam.

Her family kept moving so Mom could get a better job. And then she died, too, spring of freshman year, not long after they'd moved to Miles City. Their grandmother, Baba Irene, had come to take care of them and keep house for the parish priest, Father Michael Leary. Two and a half years in the same house, in the same school. Carrie had almost believed they would stay put.

But when Father Mike, as the girls called him, was transferred to Billings last summer, Baba said the priests at St. Patrick's needed a new housekeeper, and the opportunity was too good, for her and for them, to pass up. So they'd moved again.

It was going to be the last time. She'd graduate in the spring, and no one would ever force her to pack up and pick up again.

"VPL," Mary Ellen said, and Carrie resisted the temptation to tug at her bottom. These uniforms were beyond ugly. But Mary Ellen was snickering at Lindsay Keller, standing at the serving line, the ball in hand. Lindsay paid no attention. She wasn't as good as Carrie, but she managed three decent serves. Then the whistle blew and they all surged toward the locker room, the girls stuck holding volleyballs veering out of formation to stash them on the carts.

In the locker room, Sister positioned herself near the door, clipboard in hand, eying them fiercely. They hadn't had locker room monitors at her old high school and Sister's vigilance struck Carrie as strange, but the other girls didn't seem to mind.

Do what they do, she told herself. *Act like they act.* That was the secret.

The cramped room had one window, high above a bank of gray metal lockers and never open. The sweet-sour smell of fresh sweat mingled with the grassy scent of baby powder and the popular colognes: lemon, musk, and a hint of Grey Flannel one of the girls must have swiped from her father or an older brother.

Carrie waited her turn for the mint green–tiled showers, then stuck her arms and feet in the water. What Baba called a spit bath. She slapped a trickle of water under her arms, recoiling at the chill. One reason few girls took actual showers was that the water never warmed up.

She wrapped her thin brown towel around herself, clutching it tightly in front, and slid the shower curtain aside. She had one foot poised to step over the ledge into the main room when Sister's shrill tone pierced the air.

"Miss Old Horn," Sister Claire barked, and the babble instantly stopped.

Carrie took in the scene: Charlene Old Horn standing rigid next to a wooden bench that ran the length of the room. Long black hair in a ponytail, arms crossed over her small brown breasts, wearing nothing but white underpants dotted with pink hearts. The nun shaking a pink towel at her. A dry towel. Only Charlene's feet were wet.

Sister's eyes blazed. Her scrutiny moved from one girl to the next, some sitting, some standing. Two or three wore bras and underpants; some were partly dressed. Others, like Carrie, were wrapped in towels.

"I suppose you think this is funny," Sister said, her lips pushing forward as she spoke. "You bold girls. Laughing off cleanliness, going back to class smelling like the sewer, spraying your cheap cologne to cover up your stink." Her attention paused on the opening to the shower rooms, and Carrie froze, the thick, wet air drowning her lungs. Sister scanned the room, then settled her attention back on the shivering Charlene.

"Did they not teach you any better on the reservation?"

Someone made a noise, and Sister snapped her head toward the sound.

"Do you have something to say, Miss Keller?"

"Yes, Sister, I do," Lindsay said, stretching taller, though she was at least four inches shorter than Carrie's five eight. She was almost fully dressed, in a tan corduroy skirt and striped sweater, her feet bare. This school didn't require uniforms, except in PE, although jeans and tennis shoes were off-limits, even for the boys, who didn't have to wear hideous PE uniforms. "Just because Charlene's the only Indian in the class doesn't make her any different from the rest of us. And you had no right to tear her towel off."

The room went dead quiet but for a muffled chorus of gasps. One girl stifled a nervous laugh. "Shut *up*, Lindsay," Carrie heard Mary Ellen Simonich mutter, and she saw Jana, half naked, reach for her sweater. She glanced at the clock. They were going to be late for the next class.

"I don't suppose you showered either, Miss Keller," Sister said, her eyes boring darkly into the girl who'd dared reproach her.

Lindsay did not respond.

Sister glanced at the other girls, standing stone-still. "What are you all gawking at? Go on, get dressed, get out of here. Except the two of you." She glared first at Lindsay, then Charlene. "You will strip and go to the showers. You will stand there for three full minutes. And I'll not write you late slips for your next classes." She pulled a stopwatch from her skirt pocket.

Tension broken, the girls began to move, slowly at first, then more quickly as they realized they were running late. As they scurried to get away before Sister Claire's wrath fell on them. As they threw furtive glances at Charlene and Lindsay, wondering what would happen to them. To all of them, because surely it would be bleachers all period long for the rest of the month.

Carrie held the towel in front of her with one hand as she pulled her navy blue cotton pants on with the other. She couldn't let Sister see her dry legs and send her to the showers, too. She was elbow-to-elbow with Lindsay, who was removing her clothes.

"I can't believe you did that," Carrie said.

"Me neither. I'll probably get kicked out."

"No, you won't," said the redhead on the other side. "They wouldn't dare. You're the smartest girl in the class. But you'll be suspended from activities for ages."

"I don't care," Lindsay said, but her voice shook. "How could she be so mean to Charlene? Just because she's Crow." She yanked her towel out of her gym bag and headed to the showers, stark naked.

Sister was scary, Carrie thought as she clutched the towel to her chest with one hand and tugged her sweater over her head with the other. And Mary Ellen bore watching. But Lindsay and the other girls?

They might not be so bad.

* * *

The throng in senior hall had already begun to thin when the girls burst out of the gym, scattering like shiny glass marbles. Carrie's next class was on the same hallway, but Sister Claire's tirade had rattled her, and she didn't want to be late. She threw her gym bag inside her locker and grabbed her books. At the door to the English teacher's classroom, Mary Ellen pushed past her, Jana close behind.

The desks had been arranged in a circle, two deep, the only empty seats in the front row. Everybody else had their copies of *Hamlet* out. Carrie crossed the room and took a seat, glancing at the teacher, one of the American nuns, in a baby-blue polyester coat dress with gold buttons that strained across her ballooning chest. But the teacher said nothing.

"Act one, scene three," the boy behind her whispered. "Thanks," Carrie mouthed, and opened the small, black-trimmed paperback. They read out loud, each student taking a few lines, Sister interrupting to probe the archaic language. She was good at that, often pointing out the layers of Shakespeare's sharp humor. "Ribald," she called it, and actually seemed to understand why they were both amused and embarrassed.

The door opened, and Lindsay Keller walked in, her short hair damp at the ends.

"Sorry, Sister," she said as she slid into the empty desk next to Carrie's. "PE was so much fun, I stayed late."

How can she talk like that? Carrie wondered. But Sister merely smiled and nodded to the next student to continue reading.

After English came first lunch. Though only half the school's four hundred students had lunch this period, the cafeteria was crowded and noisy. If Baba had sent her to the public high school, with hundreds of students in each grade, she might have skipped lunch or huddled in a corner outside to eat a sandwich and an apple.

Friday was pizza day, not half bad. Lindsay was already at one of the big round tables when Carrie emerged with her tray and waved her over. She passed a table full of boys—she didn't know most of their names yet and was half glad that they ignored her—and sat next to Lindsay. Two girls replayed the scene in the locker room, mimicking the nun's pointed gestures with exaggerated movements of their eyes and chins.

"She talks like they do in *The Godfather*," one said.

"My mother saw her in the beauty shop last week," the other said, then giggled. "Underneath that veil, she colors her hair."

But the rest of the girls didn't join in the laughter, the mood subdued for a Friday.

"You're going to get called in," Mary Ellen said to Lindsay. "Maybe your parents, too."

"I don't care," Lindsay said. "What she did was wrong."

"You aren't going to tell them she watches us, are you?" Jana asked, glancing around the room furtively, her voice barely above a whisper. "I mean, we are supposed to shower."

Lindsay rolled her eyes. "Too bad we don't have a volleyball team," she said to Carrie. "You're good. You might get recruited for basketball, since you're tall."

Way taller than her mother had been. Everyone said her height came from her dad.

"Is Sister Claire the coach?"

"No, thank God, or nobody would turn out," Lindsay said. "The business teacher coaches the girls. The coaches all teach—state law, I guess—but he's good. And they win."

"Thanks for showing me how to serve," Jana said to Carrie. "I'd have been doomed without you. But I think we're all in trouble now." Her eyes darted nervously to Lindsay.

Lindsay reached for her milk carton. "I just said what the rest of you were thinking."

"Like that's going to save you?" Mary Ellen picked the black olives off her second piece of pizza and made a pile of black bits on her plate. Her lemon-yellow T-shirt with the scoop neck was cute with her denim skirt, but it gave her olive skin a sallow cast, and both were tight around her middle.

If there was a battle over how a kid spoke to a teacher, the kid always lost. Even if she was standing up for a classmate, like Lindsay had been. Carrie glanced at Charlene Old Horn, who was eating a bowl of drippy canned peaches and didn't seem upset.

"Be careful how much you help the other girls in gym class," Lindsay said. "If you do it too often, Claire will get pissed that you're showing her up."

Carrie nodded and reached for her pizza.

"What are you doing here anyway, Carrie West?" Mary Ellen fired her gaze across the table. "Nobody starts a new school senior year, unless they got in trouble somewhere else."

And they all knew what "trouble" meant for girls. Carrie felt her cheeks flush red-hot.

"Lay off her, ME. She's just new in town," Jana said.

"Oh, that's right." Mary Ellen pried open a carton of chocolate milk, dropping tiny bits of paper onto the pile of olives. "You know all about what goes on at the church."

Carrie looked from one girl to the other, wondering what old argument she'd somehow stumbled into.

"You don't know everything," Jana said, then turned to Carrie. "My mom's president of the Altar Society, so I heard about your family and the house."

"Not much of a family," Mary Ellen said. "An old woman and two kids."

The words stung. Her grandmother wasn't very old, barely sixty. Carrie bet all these girls had two living parents. And grandmothers who played golf or bridge and had standing appointments at the beauty shop and met their friends for lunch. Not like hers, supporting two girls by cooking and cleaning for priests. They probably all had their own rooms, too. Lacy white bedspreads and white shag carpeting, pink princess phones with their own lines. And cars—the lot outside was packed, though most were clearly hand-me-downs, except for one bright yellow Camaro.

The house Carrie, her sister, and grandmother lived in was small but sweet, on the same block as the grade school. Ginger had cried at hearing she and Carrie weren't going to share a room anymore, until she saw her room with its bubble gum pink walls and white bedroom set—second-hand, Carrie was sure, but Ginger was too young to notice or care. It had come with pink-and-white gingham bedding, and a green fake fur throw rug. Ginger was obsessed with pink and green, choosing a green jump rope for her birthday almost the same color as the awful PE uniforms. She took that jump rope everywhere.

And Baba had exclaimed over the roses, still blooming, though they'd freeze and die back soon. Baba loved roses. Even in winter, she smelled of roses.

"The house is nice," Carrie said. "My sister loves the pink room—she's eight."

"Good." Jana picked up her pizza. "Hey, who's going to the kegger tonight? It's out at that place where your brother taught us to shoot, right, ME?"

Mary Ellen waved her hand in front of her full mouth. "Yeah. You coming, Linds? You said you aren't working tonight."

Carrie glanced at Lindsay, so smart and cool. So *bold*, as Sister Claire would say, but the teacher intended the jibe as a put-down. She'd be furious that the girls took it as a compliment. Bold Lindsay wasn't going to drink cheap beer in a field with pimply boys and Duran Duran blasting from a boom box, was she?

"Andy's coming," Mary Ellen added.

Who was Andy? Names hadn't attached to all the faces yet, but Carrie didn't think she'd heard a classmate called Andy.

"Good," Mary Ellen said, though Lindsay hadn't replied. She dropped the second pizza crust on her plate and reached for her frosted brownie. "We'll pick you up. Find a ride, new girl, and you can come, too."

Jana turned red. She shoved back her chair, the metal feet scraping on the worn brown-and-tan fake-marble linoleum. She grabbed her tray and rushed off.

The clock on the wall showed plenty of time before the next class.

"What's up with her?" Charlene said, the first words Carrie had heard her utter.

Mary Ellen shrugged. "My car only seats three, and she's got a crush on my brother."

That yellow Camaro?

"Hello, girls. Carrie, nice to see you."

She looked up, startled to hear her name. Father Leary—Father Mike—had been part of their lives for as long as she could remember, although they'd seen more of him after their father went in the Army. His sandy hair was mussed, but his blue eyes twinkled. His black priest shirt had short sleeves, exposing his freckled arms.

"Hello, Father," Lindsay said. "If you're checking up on the new girl, don't worry. We like her."

A smile played on the priest's lips. "I'm glad to hear it, Lindsay, though I had no doubt."

A boy in a green-and-white sweatshirt that was much too warm for the mid-September day approached the table, shooting a quick look at Lindsay before greeting the priest.

"Hey, Father. Come to the game tomorrow and cheer us on. We're playing Lewistown. They won on a last-minute field goal last year, but we're not letting them beat us this time."

"Wouldn't miss it, Tim," the priest said. "Just be warned, I'm declaring myself neutral next week when you play Miles City." He clapped a hand on the football player's shoulder. Father Mike had moved here midsummer, but already he knew everybody and everybody knew him. Not all the priests were so outgoing. Carrie had seen the principal come out of the chapel this morning, a distant look on his face, and she suspected he'd rather read and pray than mingle.

During class changes, he stood outside his office and watched the kids like they were aliens from another planet.

But Father Mike strolled through the lunchroom every day, stopping to chat or to swipe a french fry on Wednesday, hamburger day. He seemed happy here. Maybe, Carrie thought, she would be, too.

"I'll see some of you later this afternoon," he said, glancing around the table. "We'll be talking about ethics in the workplace. Should be a good conversation." He raised a hand and moved on.

"He's nice," Charlene said. "Not like the religion teacher we had last year." She shuddered.

Lindsay wrinkled her nose before speaking. "Yeah, he was creepy. Always wanting us to confess our sins. Like we were going to tell him all about sex, or something."

"Father Leary came to see my mom in the hospital," Charlene said. "He got the nurses to let us burn sweetgrass. They said it's stinky and we had too many people in the room, but after he talked to them, they were much nicer."

"He's like that," Carrie said. "He's always helping people. Is your mom okay?"

"Yeah. Thanks."

"Next term, the topic is morality and human relationships. He'll want to talk about sex, too—you watch." Mary Ellen shoved back her chair and picked up her tray. She didn't seem to notice that a glop of tomato sauce had fallen on her yellow shirt. "If you want to come tonight, catch a ride with Jana," she said to Carrie. "She won't stay mad long enough to stay home."

Should she? Carrie glanced at Lindsay, who was bent over, fiddling with her shoe. *Do what they do,* she'd told herself. But she'd promised Ginger they'd have fun at the school playground today and make ice cream sundaes afterward. "Thanks, but I've got plans. Maybe next time."

"Suit yourself." Mary Ellen shrugged one shoulder and walked away, leaving Carrie with the same baffling feeling she got reading Shakespeare. Like the words said one thing and meant another.

TUESDAY
March 1, 2016

Lindsay unfolded the newspaper and laid it on the oak desk in her office. Smoothed it out and reread the article. Top right, above the fold, where they put breaking news. Not that the story had changed since she'd first read it an hour ago, standing in her kitchen, barefoot in her bathrobe.

The Billings Gazette—Billings police say a man remodeling a house near North Park found a wallet believed to have belonged to Father Michael Leary, rector of St. Patrick's Co-Cathedral in Billings. Leary disappeared in 1995 after taking a late-night call requesting he visit a dying woman to administer last rites.

Inside the black leather wallet were Leary's driver's license, his ID card for St. Vincent's Hospital, and a St. Christopher's medal, along with two credit cards and an undisclosed amount of cash.

Anyone with information believed to be related to the case is asked to contact Detective Brian Donovan at the Billings Police Department.

Lindsay exhaled, her breath ragged. Donovan hadn't let any grass grow under his feet. Not that she blamed him. She'd been a prosecutor. She'd expected him to call the crime beat reporter and tell him about the wallet. They'd make a trade, Donovan betting that the story would prompt someone to speak up. The reporter would hand over any unpublished details from the newspaper's files and get a scoop in exchange. Could you call it a scoop in a town with one paper? Promises aside, the cops would reveal what they wanted to reveal, when they wanted to reveal it. The guy at the Gazette was good, a veteran reporter who knew how to scout around for living relatives and chat up people who'd known the victim. But he wasn't likely to unearth anything new on his own, not in a twenty-year-old case.

But she hadn't expected Donovan to move so fast. Heck, he couldn't have gotten through the file yet—she could only imagine how big it was.

Her hand shook as she slid open the lap drawer and pulled out the plastic sleeve holding one more item Father Leary had kept close. She shouldn't have taken it, should have handed the wallet over with everything still inside, but she hadn't been able to stop herself. The photo held a secret, she was sure—why else would he have carried it, tucked behind his driver's license, next to the medal? She was equally certain Leary's secret was not the obvious one, when it came to a priest. And that exposing it now would do no one any good.

She stared at the photo, the face of a young girl she'd seen once and never forgotten.

A girl with a green jump rope.

FRIDAY
September 18, 1981

Lindsay's bag slipped down her arm as she pushed open the high school's north door, the rough weave of the strap chafing her skin. She blinked against the bright light and hitched the bag back up on her shoulder.

Behind her, the door flew open and a dozen kids surged past her down the short flight of steps, their chatter brash and bright against the clear, sunlit-blue sky. Cerulean, the art teacher called it. If Lindsay had a favorite color, that would be it. The color of promise.

Ever since PE, she'd felt like she was swimming through Jell-O, the world around her thick and slippery. All afternoon, she'd waited for the summons to the principal's office, where her actions would be dissected, her future decided.

But it had never come.

She turned toward Division, trailing the crowd, her thoughts picking up speed even as her feet dragged. At a break in traffic, a group of kids dashed across the street, but she hung back, waiting on the curb.

"You were amazing," a soft voice said, and Lindsay turned to see the new girl, the volleyball whiz with the high cheekbones and thick blond braid, a faded red daypack over one shoulder. *Carrie.* "I wish I could be that brave. Great bag, by the way."

"Brave, or stupid," Lindsay said as a white car stopped to let them cross. Ruining her future because she couldn't keep her mouth shut. "But thanks. Mary Ellen's mom gave the art class a stack of upholstery samples from their furniture store, and a bunch of us designed our own bags. I'm probably the only one who uses mine." She'd chosen it today to coordinate with the tan corduroy skirt she'd made, bias cut, almost managing to match the wale to her mother's exacting standards.

"They own a furniture store?" Carrie said. "My mom used to work in one, but she never brought home fabric samples."

"They own tons of stuff. Her dad owns the mall and a big construction company. They own a car dealership, too, and I don't know what else."

On the other side of the street, the girls cut through the triangular park wedged between the old part of town, laid out parallel to the railroad tracks, and the newer part, oriented to the Rims, high sandstone cliffs that bounded the Yellowstone River Valley and divided the main part of town from the Heights.

"You heading downtown?" Carrie asked.

"Just to the grade school. My mom's the secretary, and she's letting me take her car out to the mall. There's a sweater I was thinking of buying to wear tonight."

"You're going to the kegger? Aren't you worried about getting caught?" Carrie asked.

Lindsay had been to plenty of keggers and never worried about getting caught. This one felt different, but she couldn't say why. She was already screwed; what was one more disciplinary problem?

And Andy would be there. But he was even more trouble.

"I don't know if I'm going or not," Lindsay replied. "What's the point of parking a bunch of cars in a field and drinking warm beer and sloe gin till you puke? Although the music is good." And making out, and knowing you were doing something you shouldn't be doing.

"So that's what city kids do for fun," Carrie said lightly. "Go out to the country and puke. You don't know how small-town kids itch for the city."

"Billings isn't a real city. But there's movies and a few concerts, and we have the mall." Lindsay's bag threatened to slip again, weighted by the hardback copy of *The Canterbury Tales* the English teacher had lent her. "Hey, don't let Mary Ellen bug you. She likes to stir the pot. And she's always jealous of the good-looking girls."

"She'd be pretty if she weren't so mean. Oops. Sorry. But thanks." Carrie blushed. They were nearing the edge of downtown, where the older houses gave way to long blocks of low-slung buildings—offices, warehouses, plumbing suppliers. "Must be weird, going to school with the same kids all your lives."

Lindsay glanced at her, curious. Wasn't going to school with the same kids perfectly normal? "Her family lived on our block growing up. Then her dad bought a bunch of old farmland and built the mall. He made a ton of money, and they moved to a big fancy house up under the Rims. ME—we've always called her that—got all snooty, like we should do what she said because her dad gave her a Camaro when she turned sixteen."

"Hmm," Carrie said. "But everybody else is nice."

"You'll fit in great," Lindsay said. "Forget I told you any of that. Gossip is the devil's tongue."

"Now you sound like Sister Claire."

"*'Oh, you bold girls!'*" Lindsay said, mimicking the nun's scolding tones, and Carrie doubled over, laughing. "I don't know what's up with her. The younger girls get one of the Irish nuns for PE and she's really great, but then Sister Claire came and they stuck us with her. So much for actually having fun doing sports."

They'd reached North 32nd and the three-story, tan brick grade school. Lindsay had spent nearly half her life in that building. But life was changing, fast. They'd read Polonius's advice to university-bound Laertes today, and she had a few wise words for this new girl.

"Listen, if you do go out for basketball, you'll have to wear white socks and green shoes, and don't ever forget and wear the wrong shoes or socks in PE, or Claire will make you run the bleachers."

"Why is she so fixed on running bleachers? It's not like that's an Olympic sport."

"Who knows?" Lindsay replied. "I hate bleachers, especially outside ones. Sometimes I dream I fall through them into the Big Ditch—the irrigation canal that runs through town—and I can't swim. I mean, I can swim in real life, but not in my dream."

Why was she going on about all this, to a girl she barely knew? At least Carrie wouldn't blab her true confessions to ME, the way Jana always did.

"Want to see our house?" Carrie said. "It's down this block. Or come to the rectory and meet my grandma and my sister. If you have time, that is."

Lindsay looped her arm through Carrie's, her mental fog evaporating. "Both, if we make it quick. I've never been in the rectory. In grade school, sometimes teachers sent boys over if they were misbehaving. We always figured they got paddled, but my brother says the housekeeper made the boys cocoa, and the priest would lecture them about being respectful and following the Golden Rule. Then they'd talk baseball."

"My grandma's cocoa is so good," Carrie said, "the boys will want to get in trouble."

At the end of the block, Carrie opened the gate leading to a little square house with an arch over the front door and pointed at the yellow roses trailing through the white picket fence. "Baba—that's Serbian for grandma—cried when she saw the roses."

The fence looked recently repainted, and Lindsay flashed on an image of Tom Sawyer. *Why would anybody cry over roses?*

Carrie dumped her pack inside the front door and Lindsay followed her up the stairs to see her room, which was kind of bare, and her sister's, with its pink walls and white furniture.

In the hall this afternoon, between classes, Lindsay had heard Jana say that the Altar Society had furnished the place, and the bedroom set was a floor sample the Simoniches donated. But she wasn't going to tell Carrie that. Nobody wanted to feel like a charity case.

"It's cute," she said. "My sister and I have white furniture, too, and it feels so grown-up."

Back outside, they wound through the playground behind the school and crossed the street to the rectory, next to the church. Carrie opened the aluminum screen side door, and Lindsay followed her into the kitchen.

Whatever Lindsay had expected a cocoa-making housekeeper for Catholic priests to look like, it was not this. Old-world, maybe. Stout, in a calico dress. But Irene Danich—that was how Carrie introduced her—was gorgeous, trim with graying blond hair and warm brown eyes, in slacks and a stylish black-and-white print blouse. She looked like Carrie, only older and shorter.

She took Lindsay's hands in hers, and the sweet, woody scent of roses mingled with the more familiar smells of cinnamon and sugar. "I've met your mother, the school secretary," she said. "And I'm delighted to meet a friend of my granddaughter. Carrie, go get your sister. She's playing outside. I made *povitica* for Father, but you girls can sneak a slice."

"What's pova—?" Lindsay asked as she followed Carrie to the sidewalk between the buildings. She didn't see a little girl.

"*Povitica.*"

"Poe-vuh-TEET-suh," Lindsay repeated.

"It's Serbian. Sooo good. Sweet dough rolled and sprinkled with nuts and spices, then baked and sliced thin." She made a rolling motion with her index fingers. "Best after-school treat ever."

"Sounds great, but my mom's expecting me."

"Give me two minutes to find Ginger," Carrie said. "She plays in the church sometimes—she likes the candles. I want you to meet her—everyone loves her."

Two minutes became three, four, five. Lindsay kept glancing from church to rectory to street. Her mom hated to be kept waiting. She'd just decided to tell Mrs. Danich she had to get going, when the side door of the church flew open. Carrie emerged, half pushing, half dragging a small girl wearing the grade school's plaid jumper, her red hair coming loose from her braid. The girl sobbed.

"I'm sorry," Carrie said, her voice tight, her brown eyes blinking rapidly. "I'll explain tomorrow. Monday, I mean." Then the sisters disappeared inside the rectory.

Lindsay raked a hand through her hair. *What was that all about?*

The church bell chimed four o'clock. Somewhere close by, a car engine revved, then zoomed away.

She still had time to drop her mom off at home and take the car to the mall before dinner, if she hurried. The church door opened again, and Father Leary emerged. He wrapped one hand around the back of his neck, his cheeks flushed, a sheen of sweat on his forehead. He saw her and stopped.

"What are you doing here, Lindsay?" His tone was not unkind. She jerked her thumb toward the rectory's side door. As if on cue, it opened, and priest and teenager turned instinctively.

Irene Danich stood in the doorway, face white as the flour on her hands. "Father, you have to come."

Without a word, the priest strode toward the housekeeper, a girl's green jump rope dangling from his hand.

* * *

Carrie sat on the living room floor, the chemical-lemon scent of furniture polish stinging her nostrils. Around the corner, Baba, Father Mike, and the monsignor sat at the kitchen table with cups of coffee they didn't drink and a plate of *povitica* they didn't eat, working it all out while Ginger played in the monsignor's study with her Betsy McCall paper dolls.

Carrie wrapped her arms around her knees, straining to hear the adults plan the future.

She was nearly an adult herself. She'd made a friend—or started to. "If you make me leave this town," she'd told them a few minutes ago, "I am never coming back."

Why did they think they could uproot her without even asking what she thought?

Because they knew she wouldn't want to go. But they also knew she would—that she would not try to stay here on her own, even though she was nearly eighteen, because she would never leave Ginger.

She'd entered the cool, quiet church through the side door, expecting to find Ginger playing with her dolls by the wrought iron votive stand in the side aisle. Flames glowed in the red glass candle holders, the wicks giving off a faint waxy odor and the occasional puff of smoke as a flame flickered and died.

But no Ginger.

At the back of the church, Carrie had faced the altar and bent a knee partway, her hand flying through the sign of the cross.

At the door to the vestibule, she'd stopped abruptly, arrested by the harsh, almost menacing voices. Not loud, but clear. She gripped the doorframe with one hand and peered around the corner.

Father Mike faced a man in a camel hair sport coat.

"We know about the girl, Mike," the man said. "And you know what will happen if you breathe a word. About any of it." He stood in the shadow, just out of the late afternoon sunlight streaming through the church's open front door.

Another man stood a few feet away, arms folded across his chest, straining the shoulders of his pale blue jacket. One leg bounced, heel up, heel down. Carrie couldn't see his face, but she could see Father Mike's. Not worried or afraid.

No, his expression ran deeper, stonier.

Resolute, she thought. One of last week's vocabulary words in English class.

Who did they mean by "the girl"? What did they not want Father Mike to say? Carrie scanned the vestibule, or what she could see of it. No sign of Ginger.

Then her eyes stopped. Her heart nearly stopped, too. At the foot of the baptismal font lay a green jump rope. Ginger's jump rope.

Camel Hair walked slowly out of the church. Blue Coat, half a head taller than the other two, hung back, waiting for the priest to follow. Instead, Father Mike swept his hand in an "after you" gesture that Blue Coat could not ignore.

Carrie strained for a better view. Father Mike stood on the threshold. Outside, on the top step, Camel Hair turned for one last word she couldn't hear. In profile, he had a strong Roman nose, his dark hair thick, his skin burnished by the sun. Then he headed down the steps and out of view, Blue Coat trotting behind.

Only then did she notice Ginger's foot in her brown penny loafer and pink sock underneath the pew near the front door, the one stacked with missals and last Sunday's leftover bulletins.

Carrie darted forward, reached under the pew, and grabbed her sister's hand. Held a finger to her lips and pulled the girl to her feet. Father Mike was alone now, still staring out the church door. His shoulders began to droop. With one eye on the priest, she'd dragged Ginger into the church. They'd skirted around the rear pews, passed the candle stand, and bolted out the side door.

Now, her breath hard and hot, her muscles quivering as she huddled in the priests' living room and hugged herself, she remembered the startled expression on Lindsay's face when she burst into view, her sobbing sister by the hand. Lindsay—smart, funny, friendly. A *bold* girl, who'd dared to admit her own fears.

What would she say to Carrie? What would that brave girl tell her to do?

A hollow pit opened in her stomach.

The pit threatened to swallow her. Her dreams of belonging to a group of girls, of graduating from this high school as one of them. Her dreams of—of what? She had never allowed herself to dream much, but she had hoped that in the house with the white picket fence and yellow roses, and the pink-and-white bedroom, she could bloom.

But no. The voices from the kitchen made clear that this, too, was not the place for dreams.

TUESDAY
March 1, 2016

Just nail down a few more facts, Donovan told himself. *Wrap up the parking garage assault and move on.*

If only it were that easy.

He dumped double sugar and cream in his coffee. Another detective was on the phone in their second-floor office. They exchanged silent acknowledgments—a raised chin, a lifted hand—and Donovan grabbed a pad and pen from his desk. Headed for the solitude of the adjacent conference room. Closed the door and set his hot coffee on the table amid the boxes of files from the cold case.

They'd tracked the would-be assailant to a scuzzy motel that rented rooms by the week and strip-searched the place. Not much to find.

Hadn't taken long to confirm that he'd left a past as nasty as Donovan had expected, and as punk.

Donovan called the newspaper reporter again with an update. "Charges should be filed in a day or two," he told the man. "He'll be going from a hospital bed to a jail cell. Any chance you can run a sketch of the tattoos, based on the photos?" He'd bet a week's worth of caffeine that there had been other attacks, even in the short time the scuzzball had been in town. Some victims weren't the cop-calling type. But a scorpion tattoo running up the neck and another on the arm that looked like a prison job—art like that was one of a kind. And if you'd seen it on the arm that held a knife to your throat, you'd remember.

His job was to give the prosecutor enough evidence to file charges that would stick. More victims telling similar stories would improve the odds, add pressure for a plea. He hated seeing these cases going to trial, the victim raked over the coals one more time. A plea and a stiff sentence, ASAP, were the martial artist's best chance of getting back to normal life. Although as Donovan knew too well, life would never be the same.

The reporter had tried squeezing him for more info on the Leary case, but at this point, Donovan had nothing to give. He tacked a fresh map of the county on the wall and stuck a red pin on St. Patrick's Church.

He was going to need a lot of coffee.

FRIDAY
September 18, 1981

Lindsay tugged the creamy white V-necked sweater over her head and tossed it on the bed. She'd left the tags on—she could take it back tomorrow. The bookstore manager had let her trade for a day shift Saturday so she could go to the football game. If her mom let her drive.

They hadn't said she couldn't drive tonight. They hadn't said she couldn't go out. They'd been remarkably calm, which was worse than if they'd ranted and raved and grounded her until she turned forty, thin and gray like the spinster heiress who lived alone in the crumbling brick mansion near the high school, hardly ever left home, and was rumored to exist on cat food and demon rum.

She ran her hands up and down her arms, then yanked the gray Eastern Montana College sweatshirt out of the laundry basket by its navy collar and pulled it on. Slipped out of her new jeans and folded them carefully.

Her parents had gone to the Rainbow to "chew the fat," as her dad liked to say. She ought to go out and celebrate not being grounded for life.

But the craziness in the locker room had her roiled up inside, and the last thing she wanted to do was sit in the front seat of the Camaro while Juice Newton sang about the Queen of Hearts and

41

Andy Simonich tried to wriggle his hand down her pants with the damned gear shift in between them. Guys thought muscle cars were so hot, but bench seats made the whole kiss-and-feel thing a lot easier.

Her hairbrush sat on top of the white dresser, almost identical to the dresser in Carrie's sister's room. What had possessed her parents to buy the white bedroom set years ago, she could only guess. A sale at Simonich Home Décor, combined with an attempt to make their girls more feminine by giving their shared bedroom a touch of elegance? It hadn't worked. Neither of them were girlie girls. Her sister, ten years older, had said she didn't want it. Lindsay didn't hate it. Maybe she'd keep it for some future daughter.

She glanced in the mirror. Maybe she should let her hair grow. Other girls were wearing long layers. She twisted a dark lock around one finger, but when she pulled her finger out, the hair hung limp.

The radio announcer finished the weekly livestock report, and music blared. The Pointer Sisters' "Slow Hand."

Oh God. She reached down and yanked on the cord. The plug spat out of the wall, whipped around, and smacked her in the thigh. She let out a yowl and sank onto the bed, one hand on her leg, the other clapped over her mouth.

Her big mouth that had gotten her into this mess. But she wouldn't take back what she'd said in the locker room even if she could, because Sister Claire, the *bitch*, was wrong.

Like any adult would ever see it that way.

She'd picked at her dinner, pork chops baked with rice and canned peaches. "Lindsay," her mother had said, putting down her fork. "When you're not eating your favorite dish, something is wrong. Out with it."

Lindsay forced herself not to fidget, even though the chair seat made her butt hurt, instead twining one bare foot around the other. She debated pretending that she was upset over the strange incident at the church. It figured that her mother, the school secretary, would know the priests' new housekeeper. But Pat Keller would never believe that her younger daughter was too upset to eat just because the new girl had found her little sister jumping rope in the church.

Besides, they might get a call from the principal, and they'd be even madder that she hadn't told them first.

"In PE today. Well, in the locker room afterward." She told them everything—about the fake showers and how Sister Claire ripped off Charlene's towel and made a mean comment about the reservation. Word for word, she told her parents what she'd said and how Sister had replied, then made the two girls shower with soap and cold water while she timed them.

Almost everything. She didn't tell them Charlene sobbed the whole time, or that she'd walked the girl upstairs to history class before racing back down to English, her favorite class, and bursting in late.

And she didn't tell them how the nun's black eyes made her feel. Like she needed to turn away but couldn't because those eyes would follow every move.

Like they saw through her skin.

Later, after lunch, she'd seen Sister Claire in the hall, talking with one of the freshmen boys, and it was as if she'd become an entirely different person. Gentle, almost sweet. Too weird.

"I've worked with Marvin Old Horn for twenty years," her father said. "Hell of a welder. That family hasn't lived on the reservation for ages."

"Walt, that's not the point," her mother said. "Too many in this town still treat Indians like dogs. A nun, of all people, should know better."

"I know that, Pat," her father replied, his tone making Lindsay squirm. It wasn't unusual for her parents to snap at each other on the way to eventual agreement, but the sharpness made her want to slink away.

"Especially since she's from New York. You'd think she'd understand about the races. So what are we going to do about this?" Her mother fixed her glare on Lindsay. "You shouldn't have sassed a teacher."

"I didn't sass. I just told her—" But there was no point repeating herself, and if she tried to leave the table, her father would tell her to sit down and show her mother some respect, young lady, and then she'd be in real trouble.

No matter how much parents and teachers said they wanted you to speak your mind, they didn't. Not really. It was one thing to make a smart remark about President Reagan or Dan Rather, but you couldn't criticize someone you actually knew. You couldn't say they'd been wrong, that what they'd done violated all the principles you'd been taught about equality and justice before the law and in the eyes of God. Even if it was true, that kind of talk got you nothing but trouble because you threatened the power structure. And nobody in power could accept that, whether it was government or school or your parents at the dinner table.

It wasn't supposed to be like that. Lindsay vowed to be different.

"You'll get suspended and lose your scholarship," her mother had said.

"They'll let it blow over," her father replied. "How many girls heard that nun? Fifteen? Twenty? They can't deny it. They'd have to send her back to her own convent. I bet she knows that and keeps her trap shut. Maybe I should talk to Marvin Old Horn next week."

"Dad, no," she said, and her mother agreed. Lindsay asked if she was grounded, almost hoping the answer would be yes.

"No, Lindsay," her mother replied. "You're nearly an adult. You decide for yourself what you think is best."

Which hadn't helped at all.

Then they'd finished dinner, and she'd washed up while her parents went out. She could picture Mr. Stenerud behind the bar at the Rainbow, and other adults she knew shooting pool or shooting the breeze. Not Mr. and Mrs. Simonich—now that they were rich, they went to the Elks Club.

She rubbed at the red welt on her leg and slipped on a pair of cutoffs. Then she dug *The Canterbury Tales* out of her bag and made for the hideaway, the old garage between the house and alley that her dad had remodeled into a rec room. When she was little, she'd loved curling up in the corner with a Nancy Drew or *Little Women*, but her brother and sister had sent her skedaddling when their friends came over. The place still had that forbidden feel.

The evening was warm, so she left the side door open and tossed the heavy green hardback onto the brown-and-gold floral couch. Peered in the old white fridge and reached for a Coke, then took one of her dad's beers instead. She popped the cap and tossed it in the battered red-and-white metal bucket where bottle caps mingled with the remains of her brother's marble collection. Flopped on the cushions and took a long swig. Wiped her mouth with the back of her hand. Beer was okay cold like this, but one bottle would be enough.

"When that Aprill with his shoures soote
The droghte of March hath pierced to the roote . . ."

She read the first page slowly, out loud, immersing herself in the sounds of the Middle English, then flipped to her bookmark. *The Clerke's Tale.* She pictured herself among the pilgrims as they made their way down the road, then sitting at a plank table in the inn, nursing a tankard of ale while her companions spun their tales, allegories of history and morality. Tales that were also, as her English teacher said, occasionally quite ribald.

"Bookworm, bookworm. Lindsay is a bookworm."

She started at the old taunt, nearly knocking over the half-full bottle of beer in her attempt to hide it beneath the skirt of the old couch.

"You're not dressed." Mary Ellen parked her hands on her hips, pushing back the tails of her long russet sweater, the height of fashion, worn over tan brushed denim pants. Lindsay would have killed for those Frye boots.

"She's not dressed? Let me see." Andy's tone was half teasing, half serious as he pushed through the doorway and stood behind his sister.

"I—I'm not going," Lindsay said. Should she lie and say she was grounded? *No.* She wanted to be treated like an adult; she had to act like one.

"Why? You chicken?" Mary Ellen's nose wrinkled. "This place is a dump, Linds. You should fix it up."

"You liked it fine when we were kids."

"I can't believe we used to live down here." Mary Ellen spotted Lindsay's beer and took a swig. Made a face. "This is warm. So you coming or not?"

Everything welled up and pushed against Lindsay's ribcage, like a funnel cloud bursting to escape.

"No. I am not coming." She reached for the book that had fallen to the floor. "I can drink decent beer here, thank you, instead of chugging cheap stuff and getting my feet all muddy in some old field with the radio playing while the guys shoot beer cans with their BB guns. You go worry about the cops and whether the farmer will throw you out and all that other crap."

"Well, *fine*," Mary Ellen snapped. "You're so holy, you stay home by yourself and read some old dumb book that fat nun gave you. I know what you're doing, trying to make up for getting us all in trouble by brown-nosing."

"I didn't get anybody in trouble," Lindsay said. Besides, she'd been given the book days ago. "You stood there and heard Sister Claire say those terrible things—"

"Lindsay." Andy stepped into full view. Fine view, six feet tall, those broad shoulders in his letterman's jacket, the big hands made for football and other fun. The thick, dark hair she could practically feel. His deep brown eyes bore into her, and she clenched her teeth to suppress a shiver, tucking one bare foot beneath her other thigh. "I was hoping you would come."

She'd known Andy all her life. When the Simoniches lived down the block, Andy and his gang of neighborhood boys had made it their mission to terrorize his sister and her friends. They'd kidnapped the girls' Barbies for ransom, spun tales of boogie monsters and witches who ate children, and swore the chicken chop suey served in the school cafeteria was made with rotten rattlesnake meat. Then the boys had lost interest, turning their attention to sports and cars and forgetting all about those little girls.

Until one day, the girls weren't little anymore, and the boys' blinders fell away.

Mary Ellen shook her head, the layers of her hair falling perfectly into place. "Don't bother with her, the loser. We'll go get Jana instead. She never acts all stuck-up for no reason."

The chill took over, but Lindsay didn't dare let it show. Jana'd had a crush on Andy at least as long as Lindsay had. She'd make a play for him, and why not go for the girl who was there instead of the one who stayed home drinking purloined beer she didn't even like and reading dead poets nobody understood? Jana was pretty, in a bland way, and a lot nicer than Lindsay, truth be told. Plus she wouldn't mind being smarter than her boyfriend. Lindsay laughed inside, acknowledging the truth.

She watched Mary Ellen glance around the converted garage one more time, her disdainful gaze settling on the liquor shelf. She grabbed the only full bottle, Canadian Mist. "You were going to bring this anyway, right?"

Put that bottle back. Her dad might not miss a beer, but a full bottle of whiskey, he'd notice. And then she'd really be in trouble. But she was so sick of ME and her snot—how, why, when had her old friend changed so much? Lindsay just wanted her *gone*.

Mary Ellen glared, daring her to speak. But Lindsay kept her mouth shut, and after a long moment, the other girl let out an exasperated sound and stalked out of the garage, the bottle swinging in her hand, her long sweater flapping behind her, boot heels echoing on the concrete walk.

Lindsay's teeth clenched, her throat hot. All those years living on the same block, sitting in the same classrooms, reading the same teen girl magazines and swooning over the same pop stars—she and ME had sworn they were sisters, closer than blood. She'd loved her. But now, she barely recognized her old friend—or the boy who'd flirted around the edges of her life for as long as she could remember.

"You sure?"

Until he spoke, she'd forgotten Andy was there, standing in the silence his sister had left behind. He drew his shoulders back, broadening his chest, and his vision traveled slowly down her body.

From outside, in the sprawling juniper, the chorus of chirping crickets nearly drowned out the pounding of her heart. A part of her had always believed she and Andy were meant to be together. But he was a fantasy, like a boy in a book or on TV, who'd worked his way into her dreams because he was *there*. Because he was older and drove a fast car and had a job, even if he was working for his dad. He seemed so alive. So sexy and dangerous.

But none of that was real.

She reached for her book. "I'm sure."

TUESDAY
March 1, 2016
Portland, Oregon

"Aye, come aboard, mateys!" The captain spread his black-booted feet wide, hands on his hips, a rakish tilt to his black tri-corner hat. The children and their parents were in costume, too, sporting swords and eye patches, pirate hats bobbing as they paraded up the gangplank to the wooden decks of the ship, safely docked inside a warehouse turned party palace.

Carrie stood beneath a fake palm tree and watched the captain bend down to stage-whisper into her grandson Asher's ear. "Ya better have fun, matey, or I'll make you walk the plank, with alligators nipping at yer toes."

"Arrrgh!" Asher yelled.

Carrie smiled as the little boy bounded up the gangplank to the deck, where Diana, her daughters' stepmother, clapped in time with the bagpiper's tune. This party was Diana's brainchild. She had scads of money and loved lavishing Carrie's two girls and only grandchild with things Carrie could never afford. Buying their love, she'd groused at first, but Diana and Todd had been married nearly five years now, and Carrie had to admit that the other woman had never interfered with Carrie's relationship with Ali and Jessica, or Asher.

And while Carrie's mind boggled at the thought of spending so much on a four-year-old's birthday party, who knew how many birthdays this four-year-old would have? Asher was lucky to have a step-grandmother willing to make his party special.

God only knew, her sweet little pirate deserved a bit of luck.

A female buccaneer with a white parrot on her shoulder approached. "Come aboard, Mistress. We're about to set sail." The parrot squawked. Carrie tugged on the velveteen lace-up corset meant to turn her into a busty, lusty eighteenth-century bar maid, hitched up her skirt, and took a step toward the gangplank.

Behind her, a door opened.

"Auntie Ginger!" Asher shouted from the deck. "Hurry! Anchors aweigh!"

Carrie stared, disbelieving. Then she rushed to meet the baby sister who'd just turned forty-three, and they flung their arms around each other.

"You came!" Still gripping Ginger's shoulders, Carrie stepped back for a closer look. Too thin, from all that travel in dangerous places. "Why didn't you tell me you were coming to Portland?"

"Auntie Ginger!" Asher called again. "Grandma! Come on."

No time for talk when sword-swinging pirates were in charge. Carrie grabbed Ginger's hand and they dashed aboard the pretend pirate ship. Ginger scooped up Asher, still holding him on her hip as she embraced her nieces.

Then they turned their attention to the captain, who divided the partygoers into teams. One young pirate climbed to the crow's nest atop the mast and, with prompting from a crew member, spied another ship. A mock invasion followed, and the prisoners were led to a giant slide down to the lower deck.

Carrie sat at the top of the slide and nestled the small boy in her lap.

"Don't be afraid, Grandma," Asher said. "It's like at the park." And down they went, the ride almost too short for her to remember that he wasn't a normal child, doing normal things.

Back on the upper deck, the parrot landed on a child's shoulder, prompting shrieks of surprise and delight.

Carrie perched on a crate of pirate booty, Asher next to her, as a wench taught the other adults a jig. Ali sparkled in a red velvet skirt and a creamy off-the-shoulder top, and Jamal, Asher's father, made a handsome pirate. As the boy leaned against her, his black curls tickling her chin, she could feel his vibrating vest under the flowing white shirt. He hadn't wanted to wear the vest, but Ali had insisted—the excitement could easily trigger a coughing fit. Ali never took Asher anywhere without inhalers in her purse, and always made sure Carrie had a stash when she took him for a few hours. Carrie's lungs were fine—they had no idea where Asher's cystic fibrosis had come from—though at the moment, her chest was about to burst with love for her precious grandson. And with pride in Ali for how well she coped with his illness. But at the edge of Carrie's mind clung a dark, spidery anger that this vicious disease had crawled into their lives.

"Ahoy, ahoy!" a swashbuckling six-year-old yelled, and rapped his prosthetic leg, disguised as a wooden peg, on the ship's deck. The family were Syrian refugees, and the boys had been roommates last fall. About half the children here tonight were kids Asher had met in the hospital, though you couldn't tell from the noise level. Or from the way they threw themselves into the fun and games. Their resilience amazed her. They didn't know life without inhalers and masks, chemo ports and wheelchairs.

To themselves, they were just like any other kids.

"Don't let the pirates scare you, Grandma," Asher said. "They like to yell, but they won't really hurt you."

"Thank you for the warning," she replied, matching his serious tone. Then he dashed off to join the other children.

A pirate girl, a bandanna tied around her bald head, marched up to Carrie. A butterfly covered one cheek. The face painter who'd greeted them on arrival had done a brisk business in mustaches, beards, and fake scars, though some of these children bore their own scars. Obviously, this girl had chosen a theme of her own. But who could say there weren't butterflies on pirate ships?

"You're Asher's grandma, aren't you? My mother said to thank you for the party."

Carrie opened her mouth to say she had the wrong grandma but stopped herself. No point confusing the child. "You're welcome."

The girl leaned in, her voice a conspiratorial whisper, or maybe just husky from chemo. "It's the first birthday party I've ever been to on a pirate ship. Even if it isn't real."

"Me, too," Carrie whispered back. The girl grinned—she'd lost a front tooth—and sped away.

Had there been pirate parties when she was a child or when her girls were small? Not like this, anyway. Her mother would have loved putting on a costume and playing the part. Though tonight was a night for joy and laughter, she couldn't help but feel a twinge of sadness for all her mother had missed. For what they'd all missed.

They docked at a desert island. On the sandy shore, Ginger showed a young pirate tethered to an IV stand how to take a selfie. Someone—Father Leary?—had given Ginger a camera the first Christmas after they moved to Portland thirty-five years ago. Curiosity had turned to obsession, then become her occupation. When Ali and Jessica were small, Aunt Ginger had sent them fat manila envelopes of photos from around the world, her lens focused on the beautiful and sublime, the weird and intriguing. Now she did the same, via email and Instagram, for Asher. Ali had printed out his favorites, and they'd made a collage that hung on the wall next to his bed.

Photo lesson finished, Ginger stood beside her. "Can you believe this?"

Carrie slid an arm around her sister's waist. "Why didn't you tell me you were coming?"

"I wasn't sure." Ginger raised one shoulder, elegantly clad in a white silk tunic, a black-and-silver shawl over her shoulders. Her slim black pants were tucked into knee-high black boots. The Nordstrom version of a pirate costume, plus an eye patch a crew member had given her. "You know how it is."

Carrie knew. She'd have believed her sister led a life of glamour if she hadn't also seen the nightly news and the websites of the charitable organizations Ginger often worked for, documenting blood, filth, and strife.

"You're rocking the eye patch," Carrie said. "And I love your hair long." The soft red curls hid the shrapnel scars on her neck. When Ginger had called from the Army hospital to say she'd been wounded by an IED but she'd be fine, don't worry, Carrie had nearly screamed at her. *Why the hell did you have to go to Syria? Couldn't you take pictures here, in the US, where you'd be safe? And why didn't you tell me?* But of course, that was why Ginger hadn't told her. That's what big sisters do, right? Overreact when the younger ones put themselves in danger?

They didn't look a thing alike—tall, sturdy blond Carrie with her broad peasant face, and short, wiry Ginger with the hair that gave her the nickname. But they shared their mother's nose and the one crooked tooth neither had ever bothered to have straightened.

They watched Asher and the other children play a treasure hunt that led to a trunk of gold-covered chocolate coins.

"I can't believe how good he looks," Ginger said.

"Ali works so hard, keeping him healthy. And the treatment has really come a long way. If it had been you or me, or even one of the girls"—Carrie's voice cracked—"there wouldn't have been much hope."

Ginger pulled her close. "It's not your fault, sis."

"That's not how it feels."

"I know. But obviously Jamal carries the gene, too, and even then, it was still a long shot, right?"

"One in four, if both parents are carriers."

Genetic guilt, her older daughter had labeled her reaction, a remark Carrie chalked up to too many psychology classes. She and Ali had the gene, of course, but Jessie didn't. One worry gone, thank God.

We are supposed to take care of our families. She had created the family she'd always wanted, only to pass on genes that could destroy it. When their parents died, Baba had been a saint, stepping in. But she'd never talked much about their heritage, let alone their genetic flaws. If Carrie had known she carried the CF gene, would she not have had children, or urged Ali to make a different choice as a pregnant nineteen-year-old? Would she have wanted the world to never hear Asher's laugh or see his gap-toothed smile? But you didn't get to choose your trade-offs.

In high school, Ali had done a genealogy project. With help from Todd's mother, she'd traced the paternal side of her family back to Germany, before the Civil War. Made a family tree that covered the kitchen table. But Carrie hadn't been able to tell her anything about the Wests or Daniches. When she'd been a kid and asked Baba about the family, Baba had replied, "We're Serbian. We crave meat and potatoes. There's nothing else to know."

After the last crisis, the specialist had said Asher might qualify for an upcoming drug trial, but the application asked for more details about the family's medical history than they could provide. Carrie had dug out the family tree, hoping Ali would finish it. But Ali had her hands full with therapy appointments and doctors' visits, plus work. "Besides," she'd said, "I don't see how knowing whether our third great-aunt had the disease could help Asher."

It will help me, Carrie had thought. To know how guilty I should feel for passing on the gene. For not knowing the family history, not having asked more questions. Todd's family had trunks full of letters, journals, all kinds of records. But all the childhood deaths in their line came from epidemics or accidents. There had been no hint of children with lung problems.

Focus on the good luck, not the bad, Carrie reminded herself now. "Asher is so determined, so full of life," she said as the pirate crew steered them toward the Jolly Roger birthday cake. "Ali and Jamal are handling it beautifully."

"Take some credit, sis," Ginger said. "You raised her. And look at all you do for them."

A bitterness grabbed hold of her tongue. "You can say that. You haven't raised two kids. You haven't had your heart broken, over and over, by love and fear and worry—" She broke off, her pulse racing, her cheeks burning. "I'm sorry. That wasn't fair."

"It's okay," Ginger said. "Come to the hotel with me. We'll catch up over drinks and stay up too late. You can take a Jacuzzi and order Belgian waffles from room service."

"I was hoping you'd come home with me. My guest room might not be as luxurious as the Heathman, but it's not bad."

Ginger pressed her lips together. "Next time."

But it would be the same next time, Ginger refusing her invitation yet again. Carrie had seen pictures Ginger had taken of tar paper shacks in Rio and Nairobi. She never hesitated to wade into squalor. The bungalow in Northeast was cute and comfy, even though the upstairs plumbing had been acting up lately.

What did her beloved sister have against her home?

She let out a long, slow sigh. "It's tempting, but I can't. I'm replanting the rose garden at the Grotto this week, and tomorrow afternoon, I'm taking Asher to therapy."

Ginger put her hands on Carrie's shoulders. "Getting him better is what matters, sis. Not where this rotten disease came from."

Ali sashayed toward them with plates of cake and plastic forks. A white parrot feather caught a breeze from a hidden fan and floated high above the cake table, then plummeted into the lap of a young girl in a wheelchair.

The captain swung his sword like a conductor's baton, leading the partygoers in song. "Happy Birthday, dear Asher. Happy Birthday to you!"

"Wipe that black frosting off your face," Ginger said. "There's a photo booth yonder in the stocks."

Carrie groaned. "In this getup?" But she had so few pictures from her own childhood. Did she want her girls to look back, their own children and grandchildren on their laps, and wonder where they'd come from? No, she did not.

She looped her arm through that of the elegant adventurer beside her.

Anything for Asher. Anything for her girls.

TUESDAY
March 1, 2016
Billings

At her office desk, Lindsay studied the photograph from Father Leary's wallet, excavating from the rubble of memory the red-haired girl's tear-streaked face as her older sister dragged her from the church to the rectory. Their names were gone, buried by the weight of time.

To be fair, the days after the incident in PE and her walk downtown with the new girl had been hell. She still hated driving down Black Otter Trail, seeing the mangled yellow Camaro in her mind's eye. Scott always said it was probably worse in her imagination than in real life, but in her years as a prosecutor, before she met him, she'd seen plenty of wrecked cars up close. Her imagination couldn't make it worse.

And every thought of the accident tortured her with unanswerable questions. Would Mary Ellen be alive if Lindsay had stopped her from grabbing the bottle off the hideaway shelf? Or if she'd gone along?

Her dad had never said a word, no doubt thinking she was punishing herself more than he ever could.

Everybody knew the cause of the wreck was speed and alcohol. The drinking age then was nineteen and Andy had been legal, but he and Jana had both sworn he didn't provide any alcohol that night, so no charges were filed. Whether they lived with guilt for letting Mary Ellen get behind the wheel, she didn't know. Attitudes had been different then, hers included. But kids still drank and drove, and ignored seatbelts, so she'd hammered the designated driver thing into her own girls, though that hadn't kept her from worrying.

At Mary Ellen's funeral, she and Jana had clung to each other, sobbed together, mourned together. Bit by bit, their need to find comfort in each other had eased. In all the years since graduation, they'd only talked about Mary Ellen a handful of times.

As the weeks after the accident stretched into months and years, she and Andy had exchanged little more than casual greetings, even at his and Jana's wedding three years later. Poor Andy, too dumb to realize that good looks and a standout high school sports career weren't much of a foundation for adult life.

But that first week, the school had been a whirl of emotion. The halls had been shrouded with grief. It had not been unusual to see a girl slumped against her locker in tears, a damp-cheeked friend beside her. The football team had dedicated that weekend's game to Mary Ellen and then lost, their only loss of the season.

No wonder she had forgotten the girl with the Pippi Longstocking braids and her sister. She studied the photo.

What were their names?

Lindsay had written her daughters' names—Chelsea and Haley—on the back of every school photo, along with the year and grade. But whoever gave this photo to Father Leary hadn't done that.

Most people only carried a child's photo if they were related. Who was this child to Father Leary, and why had he kept that picture in his wallet all those years?

Why never a newer shot, and why not a picture of both girls?

Now that she focused on that day, Lindsay remembered Father Leary coming out of the church, clearly rattled. What had happened?

She could turn the photo over to Detective Donovan, tell him it had gotten lost on her desk as she sorted through the contents of the wallet. Withholding evidence was a serious ethical violation. But she wanted to believe in the Father Leary she remembered and the photo made her doubt that image.

Doubt did not sit well, in her stomach or her mind.

She reached for her bag, a deep raspberry leather tote the girls had given her for Christmas. She told Carla she was taking a few projects home, though the expression on her secretary's face said *yeah, right.* Carla Gutierrez could read her boss like a book.

As she wound the Prius through downtown, Lindsay pictured Father Leary patrolling senior hall in the days after Mary Ellen's death. Other teachers had walked the halls, too, their faces pale as they struggled to console stricken students. She could still hear Sister Claire telling them God had a plan and that "the poor soul" was in a better place now. As if Mary Ellen hadn't been seventeen with her whole life ahead of her. The nun had urged them to run off their grief—not bad advice, though not exactly brimming with empathy. At least she'd let them run through the neighborhood instead of up and down the bleachers.

Father Leary had presided over ME's funeral with grace, and in their small-group religion seminars, he'd let them talk freely. When Jana broke down, triggering tears in even the most stoic kids, he'd hauled out boxes of tissue. And he'd listened patiently when Lindsay railed against God, no longer sure she wanted to believe in Him if He was going to let such terrible things happen.

In her driveway, she waited for the garage door to open. Inside, she turned off the engine, then sat, the leather bag in her lap.

Why could she not shake the feeling—a feeling triggered by the wallet and the photo—that the girls in the church, the crash after the kegger, and Father Leary's murder fourteen years later were connected?

Impossible, she thought as she entered the kitchen, greeted by the smell of something simmering on the stove. A cookbook lay open on the counter, next to an open bottle of wine. Since Haley had come home at Christmas break and announced she was switching schools, she'd been obsessed with cooking. Where that had come from, Lindsay had no idea. She lifted the lid on the kettle of French onion soup and sniffed. Spooned up a taste.

Far better than any dinner she might have planned. But then, she expected nothing less from Haley, who'd always excelled at anything she tried. Which made her abrupt change of schools all the more puzzling.

She glanced at the wine, then took a bottle of Pellegrino from the fridge. The minerally bubbles slid over her tongue and pricked her dry throat. From the kitchen window, she watched a hawk circling between their backyard and the Rims, a quarter mile north. It flew with purpose. On the hunt.

Upstairs in Chelsea's old room, now the TV room, she pulled the 1982 yearbook off the white bookcase, part of the bedroom furniture she'd had as a child. Grabbed the three earlier volumes—if she was going to trek down Memory Lane, might as well take the scenic route. Across the hall, a low, rhythmic beat pulsed through Haley's closed door.

"It's all about that bass," Lindsay sang, swinging her hips as she carried the books downstairs to the breakfast nook, a bench and table Scott had built when the girls were little. The glass doors opened to the backyard. He'd hung a swing off the maple and added links to the chain as the tree grew. When had anyone last swung on it?

Next to the fence on the east side of the yard, peonies poked up their fringe-topped shoots and tiny green leaves dotted the spirea branches. One year for Mother's Day, Scott and the girls had turned an old metal spring, bits of pipe, and a broken brass faucet into a dragonfly sculpture that still stood by the back gate.

Planting, weeding, remembering. The simple pleasures Mary Ellen had not gotten to enjoy. Would they have stayed friends, had ME lived and grown out of her teenage Queen Bee role, or would their friendship have slipped away, as so many did? ME had been smart. She—not Andy and Jana's sons—would have taken over Jerzy's empire.

Was she too hard on Andy in her memory? Other than the occasional lunch with a few girls—*women*—from their class, Lindsay hadn't seen much of Jana in ages. Not until she called a few weeks ago to ask Lindsay for legal help selling the Rainbow. Jana had run the business for her dad, and it was obvious from the financials that she'd done a good job. Old Pete had decided to retire, and Jana's boys weren't interested. The older two had good jobs working for Jerzy Simonich, their other grandfather, and his holdings were worth a lot more than the bar. But Jana hadn't ever seemed to care about the top-of-the-line cars Jerzy had given her and Andy or the fancy house he'd built for them when he developed the new golf course. Generosity, or keeping them close by keeping them in his debt? Could have been either one, with Jerzy. Motive wouldn't have mattered to Jana. She believed in family.

Still, Lindsay hadn't been surprised when Jana and Andy divorced. Must have sucked, she thought as she took another sip, to marry a man for his prospects only to discover that he had no ambition.

Of course, Lindsay had realized that ages ago. And she'd always suspected Andy and Jana married out of shared grief, not love.

Lindsay opened the dark green yearbook, its endpapers plastered with signatures and sentimental notes. A big heart and "Love Ya, Linds!" from Charlene Old Horn. "We're off to Carroll!" from a future college classmate.

The girl from the church—tall, striking, with thick blond hair and a wicked volleyball serve—wasn't in the yearbook. No unfamiliar name jumped out in the index, and Lindsay didn't see her face in the group photos.

In the emotional chaos that followed the wreck, she had barely noticed the girl's absence. By the time they'd decorated the class float for the Homecoming Parade, unified by tragedy, she'd completely forgotten her.

Homecoming, the state football championship, college applications—all of senior year had been blurred by Mary Ellen's death.

And there was no denying that the locker room confrontation with Sister Claire had dogged her for months, as though she might be summoned at a moment's notice and disciplined.

But she never had been. As if nothing had happened. As if, after the shock of a teenager's death, one senior girl's moment of defiance was inconsequential to everyone but her.

She flipped past the dedication page—to Mary Ellen, of course—to a black-and-white photo of Father Leary and the principal celebrating the First Day of School Mass in the gym. Her mind's eye saw the festive green and white vestments, the school colors.

They had no idea, none of them, what changes lay ahead.

The cat landed softly in her lap and Lindsay's hand went automatically to the sleek, orange-striped back. Haley's cat, Ms. Wriggles, a shelter kitten picked out for her tenth birthday, the only one to welcome her home without asking any questions.

She heard the whir of the garage door opening. *Scott.* Wriggles raised her head an inch, then burrowed deeper into Lindsay's lap. The claws might not do her skirt any favors, but the warmth was comforting.

They'd all been surprised when Father Leary was transferred at the end of the school year. The diocese liked to move priests around back then, to keep them from getting too entrenched.

Now they all knew another reason priests had been moved. Lawyers for abuse victims had used those frequent reassignments to show that church officials knew, or at least suspected, particular priests of pedophilia. An ugly word no one had used in those days.

Not Leary. Surely not Leary.

But you couldn't say for sure, could you? Like the neighbors interviewed on the news after a mass shooting, who inevitably said, "We never knew. He was always so nice."

Where had Leary gone? Not far—Lewistown? Somewhere that still had a Catholic high school. By the time she'd moved back to Billings as a young prosecutor, that school had closed and he'd moved back, too. The shepherd returning to his flock.

She turned the pages methodically, not really seeing the pictures. In 1995, when Leary disappeared, she'd been living in Helena, the capital. An assistant attorney general married to an artist, caught up in her own life. Chelsea was two and a half, Haley on the way, when the news broke and quickly turned into a murder investigation.

Who would kill a priest?

Who would stash his wallet, everything intact, in the basement of an old house where it lay hidden for more than twenty years?

"Hey, babe. You bug out early?" Scott's gaze took in the yearbooks scattered on the table as he leaned in to kiss her, his afternoon whiskers scratchy. "Tough day?"

Yes, but not the way he meant. She'd worked on the Rainbow Bar transaction and met with her client on the financing proposal for the old theater—the kind of details she handled every day. No one had made unreasonable demands; no deals had threatened to fall apart. No, it was her head that was giving her trouble today.

"I just felt like playing hooky. I'm enjoying watching the sunlight on the Rims."

"Mmm. Nice. Glass of wine?"

She glanced at the clock—past five thirty already—and nodded.

He headed to the kitchen. "What's with the yearbooks?" he called over his shoulder.

"Just reminiscing."

He set two glasses of red on the table, along with a plate of brie, crackers, and a sliced apple. Much as she loved his smile, it was his eyes that got to her, even after twenty-five years. He could make almost anything, but metal and glass were his main materials these days. Intricate gates and railings, welded sculptures, giant ethereal forms that defied description. They saw the world so differently. And yet, they fit together.

"Hey, you guys. What's up?" Haley sauntered into the room, her dark hair loose, wearing an old red-and-black flannel shirt of Scott's over black leggings. Lindsay was always struck by the grace of her movements, earned by years of dance lessons. Chelsea, three years older, had never been interested. Haley scooped up the cat, who let out a soft mew of protest, then settled into her girl's familiar warmth. "Yearbooks, Mom? You never go all nostalgia."

"Did you see the piece in the paper about the priest's wallet? My client found it." She filled them in. "Father Leary was the best religion teacher in the school."

"Oh, the one who disappeared, and then . . ." Scott drew a finger across his throat, then saw the look on her face. "Sorry. Didn't mean to be crass. They'll reopen the case?"

She nodded and picked up her glass. Houses, basements, hidden clues. The images chased each other through her brain.

Stop it. This isn't fiction. And you're not Nancy Drew.

"Creepy weird," Haley said. The cat in her arms, she hooked a foot around a chair leg and pulled it toward her.

"Anyway, it got me thinking about high school," Lindsay said.

Scott reached for the open volume. A yellowed newspaper clipping fluttered out and Haley grabbed it. Scott turned to Lindsay's senior portrait. "Still pretty cute." He leaned over and kissed her on the lips.

Haley studied the clipping. "Is this the girl who got killed? The one who was your friend, then got all snotty and stuck up. The reason you're death on drinking and driving."

She made it sound so simple. Maybe it was. Maybe Lindsay was complicating things unnecessarily, dredging up guilt where there was none.

Having Haley home was lovely, but what parent wouldn't worry when a kid transferred midyear, without warning, from a great school in another state to the local college, blocks away? She still thought of Montana State University–Billings as Eastern Montana College. MSU-B sounded like the ID code for a rat in a psych lab.

She sighed. Kids change direction. She'd changed senior year. They all had.

"That the wine I opened for the soup?" Haley pushed back her chair. "You leave a glass for me?"

"You're not legal," Lindsay said.

"One glass won't hurt her," Scott said at the same time as Haley spoke. "God, Mom. You act like I've never had a drink before."

What the . . .? Her gaze darted between the faces of her husband and daughter, staring at her, challenging her. When it came to the girls, she and Scott had always been on the same page.

The flush of anger and isolation left as quickly as it had come on. She was overreacting. This wasn't Mary Ellen all over. And Haley wasn't going anywhere tonight. She never did.

Truth be told, Lindsay wanted Haley's company right now, so she didn't have to tell Scott the real reason she was digging around in the old yearbooks and the fragments and shards of memory. Not that she didn't want to tell *him* particularly; she didn't want to tell anybody. Not yet. Not until she figured it out herself.

Because there was some connection she wasn't seeing. She could feel it, but she couldn't identify it. Instinct could be a powerful tool, if you knew how to use it. The best lawyers did.

Did she?

She held up her hands. "All right, all right. I'm being overprotective. It's in my job description." She stood and stacked the yearbooks on the kitchen counter. "Now what can I do? Make a salad?"

A few minutes later, they sat at the dining table. Where Haley had found the terrific French bread, Lindsay didn't know.

"We're sure eating better since you came home," Scott said to Haley, but he gave Lindsay a wink. Her own mother's cooking had run to casseroles made with Campbell's soup and tacos spiced from a seasoning envelope, so when she first discovered as a young adult how good food could be, she'd taught herself to cook. And Scott was always up for making things, whether the materials were clay or flour.

"What era are you studying in art history?" she asked. "This soup is great, by the way. Rich, herby stock."

"Um, the Renaissance," Haley said. She ripped a piece of bread in half.

"I thought you studied that last term," Scott said.

"Yeah, but the classes overlap. Happens when you transfer." Haley took a bite, not looking up.

"I still don't understand why you transferred," Lindsay said. "I thought you liked Reed, and you loved Portland."

"I wanted to be home," Haley said. "I keep telling you."

She had assured them nothing had happened in Portland. She hadn't been attacked or assaulted, as you worried about with a girl, and she wasn't pregnant. It wasn't, she'd insisted, about a boy.

So they had their answers. They should be content. But it was hard to watch your kid struggle, even when you knew struggling to find your way was part of growing up.

Haley wiped her soup bowl with the last of her bread. "Tell me about her—Mary Ellen Simonich. You were friends, then everything changed. Why?"

"She . . ." Lindsay gave her wineglass a twirl, thinking. "She went through a mean phase. She'd have grown out of it, I'm sure. Gone to college, maybe taken over her dad's company. She had the head for it, unlike her brother."

"Why does everyone always compare siblings?" Haley said, her brow furrowed, her tone verging on petulant. "It's so unfair."

"I didn't say a thing about your sister," Lindsay replied. "You asked me about Mary Ellen, and—"

"No, but you're thinking it." Haley picked up her bowl and scooted her chair back. "I'm going to my room. I've got reading to do."

Moments later, they heard her footsteps on the stairs. Scott went into the kitchen and returned with the wine and a plate of cookies Haley had set out, chocolate-almond shortbread.

"I know, babe," he said as he refilled Lindsay's glass. "I wish she'd talk, too. But did you tell your parents everything when you were her age?"

Lindsay thought about the yearbooks and Mary Ellen's picture in the yellowed clipping. No, most definitely not.

Not that it would have changed a thing.

SATURDAY
April 3, 1982

"Lindsay! We found the cutest dresses. You've got to come see them." Jana Stenerud practically clapped her hands in excitement.

"Um, Jana, I'm working." Lindsay gestured toward the bookstore walls, one hand on the rolling cart filled with paperbacks waiting to be shelved. Science fiction wasn't her section, but when shipments arrived, they all pitched in. It was like a puzzle, moving old books to make space for the new, alphabetical by author.

"Well, duh, but you get a break, don't you? Or lunch?"

"Are you going?" Charlene Old Horn said. "To the prom?" The two other girls with them had wandered off.

"I don't think so." Lindsay pried a misplaced romance out of the wire rack and set it on the cart, spine up.

"Me neither," Charlene said. "But I like trying on the dresses. Maybe we can go to a movie that night."

"I thought Tim Bradford asked you," Jana said. "We could double-date."

Lindsay caught her lower lip in her mouth. "I haven't told him yes or no yet. I might have to work."

"You could get the night off." Jana glanced around the store as if she would ask the manager herself.

The last thing Lindsay wanted was to go to the prom with Tim Bradford, and she sure as heck didn't want to double-date with Jana and Andy. Even worse, they'd have to take Tim's parents' station wagon because it had room for back-seat passengers. Andy's red Camaro, like the wrecked yellow one, had a back seat barely big enough for groceries. When Mary Ellen had driven, Lindsay always refused to sit in back, instead smashing into the front with Jana. Like Jana and Andy had done that night last fall.

But now that she'd fibbed about having to work, could she go to a movie with Charlene? That would be more fun.

"You'll change your mind when you see the dresses," Jana said.

As if.

The bookstore manager appeared in the aisle. "You're due for a break, Lindsay. If you want to run down and look at dresses, go ahead. Fifteen minutes."

Five minutes later, she was standing in the junior shop as the other girls rifled through the racks. Was Jana serious about that green satin with the ruffled V-neck? How could she stand the color, after four years of bright green PE uniforms, of bright green everything?

"You'd look great in this, Lindsay." Maura McCall held up a slinky electric-blue number, a sleeveless tank style with a rhinestone-studded band around the scoop neck. "Even though you're short."

Lindsay's hand reached out instinctively. Stretch jersey, swimsuit material. Her parents would never let her out of the house in it.

"I thought you were making a dress," Jana said. She held up a pale yellow dress with a high ruffled neck that looked like something Cinderella's stepsisters would wear. "And now you're not going?"

Lindsay shrugged. "It didn't fit right." Truth was, she'd abandoned the project, hating the thought of carnations dyed unnatural colors and boys in rented shoes, dancing to John Cougar songs played by a band that couldn't hold the beat. Although she did like Cougar, and Toto. Music was pretty good right now.

"You don't have to sacrifice your entire senior year, honey," her mother had said when she'd found the half-finished dress crumpled on the floor of Lindsay's closet. "You're allowed to have fun, even if Mary Ellen isn't here to pal around with anymore."

Her mother didn't know. *She just didn't know.*

"I have to get back to work." Lindsay thrust the blue jersey at Maura and sped out of the shop, the soles of her sandals squeaking on the tile as she raced down the mall.

She skidded to a stop in front of Herberger's shoe department, twenty feet from the bookstore entrance. Her mouth went dry. Her fingers flew to her puka shell and jade choker, a consolation prize her parents brought her from their midwinter week in Hawaii.

When she first started working in the bookstore last summer, she'd found herself constantly glancing out into the mall, hoping Andy Simonich would happen by. She hadn't taken the bookstore job because his dad owned the place and he worked for his dad, learning the business; that connection had been icing on the cake. But last fall, after the accident, she'd been so afraid of running into him that she nearly quit. She worked nights and weekends, though, and he worked weekdays, so it had been okay.

Besides, she loved books, and if she was going to Carroll instead of a state school, she needed to work. And why let the possibility of seeing him scare her off? He was as much to blame as she was.

Then she had seen him. The first time, right after Christmas, she'd been refilling the paperback dump out front when he and Jerzy emerged from the vacant space across the way. She couldn't hear their conversation, but Jerzy was pointing at this and that while Andy acted like he was listening. As Jerzy talked, Andy had turned toward the bookstore and he'd waved. She hadn't known how to respond, with the longing and anger, the sorrow and guilt, all twisted up inside her. It was easier to pretend she hadn't seen him.

One evening a few weeks ago, he'd come in with a complaint from the garbage men about boxes that hadn't been broken down. She hadn't believed him—the manager had insisted they flatten every box and even taped a reminder to the back door. It sounded like a made-up excuse to see her, which was flattering and terrifying. They could be friends again, maybe, but date him? *God, no.* She'd been so relieved when a customer walked in and she could get away.

Why did she never know what to say to him anymore? Because of the accident they'd never talked about, or because they used to like each other but that had ended, too? Or most likely, because seeing him made her think of ME, and that just plain hurt.

If she was going to be a lawyer, she'd better learn how to talk to people about something besides the latest Ken Follett novel and the best Crockpot cookbook for a wedding shower. She'd restocked the personal growth section, hoping for a book that would help her, but nothing said "How to talk to the boy you once thought you'd marry but now can't face because you helped kill his sister."

Now here he was again, even though it was Saturday, talking with Father Leary and blocking her path. Her fingers gripped the choker, rolling the jade bead in the center. Andy's back was to her, and she could see how his shoulders strained the seams of his sport coat. His neck was deeply tanned. She'd heard he went golfing in Palm Springs with his dad last winter. His mother still wasn't leaving the house.

Father Leary pressed his lips together, nodding as Andy spoke. The Simoniches were his parishioners. Andy hadn't been his student, but ME had, briefly. And Father Leary was the kind of priest who would check in with his flock—who would think of his parishioners as his flock, to be shepherded through the pain of this world, guided by the promise of glory in the next.

Just because it sounded like a crock of shit to her didn't mean it wasn't true to him.

Andy raised one hand, still talking, and the lines on Father Leary's forehead deepened. Then the priest noticed her. His chin rose, and he raised his own hand in greeting.

Crap. No way now could she sneak past them into the bookstore.

"Lindsay Keller, looking like a spring day despite the chill in the air," Father Leary said, and his tone made her wonder if he wasn't glad of a reason to get away from Andy.

Projection, that was called, according to the psychology text-book she'd found in the library. It was not a good thing.

Her hands automatically smoothed her skirt.

Andy spun around. At the sight of her, he blinked rapidly. "Lindsay. What are you doing here?"

"I work here." She gestured. A deep flush crawled up his neck and settled on his cheeks.

"Well, yeah, I know, but—" His eyes darted to the bookstore, then back to her, then settled on the priest. "Father, I thank you—my family thanks you—for your . . ." He paused, as if searching for the word. "Your loyalty."

"You are always in my prayers."

Andy sped away down the mall. Lindsay watched, confused. Despite Father Leary's closing words, their prior conversation no longer seemed so pastoral.

"I interrupted," she said. "I'm sorry."

"Nooo. Not at all." The priest extended an arm toward the book-store. "What's new in my favorite section?"

She led the way, grateful to trod on safer ground. It must get tedious at times, even for a priest, always consoling people for their losses.

But not hers. Not today. It wasn't just the loss of ME and her childish daydreams about Andy. She mourned the loss of days when a boy could treat her like a friend, call her names, and make her laugh and squirm at the same time.

Simpler times, her mother called them. A casualty of growing up that almost made her want to refuse, like Peter Pan and the Lost Boys.

A lost boy.

That's what Andy had looked like. Not like a man with a job and a multimillion-dollar property to help manage.

"Any new *Star Wars* books?" Father Leary asked as he followed her to the sci-fi section, the book cart right where she'd parked it.

"No, sorry. The last ones were the Han Solo adventures, and you've read those." He was younger than her parents, but he had to be forty. "They don't seem like priest books, you know?"

"Because they're made-up, fantastical tales featuring space-ships and light sabers and bizarre creatures not seen in biblical days?"

She nodded.

"In my classes in Miles City, before I came here, the kids and I talked about the themes in *Star Wars*," he continued. "Very popular discussion. I'm already looking forward to next year, when the third movie comes out. We might make a field trip, arrange a special showing. Of course, you'll be away in college then, studying serious literature." His smile gently teased her.

Father Leary never talked down to the students. His classes with the seniors this past year had veered away from what she thought of as religion—church history and doctrine, the Blessed Trinity, how many angels can dance on the head of a pin (six if they're skinny, four if they're fat). Instead, he'd focused on what he called practical ethics, challenging them to identify their core principles and discuss how to use them in making daily decisions about life. His approach had made the big, daunting world outside the school's yellow brick walls seem more manageable.

And yet, it hadn't protected her from the big questions the car wreck had raised.

Talking to Father Leary about her true feelings would have meant confessing her sins. All of them. In the Church's world, there was no absolution without complete disclosure, to an intercessor, of every sordid detail. Remorse wasn't enough.

"Good and evil, sacrifice, harnessing the power within," he went on. "And the necessity of reliable friends."

Did he know what she'd done, letting ME take the bottle? How could he?

She used her sandal to toe a chunk of green goo stuck to the brown tweed carpet.

"Oh, a new Windhaven. Not my favorite series, but I do like George R. R. Martin." He took the book off the cart but didn't turn it over to scan the back cover, as people usually did. Instead, he looked her squarely in the eye. "Lindsay, I understand what you all are going through. You more than your classmates, because you and Mary Ellen were so close."

More than his words, it was his tone that froze her in place.

"I've never said this in class, but I lost a friend when I was your age. It wasn't my fault, but I felt responsible for a long time."

But that's the difference, she thought. *It* was *my fault.* "What happened?"

He shook his head. "I won't burden you with the details. I just want you to know you're not the only person to feel the way you do. I say that not to minimize your pain, but to reassure you that it does get easier."

Her throat spasmed, hot and swollen.

He put the book back on the cart. "I need to replace one of my Dune books. I loaned it to a student last year and never got it back. There it is." He plucked a copy of *The Children of Dune* from the shelf and held it in the "decision-made" grip. "I'll read a few pages while I wait for my movie."

"What are you seeing?" she asked as they walked to the front counter.

"*Chariots of Fire.*" at her look of surprise, he grinned. "I enjoy history almost as much as science fiction. Besides, it has a strong moral theme."

Uh-oh. That meant she'd better see it, because they would talk about it in class. She rang up the sale and handed him his change. He refused a bag, sliding the book into the pocket of his black jacket. Then he raised his plain, freckled face to her.

"Lindsay, we are always harder on ourselves than on anyone else."

"If that were true, Father, then wouldn't the world be a better place? Wouldn't everyone work to be kinder and more thoughtful, and never flip anyone off or drop their gum on the carpet?"

His lips curved, not quite a smile. "I suppose I mean thoughtful people with a good brain and a kind heart, like you."

She swallowed and fiddled with a paperclip, staring at the countertop. *He does know,* she thought. *Did Andy tell him? Or Jana?*

Though Jana hadn't been in the hideaway, might not know that Mary Ellen took the bottle of whiskey to taunt Lindsay, and that Lindsay hadn't stopped her.

Father Leary raised his hand as if in benediction, and though he did not make the sign of the cross, the familiar sense of belonging and blessing welled up in her. She watched his black back as he strode out into the mall.

Then she went to find a razor blade, to scrape up the dried gum.

WEDNESDAY
March 2, 2016

"**Y**ou're sure he'll make it?" Donovan asked the surgeon as they left the parking garage asshole's room in the ICU. The PGA, as he'd dubbed the creep. Though the patient was still unconscious, Donovan had been allowed a quick look. An ordinary guy on the scrawny side, except for the tattoos. You could never tell who the bad guys were just by looking. "'Cause I can't charge a dead guy."

"No reason to think he won't make a full recovery." The surgeon looped his stethoscope around his neck. Medium height and build, like Donovan, but maybe ten years older, with a tan from a winter vacation. "Blunt force trauma skull fractures aren't usually hard to repair, but the fragments did make this one tricky." He shrugged one white-coated shoulder in a way that said, *"For lesser mortals."*

A nurse in blue cotton pants and a top printed with tiny teddy bears walked by. Seemed like the wrong uniform for this floor, but whatever made her happy.

"So that's why he's still out of it?" Donovan asked. "And why the surgery took so long?"

The MD nodded. "The coma doesn't worry me. Not unusual. Of course, we're keeping a lookout for intracranial bleeding."

"Find any?" He was inviting a short lecture, but it could be useful in explaining the injuries to the prosecutor and making his case to throw the book at the scumbag. Aggravated assault, assault with a weapon, attempted robbery—a smorgasbord of felonies to choose from. Donovan liked assault with a weapon, but that wasn't his call.

The MD leaned against the nurses' station and held up his hands as if cradling a small ball. Or a cantaloupe. Pathologists always compared the brain to a cantaloupe, but doctors with living patients were a little more tactful, in Donovan's experience. "Three types of bleeds. They all put pressure on the brain. Epidural bleeds occur between the dura, the membrane that protects the brain, and the skull itself. Common in skull fractures, where the bone fragments can tear the arteries, letting the blood fill up the space. Subdural bleeds are similar, but they occur between the membrane and the brain." He paused, checking to be sure Donovan followed.

"With you so far."

"Those typically show up right away and are usually easy to repair. The third type of bleed is intracerebral, meaning in the brain tissue itself. Harder to detect, and they can develop days after impact."

"So you're saying it's a good thing when the skull cracks, and relieves that pressure?"

"You might think so, but no." The surgeon dropped his hands and rested one elbow on the counter. "The pressure isn't necessarily in the same area, and of course, the fractures are usually quite small. That's why we have to get in there quickly. And we did."

That was good. The world would be better off without scum like the PGA, but the case could get complicated if he died. The prosecutor would go double cautious, and if there was reason to doubt that the victim—a woman trained in martial arts—had acted in self-defense . . .

Donovan knew too well the lasting impact of killing a man. She didn't deserve that.

Truth be told, he didn't want to be deprived of the satisfaction of seeing the sleazeball sent down for a long time. They'd found a record of assaults in Wyoming and Colorado that would earn the creep a good, stiff sentence.

"When I first saw the extent of his injuries, I was concerned about the brain stem, which leads into the spinal column." The MD turned his head slightly and tapped the base of his skull with one finger. "Damage or pressure there can cause loss of consciousness, and if it's severe, shut down respiration and lead to paralysis or death in fairly short order. Bodies aren't meant to slam into concrete."

"And they aren't meant for attacking innocent women going about their daily business, either."

The man held up his hands. "Hey, I just fix 'em. What happens next is up to you. Point is, your guy suffered no damage to the spinal column. He should be able to walk into the jail and into the courtroom, though how much he'll remember, I can't say."

Though the eyewitness hadn't seen the entire incident, what he'd seen matched the victim's account to the T. The less the PGA remembered, the better.

"Good. Thanks."

"One more thing." The doctor asked the woman seated behind the counter to bring up the photographs in the medical record. She did, turning the monitor toward them. He leaned in, pointing with the end of his black pen. "There. I might be able to say that the bruising on his torso, just above the seventh rib, the one that fractured, is consistent with the reported kick."

Yes, Donovan wanted to shout. "But ribs can break for other reasons, too, right? Like in the fall he took." He was playing devil's advocate.

"The fractured rib is in the front." The doc managed to avoid smiling, knowing his testimony would confirm the woman's story. "Nothing else of note. Fractured humerus—the upper arm bone. Cuts and bruises."

Donovan pictured the scene. The guy had been reaching for her shoulder bag, grabbing the strap, when she took him out. Protecting herself and her property. The bag had flown across two empty stalls and landed on the roof of a Grand Cherokee. The guy hit the floor. Good chance his outstretched arm cracked then.

"How long till we can talk to him?"

The MD shrugged again. "The brain's an unpredictable thing. We'll call you when he wakes up. Meanwhile, we'll keep an eye out for bleeding and treat his pain."

Donovan held out his hand. "Thanks, Doc.

Too bad there was no easy fix for the victim's pain. It ought to be a rule that the bastards suffered as long as their victims did. Maybe it was a rule, if you believed in God and hell and the afterlife. Some days, most days, he wasn't sure what he believed about all that.

But he did know some justice was possible. That was the root of the job, after all.

And he had a job to do.

SUNDAY
May 30, 1982

I t was true what he'd been told when he started teaching. Each class had its own personality, shaped by shared experiences. From his chair on St. Patrick's altar, Father Leary studied the seventy-five seniors filling the front pews, their faces as bright as their caps and gowns. They were forever changed by tragedy. He'd been astonished by the discussions that continued all year long in his basement seminar room—by the depth of loss, yes, but also the growth in understanding.

That was the goal, the reason you taught. To spark that growth and guide it.

But certain personality types recurred with remarkable consistency: the clown, the athletes, the academic standouts. The kids with the ability to make anyone feel included, and the kids determined to make themselves bigger by making others smaller.

He should have grasped that twenty-five years ago, when he'd been part of a cadre of cocky, overconfident boys who lived in each other's back pockets. Would things have turned out differently had they not gotten trapped by guilt?

Logically, he knew he and Tony hadn't been responsible for Ed's death, despite the foolish games they'd been playing. It could have happened to any one of them. When Ed hadn't surfaced after the last dive, the other two had plunged back into the lake again and again, searching desperately, to the point of exhaustion. Later, after the professional divers found the body, the coroner said their buddy had broken his neck diving off the rock and died instantly.

That hadn't stopped Ed's family from blaming him and Tony, and it hadn't stopped them from blaming themselves. With the perspective of time and other tragedies, Leary understood that blame is easier than forgiveness. And that it can be easier to let anger control your choices than to let it go.

Sometimes, he had learned, tragedy can handcuff you.

At least, that's how it had been for him and Tony. He prayed these kids would be spared that fate.

But despite the differences between the classes, the student speeches were so similar that he was glad he only had to listen once a year. One bright kid after another, proclaiming that the world was theirs and pledging to live life to the fullest, without any idea what that meant.

Although this class was different that way, too. Senseless death had made them more thoughtful, more cognizant of life's fragility. Its fickleness.

The first speaker, chosen by the class, delivered a message about as deep as that on the greeting cards designed for the day, though it was funny. The boy's black-and-white high-top Chuck Taylors poked out from beneath his flimsy green gown.

Leary's mind drifted to the transfer orders in his shirt pocket. His duties here would end in ten days, and he was expected to take over St. Leo's in Lewistown on July 1, as co-pastor and high school religion teacher.

Thank goodness the rural town a hundred miles north had a movie theater. He'd laughed it off when a parishioner expressed concern over seeing a priest at the movies, especially science fiction fare the woman considered inappropriate for a priest, until the complaint reached the bishop's ears. Leary had replied that he enjoyed popular culture and needed an occasional break, and besides, it gave him something to talk about with the kids.

All true.

When he wrote today's sermon, he'd had to resist the temptation to sprinkle in too many of the movie references he used in class. Best not to overdo the talk about Indiana Jones's search for the lost ark as the search for God in the self, or to recast the battle between Luke Skywalker and Darth Vader in terms of Christ and the devil, and the struggles of ordinary humans to stay on the side of the light. Not that *Star Wars'* mythic roots weren't consistent with sound Christian doctrine, but some in the audience would wonder if he'd been tippling the communion wine.

The new parish would offer the familiar small-town Montana mix—a place where truckers and welders lived next door to bankers and pharmacists, and farm and ranch life was central to both the economy and the community. Good people, salt of the earth. His people. Frequent moves were standard practice, although he'd only been in Billings a year. Had the truth about his past finally come out? Leary had harbored the fear day and night, though not for himself. The bishop had said nothing.

And while change wasn't always easy, he had taken a vow of obedience and humility. A vow he meant to keep.

The transfer orders gave him time to devote himself to prayer and reflection, to examine his conscience and atone for his sins. A Jesuit friend in Portland had offered him their guest house. He could visit Irene and the girls.

The girls. Carrie ought to be in this class. The abrupt uprooting had been harder on her than on Ginger, still just a child. How could he not think of them today? He had brought them to Billings, after all, and it was his error in judgment that had forced them to leave. Major events evoke memories of other major events, especially those that shift our transit and put us on a different course. They'd talked about that very thing last week in senior seminar.

"And I want to thank our English teacher," the boy at the podium said, "for making us memorize poems. I memorized Robert Frost. 'Two roads diverged in a yellow wood, and I—I took the road less traveled by.' But now I'm lost, and I really wish she'd send out a search team because I don't want to miss my own party tonight. There's gonna be cake."

The crowd chuckled, and Leary smiled.

He could fly to the coast, not drive, so he wouldn't feel obligated to stop at the state prison. Dear God, what was happening to him? He couldn't even tell if his invocation of the Lord's name was in prayer or despair. The line between sometimes grew faint.

What sort of pastor was he, avoiding his flock?

But then, Tony, aka "the black sheep," had never been one of the faithful.

Neither had he, God forgive him.

Leary forced himself to train an interested gaze on the speaker.

Tony's sins were unforgivable, to man. God had greater capacity for forgiveness, infinite capacity, and it was Leary's most solemn prayer that when his own time came to talk with the Maker, to plead his case to share in the eternal life of Jesus, despite his own grave sins, he would be granted a fraction of that grace.

Because in addition to everything else, Leary had nearly committed the worst sin a priest could commit. And not against just any man, but against his childhood best friend, the man he himself had wronged. That night, not quite nine years ago, when Tony broke down and admitted everything he had done on that lonely road in the western part of the state, he'd been seeking one thing from his friend. The one thing only a priest could give.

Leary had been so shocked that he nearly withheld the sacrament, the gift of intercession. Especially when Tony refused to reveal the reasons for his actions to the sheriff and prosecutor. Leary understood why. Still, his own hypocrisy stung him.

A round of applause drew Leary back to the present. He raised his hands to join in. The speaker gathered up his notes and danced a jig on the altar before bounding down the steps.

Then Lindsay Keller strode confidently toward the podium in her high-heeled sandals. She was the salutatorian, second in the class, although he thought she had a more capable mind than the stodgier, predictable girl who'd finished first. She scanned the audience and unfolded a single sheet of lined yellow paper.

He'd been surprised to see her so obviously attracted to the Simonich boy a few weeks back, in the mall. Andy had graduated a year or two ago, so Leary hadn't taught him, but the boy had those good looks tinged with a hint of danger that drew the girls. Much like Tony in their high school days, with his full lips and brooding eyes. Unlike his own face, the one the parish priest had called the map of Ireland. Even as children, the adults had him destined for the priesthood and Tony marked for the opposite.

And Jerzy, older, but part of their crowd? Jerzy had conveniently been occupied when Leary dropped by the house the other day to check on him and Barbara. She felt keenly the loss of this milestone, a child's graduation, and they'd prayed together for Mary Ellen and the entire family.

"None of us expected, when we walked into senior hall last September, how much this year would change us," Lindsay said to the assembly of students, family, teachers, and staff. "We were children then. We are children no more."

A soft sound rustled through the pews. The air grew quieter and more serious.

"In September, Sandra Day O'Connor became the first woman appointed to the Supreme Court. When she graduated from Stanford Law School in 1952, she was offered one job, as a legal secretary. In October, President Anwar Sadat of Egypt was assassinated. In November, Luke and Laura got married."

Laughter at a reference Leary would not have understood had he not spent so much time with teenage girls who followed the soaps, even though they rarely got to watch them.

"In January, Red Lodge Mountain closed because there was too much snow for skiing. In March, the Vietnam Veterans Memorial opened in Washington, D.C. Some of the top songs were 'Bette Davis Eyes,' 'Endless Love,' 'Nine to Five,' and the phone number you will never forget, 'Eight-six-seven—'"

"'Five-three-oh-nine,'" the kids sang.

"Stephen King, John Irving, Colleen McCullough, and Robert Ludlum topped the bestseller lists. And Father Leary's favorite movie?" She held out her hands and said the words along with her classmates. "*Raiders of the Lost Ark.*"

"These are the touchstones of the last year, along with winning three state titles, in football, gymnastics, and girls' golf. But none of us will ever forget that weekend in September when our classmate, Mary Ellen Simonich, was killed, and Jana Stenerud injured."

He'd known she planned to talk about the accident, but just what this brave girl—this *bold* girl, to borrow a phrase from poor Sister Claire—would say next, he had no idea.

"What we have learned is how to keep going when our hearts are breaking. How to make a new plan, how to dream a new dream. Facing tragedy so young will not prevent any of us from facing it again." Her voice cracked, and Leary leaned forward an inch or two, silently urging her on.

Her shoulders rose, and she took a deep breath before continuing. "But the lessons our experience has given us—to rely on each other, and to trust in kindness and the power of love—will see us through those future dark times as they have seen us through the dark days of the past."

Today, these kids felt so close. And yet some of them would never see each other again.

Then she surprised him. "We couldn't have done it without our own Father Mike, Father Leary, who listens to us talk about everything under the sun without blinking and without calling the cops. Or our parents." A low ripple of amusement spread through the church, and he bent his head to hide the flush that was the curse of his fair skin.

"We've been talking today about the good things ahead, the joys and successes. And they will come. Every one of us will be faced with more opportunities than we can imagine to practice the lessons we learned this year. Because of the examples of our friends, our teachers, and our families—the examples all of you have given us—we will know what to do. Thank you."

The crowd applauded, the students standing, as she stepped off the altar, the bright green gown sweeping behind her. From his chair beside the golden tabernacle, Father Leary clapped along with them.

May the Force be with you, Lindsay Keller.

WEDNESDAY
March 2, 2016

D onovan shucked off his coat and started the coffee. After the visit to the ICU, he needed a good jolt. He'd missed shift change, the busiest part of the day. But even at its busiest, the Billings PD was quieter than any station he'd worked in back east.

The quiet out west had unnerved him, on that first trip when he and Beth flew out for her interview at the college and to scope out openings in law enforcement. A few weeks later, they drove into town with the kids and the dog, jobs waiting.

A man could love both calm and storm, couldn't he?

He poured a cup and doctored it. In every moment not focused on the parking garage attack, he'd studied the old files: patrol reports, detective's notes, lab results. They made special software for organizing cold cases, but Donovan relished sorting it out himself, combing through every detail.

Roy Small had been a meticulous investigator and file keeper. Donovan had worked with him briefly when he first joined the department. The older man was helpful, though too close to retirement to want to mentor yet another young detective. Now his wife was in treatment for cancer—Donovan had run into him at the hospital a few weeks ago.

He reached for the notebook labeled "Exhibits." Photocopied the file shot of Leary's face and tacked it next to the map on the wall. Sipped his coffee and studied the priest's features. Plain, open, sincere.

What did you do, Father? What did you know?

Asking questions wasn't blaming the victim. He was hunting for gold, buried in the muck.

But the face in the photograph was just a face. It wasn't talking; it wasn't telling him a thing.

He reread the forensics reports. On TV, lab tests solved everything. DNA magic. Never mind that DNA did little good without a suspect's sample for comparison. Matches were a crapshoot.

Leary and Donovan, they needed some of that Irish luck.

He spent the next hour poring over witness lists, statements, and lead sheets. He reread the statement from the mechanic at the all-night gas station. Donovan found the address, in the Heights, and stuck a pin on the map. From a bird's-eye view, the Heights looked like part of the city squeezed out of a toothpaste tube, as though the Rims and the river had tightened around the streets and squirted them out in a splattery blob on the alkali flats northeast of town.

The witness had been eating his lunch—at three AM, but midday to him—when the priest came in. Leary said he'd been summoned to give last rites to a dying woman, but the place was hard to find, and he'd been told to call from the gas station and someone would meet him. The pay phone was out of order, so the priest had come inside to use the office phone. He'd pulled a note out of his pocket to dial the number, but the witness had gone to the john. "To give him a moment of privacy, you know? A priest doing his sacred duty and all."

A few minutes later, the mechanic was under the hood of an old farm truck, changing the rings—"I could sit on my ass, nobody would know, but I'd rather keep busy"—when he heard what sounded like a truck pull in. Didn't see it, being busy, but he heard Leary call out a greeting. He did not hear the reply.

Nearly twenty-one years ago, but the mechanic might still be around. Meanwhile, there was video—an honest-to-God video from the station's single security camera. Donovan took the black plastic videotape downstairs to a room full of ancient equipment. Turned on the VCR, but nothing happened. Checked the plug and wires, then found a sticky note on the floor underneath the shelf, saying *"Needs repair."*

Donovan swore, then trekked back upstairs, made a call, and grabbed his coat. Hot-footed it to the sheriff's department two blocks away, where a deputy set him up with a working VCR and stood beside him to watch the tape.

"Dead man walking," the deputy said, and Donovan suppressed a shiver. *Exactly.* Three o'clock in the morning and there was the priest, fifty-one years old, with no idea that he had hours to live. Or so they guessed.

Bad light, distant, and grainy, but it had been good enough for a positive ID on Leary. No sound from those old cameras. The same tapes got used over and over—they'd caught a break that this one had been found.

"I always wondered," the deputy said, "if he diddled somebody who grew up and took revenge."

"Department looked at that when he disappeared," Donovan replied, "but nothing came to light." Still, he kept the ugly possibility in mind.

On the screen, Father Leary leaned against his car, an older black Buick. A few minutes later, he straightened, took a couple of steps, and held out his hand. Donovan watched the priest's lips move before he left the camera's frame. The person he'd been speaking to did not come into view.

Odd, that. As if he knew where the camera was and had deliberately kept himself and his vehicle out of sight. He, or she.

Then Leary came back into the picture, climbed into his car, and drove off. The mechanic had heard both vehicles leave and presumed the priest had followed the truck. From the sound, he'd guessed they'd gone north on the highway, aka the Roundup Road. Logical.

It had been early October, warm enough for Leary to wait outside. The truck showed up so quickly that it had to have come from close by.

Leary must have known the driver.

Who, Father, who?

Outside on the sidewalk, the March air cold, the skies bright and clear, Donovan pondered. Who called a priest out in the middle of the night to administer a sacrament, and never said a word when the man disappeared?

The killer—or someone covering for him.

And where, in all those pages, was the name or the detail that would lead him to it?

Back at the station, Donovan stored the tape, told the desk sergeant about the busted VCR, and made a new pot of coffee. Some days, he thought he was the only cop in the place who knew how.

Sat at his desk cradling the hot mug, feet outstretched. *A priest.* Jesus Christ. The voice of his mother that lived in his head chided him for taking the Lord's name in vain. But if there were ever a time, this was it.

The mechanic's statement sounded straightforward, but people sometimes remembered details later for no obvious reason. Or a new development might spark an "Oh, that's what that means" moment. You never knew.

He called the desk sergeant and asked for an updated witness list. Civilian staff would do the work—addresses, phone numbers, and next of kin if they'd passed on.

Even the dead could talk sometimes. Cop world buzzed a few years back when a decades-old case was solved in Chicago. A woman on her deathbed confessed that she'd lied to give her son a false alibi in the murder of a neighborhood child nearly fifty years earlier. After her death, her daughter told police, who tracked the long-lost brother to Seattle. The secondhand confession had been enough to convict the man, a retired small-town cop, though no doubt the scumbag would appeal.

So, you never knew.

Small's notes detailed the search of the gas station's phone records. One call had been made around three AM, to a pay phone outside a closed casino a mile away. They'd followed the leads and asked all the right questions, but come up empty. Roy Small had contacted every funeral home and hospital within a hundred and fifty miles, searching for the dying woman. He'd put a request in the newspaper for help from doctors or relatives. If she'd miraculously recovered, wouldn't her family have come forward to praise the priest who'd saved her, then disappeared?

Small had concluded the call to the rectory had been a hoax, a ruse to roust the priest, and Donovan had to agree. But not any priest. Father Michael Leary. It was personal.

Donovan typed up a to-do list, as much to satisfy the chief and his lieutenant as to organize his thoughts.

And then, it was time to put this investigation under his feet.

* * *

Donovan parked downwind of the high school. Some of the other cops still razzed him now and then for saying "pahked" and "cah." Josh would be starting here next year. He'd surprised himself, agreeing to put the kids in Catholic school, but Beth had convinced him. It was less about religion and more about morality, academics, and the small class size that made a kid less likely to get lost in the crowd. Josh was a kid who could get lost.

On the eighth-grade parents' tour a few weeks ago, they'd visited the science and music rooms, walked down freshman hall, and sat in the library for a presentation. Now, as he finished his perimeter circuit and opened the glass door on Division Street, he took a deep breath and imagined himself as the priest. One of those people, if he guessed right, with both an extroverted side that craved human interaction and a private side focused on the inner life. The spiritual life.

And some kind of secret life?

At the office, he showed his badge.

The secretary sucked in her breath. "You're here about Father Leary. I saw the story in the paper. That poor man."

The priest, not the man who found the wallet. "You knew him, then."

"Such a lovely spirit. Always had a kind word and a smile on his face. We were heartbroken. So glad you're reopening the case."

"Do you have a list of faculty and staff who worked with him?"

"Of course," she said, sliding into administrative mode. "He was assigned here briefly in the early 1980s. Before my time—I came in 1989. He came back shortly after that and stayed until . . ."

Until his death. "Anyone from the 1995 school year still here? Besides you."

She tilted her head, running down her mental list. "Sister Delphina went back to Ireland and passed away a few years ago. Sister Claire, one of the PE teachers, moved to a retirement community her order runs in New York. Sister Mary Teresa left the convent. She married the widowed father of a student and they moved to New Mexico. I get Christmas cards. One or two lay teachers moved to the public schools. Some of the retired folks pop in now and then."

"I'd appreciate as complete a list as you can give me," he said.

He clipped a "VISITOR" pass to his lapel. A wide glass trophy case dominated the wall outside the office—for a small school, they'd won a lot of state titles. Josh had no interest in sports. Neither did Nora, but he wasn't worried about her fitting in—his girl could make a friend in a hollow tree.

Outside the chapel, he took a deep breath. Brian Donovan was not a churchgoing man, but you went where the job took you. Inside, a bowl of holy water was mounted on the doorframe. A small red candle glowed on the altar, indicating the presence of the body of Christ. The place smelled of candle wax and furniture polish, with a hint of teenage BO. He slid into the last pew.

Early in his career, he'd been taught that it wasn't enough to study the scene of the crime. You had to study the scenes of the victim's life. That's where the energy is, where you begin to understand a man or woman. It sounded woo-woo airy-fairy when you tried to describe it, but it was like when he was a kid and walked into the kitchen after his parents had argued. He could feel the tension, even when he hadn't heard a raised voice or seen a dark eye. You knew, somehow.

He ran a hand over the well-worn seat of the pew. Twenty years was a long time. If all the cells in our body regenerate every seven years, and yet we're still the same person, that was equally true of a room, despite new paint and carpet. While the quilted banner that hung behind the altar looked fairly new, you didn't change out the crucifix because you'd gotten tired of the old one or it wasn't this year's shade of gold.

No. Father Leary had presided over this space. He'd stood on the altar. He'd opened the tiny doors of the tabernacle and slid the consecrated hosts in and out. He'd recited the ritual words, offered up his prayers, guided the pleas of the students and teachers and janitors as they made their whispered way to heaven. Despite himself, Donovan bowed his head.

Minutes later, he was strolling down the hallway, glancing in classrooms as he passed. Some students listened while others bent over notebooks, scribbling.

The bell rang and doors flew open, spilling kids into the halls. The flood of movement nearly pinned him against the wall, giving him a chance to watch. Teenhood involved a lot of touch—casual punches and shoves between the boys, openly affectionate gestures between the girls, who threw their arms around each other or picked a hair off a sweater without the slightest self-consciousness.

He felt himself sixteen again for a moment, his body holding fear, strength, anger, and desire all at once.

Then the wave passed and all was quiet.

He found the stairs to the lower level, remembering the catacombs of his own Catholic high school. In the basement, a door stood open, the small room empty. A crucifix hung on one wall. Two long, scarred tables had been pushed together, surrounded by a dozen chairs. The walls were scarred, too, the paint chipped by chairs carelessly dropped, the baseboards scuffed by shoes as boys rough-housed.

He pictured a group seated at the table, Father Leary at the head. Roy Small had talked to the kids about the investigation, asked about the priest, how he treated them, what they knew of his private life. Donovan could almost see them squirming. But according to the file, no students or faculty had even hinted to Small that Leary had abused these kids.

Neither had Lindsay Keller, who'd sat in these chairs years earlier.

He had no reason to think she knew anything about the murder. But the wallet showing up after all this time—wicked strange.

"Thank you," he told the secretary a few minutes later as he traded his pass for the list of teachers and staff in 1995. She'd high-lighted the names of those still in town in yellow, the deceased in pink. "This will save us a lot of work."

Outside, he turned up the collar of his topcoat and strode across Division. He could drive to St. Patrick's, but despite the chill, he wanted to walk the route Father Leary had taken. The weather had fooled him today, as it often did—the sky clear and the sun bright, though the temperature was barely above freezing.

A few blocks later, he reached the grade school, the center of his children's life away from home. He glanced up at the windows, then cut through the playground, quiet for the moment, to the next block. Stood on the sidewalk, gloved hands in his pockets, staring across the street at the rectory and cathedral. What had Leary's last day been like, that Monday in October 1995? What had he done, who had he seen?

Why had it seemed like a good idea to answer a call to bless a dying woman in the middle of the night, in a place he wouldn't be able to find alone and that wasn't even in his parish?

Because that's what priests do.

Like many old churches, St. Patrick's hugged the sidewalk, a stained-glass window with an arched top its face to passersby, a rose window above. Instead of a single grand entrance, two short flights of steps led to doors on either side of the façade. He climbed one and entered the vestibule, surprised to be greeted inside by a set of plain glass doors, clearly temporary.

Oh, right. The Doors of Mercy. Pope Francis had declared this the Year of Mercy, emphasizing forgiveness and compassion. The kids had brought home a flyer on the project, and there'd been a special prayer service when they dedicated the doors. He'd stayed home and done yard work. But he understood the message. To pass through these doors meant leaving judgment behind.

He was not here to impose judgment, but to bring a man before society's judgment. Render unto Caesar and all that. If he crossed into God's territory in the process, tough luck for the Big Guy. Donovan strode through the doors and into the nave.

A man in black knelt in the front pew, head bowed, folded hands resting on the rail in front of him. The current rector.

Donovan slipped off his gloves and rubbed the warmth back into his hands. If you went by size, St. Pat's was more church than cathedral. Ornate by modern standards but nothing like the gilded curlicues he'd grown up with. On the altar, murals of angels flanked the gold tabernacle, and the pale blue arched ceiling and tall, clear glass windows filled the nave with light. All designed, he knew, to direct the attention of the faithful to higher things.

How had Father Michael Leary felt about this place?

According to the case file, Mike Leary had been the third son of a coal miner who struggled to make a living after the mines closed in the 1930s. The elder Leary later found work blasting rock for the Beartooth Highway, a winding mountain pass with breathtaking vistas that looked, to Donovan's New England eyes, like something only a goat or a crazy man could have imagined.

Had Leary's vocation been a calling, or security after a hardscrabble upbringing? When he put on his priestly garb and stood in front of his flock, had he felt blessed or burdened? Was it sometimes just another job? The expectations had to weigh a man down, now and then. Maybe that was why so many priests took to drink.

A priest's work wasn't all that different from a cop's, in some ways.

In the back of the church, a series of brass plaques commemorated donors. If walls could talk . . . If he believed the file, Leary had been popular at both church and school, aside from the occasional complaint about a dull sermon or a lower than expected grade. The then-bishop had told Small he chose Leary to fill the unexpected vacancy in Lewistown because he was both a good parish priest and a good teacher.

All the praise was almost too good to believe.

Small and his team had talked to half the city and identified not a single viable suspect.

If people had not wanted to speak ill of the dead then, could Donovan loosen their tongues now?

Next to the plaques were the confessionals, not used much since the communal rites of penance had been established. Hard to imagine sitting inside, listening to the best and worst of humanity. Had the worst grown worse over the decades? Doubtful. It seemed like the world was broken now, but it had probably always seemed that way.

Donovan turned up the side aisle, a votive stand against the wall. Thought briefly about lighting a candle for his old man, then decided not to waste the wax. Up front, the priest, older but not elderly, crossed himself, then left the pew and started toward the side door.

"Spare a moment, Father?"

Father James Coletta looked up, his dark eyes wide. His bushy white brows rose. "Detective. Brian. I have a lunch date with a parishioner, a major donor—you know how these old buildings always need work—but we can talk as we walk." He gestured toward the side door. The implications were obvious: Donovan had been expected. And a murder investigation was not a subject for this solemn, sacred place.

Fine with him. The sooner they got on neutral ground, the better.

"I won't take much of your time, Father. How long have you been here?"

"I came as an assistant twenty-three years ago, and I've been pastor for thirteen. I have been blessed to serve a deeply engaged flock, and I hope the bishop sees fit to keep me here as long as I'm able."

"So you worked with Father Leary."

Coletta paused on the sidewalk between church and rectory, though he wore no coat. A gust whipped a wisp of white hair across his brow. "The last priest standing."

"What do you remember about that time?"

"The night Mike disappeared, I took the call, as you surely know." The priest lifted his face to the heavens, as if beseeching his God. Or simply searching his memory. "I always thought the caller sounded familiar."

Donovan's heartbeat sped up. "From the confessional, perhaps?"

The priest's full, faded lips pressed together. "Perhaps. Or as one of three hundred voices, worshipping together on a Sunday morning. We rotated taking late calls and it was my turn, but she asked for Father Leary specifically." He focused on Donovan. "I'll confess, I didn't mind—I'd failed to dodge in a game of sixth-grade dodgeball and had a cast on my arm that made driving tricky. I gave up trying to identify the caller years ago, when I realized I was listening to my parishioners so I could compare their voices to a vague memory instead of hearing their problems and prayers."

"No reason to feel guilty, Father. All you did was convey a message."

"If I had been able to remember," the priest said, "you might have solved this case years ago. I wonder, Detective, does the Lord forgive us when we cannot forgive ourselves?"

"Above my pay grade, Father." Donovan reached inside his coat and drew out a folded piece of paper. "This is the list of priests and staff you gave Detective Small after Father Leary's disappearance. Could we get an update? Any deaths, new addresses. Any other details that could be relevant."

"Certainly." The priest slipped the folded list into his pocket.

"Father, do you recall Father Leary saying anything about losing his wallet?"

"Not a peep."

"It's been a long time. Any theories?"

The older man met his gaze. "I won't say Mike Leary didn't have his struggles—sometimes I think the call to the priesthood is God's way of forcing us to confront our weaknesses head-on. But Mike dedicated everything he had to serving God and His people. If he died because of it, then he is a martyr for the faith."

"And if his death had nothing to do with his work?"

Father Coletta laid a hand on his arm. "That's your department, isn't it?"

It took Donovan a moment to realize it was the wind that stung him in the face.

WEDNESDAY
March 2, 2016
Portland

The boot that came with her rented costume was rubbing a sore spot on Carrie's heel. She turned the key and hobbled into her bungalow, dropping her bag on the red fir floor. She slumped onto the chair beside the door and began tugging.

Ohhh. So much better. She wriggled her toes, then cradled her bare foot, massaging the heel. No blister, thank God. A professional gardener needed her feet in good working shape.

She pushed herself up and tested the foot. Not too bad. She unbuckled the wide belt and tossed it over the back of a kitchen chair, then made a cup of chamomile tea.

The pirate party had been a hit. Asher sat on her lap to wave goodbye to the last of the children, then fell asleep as his father carried him to the car. He'd barely stirred when she leaned in to kiss him, her sweet grandson.

She padded back to the living room, the full skirt swooshing around her ankles. When had she last worn a skirt, let alone a long one? She sank onto the sofa, the mug warming her hands.

Though the garden was her passion, Carrie loved the house almost as much. It had been run-down when they'd bought it twenty years ago, but they'd sanded and painted the woodwork and restored the floors. The couch was a yard-sale find, and she'd taken an upholstery class to recover it. Granted, the place could stand a good dusting, but she'd been too busy with work and Asher to think about that.

Her sister had no reason to turn up her nose at Carrie's house.

She sipped the brew, made from home-grown flowers. Ginger had sent the rug from Kazakhstan and taken the photos that hung on the walls—the Taj Mahal, Dal Lake in Srinagar, Chichen Itza in Mexico. Family pictures crowded the bookshelves that flanked the fireplace.

She set the mug on the coffee table, on top of a gardening magazine, then crossed the room and picked up a gold-tone frame holding a faded Polaroid. The only picture she had of the four of them, she and Ginger with their parents. They'd gone on a picnic down by the river, in some long-forgotten Montana town. Dad had taught her how to catch pop flies. After he died, she'd snuck the snapshot into her room. Her mother must have seen it but had never said a word.

"Which one of you passed on these genes?" she asked, but Tony and Tina West could not reply. They were long gone. "Did you have any idea?"

She set the picture down next to her grandmother's perfume bottles—a pale green flask, a tall hexagon, and a third bottle in a teardrop shape, each topped with a gold cap. Yardley's Red Roses, through the years.

Two more photos sat on the shelf. In one, her mother held baby Ginger, while Carrie perched on the arm of her chair. In the other, she and Ginger stood beside Baba outside the house in Billings. Carrie had held such hope for the place, certain it would be their last move. There had been some nice girls in the class, and she'd begun to make friends. But then they'd had to leave. She knew it had to do with Ginger and the men in the church, but no one had ever trusted her enough to tell her why.

And so she'd started a new school in Portland, a month into senior year, the other kids too preoccupied with getting out of school to pay any attention to her.

Had Baba known about this ghastly disease? What about the Wests, her father's family? Carrie had a half-forgotten memory of meeting an old woman in a dark, cramped room. An unhappy room.

A gust of anger tore at her. Anger at loss, at secrets, at things she needed to know that no one had ever told her.

Maybe Ginger was right, that what she did for her family mattered more than genes and history.

But she couldn't escape the hunch that there was a critical connection. *Antiques Roadshow* was fun, watching people haul in family treasures and garage sale finds, but when the *Genealogy Roadshow* first came on, she'd thought it sounded silly. Why would anyone care about people they'd never met, digging up dusty details about distant relatives? She'd become captivated as the researchers introduced ordinary families to ancestors with stories full of twists and drama. And often, the modern story mirrored the past, even though it had been long forgotten.

Carrie headed upstairs to what she always thought of as the guest room, though it had done dual duty as an office and the girls' playroom. When Ali got pregnant, Carrie had imagined her grandchild spending the night and spreading his Legos and trucks out on the rug.

Not yet, not with Asher's uncertain health. *Soon.*

A half-finished Superman quilt lay in a basket next to her sewing table. Ali's old family tree stretched the length of the table, the curled corners weighted down by gardening books and Jessica's cross-country trophies.

She traced her fingers over the names and dates, details noted in Ali's small, neat printing. One side of the tree was largely blank, naming Carrie and Ginger, their parents, and Baba Irene. Ali had filled their leaf-shaped balloons with a few sparse morsels: Irene kept house for Catholic priests. Tina never lost a game of gin rummy but died of cancer at thirty-two. Tony served in the Army and was killed in Vietnam.

Though Ginger had never said so, Carrie had long realized that his death was what drove her. Ginger honored the battlefield fatality of the father she could not remember by becoming one of the few women photographers known for venturing into war zones.

Carrie traced a finger along the branches. The first time Asher had called her Grandma, she'd been overwhelmed by waves of pure love. Then the disease had struck. She glanced at the bookshelves sagging under the weight of articles on cystic fibrosis and books on coping with childhood illness.

And three of Shakespeare's plays in paperback, bought second-hand when she was in high school in Billings, among the few things she'd kept from then.

We've always been running, she said to herself. My mother, Baba, Ginger. I tell myself I've broken the streak because I've stayed in Portland for thirty-five years. But I've been running, too.

Time to stop.

THURSDAY
March 3, 2016
Billings

"Let's not worry about what he'll say until he wakes up and starts talking," Investigations Lieutenant Nita Hansen said. "No one's gonna believe a guy with his record walked up to a lone woman in a parking garage to ask for directions to the beauty parlor."

Donovan sucked in his cheeks, hands clasped on top of the PGA's file. She was right, as usual.

"Okay, so you want to be a worrywart on this case," the lieutenant continued. "Fine. Just don't get too attached to the victim. Our job is to uncover the truth, not take sides. Now, let's go over what you've got."

The patrol officer who'd assisted in searching the attacker's short-term rental joined them, and they ran down the case in detail.

"Landlord's after us to release the seal on the apartment," the patrol officer said. "He's losing money, blah blah blah. Fat chance."

"He knows the drill," the lieutenant said. "This isn't his first scumbag tenant. Besides, the rent's paid through the end of the week, right?"

The officer nodded. "Place went up in flames, it'd be civic service."

"Good statements you got from the vic and the eyewitness, Donovan," Lieutenant Hansen continued. "And good info from the doc. Soon as we hear from forensics on the prints and blood spatter, we can turn this over to the prosecutor."

"Routine, right? They won't seriously consider charging her." It was self-defense, plain as day. To him anyway. He'd called the vic this morning, to keep her posted. She sounded calm enough, but what turmoil bubbled underneath the surface?

"Not our call." The lieutenant stood. "We're done. Good work." The patrol officer bolted out the door. Donovan hung back to let the boss pass.

She put a hand on his arm. "If you think telling her you once killed a man to defend yourself and your fellow officers will help her process her feelings, go ahead. But don't make this about you. It's not."

Damn. She was right about that, too.

A few minutes later, he pulled out of the police garage, pausing at the exit to put on his sunglasses, then drove out into the bright winter day.

The triangular North Side neighborhood lay tucked beneath the Rims. Patches of snow blanketed the base of the gnarled cottonwoods, even while buds began to swell at the tips of the branches. In a block of well-tended older homes with arched doorways and curved front steps, you might spy a log cabin so encrusted with dirt and moss that you thought it roofed in sod. A neatly tended cottage from the thirties might border an overgrown patch occupied by a rusted-out pickup and a spindly lilac hedge. He passed a lot that held nothing but a teepee frame and a shed sided with mismatched sheets of rusted metal.

A neighborhood ripe for gentrification. Some neighborhoods were always ripe.

His target was easy to spot, the exterior sheathed in Tyvek. An oak door and heavy brass hardware broadcast the remodelers' ambitions. As he crossed the torn-up lawn, he heard the rhythmic whistle and thwack of a pneumatic nail gun and glanced at the roofline, alert for flying debris.

"Help you?" a voice said. A man in a pair of mud-spattered Carhartts came down a ladder, his face wind chapped, cheekbones sun ripened. Sweat dripped from beneath the black-billed red ball cap sporting the inverted double horseshoe logo of the Billings Mustangs.

Donovan held up his department ID, the gold shield glinting. "Detective Brian Donovan, looking for Trevor Morris."

"Ahh." The man wiped a big hand on his pants, for all the good it did, and held it out. At roughly six feet, he had a few inches on Donovan, and a broader chest and shoulders. "That'd be me. You here about that priest's wallet?"

"Yeah. Anything you can tell me would be helpful."

"You're welcome to take a look, but there's not much to see. We moved the house." Morris yanked off the cap and wiped his forehead with his left arm, then slapped the cap on his thigh to get rid of the dust and stuffed it into his hip pocket. "But I can show you around real quick. This way."

In back, a weathered set of temporary steps led to a wood frame screen door, propped open with a two-by-four. "Watch the stick," Morris said, stepping over it, and Donovan did the same. To the right of the tiny entry stood the kitchen, a work in progress. Beyond lay a dining space and living room, the oak floors covered in clear plastic, the walls freshly Sheetrocked, the mud finished to look like plaster.

Morris pointed at a brick fireplace, the mantel stripped to bare wood. "Buyers today demand classic architectural features, but they also want extra power outlets and double-pane windows."

"Quite the project."

"More than we bargained for, truth be told. The basement was jammed with old wooden crates, dead appliances—you name it. After we jacked the place off the foundation, we hauled the crates to our shop, and the one with the wallet got mixed in with our stuff. I suppose you want us to open them all now."

"I'll send a couple of officers to take them off your hands. Find anything else interesting?"

Morris shrugged. "A stack of *Life* magazines from the 1950s. Glass doorknobs—we can always use those. Extra hinges, drawer pulls."

Donovan nodded, surveying the place. No ghosts. No hint of the dead priest's presence. Had too much changed?

"Thanks. I've seen what I needed to see." He followed Morris back outside. "Should be sweet when you're through. Who'd you buy it from?"

"City, on a tax sale." At Donovan's puzzled look, Morris explained. "House gets too run down to rent, owner stops paying taxes. Eventually, the city files a tax lien, and if the owner doesn't pony up, the city forecloses and takes title. Some properties you can get for back taxes; this one had potential, so it went to auction, but we still got it dirt cheap."

Donovan added a note to his mental list to check the ownership history. "How long you been in town?"

"Three years. Hey." He held up both hands, palms out. "I didn't even know that priest was murdered until I saw the story yesterday."

"So why did you think the police would be interested in that wallet, and why did you think you needed a lawyer?"

Morris took a half step back. "No, man, I swear, I told her the truth. A guy's ID, that's important, and you want to do a good deed for a priest, right? I didn't have time to track him down. And no offense, but parking around the police station is a bitch. Then I was zipping along Montana Avenue, and I thought of Lindsay Keller. She did some contract stuff for us. A car pulled out, I pulled in, I popped up to her office. My partner saw the piece in the paper. When he said you thought it was murder, I about shit a brick."

Donovan held up a hand. "It's okay. I'm not accusing you. I know you were a ten-year-old in California when Father Leary disappeared."

"You checked me out?" Morris said. "Well, I guess you had to."

"It's quite the story," Donovan said, and told him about the dead priest who'd once owned the wallet.

"Jesus Christ," the builder said, paling under his winter tan. "Who would do such a thing?"

"My question exactly."

TUESDAY
June 15, 1982
Montana State Prison,
Deer Lodge

The prison guard, his freshly shaven head pink and shiny, gestured Leary forward, bypassing the visitors' line.

"No reason for you to wait, padre. Special dispensation for the clergy." He unzipped Leary's black case for a cursory inspection. "Visiting an ex-parishioner? You can't save 'em all."

Leary hated being called "padre," but he kept his face neutral. "No, but the Lord can." He didn't dare reveal that he'd come to see a boyhood friend. A juicy nugget like that could easily become a cellblock taunt, dropped by a vengeful guard.

He'd done enough to hurt Tony. Of course, Tony had caused plenty of pain himself, but that was no excuse. One sin did not excuse another.

He picked up his sacrament case and followed a second guard, a tall, bulky man who reeked of Old Spice, through a heavy steel door that closed behind them with a blood-chilling clang. It had to be devastating, to know that door would never open for you until the warden said it would.

Life inside was life redefined by the loss of freedoms so simple they barely registered. Like the ability to open and close a door on your own.

They walked down a painted cinderblock hallway and through another steel door. This was the new prison, out in the country, surrounded by cattle and crows. A Holiday Inn compared to the sandstone monstrosity built in territorial days, now a tourist attraction in town.

The guard ushered him into a windowless room, eight by eight. Even here, away from the cells, fear and isolation chilled the air.

Leary laid his case on the battered metal table bolted to the floor. In the distance, another door banged shut, and after a moment, two sets of footsteps grew closer.

Then Tony stood in the doorway, hands cuffed in front of him, the beefy guard practically shoving him forward with his thick chest. Tony's shadowed eyes widened and his full lips parted slightly; then the curtain fell, his face clamped shut. They had not told him who his visitor was, in one more official exercise of control.

"You need anything, Father, you bang on this door," the guard said. "Don't let this stringy piece of crap give you no guff."

Leary found his voice. "I'll thank you to treat him like a human being, Officer. At least while you are in my presence. We are all sinners, and we are all God's children."

The guard smirked. "If you say so, Father." This time he did push his charge, his palm flat against Tony's back. Tony staggered, then caught himself. The door closed, the guard's ear visible through the small, wire-hatched window.

Tony sat awkwardly, cuffed hands in his lap.

"Good to see you, Tony." Leary sat across from Tony, mirroring his posture. The mix of toughness and vulnerability in his old friend shocked him. He had not been prepared for such hatred, or such longing.

He had not been prepared for much of what had happened between him and Tony.

"You look good," he continued, ignoring the sour mix of BO and stale cigarette smoke.

A long silence, then Tony spoke, his voice raspy from disuse. "What are you doing here, Mickey?"

The childhood nickname stabbed Leary in the gut. He forced himself to breathe out slowly, unclenching, calling on all that was holy to help him. "They're giving me a new parish—you know how they move us around—and I've got some time off. I'm driving out to a retreat center on the coast. Thought I'd stop on my way." He had sworn he'd fly, to avoid this visit, but in the end, even he wasn't that much of a coward.

Tony's head jerked up, his eyes narrow. "You're taking the girls, right? To your new post? You promised me, Mickey. When Tina was dying, you promised you'd keep them close."

Leary felt like he was swallowing razor blades. "The girls are fine, Tony. Irene took them out of state last fall."

Tony glared, a hard prison glare. Lord knew he'd had plenty of opportunities to learn it—more useful than the quick, disarming grin that had gotten him in and out of so many scrapes in their youth. "You son of a bitch. You goddamned, self-righteous, crucifix-up-your-ass son of a bitch."

"It wasn't like that, Tony."

"How was it?"

"You know how it was. I had no choice about moving to Billings, and I knew the danger. But Irene thought the girls should have the opportunity to live in a bigger town, go to better schools. And we'd all promised Tina . . ." He trailed off. "I never believed he meant any real harm. Until he came to see me."

He continued, under Tony's dark glare. "He knows about Ginger, Tony. How—" He ran a finger inside his collar. The thin vinyl padding on the metal chair was useless. "But he knows. Irene and I decided—"

Tony's eyes narrowed. "You promised you'd keep them safe. You goddamned—"

"Keep it down," Leary pleaded. "That guard hears you, he'll haul you back to your cell, and he won't be gentle. They are safe. I made sure."

Irene had sworn she wasn't going to hide when she and the girls had done nothing wrong, but she'd agreed to take them to Oregon and accepted the housekeeping job the monsignor arranged in a community of women religious outside Portland. It came with a separate residence on the property, big enough for the three of them. He'd sent a gift for Ginger's birthday this past March, and she'd enclosed a snapshot in the girl's thank-you note.

He drew out his wallet. "See? Last spring, on Ginger's ninth birthday. Isn't she grand?"

But Tony couldn't reach for the wallet, couldn't take the picture in his hands. Leary pulled out the photo, the little medal still in the plastic sleeve, and pushed it across the table. Tony leaned in, then sat back, eyes welling.

"The coast." Tony plucked the word from the air, his voice soft. "I never seen the ocean."

"You know there's a way out of this madness. Out of here. You can turn state's evidence, or whatever it's called. There's no statute of limitations. You don't have to wait until you're eligible for parole." After all they'd done to save a life, all those years ago, how could Tony have taken one? Only, he knew, under the greatest compulsion.

"Quit dreaming, Mike."

"I have some influence."

"And he has more."

The two men stared at each other until finally, Tony raised his bound hands and scratched his chin. "You want me to grouse. To snitch. It's a death sentence, and not just for me."

"They wouldn't. He wouldn't."

"You think you know him, Mickey. But you don't. Not really. You think he's a decent man who crossed the line, outta anger and greed. It ain't nothing like that. You're too innocent, too holy to understand."

"I'm not holy. And I'm sure as hell not innocent. You, of all of people, know that."

Betrayal mixed with pity on Tony's face. "Mickey, you slept with my wife while I was in jail. You got her pregnant. That's bad. But it ain't evil." He sat back. "It ain't even close."

Leary exhaled, then reached for the picture. Slipped it into his wallet, then reached for his sacrament case. No point offering a blessing that would be refused.

"And take your religion with you, Mickey," Tony continued. "It don't do any of us any good anymore."

The deep heat of humiliation flared in Leary's chest. He stood. "I'll go, Tony. But please. Do one honest thing in your life. For the girls. Tell the truth."

On his way out, he vowed to do the same. No matter how long it took or what it cost him.

FRIDAY
June 18, 1982
Portland

The City of Roses was in full bloom. In every corner of the Grotto, as the Sanctuary of Our Sorrowful Mother was called, roses bloomed. Other flowers, too, though Leary could not name them—pink and purple, white, yellow, splashes of color amid the evergreens that grew without thinking along the stone walls and cliffs of the abandoned quarry. No such lushness in eastern Montana. Big Sky Country, the dry prairies stretched open, the earth broken by buttes and gullies. Places where a man could lose his way and not be found.

As Leary had lost his way.

The Pacific Northwest had a wholly different feel. Moist and primal, home to elemental forces with the power to nurture the wounded spirit.

He hitched up the legs of his black trousers and knelt on the hard stone steps. In the cove stood a replica of Michelangelo's *Pietà*, its grace and power almost overwhelming. Only by God's mercy did humans deserve such beauty.

He clasped his hands, elbows tight to his body, and bowed. But prayer would not come.

At long last, a young girl's high notes broke into his thoughts. "There he is! Father Mike!"

He stood and held out his arms for the girl who threw herself at him. *Ginger.* He drew her close, felt her arms around his waist, kissed the top of her head. The small Instamatic camera he'd sent her for Christmas dangled from a black wrist strap. Inches taller than she'd been in September, she smelled like lavender soap with a hint of roses.

Tina had smelled like that.

Ginger danced around him, and he had to stop himself from snatching her close. She bounced on her feet, chattering happily. He opened an arm to Carrie. The older girl's expression was stoic, a vein at her temple throbbing. She gave him a quick embrace before pulling away.

"So much like your mother," he said, his ache for the long-gone Tina always with him. "Though you have your father's height."

He turned to the girls' grandmother, seeing in her features how Tina would have aged—they had the same high cheekbones and piercing eyes. Past sixty now, Irene was still lovely. "Thank you for meeting me." He held out both hands and she took them, the space between them a bottomless chasm.

Then she dropped his hands and stepped back, her granddaughters instinctively drawing close to her.

In Montana, she'd been a burdened woman, all shades of gray. Now, she appeared set free, her silver-blond hair held back loosely with a clip of sparkling blue stones. She saw him notice and her hand went to it.

"A gift from the girls."

"It suits you." And it did, complementing the warm brown eyes. Tina's eyes; Carrie had them, too. He could not take his own eyes off these three who were all he had left of the woman he had loved, in a way he had vowed not to love, a love he had never been able to escape.

They sat on a bench well back from the shrine, and he reached into the side pocket of his black suit coat.

"For the graduate." He handed Carrie a small flat box, unwrapped. She glanced at her grandmother, then lifted off the lid to reveal an oval gold bangle, *"Carolina"* engraved in script on the outside. Inside, block letters read "GRADUATION 1982." She clicked open the clasp and slid it on, then held out her arm to admire it. Her smile came slowly but was genuine.

"I love it. Thank you."

"Congratulations. And for you, Irene. Forgive the fancy wrapping." He handed her a flat white paper bag from the bookstore in the mall in Billings, the top folded over and taped. "The Keller girl suggested it, when I told her you enjoyed mysteries. It's not new—I hope you haven't read it already."

She frowned briefly, but then slid the book out of the bag and turned it over to see the cover. "Oh. Agatha Christie's autobiography. Yes, I—I'm sure I'll enjoy it. Thank you."

Beside him on the bench, Ginger squirmed, hands squeezed tightly in her lap. He made a show of finding one last box in his pocket. "Don't worry, little one. I didn't forget you."

Another unwrapped jeweler's box. Ginger popped off the cardboard top and with one finger, pried out a flat plastic case with a clear lid.

Her grip loosened and her shoulders sagged as she stared at the small gold medal inside, and Leary knew in an instant that he'd miscalculated.

"It's St. Christopher. Patron of children and travelers. See, I've got one, too." He pulled out his wallet. Flipped over the plastic sleeve holding Ginger's picture and showed her the medal, tarnished with age. All the boys in his confirmation class had been given identical medals. He'd found hers in the parish gift shop, shiny and new.

"I thought he wasn't a saint anymore," Carrie said.

"Once a saint, always a saint," he replied. "God doesn't give up on anyone."

For the briefest moment, the birds seemed to stop singing.

"Say 'Thank you for the gift, Father,'" Irene prompted. "It will serve you well."

"Thank you for the gift, Father," Ginger repeated. She handed the plastic box, unopened, to Irene. "Can we go light a candle for Mama? And for Daddy? Then I want to take pictures with my camera."

Carrie stood. "I'll take you." Hand in hand, the girls headed for the wrought iron racks of candles glowing at the base of the rock wall.

"Funny how the simple act of lighting a candle can bring such comfort," Irene said, watching them go.

"The power of ritual," Leary replied. "Practices repeated for generations, millennia even, with the intention of bringing us closer to God. And it works."

"Sometimes."

"Sometimes." In wordless agreement, they started down the path. Leary matched his steps to Irene's, her low-heeled black pumps making a soft sound on the crushed gravel. Did the scent of roses come from her, or the gardens?

"I admire what you've done for the girls."

"I don't need your admiration, Mike." Irene's tiny pearl drop earrings swayed. "They are my family. They will always have a home with me."

A home. The last thing Tina, God rest her soul, had wanted on this earth. And he could not be part of it, for their safety or the sake of his vows.

A few steps later, he spoke again. "I stopped to see Tony on my way out."

Out of the corner of his eye, he saw her jaw tighten. She said nothing.

"I had to tell him you'd left Montana, though I didn't tell him where you'd gone. He cares deeply, Irene, about all three of you."

One hand flew to her throat, pinching the skin, her other hand cradling her elbow.

"I begged him," Leary said, "to put an end to all this. To speak up. In exchange, he could be released. He could be reunited with his family."

Irene stopped, her soles scraping on the path. "We are not his family. He forfeited that claim when he killed a man."

Leary swallowed hard. "In the eyes of the law, he is Ginger's father. And in the eyes of God—"

"Since when do you care about the law? Or about God, for that matter?"

"I loved her, Irene. Since we were kids. You know that."

"What I know is that you and Tony gave my daughter nothing but heartbreak. All she had left was the girls. Look at them." She flung a hand toward the alcove where Ginger stood on tiptoe, reaching for a candle with a lit punk. Carrie stood behind her, one arm ready to catch her sister if she slipped. "They are all that is good and holy in this world. Tina might have beaten back the cancer if the two of you hadn't broken her spirit."

"Irene, let me—"

"Tony Woijowski should rot in prison for leaving that man's children fatherless and abandoning his own family. Even if he tells the whole truth, that's where he belongs. I shouldn't have agreed to see you. Go away, Mike Leary. Leave my family alone."

My family, too, every cell in his body cried, but he knew as he watched her march toward the candle-lit alcove that there was no point throwing himself at her mercy.

She had none left, not for him. And she was right: the trouble in their lives was as much his fault as anyone else's.

Maybe more, God help him.

THURSDAY
March 3, 2016
Billings

Lindsay turned in front of the ballpark—she still called Dehler Park "Cobb Field" in her mind—and drove east on Ninth Avenue North. A working-class neighborhood only blocks from the one where she'd grown up, the North Side had become downright checkered while hers had prospered.

She slowed at the corner. A tiny square house with more bare siding than paint peeked out through overgrown junipers, the front window boarded up. A pair of those antique metal lawn chairs that blistered the backs of your legs on hot days stood in the yard, as if the occupants had stepped inside for more lemonade, thirty years ago.

The next two houses, though, had been freshly painted, the juniper neatly trimmed. Or was it arbor vitae?

She glanced at the sticky note with the address she'd stuck on her steering wheel. Next block, east side.

A dark red pickup sat out front. Bundles of shingles dotted the newly sheathed roof, the exterior wrapped in Tyvek, stickers on the new windows. She knew those stickers from their own upgrade. You could scrub them for years before the glue wore away.

A new door—Craftsman style. Classy. Pricy. Trevor Morris and his partner must have visions of a buyer with a fat checkbook.

They'd bought the place for next to nothing, but it looked like they were replacing next to everything.

But beneath the newness, the house was so familiar. No roses, no white picket fence, but it looked just like the house near St. Patrick's, the house with the pink bedroom under the eaves. Was it that house? Or a twin, built from the same plans?

A horn startled her, and she glanced in her mirror. The driver behind her glowered. She sped to the end of the block, then parked.

A thump on her window startled her a second time, and her hands flew up.

It was Trevor. She let out a long, shaky breath and rolled down the window.

"Hey, thought that was you. Come by to check out the project?"

She turned off the engine. "I'm curious what you guys are up to."

Her heels weren't meant for broken sidewalks, and she picked her way to the house with care. On the rebuilt porch, a golden oak door glowed beneath the rounded arch.

"It's magical," she said, meaning it, though her pulses were racing. "Hansel and Gretel could live happily ever after here."

He pushed open the door. She stepped inside, her foot sliding on the clear plastic sheeting.

"Okay, so the magic stops here," he said. "But you can imagine." He described the layout—compact but practical, with plenty of features her real estate agent pals would call "old-world charm." "Sorry I can't show you the second floor. The varnish on the stairs isn't dry yet. We completely redid everything, down to the studs. Added a bath, turned three bedrooms into two. You should have seen the walls in the smaller room—Pepto-Bismol pink."

Lindsay felt the house spin, like Dorothy when the tornado struck. They were definitely not in Kansas anymore. She steadied herself, a hand on the wall.

"Hey, you okay?"

No, she was not okay. *She had to get out of here.* "Yeah. Sorry. Paint fumes get to me sometimes." The lie came easy.

The pink walls. Not even a twin house would have had the same pink walls.

Trevor ushered her back outside, jabbering about the landscaping plans. *What the heck was going on?* When he'd said they were moving a house, she'd never imagined it had been this one. Bought from the city on a tax sale, after an out-of-state company that bought up neglected properties let it go. She hadn't had any reason to check the ownership history, had never looked at the property. Hadn't the church owned it way back then? The church paid its taxes and it never sold anything. Or maybe she'd misunderstood, and it belonged to a parish family who had let it fall into ruin.

That was a lifetime ago. How had Father Leary's wallet gotten into a box in the basement?

"You're the second person to drop by today," the builder was saying. "The detective you gave the wallet to. What's his name? McDonald, Donnelly . . .?"

"Donovan came by?"

"Yeah. Checking out the place, same as you."

She wrapped her arms around herself and stared at that rounded arch. "Someone must have loved this house once."

"Long time ago," he said. "It was a wreck. Whatever this house's history, I'm glad we get to rewrite it."

She held out a hand. "Thanks for the tour. I can see your new motto now—'Rebuilding the Magic City, one house at a time.'"

"Hey, that's not bad. Watch that sidewalk," he called after her.

Back in her car, she gripped the steering wheel. This *was* the house. They had lived here—*there*, by the grade school, the new girl who came senior year, with her little sister and their mother. The memories trickled back, one clouded image, then another. *No*, not their mother. Their grandmother, the priests' new housekeeper. Where had they come from? Some small farm or ranch town.

The girl in the picture in Leary's wallet had loved that pink bedroom. And her green jump rope.

September 1981. Right before the accident. Lindsay had been standing in the walkway between the rectory and the church. Her classmate had come rushing out of the church, tugging the crying child after her. Pausing long enough to say she'd explain later, before disappearing into the rectory.

"Later" had never come.

What was her name?

And then, Father Leary had emerged from the same door, the jump rope in hand.

Not your problem, she told herself now. *You don't have to get involved.*

Yeah, right. If there was one thing Lindsay Keller knew for sure, it was that you can fool yourself some of the time, but you can't fool yourself all the time.

THURSDAY
March 3, 2016
Red Lodge, Montana

"I'm sorry, Detective, I never met Father Leary, God rest his soul." Father Santos touched his hand to his heart. They were standing in the vestibule of the Church of St. Agnes in Red Lodge. "The parish counts itself blessed to have a local boy called to serve Our Lord. We hold him in our prayers."

"Twenty years is a long time to pray."

"God never stops listening, Detective. Perhaps your presence signals that our prayers will be answered."

Point for the padre, Donovan thought. What had brought this small, welcoming man with jet-black hair to the tiny mountain town just north of Yellowstone Park?

"I understand that he was survived by two brothers, both gone now. I'm hoping to find other relatives, to let them know we've reopened the investigation. Any chance you can shorten my search?" He'd already walked the block where Mike Leary grew up, full of tidy homes so unlike the house in Billings where the wallet had been found. Talked to a neighbor, who hadn't known the family. A couple from Arizona had replaced the house with a duplex a few years ago, a combination rental and vacation getaway.

"I suppose it's a long shot. He was the youngest, and he'd be past seventy," Donovan continued. He knew exactly how old Michael

Leary would be, but precision could put people off. Or alarm them. "But then, priests specialize in long shots, don't they?"

Santos gave him a canny eye, his lips firmly closed but gently curved. "As do detectives. Let me make a call."

He followed as the priest speed-walked through the church hall to an office dominated by a desk, elegant in an old-world way. Walnut, or mahogany? Donovan had never been any good at identifying woods—in his family's apartment on the top floor of a triple decker, they'd had chipped Formica and warped particle board. He'd even flunked shop class. "How do you flunk shop class?" his old man had bellowed. "Your brother cut off a finger and he still passed." The old man had bellowed a lot. Might be why he croaked a day after turning fifty, much wailed over and not much missed. And his brother hadn't actually cut off a finger, just nipped the tip. You could barely tell.

The priest gestured to a chair, black hair flopping over his eyes. Filipino, Donovan decided, though he spoke with no accent. Native-born, or brought to this country very young? Half the parishes in Boston had immigrant priests now, according to his mother. Same as always, but from a different shore, across a different ocean.

Donovan took one of the matching red velvet chairs, the carved arms the same dark wood as the desk, the ends just right for resting a curled hand. The priest punched a number into his battered phone, then explained his mission to the voice on the other end. A minute later, he slipped the phone into the pocket of his black trousers.

"They live a few miles out of town, up the West Fork. You can follow me out there. Otherwise, you might never find the place."

The echo of Father Leary's last night had to be unwitting, but that didn't stop the shiver shooting up the detective's spine. "*Someone walking on my grave,*" as his old gran would have said.

After winding through the canyon above the rushing water, Donovan parked beside the priest's black SUV—was it canon law that priests had to drive black as well as wear it?—and followed the man up the curving slate walkway. No mere cabin, this. A log showpiece, tastefully landscaped with deer-proof foliage, the walkways cleared of ice and snow. One of the pine double doors opened, and a fiftyish woman with close-cropped platinum hair and red glasses stood on the threshold.

"She's expecting you," Meg Leary said after introductions, "though neither of us can imagine how she might help."

She led the two men into a spacious living room. As an artist's husband, Donovan knew immediately that the paintings and rustic pottery were not some decorator's idea of a Montana log home. Whoever had collected these pieces knew what he or she liked.

The two-story windows opened on a spectacular view of the creek. A stone chimney climbed one wall, the head of a papier mâché bear mounted above the half-round bark-clad log mantel. But Donovan's attention was drawn to the tiny woman installed in a mahogany leather throne—a recliner, he assumed. His first impression was of royalty. Easily eighty, though a golden braid of hair wound around her head, her blue eyes as clear as a twenty-year-old's, piercing and bright. The hand she extended was veined and trembled. He took it as though it were a baby bird.

"My mother-in-law is having her daily dose of Maker's Mark, but if four o'clock is too early for you gentlemen," Meg said, "I can make the best espresso you've had all day."

They accepted the offer of coffee, and when it was served, Donovan told the story of the wallet and its unlikely discovery.

The trembling in Anna Leary's fingers stopped when they wrapped around her glass. She took a sip, then held it in her lap with both hands. "Mike was the youngest of the three boys. My husband, Bill, was the eldest. We were living in the north of England when it happened. They couldn't tell us officially that he was dead until much later, but we feared the worst, and when weeks went by with no sign of him . . ."

Her voice trailed off as she gazed back in memory. Donovan registered the strains of classical music coming from a sound system he couldn't see.

"The grief and worry tore Bill apart," Anna said. "But there was nothing we could do, and with no body, no funeral. Bill was a mining reclamation engineer, working on the closure of a coal mine in Yorkshire. When we came back to the States a few months later, the family gathered for a service. A celebration of life. Mike was truly loved, Detective. Devoted to God and his people. He had his moments of doubt, I know, but they only confirmed his faith in God and his vocation."

Out of the corner of his eye, Donovan saw Father Santos cross himself.

"Where was the middle brother? What was his name?" He knew all this, from the file. Both brothers had been cleared, but you had to ask.

"Frank. Texas. Oil and gas engineer. He came right up and kept us informed."

Two engineers and a priest. The seen and the unseen—the Leary boys had it covered.

"Mrs. Leary, are you aware of any connection between your brother-in-law and this house in Billings?" Donovan held out copies of the photo he'd taken at the renovation site and a "before" shot the contractor had emailed him.

The old lady set her glass aside. Drew the photos close to her face. Squinted. Shook her head.

Donovan sighed inwardly. Another long shot missed.

"The detectives interviewed your husband and his brother several times," he said, "but neither of them had any idea what might have happened. Memory being what it is, I wonder, do you know if they recalled anything later that they didn't think to tell us?" As time passes, witnesses lose their reluctance to speak. Relationships change. Mortality looms larger, and few people want to carry to the grave a secret that could right a wrong.

The old lady's eyes dimmed. "They're all gone now," she said, as if she couldn't quite believe it. "We didn't speak of Mike much, not for years. Too painful, and we were busy living our lives, raising our children. They called you—well, not you, you're much too young." She gave him an indulgent smile. "They called your office every few months. Put up a reward on the fifth anniversary, along with Ed

Simonich. No, that's not it. Ed was the one who drowned. When Bill, my husband, was failing, and his memory was coming in and out, he told me he finally understood how Jerzy felt about losing Ed."

"Jerzy? Jerzy Simonich?" He'd seen the name in the file. Chair of the parish council at the time, major donor, still a prominent figure in town.

"That's it. A friend of Mike's, I think. I met him at the memorial service. With both his brothers gone," Anna Leary said, "my husband felt a bit lost. I'm the last of seven myself, so I understand. Even when you've been blessed with children and grandchildren, a hole opens when the last of your siblings dies. There is no one left on this earth who knows you in quite the same way. No one who shares your earliest memories. Even if you aren't close—and the Leary boys were, but they chose such different lives. There was so much Mike couldn't talk about."

Now what took her there? He glanced at Santos, but the man's face betrayed nothing. Donovan turned back to Anna. "Did you have the impression that Mike was keeping a secret? Something he would have told his brothers, had he not learned it in the confessional?"

To whom did a priest confess? In whom did he confide?

"I'm sure he had many secrets, Detective, professional and otherwise. Don't we all?" The old woman gave him another queenly smile and reached for her glass, the amber liquid diluted by the melting ice. "In his last few weeks, my husband lived mainly in the past. We'd given up our home and moved in here, with our son and daughter-in-law." She gestured to Meg, who sat in the corner sipping her own espresso, though Donovan had seen her add a shot of her mother-in-law's whiskey to her cup. "Time didn't move forward for him. What happened eighty years ago was as recent as breakfast. He talked to Mike and Mary Catherine as if they were here."

"Mary Catherine?" A new name.

"Their sister, eleven months older than Mike. A sickly child from birth—I never knew what the problem was. Medical care was hard to get during the war, but they did everything they could. She died before she was two."

"She'll be in my prayers," Father Santos said.

"Thank you, Father," Anna replied.

An admirable conviction, that prayers mattered, but did the soul of Mary Catherine Leary, dead these seventy-some years, truly need anyone's prayers? Maybe prayers for the long-gone were reabsorbed into the spiritual atmosphere, like unattached protons or whatever those particle things were called. Floating on the ether until they found someone in need who had no one to pray for them. Donovan had always thought prayers more comfort for the living than help for the dead.

Too much caffeine. "Mrs. Leary, can you tell me anything more about Mike? Or tell me who else we should talk to?"

"Have you spoken with Tina Danich? That's probably not her name. She married—" The woman held up a hand, wriggling her thin, ringed fingers. "She married Mike's best friend, and it broke his heart."

"Is that why he became a priest?"

But Anna had wearied too much for further talk. Maybe the best friend could tell him, if they could track the man down.

Donovan thanked their hostess and put his card in her hand.

"You were right about her memory," he said. "And your espresso."

Outside, Santos stopped on the front walk. "We've got all kinds of *iches* in this community, descendants of mining families, but Danich . . ." He shook his head. "I'll ask around."

"Thank you, Father."

"You are doing God's work. I will pray for your success." He took Donovan's hand in both of his, and the detective was surprised to feel himself held in a warm light.

The courthouse and historical society were both closed by the time Donovan drove back through town. He stopped at the cemetery and found the Leary plot, a big one holding several generations. He strolled down the next row, reading the names. Stopped at a Donovan—Rose and Patrick—and channeling Father Santos, said what passed for a small prayer in his unreformed heart.

Two plots down, he stopped again. Father Santos must not walk the graveyard much. He snapped a picture with his phone. "Michael Danich," the stone read. "Big Mike. 1917–1962. May his soul soar."

The next plot was labeled Petrovich, between them a small, flat bronze plaque reading "Cristina West, 1946–1978."

We're born alone, we die alone. And in between?

That's up to us.

THURSDAY
March 3, 2016
Portland

Better use a pencil, Carrie thought. In case I regret this.

She'd spent the morning with her crew, prepping the ground for the new rose garden. Tomorrow and Saturday, they would plant. This afternoon, she'd taken Asher to therapy, and he'd struggled, worn out by the pirate party. She was worn out, too, but finding answers would reenergize her.

She leaned into the circle of light cast by the old brass reading lamp. Even with every detail she could dredge up, the branches on the West side of the family tree would be sparse and barren compared to the fully leafed Matheson side.

Tomorrow, she'd ask Ginger what she knew. It wouldn't be much—Ginger had been only four when their mother died. But she might have gleaned some tidbits in those years alone with Baba after Carrie left home. College had been a struggle, and Carrie had given up after a year and a half. Eventually, she'd found herself working in a nursery. Portlanders loved their gardens, big and small, and she loved helping them live up to the nickname, the City of Roses. She'd met Todd Matheson on a construction project where she was helping with the landscaping, and married him on her twenty-fourth birthday.

Ali had inked in that date. Carrie penciled in their divorce and his remarriage. Their relationship had remained tense until Asher came along. Even before his diagnosis, the baby had exercised a powerful force over all the family.

No regrets. Carrie reached for a pen and traced over the dates she'd just written. She added Asher's birth and his father's name, Jamal Jackson. No marriage line. Later, she hoped.

Pen in hand, she moved back up her side of the tree. *Irene Petrovich Danich*, born Red Lodge, Montana, 1919; died Portland, Oregon, 1994. *Baba.* Seventy-five had seemed ancient then. Irene had stayed at the abbey after the girls were gone, even when the sisters no longer needed a housekeeper. Later, as death approached, the nuns had sat for hours at her bedside, with Carrie and Ginger and the Orthodox priest, reminiscing about Baba, her *povitica*, and her love of roses. The tiny, withered Mother Superior had helped prepare the body for viewing and burial.

Eyes closed, Carrie leaned back, remembering. Baba never would have left Montana if not to protect her girls, though she had loved Oregon's lushness. They'd buried her in the abbey cemetery, near the rose garden.

But while Carrie's youthful pledge not to return to Montana, the place of such sadness and upheaval, had felt like strength at the time, she recognized it now as the lashing out of a teenager struggling to make sense of loss. Of her parents' deaths. She'd long forgiven them for abandoning her—they had not done so by choice. It was time to forgive herself for her anger.

She added her grandfather's name and dates. *Michael "Big Mike" Danich, 1917–1962.* Her mother had been sixteen when he died. *Cristina "Tina" Danich West,* she wrote, her hand shaking. Born 1946, died 1978.

Carrie pushed her chair away from the table and headed for the kitchen. While a fresh pot of coffee brewed, she opened the liquor cabinet and pulled out the bottle of rum Ali and Jamal had brought over the night they picked out their pirate costumes.

Jamal had been a perfectly fine high school boyfriend, but not ready for the partner stage. When Ali got pregnant a few months after they graduated and moved in together, he'd moved out. Then

Ali lost her barista job after standing up to the shift manager once too often. Carrie had offered to let her move home and join one of the landscaping crews, though even a frugal mom couldn't support a child alone on a gardener's seasonal wages.

Instead, Ali had patched it up with Jamal, gotten a shift manager's position of her own in a different coffee house, and welcomed Asher into the world.

And Asher was beautiful, his skin a shade lighter than Jamal's, his features a combination of both parents' faces.

But the obstacles worried her. An interracial relationship. Teen parenthood. Cystic fibrosis. She worried that Jamal would leave again when it got too hard. Ali could never leave—she was tied—*bonded*—to that child. Some men acted like they had options women never had. Not that every parent didn't have their moments. But you didn't walk away.

You just didn't.

Ali didn't share Carrie's doubts. Carrie had to admit that Ali, and Jamal, too, had a maturity beyond their years. But she was Ali's mother, and it was her job to worry.

She warmed a bit of milk and mixed it with the coffee, sugar, and cardamom, then added the rum. A modern version of Baba's Christmas drink. Took a sip.

Something missing. She had forgotten to buy more cocoa after Asher's last visit, but she was able to shake enough from the bag to top the drink. Not barista quality—Ali could do better without thinking—but good enough.

She glanced at the Serbian Orthodox cross hanging by the back door, gold mounted on dark wood, the only religious symbol in the house. The cross had always hung in Baba's bedroom. How Irene reconciled her faith and that of the priests she took care of, Carrie had never known. Housekeeping had been a reliable living for a widow with a teenage daughter, and later, a widow raising two granddaughters. She'd given them a stable life, in contrast to the constant moves of their early years.

It wasn't Montana's fault that Carrie's hopes had been dashed. That she'd never fit in and was always starting over. That feeling, though, had stuck with her. It was why she had insisted on keeping this house after the divorce, and later after Jessica and Ali had both moved out.

Funny. She hated moving. Ginger hated staying put.

She opened the back door and stood on the threshold. Though the temperature hovered around fifty, the air held that hint of warmth that signaled a change.

She sipped her drink, the sugar sweetening the bitter, the rum and coffee rubbing the edges off each other. A night in a suite at the Heathman with Ginger would have been fun. But so would a night together here, wrapped in coats and heavy socks and tucked in Adirondack chairs on the deck overlooking the spring-ragged garden, sipping hot drinks and talking way too late. She'd begged off because of work, but she could have gone. Damn her stubbornness.

Ruminating over childhood moves and her relationship with her sister wasn't getting her closer to solving the mystery of Asher's illness. Her workdays would be long for the next few months. She ought to go to bed. But the research couldn't wait.

She took one last look at her garden sanctuary and closed the door. Refilled her coffee—no rum this time—and found a bag of chocolate chip cookies in the freezer.

Back upstairs, she fired up the laptop and found the genealogy website. The one that ran the TV ads with giddy men who swapped kilts for lederhosen or changed the spelling of their last names when they got their DNA results. Took a deep breath and signed up. Read the research tips twice, trying to convince herself that she could handle this.

Two hours later, her head spun with details about the Daniches, the Petroviches, and dozens of other relatives she'd never heard of, on both sides of the Atlantic. Some resources were in Serbian. Her knowledge of her ancestors' native tongue began and ended in the kitchen. At Christmas, she made *kolache*, the date-filled turnovers, and *povitica*, but her grandmother's handwritten recipes were in English, thank God. Carrie could not decipher a single speck of Cyrillic. How long since she'd had *povitica*? She should make some this weekend. Asher would love it.

Now, she peered at ships' manifests and immigration records. Studied black-and-white photographs from weddings and the carnivals held before Lent. Got lost in accounts of ocean passages and cross-country train trips. Turned blurry eyed at obituaries and census data, citizenship records and homestead claims—details she'd had no idea anyone gathered.

Her mother's birth record popped up. No surprises there. Then the Montana Marriage Index listing for Cristina Danich.

Carrie squinted. *"Spouse: Anthony F. Woijowski"*?

Who was he? How did you even pronounce it?

She laughed out loud. Simple enough, wasn't it? Born with an unpronounceable name, her dad had changed it to West before his marriage. She clicked a few more keys. *Pooh.* Name change records were not in the database.

At least that solved the problem of searching a common name like West. Woijowski shouldn't be hard to find.

Far as she knew, no one in her father's family had ever reached out to them. Not when their father died, and not when Tina followed him to the grave. There had been no birthday cards or gifts, no visits to aunts and uncles, no mention of cousins. The family breach had been so thorough that Carrie did not even know any relatives' names.

What had triggered the split? Surely something more than irritation over a name change. Some other dispute—families were rife with them. Or it might have been a small family that died out.

Her father's birth record came up with a few clicks. She breathed in sharply at the sight of her grandparents' names: Anton and Zofie, both born in Warsaw, Poland. Feeling almost adept by now, she found the record of their marriage, in Red Lodge, Montana. Her father had come along three years later. He'd been two years older than her mother, the girl down the block, the girl he'd waited for.

Of course, she knew they hadn't waited for everything. Her grandmother had admitted that the marriage had been one of necessity, quickly assuring Carrie that she was not to blame and shouldn't feel ashamed. Thank God the stigma of being born too soon after the wedding or to unmarried parents had all but vanished. Though Baba had never said so, Carrie had always had a vague impression that her grandmother hadn't thought much of her father.

She made note of a few other Woijowskis, none in Montana. Those trails could wait.

She sipped her coffee and dove into the death records. No Anthony or Cristina West. Maybe a person who legally changed their name was listed under the original. She tried Woijowski.

Nothing.

Her throat tightened. Next try, she searched for Tina West. *Ah, that was it.* The too-familiar date of death came on screen. That must mean her mother had changed her first name as well. Maybe her father had done the same. Her fingers stumbled on the keyboard, but she pushed on.

No Tony West.

She'd assumed there would be a record in his home state, even though he'd died in another country. Maybe the Army records would fill in the missing details.

But before leaving the Death Index, she put in her newly discovered grandparents' names. Anton had died in 1966, when she was two, Zofie in 1978.

Had they held her as a baby, cooed over her, remarked over family resemblances?

She stood and paced the small room, working on the memory that had been trying to surface over the last twenty-four hours. She'd been five or six. Her mother had taken her to see an old woman with disapproving eyes. Everything had reeked of must and old newspapers—the house, the woman's breath, her purple dress dotted with tiny white flowers.

What else? What else? She paused, peering into the past. The old woman glared at her, and her mother clapped one hand on Carrie's knee to stop her kicking the threadbare sofa with her shiny black Mary Janes. Finally, her mother sent her outside and told her to stay in the yard. God, she'd been glad to escape.

Her gaze landed on her garden books. *Hollyhocks.* When the visit ended and her mother stepped onto the cracked concrete porch, the old woman had seen the blossoms in Carrie's hands, the stripped leaves and the pistil and stamen she'd pinched out to make a doll on the sidewalk beside her. She heard the woman shout, saw the twisted finger aimed at her, felt her cheeks flush as deeply as the flower doll's burgundy skirt. They had hurried away, Tina clutching her hand, the dark petals dropping behind her. A block away, Tina had pointed to a pale yellow house with green shutters and a white picket fence. That, she'd said, was where she'd grown up.

Carrie clicked back to the Census records and found a listing in Red Lodge for Anton and Zofie Woijowski. Then she found Michael and Irene Danich. *The same street.*

The nasty woman who yelled at a restless child for picking hollyhocks had been Zofie, her paternal grandmother. Ashamed of her father, ashamed of her.

Why? Because of her birth and the old stigma? Or something else? She arched her back, stiff after sitting in the wooden chair too long. Her mother's album might help her recall more faces, unearth more details. People wrote names and dates on the backs of photos. These days, photos lived in computer files, posted online but rarely printed out.

She picked up her cup and headed downstairs. Rinsed it and set up the coffee for morning. She was going to need it—well past midnight already.

In the living room, she switched on the fake Tiffany lamp in the corner, picked up at a neighbor's moving sale.

She bent, searching for the album. Found it on the bottom shelf, next to a National Geographic book on Central Asia with one of Ginger's photos on the cover.

On the couch, she tucked one foot beneath her and placed her hand on the dark green vinyl cover, the embossed gold swirls reading

"Treasured Memories." An image of her mother on a brown plaid couch in their living room, this album in her hands, flashed into Carrie's mind. What town had that been? Sidney, Forsythe, Miles City? No idea.

She exhaled and opened the book. Flipped through the pages quickly. The back half of the book was empty. There were no pictures of the hollyhock hater, or anyone who might have been her father's family.

And no pictures of him. She remembered him laughing, his hand in hers. Walking her to school and waiting for her when the last bell rang. Then he'd been drafted and sent to Vietnam.

Wait. Were married men with young children drafted? That didn't make sense. He'd been home a few times, a sadder man, thin, with short hair. But he'd played with her and baby Ginger and made them giggle. Then he was gone again.

She frowned, another question nagging at her. They had no pictures of him in uniform.

Next came her mother's senior portrait, in black-and-white— long blond hair center parted and teased in back to give it a little lift, framing her lovely, serious face, a string of photographer's pearls around her slender neck. Pale pink lipstick.

Despite all the upheaval, Carrie had always known her mother loved them deeply. How different life might have been . . .

Shake it off, Carrie, she told herself. No point going there.

Carrie found pictures of her first birthday and her first day of school, then more school photos. She'd always thought herself big and awkward, but seeing the pictures now, through the softer eyes of a mother and grandmother, she saw that she'd been neither. Snapshots of Christmas trees, and Ginger on Santa's lap—where had that been? Her mother and grandmother, and a blue car in front of a house she didn't remember.

Then another, taken the same day as the shot of the three of them in the chair, which she kept on the living room shelf. Her mother wore the same blouse and slacks, and she sat while a man gazed lovingly at baby Ginger in her arms.

But the man wasn't her father. Carrie scrounged in the drawer of the side table for a pair of reading glasses.

Her breath came fast and thin. He and Tony had been lifelong friends. She knew that. Whenever they'd lived close to him, they'd seen him often. So why shouldn't Father Leary, dressed in dark slacks and a polka-dot sport shirt instead of his usual clerics, look adoringly at his friend's newborn daughter?

No reason at all. Except something else was written on his face and on her mother's.

She set the album on the coffee table. Like most of the older homes in this neighborhood, hers had an unfinished basement suitable mainly for laundry and storage. They'd painted it ages ago, so it wasn't as drear as some, despite the concrete walls and bare-bulb lighting.

The cardboard carton sat on the shelf exactly where she remembered. She swiped at the dust and carried the box of her grandmother's things upstairs.

Ali's cat had settled into the warm spot on the couch. The big gray tuxedo groaned softly as Carrie scooted him over a few inches. Ali had asked her to take him when Asher became ill. She hadn't had a pet since the girls left home, but Tux was good company.

She took off the lid and sneezed at another puff of dust. Surprising what a life boiled down to. She set aside the plaster of paris print of Ginger's hand, painted in still-bright tempura. A ceramic snail Carrie had made for Baba's birthday—why a snail, who knew?

Next, she lifted out a hardback copy of Agatha Christie's autobiography. *Why had that been saved?* Then she remembered Father Leary's last visit. She'd just graduated. They'd met at the Grotto. He'd given them gifts, and she and Ginger had gone off to light candles while he and Baba talked. She had never seen him again.

She opened the cover.

For Irene.

Life is a mystery. With sorrow and gratitude,
Mike Leary, June 1982

Sorrow and gratitude? What was that about? Her gift had been a gold bangle, engraved with her name. Jessica had worn it to a high school dance and lost it. He'd given Ginger a holy medal. Ginger had not hidden her disappointment—she'd been what, nine? Too young to appreciate it, not like a toy or a book.

A sense Carrie couldn't name was growing in her body, making her twitchy and afraid.

And then, further down in the box, the photos she remembered from her mother's dresser, in filigree frames spray-painted ivory and gold. In one, an impossibly young couple in dark suits, he a full head taller than she, smiled into the sun on the steps of a brick building. A courthouse, no doubt. Her parents on their wedding day.

In the other, they'd been seated on a button-tufted couch, both fixated on the bundle in Tina's arms. On Carrie.

After a long minute, she pushed herself up and shuffled into the kitchen. Her warm, sweet kitchen, the heart of her home.

You can deal with this. You've dealt with hard things before.

She found a clean glass and poured an inch of rum. Took a small sip and let it calm her. Back in the living room, she set the two framed photos on the bookshelf next to the photo from the picnic. From the cardboard carton, she drew out a rectangular metal box Irene had kept in the bottom drawer of her dresser. Carrie had never looked inside, not even when one of the nuns helped her clean out the housekeeper's cottage after Irene's death. There hadn't been time.

Or maybe she'd been afraid of what she'd find.

She ran her hands over the top. "Time to let the secrets out, Baba."

The box was stuffed with papers. First came Irene and Mike's marriage certificate, and her grandfather's death certificate. The girls' report cards, immunization records, other papers she flipped past.

And then, clipped together, two Petitions for Name Change, one for a minor child, filed in Musselshell County, Montana, the typed carbon copies thin and brittle. She didn't even know where that was. Behind the petitions were court orders granting the name change and ordering a change in the child's birth certificate. The Petitioner, Cristina Irene Woijowski, sought to change her name to Tina Irene

West and her daughter's name from Carolina Faith Woijowski to Carolina Faith West.

It had been her mother who changed their last name, not their father, years after Carrie was born.

The page rattled in her hand, a pain growing between her eyes. She had once been someone else. *What the eff?*

She tried a few variations of the strange name out loud and settled on two: Woy-CHOW-skee and Woe-CHOFF-skee.

Both petitions appeared to be forms filled out in her mother's handwriting. An X marked the box beside the statement "I attest that I am not changing my name in order to avoid debt, hide a criminal record, or for any other improper reason."

"Ohhh-kay, Mom. So what was the reason?" The blue carbon ink had faded, and she held the papers closer to the light. *Petitioner's husband has abandoned her and child. Name change will facilitate employment and allow petitioner to settle into a new community.*

Abandoned? She was baffled. The orders were dated in August 1969. She'd been five, about to start kindergarten. Obviously, her parents had gotten back together. Ginger was born in February 1973, and Tony was killed later that year. Somewhere along the line, he must have changed his name, too.

She read on. The order authorized an amendment to her birth certificate. She set the order down and picked up the tin box. Rifled through the papers. Near the bottom lay a small rectangular form completed on a typewriter, the embossed seal certifying it an original.

Carolina Faith Woijowski, born January 10, 1964, to Anthony Francis Woijowski and Cristina Irene Woijowski.

She ran upstairs to the guest room closet where a gray metal file cabinet held her important papers. Opened the bottom drawer. Cut her thumb on a file folder and sucked it as she made her way back down to the living room. Laid the two certificates side by side. The original named both parents, Anthony and Cristina Woijowski. But on the amended certificate, only her mother was listed, Tina Irene West.

Had she never noticed that her birth certificate had been amended or that the space naming the father was empty?

Tux rolled against her thigh, and she stroked his soft back. She vaguely remembered gripping her mother's hand, counting as she climbed a long staircase to a big room with high ceilings where a man asked her questions. She'd thought it had to do with starting school—had her mother told her that?

Had he been a judge, holding a hearing on the name change?

She flipped through the rest of the papers. In all the records Baba had kept, not one slip of paper related to Tony. He wasn't her son, but shouldn't some of his papers have been among Tina's? His birth certificate, enlistment records, the ordinary papers everyone had.

The telegram from the US Army. The official notification of his death. An obituary.

Nothing.

Whenever Carrie had asked her mom about her dad, Tina had grown so quiet and sad that Carrie had stopped asking. Freshman year, they'd studied the war. One girl's cousin had been killed, and she'd brought in a photo montage. Carrie had asked Baba to help her make one. Baba sat her down and told her the story. Tony had been returning from a mission to Laos when he disappeared with all the members of his platoon. A secret mission; the government had told them almost nothing. He'd been a hero. They hadn't held a funeral—she remembered that. And she remembered Sad Mommy, as she'd thought of Tina in those days, staring out the window for hours.

What about memorabilia—medals, ribbons, photos? Tina had sent them all to her father's mother, to give her comfort, Baba had said. "We had the two of you. She had nothing."

The grandmother who, for reasons never explained, had not wanted to know them either. "Best to let it go," Baba counseled. "All of it."

Carrie had done a report on the role of Laos in the Vietnam Conflict—never officially a war—instead. Once, in the town library, in those pre-internet days, she'd tried searching his name in the old newspapers, scrolling through reels of microfiche for an obituary or a news account. Nothing. Government secrecy, she'd supposed.

Every now and then, when she read about the war memorial or the recovery of long-lost remains, she thought about contacting the Army to learn more. What had happened to the medals and other mementos when Zofie died? Now that she knew there weren't many other relatives, she had to wonder.

But she'd never gone searching, never called. She'd remembered Baba's advice and her mother's sadness, and let it go.

They had done a good job of building a wall around themselves, her mother and grandmother. A wall of silence.

And she had let them.

She'd started this dive into the past for Asher, but it was turning out to be for her. Now, she wanted to answer the questions she'd always been told not to ask. She was fifty-two years old. It was time.

She slipped into her pajamas and grabbed the laptop. Settled on the couch, a notepad and the sleeping cat next to her, to continue the search.

A few minutes later, she found the US Army's list of fatalities from Montana. She took a deep breath and scrolled down the W's. No Woijowski. No Tony or Anthony West.

Then, her eyes sticky with exhaustion, her fingers cramped, she found her father's name on a list. His real name. With a trembling hand, she scribbled a note, then another and another. At half past two in the morning, she put the laptop aside, her throat raw with unshed tears.

Her notes were a time line of lies. Of a life gone wrong. The records were incomplete, but showed enough of a pattern for her to piece together the truth. Those early moves from one small Montana town to another had followed Tony's troubles, from one county jail to the next. He'd gone to the state prison early in the summer of 1969. That must have triggered the name change, so she and Tina could start a new life and she could start school, without the burden of a name becoming more and more notorious.

If her notes were accurate, he'd been released from prison in August 1972, and he'd gone to prison for good a year later, when she believed he'd been killed in the war.

Prison. For homicide.

Ginger was born in February 1973. Nine months earlier, Tony had been in custody.

Damn, damn, damn.

She picked up the photo album, still open to the shot of Father Leary gazing at baby Ginger.

She, Carrie, looked like their mother and grandmother. Same face, same build, except for her height. She grabbed her laptop and found a recent publicity shot of her sister, even though she knew Ginger's face by heart. Studied one photo and then the other. The slight, wiry build, the red hair of childhood now a soft strawberry blond, the skin fair and slightly freckled.

Ginger did look like her father.

Father Michael Leary.

And Carrie knew that if she wanted to find the truth, for Asher—for herself, for Ginger—she had to do what she'd sworn she would never do. She had to go to Montana.

MONDAY
April 4, 1983
Lewistown, Montana

The flames died down, giving off a thin trail of smoke.

Remember, man, that you are dust, and unto dust you shall return.

The rituals of Catholicism were a powerful draw. They set the stage, invoked the spirit, helped create the sense of history and community that a liturgical church requires. Long before seminary, Leary had known this, deep in his bones.

In fact, ritual was what lapsed Catholics most often told him they missed.

The church had a prescribed ritual for burning the fronds left over from Palm Sunday, the Sunday before Easter, when Jesus and his followers were welcomed into Jerusalem by a crowd of palm-waving believers. Days later, our Savior had been hung on the cross. The ashes would be used next year on Ash Wednesday, the first day of Lent. This fire was the final Easter duty, the moment of transformation when the cycle of birth, death, and resurrection began anew.

It was a task he had always enjoyed.

His co-pastor at Lewistown St. Leo's had joined him. Finally, the fronds had all been burned, and Leary said he would wait until the small black Weber cooled completely, then pack up both ashes and grill. The other man left to prepare for that evening's Confirmation class.

Now Leary stood alone in the church parking lot, aware that it was technically sacrilege to burn other items with the palms, which had been blessed and made holy objects.

Leary was burning his memories. Letting the sacred ashes engulf the profane. Like the English poet-priest Gerard Manley Hopkins burning his scribblings, certain they were both bad poetry and a sin of vanity, so he could rededicate himself to Christ.

To Leary, Tina's letters, the photos, and the drawings the girls had made for him over the years were holy objects, too.

But not to the Church. To make himself right with his vocation, he needed to sacrifice these relics.

He drew the bundle out of his coat pocket and made the sign of the cross over it, muttering the Latin of his youth: *"In nomine Patris et Filii et Spiritus Sancti."*

The heat seared his cheeks as he leaned over the grill, closed his eyes, and blew gently. The flames sparked back to life and quickly, carefully, he fed in the first few pages, one at a time, until the blaze took hold. Added the rest, ending with his last check to Irene, sent a few weeks after their visit at the Grotto. The check Irene had returned with the admonition to write no more.

He had complied, to keep the girls safe. Safe from the secrets of the past, which could do so much harm.

This was the closest he would come to confession. Co-pastors often served as confessors for each other, but while he and his colleague managed their shared duties and household without conflict, they rarely spoke of personal pain.

He had renounced his sin to God without benefit of intercessor. Heresy though it might be, it would have to do. He had made every attempt to shield the girls and provide for them while he could. That, too, would have to do.

One by one, the letters and photos turned to ash. The words and faces would live on inside him. As the final puff of smoke rose to the heavens, he clasped his hand to his heart.

Amen.

TUESDAY
November 12, 1985
Billings

"Heavenly Father, let my life be a blessing to those I serve. Guide my words and actions, and give me strength to do your will, in Jesus' name."

The words hung in the air of the small office in St. Patrick's rectory, mingling with the scents of holy water and old books. Leary rested heavily on the prayer bench, the wood darkened with time, the worn purple velvet barely cushioning his knees.

"Let me change my weakness to strength," he prayed out loud, "so I may right my wrongs and make recompense to those I have harmed."

He used both hands to push himself upright, feeling older than forty-one, and brushed off the knees of his black trousers. The movement was a habit, nothing more. The housekeeper, hired a few years ago after Irene left, let no dust gather on her watch.

How strange to be back at St. Patrick's, handling the usual duties of Mass and parish along with school ministry. "I understand you have quite a rapport with the young people," the bishop had said in reassigning him after the Catholic high school in Lewistown closed. "We have so few high schools left in the diocese, and I want to put your talents to good use."

Leary thought of squandered talents now as he sat at the desk, the swivel chair squeaking beneath him. Not his talents, but those of the man named in the notice from the Montana Board of Pardons and Parole that lay before him. He had been listed as a potential witness for the inmate, Anthony F. Woijowski. Whether Tony was finally willing to tell the truth, or the request was merely routine, Leary didn't know.

The notice shook in his hand. Factors to be considered in granting or denying parole, the notice said, included the nature and circumstances of the crime, the inmate's behavior while in custody, and expressions of remorse.

He exhaled. He did not know every detail of Tony's crimes. Ultimately, Tony had not made a formal confession to him, saying just enough for Leary to understand what he wasn't saying. A priest could not reveal a sacred confidence, but what of an unholy one? Days later, Tony had pled guilty, saving the victim's family the horror of a trial. Time after time, Leary had urged his friend to come clean, to tell the full story. Tony had insisted there was no other story.

"What about your wife and daughters?" he'd asked, his voice and heart breaking.

Tony had shot him a look of hardened steel, as hard as a man's soul could be. "Remind me, Mickey. Which commandment says don't covet what little your neighbor's got? That holy God stuff's your department."

He'd been stung but kept on pleading until finally Tony had told him his soul was damned and there wasn't a thing anyone could do about it, least of all Mike Leary.

He heard a soft knock on the door. "Yes, Mrs. Kuehn?" A good churchwoman, the housekeeper.

Mrs. Kuehn crossed the room, her step surprisingly light for a bulky woman, and opened the dark velvet curtains, leaving the white lace sheers closed. "You've got to be in class in fifteen minutes, Father."

At the door, she handed him his gloves and black wool overcoat. He thanked her and headed outside, blinking against the sun pushing through the November clouds. He could walk to the high school in the time it would take to find a parking spot.

Halfway down the block, a low-slung black sports car caught his eye, a bare-headed figure in the driver's seat.

He shivered with the sense of being watched, then cut through the grade school property to the next street. He glanced left, to the white house where Irene and the girls had lived, symbol of so many disappointments.

No point reminding himself not to dwell on the past. It never worked.

Some days, though, the past felt like all he had left.

FRIDAY
November 22, 1985

The Billings Gazette—The Board of Pardons and Parole announced today that convicted murderer Anthony F. Woijowski has chosen to make no formal request for parole, after an informal indication from the Board that release was unlikely. Woijowski pled guilty in 1973 to the execution-style murder a year earlier of Robert Ziegler, a married father of four who farmed outside Billings. Ziegler was run off the road north of Missoula and shot, after responding to an invitation to inspect used farm equipment.

A trucker who stopped nearby to check a tire reported observing a vehicle in a pullout; after the gruesome discovery, the vehicle was traced to Woijowski, who was arrested a week later. He confessed to the killing and was sentenced to life in prison.

No motive for the killing has ever been identified.

This was Woijowski's first opportunity to request parole. He will be eligible again in 10 years.

THURSDAY
April 25, 1991
Billings

Lindsay smoothed the knee-length silk skirt with both hands. The suit had been a splurge, a statement in caramel, the jacket's nubby fabric slightly sporty, her windowpane silk shell classic. No more of the "dress for success" color schemes that ruled when she finished law school two years ago. Now, if she wore gray or black, she put a hot pink shell underneath the jacket or added a colorful scarf. A look that said she was in charge, just as she had taken charge of this case—her first solo major felony.

The heavy wooden door behind the bench opened and she stood, ignoring the pinch on her left heel from the pseudo-snakeskin pumps, as the bailiff announced that the District Court of Montana for Yellowstone County was back in session.

The judge glanced at the jury, then at the counsel tables—Lindsay alone at one, and at the other, the defendant standing next to his lawyer, wearing a too-small navy sport coat she was sure some legal assistant in the public defender's office had found at Goodwill. Then the judge hoisted himself up the two steps to his seat, his black robe rustling.

"Have you reached a verdict?" he asked, sounding as old as the sandstone cliffs on the city's north rim and centuries more tired.

A big-bellied man in his fifties rose from the front row of the jury box. "We have, Your Honor."

Lindsay breathed slowly, her hands on the table, as she listened. Guilty, on two counts of aggravated assault, one for each of the two brothers he'd waited for outside the Rainbow and viciously attacked over a perceived slight at the pool table hours earlier, nursed with cheap whiskey.

And then it was over. The bailiff led the defendant away, and the judge thanked the jury and dismissed them. She made a note of the date the presentence report was due and accepted opposing counsel's congratulations.

She'd won. This was the work she'd wanted to do since the first time she'd watched *Matlock*. Real-life trials were so much better than TV. She clenched her jaw to keep from grinning. *No gloating.* But to be back in her hometown, working for justice, and *winning.* Oh, a thousand times more thrilling than any mock trial.

A few minutes later, she strode into the county attorney's office, resisting the urge to swing the burgundy leather briefcase her parents had given her for law school graduation. The receptionist, on the phone, gave her a thumb's-up. How quickly news traveled. As if the walls had ears.

"Good job, Keller." Stan LeMoyne, the county attorney, stood in the doorway of his office, hands on his hips, his dark tie stark against his white button-down. "Clean trial, good result. Not to say the scumbag won't appeal, but I like our chances."

Geez, can you wait five minutes to burst my bubble? "Thanks, boss." She tightened her grip on the briefcase.

"A moment of your time?" His tone gave her no choice.

In LeMoyne's office, she took one of the matching chairs and set her briefcase on the floor. The chairs weren't government issue—LeMoyne's wife worked part-time at the ritzy downtown furniture store, and the office looked like a showroom. Not crammed with books and files like hers, which was barely bigger than a closet. Lindsay tugged her skirt down so the tweedy upholstery, brownish-gray flecked with purple, didn't scratch the backs of her thighs. Gleaming shelves filled the end wall, photos of LeMoyne with local dignitaries and civic groups positioned between biographies of Supreme Court justices and treatises on criminal law and procedure. A bobblehead doll of Justice Kennedy struck a humorous note, and the picture of LeMoyne's son in his Little League uniform added just the right personal touch.

LeMoyne stood behind his desk, though he didn't sit. Through the window, Lindsay could see the city stretch up North 27th to the Rims. The credenza held a family portrait and the latest set of Montana code books. His desk was equally tidy, though the Redwell expanding file next to the fresh yellow legal pad gave her pause.

"I'm sure you've guessed what this is about."

"The Blanco case. You've made a decision."

"I have. We're putting on Dr. Thompson's complete analysis. I know you don't agree"—he held up a hand—"and I've considered your arguments carefully. It's my duty to use every resource available to ensure that justice is done. This case could hardly be more horrific. A desperate scumbag befriends a single mother with two young daughters, works his way into their confidence, then breaks into the house through a window in the middle of the night and rapes a nine-year-old girl at knife point. Threatens to kill her mother and sister if she makes a single sound. Stabs her doll in the heart on his way out. Now twelve reasonable people are going to conclude that was a pretty clear message, wouldn't you say?"

Put like that, the case did sound solid. But why would Jesús Blanco, who did odd jobs and admitted having had sex with the girl's mother, climb in the window of a house he knew was never locked?

She fingered the oversized button at the waist of her jacket. "The only evidence placing Blanco at the scene is a single hair found in the sheets. It could have gotten there in the laundry. Blanco admits—"

"The girl identified him, and the mother's testimony will support her." LeMoyne came around the corner of the desk and perched on the edge, one leg up, one shiny black shoe on the floor. Lindsay steeled herself not to lean away.

"It's true that the girl picked him out of a lineup—I was there—but she said at the time that she was about sixty percent sure, and she's said ever since that she—"

"That she can't believe Jesús would hurt her. That's not the same as saying it wasn't him."

"But she did tell her therapist it wasn't him. I'm as determined to put rapists behind bars as you are—"

He raised one finger. "Don't tell me this is racial because the defendant is Mexican. It's not, and you know it."

She knew no such thing. LeMoyne wasn't outwardly biased, but Hispanic and Indian defendants had a much harder time in Montana's judicial system than white men accused of the same crimes. "Stan, we do that girl no favors putting her on the stand and making her relive this. I know Blanco's lawyer isn't well prepared"—LeMoyne interrupted her with a snort—"but it's going to be hell on her. She turned ten last week, and she's gone back to wetting the bed and sleeping with the light on. The jury will be sympathetic, but all we have is Thompson and a tentative ID from a traumatized kid."

"Your concern for the kid does you credit. But Thompson is a respected forensic scientist with decades of experience in crime labs all across the west."

"No other expert in the country believes hair analysis is a reliable means of identification." She leaned forward, her restraint slipping away. "The probability of identity he's claiming just isn't supported. Under the *Frye* decision, the court has to consider whether the scientific technique used is generally accepted as reliable in the forensic community. Even though the defense hasn't moved to exclude it, we have a duty not to put on evidence that doesn't meet that standard."

"I know the precedents, Lindsay." LeMoyne fixed her with a hard stare, honed in the courtroom. He had a great conviction rate—and a rate of reversal on appeal to match, which he always claimed was the price of being assertive in a state with a too cautious Supreme Court. "Someone's got to be bold here. We're on the cutting edge. What better case to take a stand in than that of a monster who would rape a little girl to get back at her mother? You know it can't be his first time."

A sharp heat crawled up her rib cage. He was chiding her. Telling her that for all her logic and her passion, she would not win this argument.

But it was Lindsay, not LeMoyne, who had spent hours with the victim and her family. Who had interviewed the girl's teacher and therapist, and talked to her friends and their parents. Who had quizzed Blanco's ex-girlfriends, not one of whom had ever hesitated to leave him alone with their own daughters or seen any hint of violence in him. Lindsay had told LeMoyne all this and shared her fear that the mother was using the system to get revenge on Blanco after he'd ended their brief relationship. The mother talked more about putting him behind bars than she did about healing her daughter's wounds or protecting others, and there was a hard sheen in her eyes that Lindsay didn't trust.

And it wasn't just the mother. Thompson was too eager to push his theories about hair evidence. She couldn't prove he was outright lying, and he acknowledged that no full-scale scientific studies concluded yet that hair analysis was as reliable as, say, fingerprint evidence. A matter of time, he'd insisted. His own experience with hundreds of cases was the proof he needed. And he did have good credentials.

That the defense couldn't afford to hire an expert to challenge him didn't solve the problem for her. They had to be certain—*she* had to be certain—that the legal standards were upheld. Otherwise, they weren't serving justice. They were just getting convictions, and that wasn't the same thing.

"You'll be my second chair." LeMoyne slipped off the desk and strode behind it. "I'll handle Thompson. You take the girl. You're good with kids."

Her shoulders drooped and her stomach sank.

LeMoyne was right about one thing: she was better with kids than any other deputy in the office. This girl needed her. LeMoyne needed her, too. Any decent-sized prosecutor's office needed a woman willing to work sex crimes. But Lindsay could be replaced, and she would have trouble finding a job in another prosecutor's office without a reference from him.

His implications were clear. If she wasn't willing to go along, she could go out the door.

Get through this case, then decide. Maybe the judge would exclude Thompson's testimony. Maybe Thompson would prove more cautious, and more reliable, than she expected. Maybe, as her dad liked to say, the road would look different from the other end.

"After the silk purse you made out of a sow's ear this week, I have confidence in you," LeMoyne said, a wolfish grin on his face. He sat and picked up his pen. "Leave the door open. I'm expecting Detective Small any minute."

Confidence, my eye. You're confident I won't quit, I won't go public, I won't expose you for caring more about winning than justice.

She picked up her briefcase and rose. *You watch me, Stan LeMoyne.* Because I am a bold girl in a caramel silk suit.

FRIDAY
March 4, 2016

At seventy-five, Jerzy Simonich had a powerful build and an enviable shock of white hair. They were sitting in a small office Donovan had reached by following a uniformed security guard through a maze of narrow, brightly lit hallways, away from the canned music and cinnamon-sugar smells swirling through the mall's public spaces. He'd seen a piece on TV—*60 Minutes*?—about new uses for shuttered malls, but this one, a fixture of Billings' West End, looked vibrant and prosperous.

Well, not at nine thirty on a Friday morning, but by midday Saturday, the place would be buzzing. At age eleven, his own daughter was starting to like hanging out here, but the draw was still her friends and the movies, thank goodness, not clothes or boys.

"You doubled the reward money Father Leary's brothers put up, simply because he was your parish priest?" Donovan watched the rock of a man sitting behind the gleaming white pedestal desk. "That was generous."

"My wife's parish. I've never been much of a churchgoing man. But yes, that was reason enough. The community was in shock. We needed answers."

"And yet, none came." Donovan shifted his attention to the wall behind the developer, painted a soft gray and hung with black-framed newspaper stories: groundbreaking for the then-new mall, the first of its kind in the state; crowds on opening day; Santa with a lap full of kids that first Christmas. "Looks like this town's been good to you."

"Very good," Simonich agreed.

On the back bar behind the desk stood several trophies, each with a male figure holding a golf club or a rifle. Next to them stood a pair of gold-framed photo montages: parents, children, grandchildren, at play in the mountains, on a boat, at the ocean.

He'd run the man's name through all the databases this morning. The Simoniches had lost their seventeen-year-old daughter in a terrible car crash. Leary had presided over the funeral. The girl's brother and best friend had been passengers. The best friend had been injured but recovered; the boy had walked away unscathed.

Simonich followed Donovan's gaze to a photo of a dark-haired girl, clearly taken decades ago. A senior portrait? "She was the bright one," he said. "Good business instincts."

"The one you wish had lived to follow in your footsteps, eh, Dad?" a voice said from the doorway, and Donovan turned to appraise the new arrival.

This man was in his early fifties, his salt-and-pepper hair thick, his face flushed, tiny broken veins over his nose suggesting a life lived hard. So did the dark glare trained on his father.

"About time you got here," Jerzy told his son. "You should take a lesson from your boys."

Fathers and sons, Donovan thought as he watched the two face off. After a long moment, the younger man took a step into the room and held out his hand.

"Andy Simonich, manager of this joint." His grip was firm, his shoulders broad, though his build had begun to soften, the look of a former athlete who'd given up the battle. He shifted his eyes back to Jerzy. "That's my desk, old man."

A joke or a barb? Donovan couldn't tell. But it was the way he himself might sound if his father were alive and keeping a tight rein.

"I'd like to ask you both a few questions," he said.

Andy Simonich kept his focus on his father another long moment, then took the chair next to Donovan's. "About the late Father Leary, I presume."

"Did you know him well?"

"I was already out of high school when he came here," Andy said.

"I understand he said your sister's funeral Mass. A tragedy—my condolences."

The soft skin beneath Andy's eyes twitched and the crease on one side of his mouth deepened.

"Thank you." His voice had a sandy quality it had not held earlier. "It was a long time ago."

A heavy silence fell over the room, and Donovan let it lie there.

Finally, Jerzy spoke. "Father Leary came to the parish the summer before Mary Ellen died. My wife liked him, so we asked him to preside." He spoke slowly, the light in his eyes dimming. "His presence gave my wife great comfort."

And you? "I understand he was transferred to another parish at the end of the school year. Any idea why?"

Jerzy raised his eyebrows. "The Church in its mysterious ways."

Donovan glanced at Andy, who was eying his father, the heel of his left foot bouncing up and down.

Jerzy let out a small laugh, and Donovan wondered what the old man was hiding. But grief takes many shapes. Exercising what control he had left might be what kept it from consuming him.

So where did the dead priest come into the equation?

"Any other connection to Father Leary?" he asked. "The occasional round of golf? A martini or two now and then?" Donovan was giving the man an opportunity to confirm the old woman's fading memories.

"I was brought up Orthodox, but my wife wanted to raise the children Catholic and I agreed." Jerzy spread his big hands. "The church was running a capital campaign to modernize the place, so I stepped in. Money and building, my specialties. That led to my becoming head of the parish council. You know how it goes."

They suck you in. Donovan said nothing, and Jerzy continued. "My wife and I endowed a scholarship for an outstanding senior in our daughter's name, and as you say, we contributed to the reward fund after Father Leary's death."

But no mention of the shared hometown or the more personal link old Mrs. Leary had mentioned. Nor had Simonich volunteered those details to Detective Small during the initial investigation. And Small hadn't found out, though Donovan didn't blame him— he'd had no reason to investigate the background of a background witness.

Jerzy Simonich and Mike Leary were roughly the same age and had come from the same small town. That might mean nothing, but Jerzy's silence on the matter made Donovan curious. Borderline suspicious. This was Montana, where people bragged about those hometown ties.

"And your sons are part of the business?" he asked Andy.

Andy drew his shoulders back, a satisfied expression on his face. "My older boy runs our commercial construction company, and the younger manages our real estate holdings—retail, industrial, you name it. Except the mall and the golf course. Those are my turf."

"You must be proud of them." Donovan stood, and so did the other men. "Thank you both for your time."

At the door, he stopped. "One more question. Who was Ed Simonich?"

For the first time, Donovan saw genuine concern on Andy's face as his father paled and reached behind himself. Jerzy sank into the chair heavily, his eyes blank and unseeing.

After a long moment, he spoke, his voice thready. "Sometimes, Detective, I wonder if our family is cursed."

THURSDAY
July 9, 1992

"Hey, padre," a man wearing a faded blue ball cap called out as Leary stepped over the worn threshold. "What brings you in here?"

What do you think brings me in to the Rainbow on a Thursday afternoon? A craving for cocoa?

"Quenching the dry," Leary said, and headed for a stool at the far end of the mahogany bar, the red vinyl seat cracked, a bit of yellow padding poking out. "The usual," he told Pete Stenerud. The whiskey—Glenlivet, neat—appeared in front of him like a leprechaun's charm, poured the moment he pushed open the door.

Bar etiquette honored the distance as a quiet zone, the bar a refuge, but the chatty man in the ball cap didn't pick up on the signs. Pete did, though. The balding man in white shirt and black suspenders set a tall glass of water, no ice, next to Leary's whiskey, then slid down the bar, towel in hand, to keep the customer occupied.

Leary recognized the irony in his Thursday afternoon tradition of stopping at the Rainbow after his weekly sessions at the Rescue Mission. Most of the men who attended struggled with alcohol, and a few had drug problems as well. They needed help getting back on their feet. His thirst for strong refreshment afterward was sparked less by the demands of the men and more by the challenges of dealing with well-minded churchwomen—and God help him, they were mostly women. Some genuinely open-hearted, others judgmental do-gooders unable to see that the most useful thing they could do was shut the hell up and listen. Everyone needs to be heard sometimes. Not counseled or consoled or lectured. Just *heard*.

That, he thought, was the true value of the sacrament formerly known as confession.

There but for the grace of God and all that. A truth he knew better than most.

The door opened and three men entered, calling to the bartender for beers. He glanced at the clock, red and blue neon advertising Pabst Blue Ribbon. Shift change at the refinery. He was running late today. The door opened again.

A moment later, a graying man sat on the stool next to him.

"Mike," the man said.

"Jerzy," Leary replied.

"How you been?"

"Good, good," he said, in a way that said things might be good or not, but he wasn't going to open himself up to cross-examination. Time was, they'd all been open books to each other—Mike, Tony, Ed, and even Jerzy. No secrets, no lies. Now, that was pretty much all there was left. Despite that, Jerzy seemed to know everything. He'd always been a collector of information, a gatherer of dropped hints and stray looks, hoarding them, putting bits and pieces together, just in case. It had been Jerzy, not Tony, who first figured out how sixteen-year-old Mike felt about Tina, though she was Tony's girl. Jerzy knew the rest of the story, too. And every so often, the flick of his eyes told Mike Leary that he remembered.

Jerzy gave him that look now, and Leary's stomach turned sour.

Stay, he told himself. *You leave and he'll know you're weak.*

He knows it anyway. Even as a kid, Jerzy had an instinct for sussing out weakness. The new kid, the boy who hid a stutter with silence, the one without enough to eat at home or who dared to venture out of his place.

But Jerzy hadn't been a bully—far from it. His strength came in offering protection. Not for a nickel or a slice of onion bread from a kid's lunch box. For some future favor. For owing him.

And he always collected.

"I hear you got the contract for the addition at the refinery. Nice going," Leary said, careful to keep his interest casual.

"Don't worry—the collection basket will get its share," Jerzy said. He jerked his head in thanks as Pete Stenerud set a shot and a bottle of Bud in front of him. He didn't reach for glass or bottle. Instead, he fixed his gaze on Leary's reflection in a patch of mirror behind the bar. "I hear you been counseling my daughter-in-law."

Leary ignored the question. His conversations with Jana were off-limits.

"Ah. So it's like that." Jerzy drew the shot glass toward him, his stool squealing as he turned to face Leary. "Andy's not a bad kid, Mike. Just—misbehaving."

Leary met his old friend eye to eye. "Then straighten him out, Jerzy. Surely you can do that."

Down the bar, over Jerzy's shoulder, he saw Pete Stenerud watching them, blinking rapidly, his towel making endless circles on the same spotless surface. Jerzy's glower said Leary had gone too far, but Leary wasn't sure he cared. He downed the last of his whiskey, then stepped down and walked away.

For now.

SUNDAY
January 3, 1993
Portland

"If you want to be useful, put that camera down and burp the baby while I finish packing the Christmas boxes," Carrie told her sister. "Toss a diaper over your shoulder so you don't get spit-up on your fancy blouse. How can a college student afford silk anyway?"

"It's not silk. It's quick-dry rayon. Made for camping." Ginger set her camera with its bulky zoom lens on a shelf next to the fireplace, out of Jessica's reach, and took baby Allison from her sister. Milk drunk, cheeks soft and damp, Ali wrapped her chubby arms instinctively around her aunt's neck. Baba had gone back to her house at the abbey a few days after Christmas, and Ginger had gone with her, stopping in today on her way back from school.

"Since when do you go camping? You can't plug a hair dryer into a pine tree."

"I'm getting ready for the field portion of my photojournalism class." Ginger adjusted the diaper on her shoulder and lowered herself onto the couch. "The trip I told you about last summer. And in case you haven't noticed, I'm letting my hair go natural. Easier to take care of away from civilization."

Carrie picked up the stuffed pony Santa had brought Jessie and nabbed a stray candy cane wrapper from under the couch. Ginger's

159

red curls looked great, nothing like her own dishwater blond hair. She kept it shoulder length, tying it back at work and around the girls, who at ten months and not quite three tested their grip strength every chance they got. She'd had to give up earrings, too, except for tiny little studs their stubby fingers could only point at.

"Baba is never going to let you go to El Salvador. They have death squads."

"Not since the peace accord a year ago. Besides, Baba doesn't need to know."

"Mommy, my pony," Jessie said, hands outreached. Carrie gave it to her and perched on the edge of Todd's leather recliner, next to the tub of Christmas ornaments. They'd moved into the bungalow a week before Thanksgiving. With so much other work to do, Todd hadn't wanted to decorate, but Carrie had insisted. She was not going to have her sister and grandmother here with them for their first Christmas in their very own house without a tree and lights. Besides, it had been great fun for Jessie.

"You're not serious. You're not going to the Third World without telling her," Carrie said. "Guerilla wars don't end just because politicians say so."

"This is what I want to do," Ginger said. "Document war and injustice. Especially its impact on women and children."

"You're a student. How can they send you into a battleground? What if something happens?" Carrie pulled Jessie against her legs.

"I won't be in a battleground. I'll be following a group of medical workers. Six of us, including our professor. The camp is run by an international aid organization. Everything will be fine."

"You don't know that. If it was a place where everything is fine, there wouldn't be any point taking pictures."

"Sis." Ginger shifted Ali to her other shoulder. "You know I've wanted to do this all my life. I've been taking pictures since Father Leary gave me that Instamatic the Christmas I was eight."

"I remember. You had it with you when we met him at the Grotto." The last time they'd seen him.

"Mommy. Too tight." Jessie wriggled free, and Carrie realized she'd been gripping the girl's shoulders like the handle of a balky lawn mower.

"Don't take everything so seriously," Todd would tell her. *"The fate of the free world doesn't hang on you."*

"You're only nineteen," she said, knowing she'd already lost the argument.

"Carrie, tell me about Dad."

"What? That's a hell of a way to change the subject. Do you think I'm going to forget you're gallivanting halfway around the world to take pictures of people fleeing violence and living in tents? That *you'll* be living in tents within earshot or rifle shot of whatever the hell is going on down there?"

Ginger circled her palm over the sleeping baby's back. "I thought you, of all people, would understand how much I want this. But tell me about Dad. Please. I was a baby when he died. Sometimes I just want to know what I missed."

"Why now?"

"No reason. I—" She broke off and shrugged. "I needed my birth certificate to get my passport, and it got me wondering."

"I don't even remember him all that well."

"Where did we live?"

Carrie leaned back, clutching her elbows. They'd moved a lot, the houses and apartments blurring together. "When he died, you mean? Sidney, I think. Far eastern Montana." One of a series of towns she barely remembered. "Mom worked for a car dealership, handling title registrations and other paperwork. We lived in a tan house surrounded by big trees. The living room had brown carpet with a pattern like the maple syrup she swirled on our pancakes."

"Mom made pancakes? I don't remember her cooking."

Ali let out a soft moan. Carrie reached for the baby, her familiar scent comforting.

"Yes, she cooked. Not like Baba. The one Serbian dish Mom ever made was hamburger mixed with tomatoes and onions and wrapped in boiled cabbage. I peeled open the cabbage and picked out the insides."

Now that Ginger's lap was free, Jessie crawled into it, her pony forgotten.

"Your crib was in my room," Carrie continued. "When Baba visited, she took my bed, and I slept with Mom." Their mother had slept in satin sheets so her pajamas—what she called "her pretties"—didn't stick. The sheets had smelled faintly of the cologne she kept on a mirrored tray on top of the dresser. Carrie had loved the touch of her mother's powdery-soft skin but hated the satin, so slippery she was afraid she'd slide out of her mother's arms and onto the floor.

"Baba and Mom were always fighting, weren't they?"

Were they? "I—I think they were really different, and it was hard for Baba to accept that. Especially later, when Mom was sick. Or maybe they weren't so different, but Mom made choices that disappointed her."

"Like Dad, you mean."

"Mom was barely eighteen when they got married. Times were different then, but parents always worry about kids making such big decisions when they're so young." She gave her sister a pointed look. "Like running off to Central America to take pictures."

Ginger said nothing.

Carrie laid the baby in the sleeper that converted to a car seat and toted her into the kitchen. "Put the kettle on, would you?"

"You asked about Dad," she said as the water heated. Her sister wanted details, and it was nice to remember. "He was tall—I got my height from him. Short hair—Army regulations. He had big hands and a big smile, and he laughed a lot. Mom laughed, too, when he was around—I remember that."

"I don't remember her ever laughing."

"After he died, the light went out of her. When she got cancer, she didn't have the strength to fight it. These days, she could have been cured." A spasm shot through her jaw.

"That's when we moved to Miles City, right, after she died? Where Baba worked for Father Leary?"

"No, we moved there with Mom." Carrie massaged the back of her jaw, below the ear. "When Father Leary got transferred to the church in Miles City, he knew the owner of the furniture store, who offered Mom a better job, so we moved. When she got sick a few months later, Baba moved in to help with us. After Mom died, she became the priests' housekeeper."

Father Leary had been around a lot, first when their father died and later when cancer struck Tina. He'd been good to them, but it was no substitute.

"Ginge, is that why you want to photograph war? Because our father was killed in one? Oh, come here."

They held each other, tears rolling down their cheeks, until the kettle whistled. Carrie made coffee and they sat at the kitchen table, set with red-and-green placemats and holiday napkins, sipping from Christmas-themed mugs.

"I remember Father Leary visiting once—I don't know where we lived—and he brought a bottle of whiskey. He and Dad drank, and Mom let me stay up late while they told jokes and stories. I don't think you were born yet." Carrie had been happy because their mother had been happy.

Later, they stood on the front porch, Christmas garland still draped on the white banister. Ginger swung her heavy camera bag over her shoulder.

"I hate keeping a secret from Baba," Carrie said. "But I will, for you."

"It's like the line on the poster, sis. If you love someone, you have to let them go."

Carrie cradled Ali against her shoulder, Jessie beside her waving and calling "Bye, Auntie G."

Dorm room wisdom—one more thing she'd missed by dropping out of college. It wasn't bad advice, Carrie thought, as Ginger bounded down the steps and got into her vintage orange Beetle.

"Stay safe," she whispered. "And come back to me."

FRIDAY
January 22, 1993

The Billings Gazette—Pressure is mounting on Yellowstone County attorney Stan LeMoyne to resign, following news that the Montana Department of Justice has requested a new trial in seven cases in which former state crime lab examiner Dr. Murray Thompson testified. Sources within the department say that they were alerted to possible irregularities more than a year ago by an unidentified former employee of the County Attorney's Office.

After reviewing Thompson's record for several months, investigators have concluded that his testimony on the results of scientific analyses performed in the state lab violated professional standards.

Word also came that Thompson was fired last week from his position as a supervisor at the Oregon State Police Forensic Services Division. Officials in Wyoming, where Thompson worked before coming to Montana, have begun an audit of all cases in which Thompson testified, citing the need to "restore public trust and confidence."

Attorneys for the defendant in an eighth case from Yellowstone County, a man convicted of unlawful sexual intercourse with a minor, have also requested retrial. Thompson's testimony was critical to the conviction of Jesús Blanco, now 38. However, Department of Justice officials concluded that Blanco's conviction does not meet standards for a new trial. Blanco's current defense team maintains that LeMoyne was made aware of concerns about the competence and accuracy of Thompson's testimony, as well as the reliability of hair analysis, shortly after charging Blanco. Despite the warnings, which they say came from the former employee who had personal knowledge of the case, LeMoyne insisted on trying Blanco. "Of course he was convicted," Blanco's new lead attorney said. "Thompson lied under oath, making junk science sound like the real thing, and LeMoyne knew it. The entire trial was racially charged. He should resign and be disbarred. He's not fit for public office."

Concerns have also been raised about Thompson's conclusions in hundreds of drug analyses he conducted in several states. Thompson took the job in Oregon one month after Blanco's conviction, reportedly after being recruited and offered a higher salary. He could not be reached for comment.

LeMoyne's office issued a statement saying the county attorney is confident that the convictions will be upheld and that there is no need to question Dr. Thompson's testimony.

Montana law provides that an elected official such as LeMoyne can be removed from office by a district judge for incompetency or official misconduct. A phone call to the state bar association representative responsible for discipline against licensed Montana attorneys had not been returned at press time.

Blanco is serving a 40-year sentence at the Montana State Prison. His attorneys, who did not represent him in the initial trial, say they will request a private lab conduct DNA testing of items gathered from the alleged victim. If the results are favorable, he may seek post-conviction relief, including immediate release. It is not known how long such a process may take.

FRIDAY
March 4, 2016
Billings

"**I** don't even want to know," Lieutenant Nita Hansen said as she handed Donovan a manila envelope, "how you managed to get a rush report on a twenty-plus-year-old murder. I've been waiting months on routine cases."

Billings might have topped the hundred thousand mark a few years ago, but it still operated like a small town. The head of the state crime lab's local division was Catholic, had attended St. Patrick's as a child, and remembered her parents' anguish over Father Leary's disappearance. When she heard about the wallet, she'd called Donovan and offered to run whatever tests he needed ASAP.

"You gotta ask nicely," he said. "Even when you're the boss."

Hansen rolled her eyes and shook her head as she turned to the whiteboard and read Donovan's carefully printed notes. Next to it hung the cork board where he'd pinned the Reverend Michael Leary's last official photograph, a smiling forty-year-old with the kind of face you could have seen coming and going in the largely Irish neighborhood in Boston where Donovan had grown up.

"Wish I could give you an officer or two to help, but you know I can't. We're strained to the max. A priest. Christ." She grabbed her notepad and left the room.

But even prayer and overtime can't create evidence where it doesn't exist.

He picked up the phone. The lab director answered on the first ring.

"Hey, thanks for the rush on the Leary case," he said. "Any point in testing the wallet for touch DNA?"

"Worth a try," she replied. "We'd be looking for fewer points of contact and match than in a typical DNA test. That's the whole idea—shed skin cells leave enough material to be tested. In this case, the rough surface of the leather could easily catch the minimum number of cells. Fifteen to thirty."

"Compared to what in the usual sample?"

"Seventy-five is good, twice that is better," she said. "But our protocol requires touch DNA analysis to be done at the main lab, where the samples can be reviewed by a supervisor who's got eyes on the slides, not just the report. You'll have to wait awhile."

He grunted. Sending the evidence to Missoula and waiting for results could take weeks—or longer. "I know, I know. You gotta be extra careful with scientific stuff."

"Otherwise, it would be guesswork, not science," she said. "Keep in mind, though, degradation's a factor with a sample this old. You said it was stashed in a basement? Heat, frost, and moisture are killers. Pun not intended."

"I know it's a cold case," Donovan said. "Pun not intended. But anything you can do to speed it up . . ."

"Don't push your luck."

Which meant, as his FTO in Boston had said—as probably every field training officer on the job before technology effed everything up had said—this was a case crying for shoe leather.

Twenty minutes later, he was walking into a café on Tenth, halfway between downtown and the college, blocks from the two hospitals that were chewing up the neighborhood, lot by lot. The art faculty had held their Christmas party here, and the owner had purchased one of Beth's vases. It held pride of place behind the front counter, a tall, graceful piece with hand-carved leaves in mottled shades of green and deep blue, inspired by the work of Arts and Crafts era potters—mostly women—she'd seen on a trip to New Orleans.

The vase reminded him of all they'd been through, from the day he'd fallen for her in their sophomore year of high school, to unplanned parenthood, to the move across the country and the life they loved. They had managed, despite the odds.

That made him feel he could do anything.

Even solve this case.

He chose a round table in the corner. Once a neighborhood grocery, the place managed to be both trendy and local. As a hand-painted sign over the bakery case said " Real Cowboys Eat Cupcakes."

And retired detective Roy Small was a cowboy through and through. An old-fashioned one, who paused on the threshold to remove his hat. Donovan shook Small's big, calloused hand and was glad he'd had time to swap the metal bistro chairs for sturdier wooden ones.

"After I read the paper, I figured you'd be calling," Small said. "Besides, I do enjoy a good cup of coffee."

"How's your wife?"

The droopy flesh below Small's chin quivered. "Not good. They couldn't get all the tumor this time. Damn cancer keeps coming back."

"Can they do chemo, radiation?"

"Going through all that again, if she's only got a few months . . ." Small's voice cracked. "Next year's our fiftieth. Not sure we'll make it."

How did you talk about murder with a man whose wife was dying?

"What'll it be, Roy?" the waitress asked, a trim blonde with a black apron over her white shirt and black pants. Small ordered, and she turned to Donovan, who asked for a mug of their darkest roast.

"Never figured you for a guy who drinks lattes with hearts drawn on top," he said after the waitress left. "And mocha cheesecake?"

"As I age," Small said, patting his belly, "I seem to have traded guts for this gut. So where's that priest's wallet been all these years?"

Donovan told him about the remodeler who'd found the wallet, decided it was important, but then decided it wasn't important enough to bring it in himself and foisted the task on Lindsay Keller.

"Keller? The lawyer who quit the prosecutor's office over bogus testimony?"

Donovan furrowed his brow, leaning back while the waitress set their coffee and Small's cheesecake on the table. "I never heard that story."

"Twenty years ago, maybe?" Small said. "Keller was the rising star of the prosecutor's office. Rape case. Forensics expert swore up and down a hair found at the scene conclusively established the scumbag's identity. Keller thought it smelled and balked at putting the expert on the stand. Prosecutor insisted. She tried to get reassigned, but he wouldn't take her off the case. They called the witness, he testified, they got the conviction, and she quit. 'Course, this was all before routine DNA."

"The victim? Other evidence?"

"Nine. She'd been asleep. Sweet kid. The mother had dated the defendant, and he made a good suspect." Small lifted the wide white cup and sipped. A wisp of foam clung to his gray-brown mustache. "Turns out, Keller was bothered enough to take it to the state, and they opened an investigation. They're poking along, taking their time, when this big brouhaha erupts in Oregon about a guy in their crime lab using hair analysis to make positive identifications, even outright telling lies."

"Same guy," Donovan said.

"Same guy. By the time it all surfaced, we had DNA testing and Keller had moved on, but she helped his new counsel get the evidence retested. Lo and behold, it could not possibly have been him. County attorney got so much heat, he quit. Retired to Arizona, last I heard. Probably dead by now."

"Never heard any of that. I thought she did real estate law."

"Now, yeah." Small picked up his fork, drew the cake plate closer. "I always liked him, thought he was a good guy. County attorney, I mean. At first, I thought he got a raw deal, hounded out of office by bad press. But the more I heard, the clearer it became that he knew what was going on. And I'd swear on a stack of Bibles, no one in the PD had a clue what he was up to."

The two men locked eyes for a long moment. Every cop knew stories of cops who cozied up to crooks, or to crooked lawyers and judges. It wasn't just Boston, and it wasn't just the old days. But he sensed nothing underhanded from Small, and no resentment from the older cop of the young lawyer who'd thrown a monkey wrench into the system.

But the story did cast Lindsay Keller in a different light. "I believe you, Roy. Let's talk about Leary. You kept a clean file—makes picking it up again easy."

"That house. You're checking the ownership history, tracking down the tenants?"

"Yeah, though everything takes more time than it should. No resources to spare. Blah blah."

"We put every resource we had on that case back in ninety-five. Catholic priest, well liked. The whole department made it a priority."

"That was then, this is now. I'm going over every detail, but if there's a name that keeps you up at night . . ."

"We weren't naive. We considered retaliation for child molestation. A lot of that happened in the reservation schools and parishes, where victims were less likely to speak out. Church treated them as dumping grounds. Transfers were common back then, and we checked into every one of Leary's moves. But we never caught a whiff of dirt on him."

"What else?"

"Always bugged me that the caller asked for Leary. They had some tie—when it came to dying, they wanted *that* priest. But we never could find the connection. 'Course, it didn't have to be a parishioner or someone local. Priests know a lot of people."

"We're assuming the link was a professional one," Donovan said. "But it could have been personal. A ruse."

"Hell of a deal. Somebody knows something they aren't saying." Small pushed his empty plate away.

"Let me ask you one more thing. You interviewed Jerzy Simonich, right?"

Small nodded, his brow furrowed. "Now there's a guy with rumor attached to him, mostly about money. He's made a lot of it. Contributed to the reward fund, if I remember right."

"Simonich tell you he grew up with Leary in Red Lodge?"

"What the hell? No, he did not. Nobody mentioned that. How'd you find out? What are you hearing?"

Much as Donovan trusted Small, he couldn't share the details without breaking department policy and ticking off the lieutenant. Jerzy was lying about his history with Leary, he was sure. He should have interviewed Andy alone. Too late now—the son might not be the brightest bulb on the Christmas tree, but he knew the old man wanted his secrets kept, and he was too dependent on the family money to break ranks.

"Nothing I can share. Sorry."

Small grunted and pushed back his chair. "Gotta get back to the hospital. You call on me anytime."

A movement to the left caught Donovan's eye. A dark-haired young woman, vaguely familiar, set a coconut cake on a silver stand on top of the bakery case.

God. Coconut cake.

Hat in hand, Small followed his gaze. "Speak of the devil, sort of. That's Lindsay Keller's kid."

Donovan gave the girl a closer look. Montanans liked to say they didn't need six degrees of separation to connect people—two would do. And it was true—neighbors, Beth's students, people he met on the job often had deep ties despite coming from tiny towns all across this huge state.

But sometimes—and this was another thing he'd learned in field training—a coincidence wasn't just a coincidence.

"Good to see you, Roy. Give your wife my best. I'll be thinking of her."

"Thanks," Small said. The two men stood. "Good luck. You walking out?"

Donovan glanced at the bakery case. "You know, I think I'll have a refill and a slice of cake."

MONDAY
October 2, 1995

This time, the hearing would go forward. This time, Leary would say what he had to say. He would not be silenced.

Of course, he knew that "speaking truth to power," as the activists said, was no guarantee. The Board of Pardons and Parole could listen politely and decline to release the prisoner, no matter what the evidence. Ten years ago, they hadn't even deemed the routine application on Tony's behalf worth considering. They were unaccountable, except to God.

But at least the truth would finally come out.

Leary had sat with crime victims' families in church pews, in hospital lobbies, in the tiny airless viewing rooms of mortuaries. And in this very office at St. Patrick's. He'd heard the anguished cries: *"Let them rot in prison." "Throw away the keys."*

But it had been twenty-two years. Critical facts had never been revealed. If Tony wasn't going to talk, then by God, Leary would.

Tony believed he was protecting Carrie and Ginger with his silence, keeping them from learning the truth. Protecting Leary, too, though he doubted Tony cared about that. But Tony's wrongful deeds, evil as they were, had been in the service of a greater evil, of another's pride and greed. And revenge.

Leary had honored Tony's wishes all these years, but no more. *No more.*

God, he missed them, Irene and the girls. He had never stopped praying for them. Even Irene, who had hung the cross of one tradition on her wall and aided the servants of another, would not have asked that.

He prayed for all of them, morning, noon, and night. His life had become a prayer for them.

But they were all prisoners of the past. Leary could not believe that God would endanger any of them because he, poor sinner that he was, finally spoke the truth.

No one had told him, when he'd been a young seminarian, that being a priest meant denying yourself not merely in the flesh and material goods, but also of the freedom to follow your own counsel. He had made himself not just the servant of the Savior, but of all God's children, even when they knew not what they asked.

When this was over, he would find a way to help Tony rebuild his family. What his own relationship with them would be, only time would tell. Time, and God.

Leary took the black leather wallet out of his pants pocket and opened it. Rubbed his thumb over the St. Christopher's medal in its plastic sleeve. Marveled at the photo, taken so long ago. His heart never hurt nor swelled with love so much as when he saw Ginger's freckled face.

He set it on the desktop and reached for the gold pen, its filigree worn with use. The girls had given it to him for his birthday, before their sudden departure for Oregon. "Solid gold," Ginger had said, her eyes wide.

He pulled out a sheet of stationery and began his letter.

Dear members of the Board,

I write to you reluctantly, my prayers that those who know the full truth of the petitioner's deeds would freely disclose what they know and relieve me of this burden unanswered.

Petitioner—such a cold, blank word for his old friend. But they were all petitioners in search of mercy, weren't they?

I have long believed—am all but certain—that while the peti-tioner acted alone, he did so under great duress, and out of a debt he believed he owed another. A debt we both owed to—

He began to write the name and scratched it out. Wadded up the paper and tossed it in the trash. Retrieved it, smoothed it flat, then reached for a fresh sheet.

A knock on the door interrupted him, and the housekeeper entered before he had a chance to call, "Come in."

"Your two o'clock, Father."

Leary folded his wallet and shoved it back in his pocket. Laid the letter from the Board of Pardons and Parole on top of his unfinished reply.

"Yes, yes, Mrs. Kuehn. Thank you. Send them in."

"Just him, Father," she said with a note of disapproval, though whether of Andy Simonich or his absent wife, he couldn't tell.

"Then send *him* in."

Andy was still a good-looking kid, now in his early thirties. Same shape of head, same coloring as Jerzy. But softer. Without his father's ruthlessness.

"How are your parents? Will Jana be joining us?"

A shadow crossed Andy's face but didn't linger. "They're fine. She'll be along in a minute. Some last-minute snafu at the bar."

The Rainbow no longer bustled as it had in years past. The refineries weren't the source of business they had been—leaner and meaner, running smaller crews, the men less likely to stop for a beer after their shift than in their fathers' day. They had wives who worked and expected them to make after-school pickups or cheer for the kids at sports practice. And the men wanted to do those things. Good for them.

But the Rainbow soldiered on, despite the changes. The Steneruds, Jana's family, were part of the community in a way the

Simoniches never had been, despite their wealth. Maybe it was history or the way they got involved. The Steneruds didn't slap their name on hospital wings they'd been paid to build; they contributed beer to Knights of Columbus gatherings and pop to Little League team picnics.

He heard the front door open and close. Heard Mrs. Kuehn's greeting and a woman's reply.

The door opened and Jana slipped in, long hair flying as she slid one arm out of her coat sleeve. Her husband rose and his lips brushed her cheek.

"Sorry, Father," she said as she tugged her other arm free. Andy took her coat and draped it over the prayer bench, on top of his. They sat. Andy took his wife's hand and turned to Leary, a confident smile on his face.

A warm sense of relief flooded through Father Leary. Maybe he'd done some good, helping this couple through a rough patch. Helping them draw closer to each other and to God.

Maybe he was not a lost soul after all.

TUESDAY
October 10, 1995

O *Jesus Christ, my Lord, my God and Savior, how has it come to this?*

My one task, the task You entrusted to me, was to lead Your people to a new life in You, the life to which we are all called.

I believed I was serving You by helping to right an injustice.

I have failed.

Mike Leary lay beneath the sage and scrub pine at the bottom of a cliff—where, he couldn't say, other than north of the city, where the Rims flattened out—every inch of him covered in the fine, dry, dusty earth too thin to be called soil. He'd been dragged through the brush under the light of the waning moon, his hands bound with wire that cut deep. His shoes had been tossed into the distance, one at a time, the shoes he'd polished every Saturday night since that first week in seminary more than thirty years ago. As if he could get away, shod or not.

And then came the gunshot, not skillful or merciful enough to kill him right away.

Was I fooling myself, believing I needed to testify on Tony's behalf to make up for my sins against him? Sins of lust and envy, made worse by pride.

As if I could make up for all the hurt and pain I've caused.

But to die like this, at these hands, as a result of my own vanity? My need to be needed?

He had never felt such pain.

Would he be found alive? Unlikely. He might never be found at all, in this desolate country. First would come the mice and other small creatures. Then coyotes and ravens, drawn by the blood. Eagles and vultures would pick his bones.

He raised his head, drawn by a hint of light far above. He must have rolled into a ravine or a rock seam. Through the veil of pain, he could make out a scrubby branch, though he couldn't have said whether it was juniper or pine. He longed for the mountain forests and lakes of his youth, where he had spent so many hours alone and with his friends.

So many happy hours.

Somewhere, a hawk screeched.

Every morning of his life as a priest, he had risen before the sun to recite the Divine Office. To pray for the Church and the world, as well as himself. He ransacked his battered brain for the words.

They were gone.

He'd been taken by surprise at the gas station. "You?" he'd asked at the sight of the familiar face. "Helping a family friend," had come the reply. Why had he been willing to go along despite all that he suspected? Because he wanted to believe the best in people, even when he knew the worst. A few miles down the highway, they'd turned onto another road. His escort had pulled over and beckoned for him to get out of his car, then frisked him at gunpoint, taking his watch and wallet, but this was no robbery. Then he'd been shackled and blindfolded and shoved into the back of a pickup.

He lost count of the turns they made, the miles they drove, on a bumpy two-track, then off road.

It is too late to ask for Your mercy now.

But if I have done any good in Your name, then bring all things good and holy to Ginger and Carrie. To Irene. Give Tina peace in Your rest.

I tried, oh Lord, You know I tried, to resist my desire for her. Was it weakness, as we were taught? Or did the Church miss the point by asking Her priests to deny the body in order to serve the Spirit? I have wondered if Your purpose for us—for all of us—wasn't to unite the two, to live fully in body and Spirit. Is that the Divine Mystery your Church has failed to see?

Or just a poor excuse for my sins?

He sensed his spirit gathering itself, preparing to leave his weakening body. This was the end of his days on earth. Now, after decades of theological study and debate over the nature of heaven and hell, after years of sitting with dying parishioners, after hundreds of hours listening to the grieving, he was about to discover what God truly had in store for him.

They had been taught not to fear, but to trust in God's love.

He had betrayed that love for his own sake. And as he felt himself turn to ashes and dust, his life of prayer came down to one word.

Ginger.

FRIDAY
March 4, 2016

Still more out-of-state files on the PGA had landed in Donovan's email while he'd been out. The surgeon's office had left a message that the asshole's condition continued to improve, although it had been phrased more politely. And on his desk lay a subpoena to testify at trial on a domestic they'd sent the prosecutor the day before Christmas.

He studied Andy Simonich's card. "Property Manager," it read, followed by office and cell numbers. He flicked the card back and forth across the heel of his hand. Andy had sat motionless in the mall office while Jerzy told the story of his brother Ed's death in 1960, at sixteen. Surely Andy had heard the story before—boys swimming in a mountain lake, a tragedy.

And yet he showed no reaction. Even if he felt no grief at the loss of an uncle he'd never met, most people would listen to their father tell a painful story with some show of sympathy. Even men schooled not to show emotion. Jerzy's own eyes had dampened, his voice trembling in all the right places.

A credible story. Jerzy had not been there, by his account, but told the story as if he'd witnessed it. The details of the boys diving in, one not surfacing, the others searching for their missing friend until they were close to drowning themselves, sounded right. Still, something about the story sounded off.

"Was Mike Leary one of the boys?" Donovan had asked. A hardness crossed Jerzy's weathered features as he lifted his heavy head, quickly replaced by a neutral expression.

"He was as pained as I was," Jerzy had said, and the conversation ended.

Their paths continued to cross, Jerzy's and Leary's. The old Montana story?

Donovan had the sense that he was being manipulated. Or was he being too cynical? Hazard of the cop trade. The man had lost a beloved younger brother and a cherished daughter, both still in their teens. Perhaps the rote telling was his way of coping, even after all this time.

Donovan pursed his lips. Tossed the card on the desk, and on his screen he called up the cold case witness list and started scrolling.

FRIDAY
October 13, 1995
Montana State Prison,
Deer Lodge

indsay steeled herself for a grilling. She'd spent the last three days poring over documents from the 1991 trial and the information uncovered in the four years since, plotting out her statement. Working to strike the right note of regret balanced with justice. To steer past self-righteousness and veer away from blame and guilt.

Hindsight was damned complicated.

It didn't help that she was still queasy every morning. This baby wasn't honoring the first trimester rule.

Every step of this ridiculously long pardon and parole process, she'd worried, terrified that doing the right thing wouldn't be enough. First had come the petition for DNA testing, then the request for post-conviction relief, languishing on the trial judge's desk for months. Not until another DNA match had been made had they caught a break. Finally, she allowed herself to believe that they were on the verge of undoing a mighty wrong.

She sat in the third row of the hearing room behind Jesús Blanco and his team as the three-member Board of Pardons and Parole listened, faces unreadable. Defense on the left, prosecution on the right, like the bride and groom. Counsel from the law school's exoneration project led off, detailing the initial investigation and prosecution, and all the gaps. She chewed the inside of one cheek, expecting to be lambasted for sitting by while her boss put on testimony whose validity she'd questioned. Or alternatively, blasted for throwing him under the bus after she quit, when she finally mustered the courage to take the story to the state attorney general. Raked over the coals for questioning the criminal justice system that had once been her passion and her highest ambition, drawn and quartered for questioning a jury verdict she'd helped obtain.

But their wrath focused on Thompson, the now-disgraced forensics examiner, and LeMoyne, the former prosecutor. Neither man was in the room.

First to testify was the state's own forensics chief, new to the job, who testified that DNA tests of the fluids samples in the properly preserved sexual assault kit established to a reasonable degree of scientific certainty that Blanco could not have been the assailant. Further, he testified, results conclusively established that the semen could only have come from another man who had been convicted of two subsequent rapes in nearby counties.

The deputy prosecutor from Yellowstone County, a red-suited woman Lindsay had not met until this morning, confirmed that the state accepted the DNA results as establishing the guilt of the newly identified man, who had now been charged with this crime. The state, she said, agreed with the recommendation to pardon Blanco.

Lindsay's shoulders sank in relief. Blanco should never have been charged, let alone tried. And though LeMoyne always insisted otherwise, there was no question that being Hispanic and from the wrong side of town had been extra strikes against him. In her not-so-humble opinion.

"The victim is still a minor," the board chair noted. "I take it she is not present."

"No, sir," the prosecutor replied. "I have spoken to her mother, who understands the new evidence and is willing to accept your decision."

Damn right, Lindsay thought. She hated to perpetuate the idea that women cried rape to get revenge, but she'd always believed the mother had pointed to Blanco for exactly that reason. Though maybe the woman hadn't expected her lie to go this far.

The next-to-last witness was Detective Roy Small from the Billings Police Department. A straight shooter. She liked him. As he laid out the evidence against the new suspect, it was clear that he might be uncomfortable acknowledging the shortcomings in the case against Blanco but had the integrity to admit them. They'd given the case to the prosecutor, but what he'd done with it later—the decision to put on questionable forensics—wasn't the police department's fault.

She took heart. If Small could take his licks, so could she.

After that, the board's questions for Lindsay were anticlimactic. No, she'd been able to say with complete honesty, there had been no physical evidence, apart from the discredited expert analysis of a single hair, to place the prisoner at the scene, and no, she'd been completely unaware of the man now facing charges for the crime. The case had rested on the girl's initial identification, which the jury had accepted, and Thompson's testimony.

The board took a short break and came back with a unanimous decision. She watched counsel congratulate each other, and let the teary Blanco embrace her. But this was not her celebration.

She took her time packing up the yellow legal pad with the bullet points of her testimony. She'd geared up for the firing squad, only to find herself almost irrelevant. It was both a lesson for her ego— *you and your regrets are not the center of the world*—and a reminder that working as counsel to the Board of Realty Regulation was about as exciting as pine needles. She was good at the work, advising on complaints, statutory interpretation, updates to forms. Helena, the capital, was a good place to live. The narrow maze of cobbled streets and historic buildings in Last Chance Gulch always intrigued her, and the valley was full of places to hike and play outdoors. Scott thrived at the ceramics center built, literally, on the foundations of an old brick factory. With Chelsea a toddler and another baby on the way, the steady routine of nine-to-five was good for the family.

But what did *she* need?

Forget it, she told herself as she latched her briefcase. *No one ever promised you personal fulfillment.* The envy that flooded her as she watched the deputy county attorney in her red suit didn't matter. That life was a thing of the past. And good riddance—see where ambition had gotten her?

God. She felt completely unplugged. She'd worked and worried for years to help get Blanco released, and now that it was done, she should feel ecstatic.

Instead, she felt—*bereft.* It was a victory for no one.

The side door opened and the board members filed in after another break. She hadn't noticed the room fill up for the next case, nor seen Detective Small leave.

"In the matter of Anthony Francis Woijowski," the chairman said, shuffling a stack of papers. *Woe-CHOFF-skee.* "Case number 95-095. The petitioner is present, with counsel. The state is present. We have been given a list of witnesses. And we have reviewed the report and recommendations. Counsel, you may begin."

Woijowski, a tall, thin man, rested his folded hands on the table and stared straight ahead. Lindsay craned her neck for a better look. Even in profile, the petitioner's face appeared stony. Good-looking once, she suspected; he might have aged to distinction, had he made other choices.

She wished she could see his eyes. The eyes were part of what had convinced her of Jesús Blanco's innocence, and of the so-called expert's deceit.

But something about Anthony Woijowski's bearing told her she might not want to see what his eyes revealed.

Defense counsel rose, lips tight, leaning forward, fingertips balanced on the tabletop. "Mr. Chairman, this application is based in part on facts never publicly revealed that shed new light on the underlying conviction." Though the words were definitive, his tone was hesitant. "We had anticipated presenting testimony from Father Michael Leary, who is on your witness list. You may have heard, he left town unexpectedly a few days ago. May we proceed with our other witnesses and request a continuance until Father Leary returns?"

Father Leary? Lindsay leaned forward.

The board chair frowned. "Would his testimony go beyond the usual statements that the petitioner has found God and regrets his crimes?"

Counsel glanced at his client, who gave an almost imperceptible shake of the head. "I—I'm not at liberty to say, Mr. Chairman, but—"

The prosecutor pushed back his chair and rose. "We would object to any attempt by counsel to testify."

The chairman waived the objection away.

"My client prefers to present the details through Father Leary," defense counsel continued, his voice growing stronger. "I can say, his testimony will not exonerate my client, who has served twenty-two years, but it will strengthen the case for parole."

"I see that the warden and prison psychiatrist are here," the chairman said. "We'll hear from them, and then I'll consider your request."

Lindsay did the math—Woijowski had been in prison since 1973. Leary would have been a young priest when the crimes occurred. Had the man been a parishioner? And what was this about his disappearance? She hadn't heard anything.

A slide show of memories flashed through her mind: Leary in the high school cafeteria, stopping to chat with the seniors. Stopping by the bookstore in the mall, scouting for the latest sci-fi. Presiding over Mary Ellen's funeral and their graduation Mass.

Across the aisle, a man whispered into the ear of an older man in a camel hair jacket. Mr. Simonich, Andy and Mary Ellen's father? She still thought of Jerzy Simonich as "Mr.," the way you did of adults you'd known when you were a child.

The warden and psychiatrist testified to the petitioner's good behavior, his employment in the prison laundry, where he'd risen to supervisor, and his completion of all required prison programs.

"Has he ever expressed any remorse for his crimes?" a board member asked the psychiatrist.

"No, sir, I can't say that he has," came the reply.

Lindsay was not surprised when the prosecutor adamantly opposed the petitioner's release, emphasizing the brutal nature of the crime and its effect on the victim's family. The details would have turned her stomach even without the morning sickness. "Robert Ziegler was a young man with a young family. His wife and four fatherless children are here today."

He gestured toward the full row of seats behind him.

"They have lived without him for twenty-three years. His wife was forced to sell the family farm on the outskirts of Billings and move away. The family legacy was destroyed, a piece of community heritage lost."

Lindsay's ears perked up, and she leaned forward for a better view. She'd been a kid when the crime occurred, but had never heard a word about it. No one in the family looked familiar.

The prosecutor detailed Woijowski's criminal record, a string of petty crimes that culminated in a murder staged to look like a car accident. "He might have gotten away with it, had Robert Ziegler not had so much fight in him. He didn't die the way he was supposed to. He didn't die until this man"—he snapped out his arm, pointing at Woijowski—"until this man pulled out his pistol and executed an innocent man in the prime of life. That the Ziegler family was not utterly destroyed is a testament to their strength, their love, their defiance of evil. This man"—he pointed again—"is pure evil."

Lindsay found herself holding her breath. Despite the harsh words, Woijowski didn't move a muscle.

Why had he committed this horrific crime? The prosecutor offered no explanation. Maybe evil was reason enough.

"You'll notice we haven't heard from the prisoner himself."

"We plan to call Mr. Woijowski after Father Leary testifies," defense counsel said. The chairman acknowledged the interruption with a displeased flick of the eyes.

The prosecutor continued. "You heard the psychiatrist. No expression of remorse. This man is a vicious killer. Running the prison laundry without incident is hardly proof of reform. I can't recall when—if—this board has ever granted parole to a defendant who has refused to acknowledge the impact of his crimes." He barely paused for breath, the steam rolling now. "Robert Ziegler's widowed mother went to her grave confident that the man who took her son's life would not walk free. Let us not betray her confidence based on vague hints of new evidence from witnesses who can't be bothered to show up."

Lindsay cringed despite her prosecutorial heart. Father Leary was no flibbertigibbet will-o'-the-wisp. If he'd planned to testify, he had something important to say. If he wasn't here, there was a very good reason.

In the end, the chairman agreed to continue the matter until the board's next scheduled hearing.

"I'm giving you this leeway, Mr. Woijowski, as a courtesy to your witness." He raised one finger. "But I'm warning you and your counsel, if this turns out to be a waste of time, I'll not look kindly on you for dragging the victim's family through a prolonged proceeding."

No one sat behind Woijowski. Had he no relatives?

Lindsay stayed in her seat as the prosecutor ushered the Zieglers down the center aisle, followed by the men who'd sat near the family. Like a church procession. Mr. Simonich didn't notice her. But a step behind . . .

"Andy?" she said.

The broad-shouldered man in the charcoal-gray suit turned.

"Lindsay? Lindsay Keller?" he said, stopping in the aisle. "What are you doing here?"

She gestured with her thumb, indicating the past. "The earlier case, involving the release of the man convicted on false evidence—that was my screwup, years ago."

"The reason you left the prosecutor's office?" Andy sat next to her. "They let him off, though, right? Hey, you got a baby on board? You look great."

She could not say the same of him. Though his clothes fit well, the white shirt and dark suit coat made his skin look yellow. Might be the fluorescents. The jaunty pocket square matched his light blue tie and should have complemented the brown eyes she'd once swooned over. But his eyes seemed a little wild, the whites streaked with red, the skin beneath them dark and puffy. The heel of one raw, chapped hand pressed down on his right thigh, his left foot bouncing up and down. Too much late-night whiskey, not enough morning coffee?

"Thanks. When I heard Father Leary's name—it's been years, and I was hoping to catch up. But he's gone missing? And why are you here?"

"Oh, uh." He straightened and ran a finger inside his collar. For a moment, he looked as though he couldn't breathe. "Dad knew the family, years ago. Wanted to show his support. He doesn't like driving distances anymore."

"Sure," she said, unconvinced. Andy had a serious case of the jitters, and not, she thought, from chauffeuring his father from Billings to Deer Lodge. "How's Jana? Since I moved to Helena, I lost touch."

"Um, good. Good. I'll tell her you asked. When are you due?"

"End of January. It's our second—our daughter is two and a half. And your boys?"

"Six and nine." He opened his mouth to say more, but a voice stopped him.

"Andy. We're waiting," his father snapped. Lindsay hadn't seen him approach. "Oh. Lindsay Keller. I almost didn't recognize you, all grown up."

Andy started to rise, shoulders twitching as if he wanted to lean in for a hug or a kiss. Instead, he straightened and stood, shoving his hands in his pants pockets.

"Mr. Simonich." Lindsay kept her seat. "It's been a while."

"What brings you here?" His lip curled slightly and he flicked his fingers toward the front of the room, as if to say a pretty girl like her didn't belong in a place like this.

"I was here on the earlier case, but I stayed when I heard Father Leary's name."

A shadow crossed Jerzy Simonich's well-tanned face. "Can't imagine what happened. Not like Mike to miss an appointment. Nice to see you, Lindsay."

She watched him stride away. Andy blinked several times and nodded once, abruptly. "Good to see you, Linds."

Before she could reply, he'd hustled down the aisle to join his father. As she reached for her briefcase, she noticed a movement at the front of the room. Shoulders sagging, the defense lawyer packed up. A few feet beyond, a uniformed guard stood on alert.

And Tony Woijowski watched her, a dark look in his eye.

SUNDAY
October 18, 1995

The Billings Gazette—The Billings Police Department continues to seek information in the disappearance of Father Michael Leary, co-pastor of St. Patrick's Co-Cathedral and a popular instructor of religion at the Catholic high school.

Father Leary was last seen at 3 a.m. Tuesday morning, October 10, 1995, at a gas station on Main Street in Billings Heights, where he spoke to the attendant and used the station's phone. A few minutes later, another vehicle arrived, possibly a dark, late-model pickup, and the two vehicles departed.

Leary, 51, is 5 feet 7 inches tall, 140 pounds, with sandy red hair and blue eyes. He was last seen wearing black pants, a black knit shirt with an open collar, and a black overcoat. His car, which has not been located, is a black 1987 Buick Century with Yellowstone County plates.

"We believe Father Leary was called out to bless a dying woman," said Monsignor Michael O'Shea, co-pastor of St. Patrick's, who shares the rectory with Father Leary and another priest. "It is possible that he had an accident along the way or that he has remained with the family of the sick woman to comfort and assist them. We pray for his safety and for news of our brother in Christ."

Anyone with information is asked to call Detective Roy Small of the Billings Police Department, or local law enforcement.

FRIDAY
March 4, 2016
Billings

Lindsay drew her finger down the last document. All in order. She'd proofed every page on screen and on paper, and Carla had done the same. If they'd missed a typo or transposition somewhere—entirely possible, with all these figures—it wasn't for lack of effort.

The Rainbow Bar. An institution. Wasn't it Mae West who joked that marriage was a great institution, but she wasn't ready for an institution? Mae would have loved the Rainbow in its heyday. It had its roots in bootlegging—Jana Stenerud might be embarrassed by that bit of local color, but everyone knew her great-grandmother had been one heck of a businesswoman, parlaying a barnyard booze operation north of town into a beer hall still booming nearly a hundred years later. Half the town knew the history. And it hadn't kept the family from respectability, although their generosity to the church had helped.

Lindsay remembered the battle, early in the family's discussions about transferring the property from one branch to another, that had nearly derailed the entire project. When the hotel had closed decades ago, the upper floors became a dumping ground, storage for boxes of old photos, hardware, antique lamps and dressers, pitchers and basins. Pete had carted what he called "the junk" away years ago, clearing out the rooms for some long-abandoned plan of his own, and his sister, Rose, wanted it back. Those things belonged to the Rainbow, she insisted. Pete balked—after all, he'd run the place for decades, and he'd done the heavy work of hauling it all down the narrow steps and halfway across town to his garage.

But Lindsay had suspected there was more to the dispute, and probed gently. Though she was past eighty, Rose still smarted from her father's refusal to let her participate in the business. To her, the antiques and other items represented those lost years. Pete admitted he had no plans for them and eventually decided the junk was more headache than it was worth. The younger men in the family had carted it all back, and the sparring siblings had carried on with the deal. A cousin had created a photo display that now hung in the hallway by the restrooms—sepia-toned blowups showing the distilling and bottling setup in the barn, Model As and farm trucks loaded with contraband, and a grinning granny with her hooch-happy family.

"We're good to go," Lindsay said as she handed Carla the stack of documents. "Fire up the copier." She closed the door to her office. Opened a desk drawer and pulled out the photo of the girl.

Why had she kept it? Because she couldn't bear the thought that Father Leary had not been the man her teenage self had imagined? No one was what they seemed to be. And if her actions kept the truth from emerging—whatever the truth was—then she was no better than her old boss, Stan LeMoyne, or the church authorities who covered up the moral and legal failings of the clergy.

Still, she had the sense that there was a bigger story here, and that it wasn't her story to tell. Or to hide.

She pressed the heels of her hands against her temples. The memory of that day outside St. Pat's had kept her awake last night. She'd tossed and turned, the image of her classmate bursting out the side door, half pushing, half dragging her sobbing little sister toward the rectory, as vivid as if it had happened yesterday, not nearly thirty-five years ago. The older girl had shot her a look—she could see it without closing her eyes—filled with emotion. Fear, loss, regret, terror. Longing. Knowing.

Had the girl's face really held all that, or was Lindsay projecting backward? Making shit up.

Both girls had been terrified—of that, she was sure—and Father Leary, alarmed. But whatever had happened inside the church, Lindsay had never given it another thought, let alone rearranged the memory in her mind.

She drew a yellow pad toward her and reached for a pen.

What was the girl's name? That morning, the new girl had ticked off Sister Claire in PE by teaching Jana to serve a volleyball. The nun never liked a student outshining her. That alone would have made the girl popular.

But their attention had been diverted. Lindsay clicked her pen on and off. In the locker room, she'd spouted off after the nun's racist comments about Charlene Old Horn. The incident had hung over her all afternoon and evening, and she'd changed her mind about going to the kegger with the Simonich kids. Jana, who'd never bothered to hide her crush on Andy, had gone instead.

God, how important it had all seemed. The petty games kids played with and on each other. She tossed the pen on the desk, where it skittered to a stop against her coffee cup. Was that what had happened to Haley? Some overblown intrigue among the college set that rocked her back on her heels and sent her scrambling for home?

What was that girl's name?

The accident had occurred that night, reshaping the entire year. Lindsay had forgotten all about the new girl.

Lindsay was supposed to have been there. If she had been, she could have prevented the wreck. Or been killed.

On the yellow pad, its narrow lines and familiarity comforting, she wrote the current address of the house where the new girl had lived, where the wallet had lain hidden in the basement for decades. How on earth was it connected to Father Leary's murder?

Lindsay stood, the rhythmic ka-thunking of the copier in the next room covering the rap of her heels on the floor as she paced, tugging at fragments of memory. She needed to tell Donovan about the house.

The dream home of a girl whose name she could not remember and a girl whose face she could not forget.

Half an hour later, Lindsay left the office, the final client copies tucked inside her raspberry leather tote, and strode down Montana to the Rainbow. It was warm enough to go without a coat, and she caught a glimpse of herself in a glass storefront. The worry nagging at her didn't seem to show on her face. Yes, she looked middle-aged, but stylish, the teal silk blouse perfect with her black pants and cashmere sweater.

In the 1980s, when this part of town had been in its nadir, the Rainbow had slipped from working class to grunge—honest-to-God grunge, not the deliberate, cool grunge of rock. But a few years later, property owners along Montana Avenue started fighting back. Pete had cleaned up the joint, highlighting features like the oak-paneled back hall and repairing the black-and-white hex-tiled floors in the restrooms.

The street had taken another step upscale in recent years, despite the pockets of neglect tucked between the new and trendy. She occasionally took a yoga class in the old rummage room the church ladies used to run. The Northern Pacific Depot was back in use, its Beaux Arts style a picturesque backdrop for weddings and other grand events. Chic restaurants—some quite good—and art galleries filled the street fronts, and architects and ad agencies officed upstairs.

And the occasional lawyer, like her. She hadn't planned on putting her office on Montana Avenue, until after she'd helped a developer wend his way through the maze of permits, regulations, tax-increment financing, and other legal doodah involved in transforming a building with a past as checkered as its tile floors into a tax-generating model for the future.

It had worked, by golly. In the process, she'd developed an expertise that was serving her and her clients well. And she loved working in a building she'd helped bring back to life.

She looked up. Despite the spit and polish, the Rainbow was still the Rainbow, the classic neon sign a work of art. She pushed open the glass-front door and crossed the threshold.

Her clients sat in the far corner, an array of glasses and bottles on the round high-top. A few feet away, a row of keno and poker machines beckoned.

"Little Miss Lindsay," old Pete Stenerud called from behind the bar. Tempting to say that he never changed. But of course, he had.

Balding and stooped at close to ninety, Pete wore his uniform—dark slacks, white shirt, and suspenders. Today's braces sported toothy jack-o'-lanterns. In March.

Her mother had said a few weeks ago that Pete was losing it. *If the suspenders are a sign of senility,* Lindsay thought, *may I lose my mind with such flair.*

"What can I get you?" he said.

"Just a Coke."

"Better make that a double, missy. You're dealing with a rough crowd."

Jana slid off a stool to greet her. "Gang's all here," she sang, her tone bright and chirpy. "Look at you. All hip and fashionista. That's what comes from having daughters instead of sons. You must be thrilled to have Haley home."

At fifty-two, Jana Stenerud Simonich Stadler still had her sweet teenage smile and kind eyes, and Lindsay would know her anywhere. But when she ran into Jana unexpectedly, her first reaction was always to think the other woman ten years older. A roll around the middle, worry lines traveling her forehead, hair cut short at the beauty college. As teenagers, Lindsay had envied Jana's hair, center parted and layered like the hairdos on models in *Teen* and *Glamour*. Mary Ellen had worn hers that way, too, but it looked better on Jana. Not that Lindsay's mother had let her waste her money on frippery— that had been Pat's word—but when she got the bookstore job, she'd dropped a hard-earned dollar on one of the glossies every month. When her own girls had brought magazines home, she'd thumbed through them. You never knew what style trend would catch on or when a pop star's name might come up at the dinner table.

"She's a bright spot," Lindsay said of her daughter. She drew the thick envelopes out of her bag and greeted Pete's sister, Rose, and her son Tom and grandson Thomas. The new owners. "Congratulations. You have a deal."

Pete set her Coke on the oak-trimmed Formica table, took his seat, and raised his glass—whether it held tonic or gin, she couldn't guess. "Glad the place is staying in the family. That way, I know I'll always have a job."

"I thought the whole idea was to allow you to retire," Lindsay said as they all raised their drinks, cheering and clinking.

"It was," Jana said. "But if he wants to work, why not?"

"Jana's boys aren't interested, and Thomas is," Aunt Rose said, touching her grandson on the shoulder. "This is the perfect solution."

Thomas grinned and Jana blushed. She'd always blushed at anything, embarrassed or not, but Lindsay suspected this transition hit her hard. Her two sons from her marriage to Andy had chosen to work for his father, and her youngest son, from her second marriage, was aiming for medical school.

Lindsay turned to Jana. "I swung by an old house a client is rehabbing earlier this week, east of the ballpark. I swear, it looked just like that little house by the grade school, where—"

"That whole North Side has changed so much," Pete said. "Like a crazy quilt. I hardly recognize it anymore."

"Me neither," Lindsay said. "But the tide may be turning. My client is sure doing his part. What I really wanted to ask is, do you remember the girl who—"

"'Scuse me. Be right back." Jana slid off her stool and headed for the photo-lined hall leading to the restrooms. Lindsay could picture her standing at a white pedestal sink, splashing cold water on her face. Letting go could be so hard, even when you knew it was right.

Pete broke the silence. "They're good boys, but it does sting her that they chose their father's family business over hers. 'Course, Jerzy Simonich built an empire, not a bar with a couple of vacant floors upstairs. Marrying Jana was the only thing Andy ever did that his dad didn't tell him to do."

"I've got plans for that space upstairs, Uncle Pete," Thomas said.

Pete gave him an indulgent smile. "And they're good plans. The Rainbow is in good hands." He picked up his drink and took a long swallow.

"You suppose they can find who killed Father Leary," Rose said, "now that his wallet's turned up after all these years?"

Did Rose know something? Not that the discovery wasn't the topic of conversation all over town.

"He used to come in here every Thursday afternoon at two thirty," Pete said. "Sat at the bar and drank one whiskey. He never said, but I knew he'd come from praying over the bums at the Mission. That would make me want to drink, too."

"Pete, don't call them bums. They were decent men down on their luck," Rose said.

"Some of 'em, sure," Pete said. "But some of 'em were bums."

"Did he mention any trouble there?" Lindsay asked. After the priest dropped out of sight, rumors and theories abounded. She vaguely recalled speculation of a link to the Rescue Mission. The theory might have made sense if he'd been killed at the church or rectory, just a few blocks away. But he'd been lured out of town by that mysterious phone call.

"Most days, he wasn't in a talking mood. And it's a barkeep's job"—he shot Thomas a "pay attention to me" look—"to know when a customer wants to jabber and when he doesn't. People gravitated to Mike Leary. Priest or no—he had charisma. But when he came in here, he wanted to be left with his own self."

"He was one of our favorite teachers. He remembered what being a kid was like," Lindsay said to Thomas.

"I'm sorry I never met him," the young man replied.

They fell silent. Jana returned, squeezing behind Lindsay to get to her seat. Lindsay wanted to ask her about the little house and if she remembered the names of the girls who'd been so happy to live there, but the moment was gone.

"You knew Father Leary as well as any of us, Pete," Rose said. "And you heard all the scuttle. Who do you think killed him?"

The old man tightened his grip on his nearly empty glass. "God only knows. And He isn't talking."

MONDAY
November 20, 1995

The Billings Gazette—Billings police reported the weekend discovery of a car registered to Father Michael Leary, co-pastor of St. Patrick's Co-Cathedral, who was last seen in the early morning hours of October 10, 1995, at a service station on Main Street in Billings Heights. Leary, 51, was reportedly on his way to minister to a dying parishioner.

The car, a black 1987 Buick Century, was found in an abandoned hay shed off the Roundup Road. Billings police detective Roy Small, the lead investigator in Father Leary's disappearance, states that the front end of the car was heavily scratched, as if towed over rough terrain. No body has been found. Foul play is suspected.

The vehicle is being tested for physical evidence. Teams from the Billings Police Department and Yellowstone County Sheriff's Office are searching the area for further evidence.

A prayer service for Father Leary will be held at St. Patrick's at 1 p.m. on November 24, the Friday following Thanksgiving, Monsignor Michael O'Shea announced. "This is not a memorial service," O'Shea said. "Although we are deeply saddened by Father Leary's disappearance, we continue to pray that he will be found alive."

"We're heartbroken," Leary's brother, William, told reporters by phone from his home in England. "From childhood, Mike felt called to the priesthood. So many depended on his guidance and wisdom. We simply can't imagine who would want to harm him."

Since Father Leary's disappearance, parishioners have kept a 24-hour vigil. Other priests from the Diocese of Great Falls-Billings, including Bishop Francis Lombardi, have been on hand to counsel and pray with parishioners. Monsignor O'Shea reports that many people who knew the missing priest from his service in other towns in central and eastern Montana have visited St. Patrick's since his disappearance, to offer their prayers of support.

Anyone with information is asked to call Detective Small of the Billings Police Department, or local law enforcement. A reward is being offered for information leading to the arrest and conviction of persons responsible.

FRIDAY
March 4, 2016

Sunlight flashed off the rearview mirror as Lindsay drove east on First Avenue North.

At the junction by the fairgrounds, she stopped for the light, then headed north on Main. To her left, the Rims dropped off abruptly. She passed the turnoff to Black Otter Trail, where Mary Ellen had died, but she didn't take the detour. A different memory propelled her today.

The Prius hummed to itself as she drove through the Heights' commercial district, indistinguishable from thousands of others in suburbia, then scooted through the last light and hit the accelerator. US 87, aka the Roundup Road, was still a narrow, two-lane highway with skinny, sloping shoulders, a thin, worn-out old man of a road.

One thing she liked about Billings—and this wasn't as ironic as it sounded—was how easy it was to get out of town. Though she hadn't driven out this way since before Haley got her driver's license, when she'd hung around with a girl who lived off Wicks Lane. Four years ago, maybe five.

The country began to open up, the spaces between spots of development widening. To the east, where the canal system fed the land above the river, piles of rock edged the tamed fields. Sugar beets, alfalfa, and corn—good, dependable crops. The remnants of the last snow ran clear in some stretches of the borrow pit, slowing to a mucky brown sludge in others.

To the west, though, lay a strange landscape. Not exactly desert, not quite prairie. Twisted ponderosas and stubby junipers jutted out of sandstone mishaps, rocks that might resemble a bison from one direction and an eagle from another.

It all depended on your point of view.

She passed another white cross. Nowhere but in Montana had Lindsay seen the roadside markers, flashes of painted metal against the clear blue sky. After the accident, she, Jana, and Charlene had made frequent pilgrimages to Mary Ellen's marker. Graduation week, a dozen kids had gathered to spray-paint the post emerald green and tie on a yellow tassel with a tiny gold '82 charm.

We visit, we leave mementos, we decorate as if our loved one were still alive to enjoy our offering, because we are afraid of forgetting.

Of being forgotten.

In this stretch alone, she'd seen four.

Everywhere she looked, the world reflected those crosses back to her. Power lines and poles, weathered gray fence posts strung with barbed wire, sunlight splintering off the backs of metal signs.

How did the mind know what to remember and what to forget?

A pheasant hopped out of the ragged brush and Lindsay slowed, waving her hand at it. "Go. Fly. You have wings." The bird ignored her and strolled across her lane before finally taking flight.

The week after ME's death had been awash in tears. Classes were canceled for the funeral, and the entire senior class, seventy-five shocked teenagers, processed solemnly to the church, led by motorcycle cops. And nearly thirty-five years later, the image still made her eyes water.

She could only imagine the turmoil when Father Leary disappeared. Worse, because of the not-knowing. And because accidents happen, but murder . . .

The telltale rattle of tires on the hash marks in the asphalt told her she'd crossed the center line. "Careful, Linds," she told herself as she jerked the Prius back into her own lane.

Finally, she spotted the turnoff she'd been searching for. In the distance, the Bull Mountains loomed, all rock and shadow.

A mile in, pavement gave way to gravel. A loop of rusty barbed wire hung on a weathered fence post. Tiny clumps of wild grass poked up through the reddish-brown soil, alongside the sages.

A magpie sat atop the next post.

She pictured Father Leary on the altar at Mary Ellen's funeral, raising his arms in the heavy gold-and-white-brocaded vestments. How had he felt, called time and again to preside over tragedy? He had said they were celebrating life, celebrating the union of souls with the Holy Trinity, with God the Father, the Son, and the Holy Spirit, Amen.

Such BS. Not that she'd thought so at the time. He'd been deeply affected, but he had never seemed broken. They'd all drawn comfort from that. He had been a model of strength and inspiration.

Murder victims ought to have their own white crosses.

She'd heard, via some grapevine or another, that the shed where Leary's car was found had been torn down, the rancher too pained by the sight of it. Somewhere down this road, which dead-ended at the giant butte of striated sedimentary rock. The butte loomed in the distance, the far side glowing in the sunlight, the near side deep in shadow. Back in high school, the three girls had driven out here a few times with a lid of pot and a bottle of cheap Cold Duck. Sweet, red, and fizzy, like fermented Kool-Aid. Pot had never done much for her except make her crave Three Musketeers bars.

She'd raise a toast to Father Leary with her water bottle and pretend it was communion wine. Whiskey would be best, of course— Pete Stenerud probably still knew what brand Leary had drunk.

To the north lay a large, flat disc of sandstone, guarded by a half circle of pine and last year's yucca spears. The land appeared to drop sharply on one side. She stopped and climbed out. She didn't need to traipse across the prairie or see where Father Leary had died. All she needed was to be near, to think and remember.

All ground is holy in some way, isn't it?

A hawk soared up from the hidden gully, and another joined him. They climbed on the winds, then caught a thermal and drifted down, only to pull out as the ground approached and zoom upward.

In a flash, the way it sometimes happens, the missing piece came to her.

"Carrie," Lindsay said out loud. "Her name was Carrie." And the little girl—Ginny? Gigi? No. *Ginger.*

Father Leary had strode out the side door of the church, stopping at the sight of her. He'd gone blank, baffled. The housekeeper had opened the rectory door and called to him. His face had gone from red to pale, from fury to anguish.

The housekeeper had been the girls' grandmother. She'd been nothing like the housekeepers Lindsay knew, Aunt Bee from Mayberry or Alice from *The Brady Bunch*, although she had worn an apron over her blouse and slacks.

That green jump rope dangling from his hand had been Ginger's.

A cloud of dust signaled a vehicle approaching. It crested the hill and started down, the dust obscuring its shape and size.

Gad, Linds, what are you doing out here? She'd kill her girls for being so reckless. She sped around the front of her car to her door, fingers inches from the handle, when the driver rolled to a stop, lowering his passenger window.

"Need a hand?" the man called.

"Detective Donovan. No, I'm fine, thanks." The unmarked SUV shuddered as he shoved it into park and climbed out.

"Car trouble? Run out of juice?"

"No, no. More like head trouble." She turned toward the horizon, the butte standing guard.

Guarding against what?

The land held such secrets. *We all hold secrets,* she reminded herself, *more than we admit.* She crossed her arms, wishing for her coat. Donovan stood beside her.

"Ever since Monday, since my client brought me that wallet . . . You know Father Leary taught in the high school. We all loved him.

What you might not know . . ." She took a deep breath, steadied her words. "It seems like every few years in a small town, there's a tragedy. Kids are drunk or careless. There's a crash. And a round of funerals.

"Billings still looks small to you, I imagine," she continued. "Coming from the big city. It was maybe sixty thousand then, but the Catholic community was kind of a subset, especially the Catholic school families. Less than a hundred of us in a high school class, and most of us had known each other since grade school."

"A community within the community," he said, leaning against the hood of his Explorer.

"Exactly. Thinking about Father Leary brings it all back. There was a girl in my class. We'd been friends since practically zero. It was a Friday in September. The weather was still warm, and some kids planned a kegger out past the airport. She persuaded her older brother to come along because she knew I had a crush on him. But I was upset over an incident at school and ticked at how she'd treated a new girl in our class, so I didn't go. And she died."

She left out the detail that haunted her.

He was a good listener, Brian Donovan. Too good.

"Survivor's guilt," Donovan said.

"That's what Father Leary called it. I got through the whole mess mainly because of him. My parents didn't know what to say or do— of course, I couldn't tell them I'd planned on going." Or about the whiskey. Next time she'd been in the hangout, a new bottle sat on the shelf in its place. "Father Leary understood. He was nearly our parents' age, but because he wasn't one of them, he could see and say things they couldn't."

"Too bad more priests aren't like that," Donovan replied, and she wondered what history had turned him against the church.

"Anyway, his wallet is dredging it all up. This might sound crazy to you—cops deal with facts. Like lawyers." She let out a self-mocking laugh. "I thought if I came out here, it would be like talking to him again."

"The spot's down the road a little, then north. A bit of a hike."

"That's okay. I don't actually need to see where he died. I only wanted to feel the connection."

"I've been going over the file," Donovan said. "He left here in 1982, came back in eighty-five, and stayed until his death in ninety-five. Did you see him much after you graduated?"

"A few times. I started my career in the Yellowstone County Attorney's Office, and he was at St. Pat's then. I . . ." She didn't know what the detective knew about her and didn't much care. "I didn't last long. Washed out and took a state job in Helena, where I met Scott. We didn't move back to Billings until years later, after Father Leary's death." No reason not to tell him the rest. It had been pure coincidence that she'd been at the Parole Board the very day the priest was supposed to testify. Maybe now, after all these years, the coincidence would help them find his killer. Because life could be strange that way. "But there's another reason why his death bothers me." The sun, weak from the long winter, slipped behind a cloud, and she rubbed her arms in the thin sweater, grateful she'd worn pants today. She told the detective about sitting in the hearing room at the Board of Pardons and Parole.

"It had been a difficult day, and when I heard his name, the thought of seeing him was—I don't know. Comforting. But that was the week he disappeared. I hadn't known. The murder victim in the other case was from Billings, and there were people there that I knew. Father Leary knew the defendant. This is probably all in your file."

"I had coffee this morning with Roy Small, at the café by the hospital," he said. "He told me what happened when you were a young prosecutor."

"How I torched my career in criminal law for a dirty spic who might not have raped this girl but sure as heck deserved to be punished for something, so why not slam him when we could? That's what the county attorney thought. That's what they all thought, though maybe not Roy. They were wrong. The guy was clean and he stayed clean, hard as it is for cops and prosecutors to believe."

"We have our biases. We make our mistakes." His lips made a quick, wry twist. "Glad you were right. The system needs fighters like you."

"Humph. Fought my way right out of a job. Hey, I'm freezing, but you met with Roy on the Leary case, right? Why did my name come up? I guess you told him I turned in the wallet." Except for the photo. Which she didn't have with her. She opened her mouth again to mention it, but he spoke first.

"Yeah, and because we saw your daughter. That cake of hers was fabulous. I'm gonna have to run a couple of extra miles tonight."

"Cake? What cake? You saw *my* daughter? Haley? Couldn't be— she has art history Friday mornings, with your wife."

"Beth doesn't teach on Fridays. Studio day."

Lindsay went rigid. It's one thing when the world lies to you. That's the world's job, some days. But your kid . . .

That's another thing.

"I gotta go." She took a step toward her car.

"Wait. You ever wonder if Leary's disappearance was related to the Parole Board hearing?"

She stopped, looked back at him. "I never had any reason to think there was a link. Why? What are you thinking?"

The sun glinted off the door of his car as Donovan threw it open and reached inside. Pulled out a stack of documents and ran his finger down a page.

"The team on the case inventoried every item in Leary's office. Even the trash. No sign of his appointment book. But they did find an envelope from the Board of Pardons and Parole, postmarked September 25, 1995. An empty envelope."

"So? We know he was planning to testify for the defendant. Anthony Woijowski—I've never forgotten the name."

Donovan stared at her. "Woijowski. They called him Tony W. Who was he to Mike Leary? And why didn't we find the Parole Board letter?"

Above them, a single red-tailed hawk rode the winds.

SUNDAY
December 24, 1995

F ar be it from him to doubt the ushers' efficiency, but ever since
that morning a few weeks ago when he'd found the homeless
family sleeping in the cry room, Father Jim Coletta had made a
point of checking the locks when he came into the church for nightly
prayers.

At the center aisle, he paused, silently thanking God for His
blessings, for the opportunity to serve His people in the name of St.
Patrick.

A flood of gratitude for the example of his church's patron swept
through him. Belief was so difficult in this world, and yet so necessary.

As he approached the altar, he thought of the family who'd
taken refuge here. He suspected one of the older altar boys had left
the door unlocked on purpose. It was the kind of thing Father Leary
would have done, had he still been with them. A church committee had collected clothes and toys for the children and found the
family an apartment. A parishioner had given the husband a job,
and another had replaced their broken-down car. They attended
Mass faithfully every Sunday, though he had a hunch they weren't
officially Catholic. He had another hunch that the scholarship fund
would allow the older child, the boy, to attend kindergarten at St.
Francis next year if the family stuck around.

Not all such stories ended so well. Not everyone who sought refuge and received assistance made the most of the opportunity.

A fitting reminder on Christmas Eve.

He knelt on the bottom step. A sharp, quick pain shot through his right knee. When the orthopedist had diagnosed bursitis, he'd protested that he was too young, and they'd both laughed. A knee injury, a priest's occupational hazard.

Easter might be the most important day in the liturgical year, the celebration of the Risen Christ who died for our sins and ensured our salvation. But in his heart, Jim Coletta enjoyed the Christmas services more. He loved seeing the sanctuary so full, especially on Christmas Eve.

And the pure joy of the children—what greater gift? No matter that their excitement was mainly over Santa Claus. Although when the little ones gathered on the altar with him earlier tonight to sing Happy Birthday to Jesus, he'd been absolutely convinced that they understood the true meaning of Christmas, perhaps better than their parents.

Perhaps better than he did.

He bowed his head.

A few minutes later, he put a hand on the upper step and pushed himself up. Joy could be exhausting.

His brow creased. What was that in the crèche? The chief usher had laid baby Jesus in his straw-lined manger this afternoon, and the children often made unexpected additions. That holy night had been ages ago, but not even the Gnostic gospels mentioned a stegosaur or triceratops attending the Savior's birth.

He crossed the altar to inspect the nativity scene. Aside from the dinosaurs and a pair of Lego sheep, there was nothing unusual in the display.

But what was that in back?

He parted the straw. A black leather bag lay on the floor of the manger, well behind the figures of the shepherds and the Holy Family.

He had a bag like that. It held his sacramental kit, for visits to the sick and dying. But his sat on a shelf inside his office. He had tucked it there after making his hospital rounds two days ago. Hadn't he?

His eyes narrowed in the dim light and he reached for the bag. Not his—smaller, with a wear spot on one corner. The zipper stuck, but he waggled it open.

Inside lay all the familiar paraphernalia: the silver cross, the purple stole, the vial of holy water. Even the gold-plated pyx that resembled a woman's compact and held the communion hosts.

And stitched to the lining, a tag with a name.

As if he'd been punched in the gut, Father Coletta staggered backward. He tottered on the edge of the step, pain shooting through his leg, fingers automatically making the sign of the cross.

He was holding a dead man's kit. Father Leary's. His brother in Christ, who had died without benefit of the sacraments for which he had lived.

Who had died unblessed.

What would St. Patrick say of that?

WEDNESDAY
February 14, 2001

The Billings Gazette—The Billings City Council Monday night approved a publicly financed loan to Simonich Properties for the purchase of the historic Babcock Theater downtown. Andy Simonich, spokesman for the company, developers and owners of the Billings Mall, the largest indoor shopping center in the state, said that he and his father, Jerzy, have long eyed the shuttered building and plan a complete refurbishment. Hailed as one of the finest houses between Minneapolis and Seattle when it opened in 1907, the Babcock marked the city's expansion north and west from the Northern Pacific Depot and other businesses along Montana Avenue.

Plans include replacing the stage and seating, installing new sound and lighting systems, and an upgrade of the lobby, as well as improving backstage areas. "It would not be possible for us to save this nearly century-old gem without the city's participation," Simonich said in an email to the Gazette. "We look forward to bringing a wide variety of entertainment to the region."

TUESDAY
June 25, 2002
Portland

C arrie spotted the shiny red car in front of the bungalow and muttered under her breath. The streets in this neighborhood were narrow, the homes older and mostly without garages. Some didn't even have driveways. Add in Portland's hills, and parking was impossible. Ten years in this house next Christmas, and the congestion had only gotten worse.

And some people just did not know how to park.

She squeezed her big white work van past the red car, which was too close to the driveway and too far from the curb, and wriggled into her driveway. Inched back and forth a few times, then gunned up the incline.

The door of the garage—built for a Model T, like the driveway—hadn't wanted to close all the way last night after she loaded the van for today's job. Todd always said, "Sure, you bet," when she asked him to fix something, but then he let it slide, and when she reminded him, he complained about spending his free time doing the same kind of work he did all day.

She was lucky that way, getting paid to muck about in the dirt. The front garden had finally come into its own. First, they'd ripped out the rat's nest of ivy that had thrived under the previous owner's neglect. A literal rat's nest—the thought of the creepy critters made her shudder. Next, they'd shored up the concrete retaining wall and refaced it for an old-world look. Then came a truckload of compost, perfect for the roses, to nourish the tired soil, and she'd built an arbor from branches pruned in the overgrown backyard. This was the Rose City, after all. And Carrie adored roses, from the old-fashioned grandifloras to the trendiest of teas and trees.

The pink lavender gave off a sweet fragrance as she brushed its floral wands. At the corner of the house, the eight-foot-high buddleia was about to burst into bloom. She'd kept most of the plants that had come with the house, moving them around for better light and views, but that one's roots had run too deep, and she'd left it alone.

The front door burst open, and Ali flew out.

"Mommy, Mommy, look who's here!"

Carrie crouched, arms wide, as Ali, all of ten, threw her lithe little body at her. *God, how good that felt.* Behind her came Jessie, who grabbed one white porch pillar and swung a bare foot in the air. Another figure, no taller than twelve-year-old Jessie, with a head of red curls, followed.

"Ginger?" Carrie set Ali firmly on her feet and stood. "Is that you? Oh my gosh. I thought you were in Nepal."

Ginger trotted down the brick steps and the sisters embraced.

"Is that your red car?" Carrie said. "And what's that on your face?"

Ginger reached up to wipe away a dusting of flour. "It's a rental. I was due for a break. And Portland's so pretty this time of year."

"We made *povitica*," Ali said, though it came out pole-tuh-VEET-suh rather than poe-vuh-TEET-suh.

"Like Baba used to make? How did you learn—and since when do you bake? Or cook? Do you even have a kitchen in your tent or whatever it is you live in?"

"C'mon, sis." Ginger spoke lightly, though her expression had turned guarded. "You know I have an apartment in New York, and yes, it has a kitchen."

A shared apartment where Ginger didn't spend much time and that Carrie had never seen. But that didn't matter. Her sister was *here.*

"The garden looks fantastic. Where did you get your green thumb?" Ginger leaned down to sniff a yellow peace rose.

Same place you got your rootlessness. "How long are you staying? And why didn't you tell me you were coming?" Carrie snapped off a spent blossom and tucked it into the pocket of her work pants.

"A few days. I wanted to surprise you."

"Consider me surprised." She sat on the bottom step to unlace her work boots. Her green thumb made for hot feet. "Jessie, could you bring us some lemonade?"

"And poletuhveetsa," Ali said, following her sister into the house.

"Hey, neighbor," a woman called from the sidewalk, and Carrie raised a hand. "Got a moment for a quick question? About my azalea."

Neighbors asked her plant questions all the time. She never minded; some had become clients that way. Todd called the garden her portfolio. It was her refuge, tending it her therapy.

She introduced Ginger to the neighbor, Ellie.

"You're the photographer," Ellie said. "She brags about you and your work all the time. She's very proud of you."

They talked azaleas while sipping lemonade and nibbling the *povitica*, warm and sweet, full of cinnamon, walnuts, and raisins.

"Sounds like too much shade," Carrie said, after hearing Ellie's description of poor growth and sparse blooms. "They like it cool, but if the shade is too deep, they don't get enough oxygen."

"Photosynthesis," Jessie said, with a knowing nod.

"You might need to move it or cut back the surrounding plants. I'll come over and check it out later in the week."

"Thanks. You're a godsend. Which one of you braided Jessie's hair? It's darling."

Carrie reached out and stroked Jessie's French braid, still tight after a full day of summer camp at the city park. The girls got their thick blond hair from both parents, but it was already obvious that when the roundness of childhood dissolved, Carrie's strong features would emerge on both their faces.

"My mom did it," Jessie said. "Her mom taught her."

Ginger's blue eyes widened as she turned her gaze to Carrie. "Mom taught you?"

"Is she a hairdresser?" Ellie asked. "That would be a fun mother to have."

Todd's truck pulled into the driveway. "Red!" he called out the window. "What are you doing here?"

"She died young," Carrie told Ellie. "When I was fourteen and Ginger five."

"Oh gosh. I'm so sorry to hear that. Thanks for your advice on the plant." Ellie set her lemonade glass on the tray and pushed herself up. To Ginger, she said, "Lovely to meet you. What's your next project?"

Ginger shot Carrie a glance, blinking rapidly before replying. "I'm starting a new assignment in East Africa. In about a week."

"But you just got here." Carrie heard herself whine and cringed inside.

"It's what I do, sis," Ginger said. "I go places and I take pictures. Pictures the powers that be can't ignore."

"I know. I just wish we could see more of you."

"Safe travels," Ellie told Ginger, then called a greeting to Todd and headed back to her own yard.

"Mommy," Ali said, leaning heavily into her, "don't die young."

Too late for that, Carrie thought as she drew Ali onto her lap. She was already older than her mother had been when she died. "Oh, baby. Don't worry. Don't you worry."

SATURDAY
March 5, 2016
Billings

*A*nthony Woijowski. After all the variations on the name that he'd heard in the last eighteen hours, Donovan understood why the man had been called Tony W. The scumbag had been convicted of half a dozen crimes from 1963 to 1972, when he hit the jackpot: deliberate homicide. His prize? A life sentence on state hospitality, such as it was.

But none of the convictions had been local. The files were too old to be fully computerized and too fat to scan, and no one could ship him anything until Monday. Even then, deliveries might be delayed by the late-spring storm threatening to drop a foot of wet, heavy snow across south-central Montana.

He scanned his notes, neatly printed on a yellow pad. Millennial he might be, but Donovan liked writing by hand sometimes. Slowed him down and showed him connections he might otherwise miss.

His bare-bones dossier on Tony W painted an ugly picture.

According to prison records, Tony had first come up for parole in 1985 but hadn't applied. Too long a shot, even for a risk taker like him. Ten years later, in 1995, he applied but withdrew his request partway through the process. Chances had come and gone since then, but he hadn't taken them.

Why not? And what had Father Michael Leary intended to say at that 1995 hearing?

A priest testifying for a former parishioner—not uncommon, he supposed. He ran down the roster of Leary's assignments, comparing it to his chart of Tony W's arrests, to see where they might have met.

So much for that theory. Never in the same place at the same time.

Yes, they were, he realized with a start. Not as adults. But both Anthony Woijowski and Michael Leary were born in Red Lodge in 1939.

Boyhood friends who took completely different paths? A staple of gangster movies, old and new. But clichés are sometimes true. Donovan had come close to being one himself.

And what about Jerzy Simonich?

The snow had already begun in the mountains. Even in his heavy rig with studded snow tires, the sixty-mile drive to Red Lodge was unadvisable. The phone was a poor substitute for a face-to-face interview, but this felt urgent.

"I'm happy to ask if she recognizes the name," Mrs. Leary the younger told him when he made the call and his request. "But you know, Anna didn't grow up here. She met my father-in-law while he was a young engineer working abroad and she was nanny to another American family. They didn't spend much time in Montana until they retired. Summer vacations and holiday visits, mainly. Hard to imagine she'd have known Father Mike's childhood friends."

"She may have heard family stories. Your husband, too."

"He's out shoveling some of that 'partly cloudy' that was forecast. I'll have him call you."

Donovan put the receiver back in its cradle and warmed his hands on his coffee mug.

Twenty minutes later, after a return call dashing his hopes that the Leary family might know who Tony W was to Father Mike, Donovan approached the front door of the rectory. Father Coletta stood in the doorway, watching a woman hurry to the white Cadillac SUV parked at the curb.

"Conflicts on the parish council," the priest said. "I think we have suffered a mistranslation of the Scriptures."

Donovan waited.

"I think what Jesus actually said," Father Coletta continued, his bushy brows wagging, "was 'Wherever two or more of you are gathered in my name, there will be a problem.' Come in, Detective."

When he he'd been eight or nine, his mother had pleaded with his father to go to counseling with her. Hell, no, the old man had yelled. No sissy, skirt-wearing priest was going to tell him how to take care of his family. His mother went anyway, but it hadn't done any good, not that Donovan could see. She'd been powerless to stop the drinking and yelling. The old man had never hit her, far as Donovan knew, though he'd gone after his brother once. She'd stepped in, and it never happened again.

But young Brian had lived in fear. They all had. Why she hadn't found another counselor, not connected to the church, he'd never understood. Maybe she knew, subconsciously, that an educated professional woman would urge her to leave, and that was the one thing she could never do.

He exhaled heavily and stepped over the threshold.

"Working on Saturday?" Coletta asked as he led the way down the hall.

"As are you, Father."

"Never off duty," came the reply. "We have that in common. It's a calling, not a job. Most days."

In his office, Coletta gestured to a chair and walked around the desk. His black cardigan was missing a button.

How much had the place changed since Father Leary's day? How much remained the same? Bookcases filled one wall, overflowing. Donovan read a few titles as he laid his coat over the prie-dieu. *The Letters of St. Augustine.* Handbooks on marriage counseling.

His old man had a point when it came to the irony of celibates counseling couples. But he supposed a certain outsider perspective might be useful.

"How's it going, Father?"

"One day at a time, Brian. One day at a time." Coletta moved a book on the church and the LGBT community to the other side of the desk. "I hope my experience in rehab makes me more compassionate. Thank God for a second priest in the parish. I'm on my own this week while he visits his parents. And the parishioners have been very understanding."

"Problems with the parish council aside?"

"Touché. You're here about that list, aren't you? I asked the head deacon to update it for you. It's here somewhere." Coletta shuffled through a stack of papers. Held a page in the air, triumphant. His glasses slipped down his nose as he skimmed it, large frames long out of style, lenses badly smudged. "Twenty years bring a lot of changes. Monsignor O'Shea, alas, is deceased. Most of the other priests working in Billings in 1995 have died or retired. Father Schwartz is retired, but he lives in the apartments behind St. Thomas."

The church in the West End, near Donovan's home. Doubting Thomas.

"Father Chapman would have known Father Leary, but I'm afraid his memory is gone. Alzheimer's. We had better luck updating the list of deacons and other volunteers. Some gaps there, too, though." Coletta gave the list another once-over, then passed it to Donovan.

"Do you still have a housekeeper?" Donovan asked. He hadn't seen one. But then, it was Saturday.

"I'm afraid not. These days, most of us are lucky to hire a woman to come in and clean every week or two. And I'm blessed with churchwomen who drop off a casserole or cookies now and then. Even in Father Leary's time, we ran a lean operation compared to the old days, when the church had ample resources." Father Coletta smiled slightly, tilting his head. "It's a different mission now. We do have administrative staff, and that frees me up for individual ministry. But the personal is political, as the feminists taught us. Even here in Billings, our parishes are more diverse. We deal with social justice issues on the ground, so to speak."

Donovan ran his eyes down the list.

A name and a pair of dates snagged his eyes. "Irene Danich. She wasn't here long."

"No. She came here about the same time as Father Leary, in 1981, but didn't stay. Why, I don't know. Before my time." The priest sat back. "That was years before his disappearance."

"Any idea where she went?"

"No. But there is someone you might talk to. He's getting on, but still sharp as a tack. Very generous. Knows everyone. Organizes an annual prayer service on October tenth, the date Father Leary disappeared." He scratched a name on a yellow sticky note, reached across the desk, and slapped it on the list of former church personnel.

Donovan read the name. Why did everything seem to come back to Jerzy Simonich?

* * *

"You worked the early shift today, I take it?" Lindsay said.

Haley stood in the kitchen doorway, her black cotton pants dusted with flour, keys dangling from one hand. Her wide-eyed gaze darted from one stone-faced parent to the other.

"I don't know what to ask first. Why you lied to us about changing schools. If you honestly thought we'd never find out. What you did with the tuition money." Lindsay picked up one of the envelopes that lay on the breakfast nook table. She'd have uncovered Haley's deception sooner if she hadn't been too busy at work to open her own bank statements. "I gave you a check for three thousand dollars when the term started seven weeks ago. It hasn't cleared."

"It—it's in my sock drawer," Haley said.

The cat jumped down and circled Haley's feet.

"At least this explains why you've been dodging us. Telling us you've got early classes when you're out of here before dawn to chop peppers and crack eggs. Hiding in your room at night, letting us think something terrible had happened."

"I never said that. Whatever you thought—"

"We thought," Scott said, "you would tell us the truth."

"This is why I didn't tell you." Haley threw up her hands, the keys rattling. "Because I knew you'd make a big deal out of it."

"It is a big deal, Haley," Lindsay said. "And don't try playing victim with us. You want to be in charge of your life, fine. You have to own up to the consequences."

After her conversation with Detective Donovan yesterday, Lindsay had called the cafe's owner, a former client. She'd helped the woman find financing to convert the long-vacant space, originally the corner grocery a short bike ride from her childhood home. The café thrived, serving the neighborhood as well as hospital staff and visitors. "She's a talented cook and a promising baker," the woman had said. "I assumed you knew she was working for me."

What else had she been clueless about?

Lindsay had harbored no illusions that they would be immune to kid problems, and on the grand scale of things, this was barely a blip. But it was still a shock. Haley hadn't just kept a secret. She hadn't just kept her troubles to herself until she got a handle on them.

She had *lied* to them.

She must have been terrified that they'd find out. *Good. Serves her right,* Lindsay thought, knowing it was unkind but in this moment, not caring. They had been genuinely worried.

"I didn't want to disappoint you."

"Honey, you didn't disappoint us. You lied to us," Scott said. "There's a big difference."

Lindsay picked up her coffee cup. Empty. She set it down with a loud clunk.

Haley leaned against the wall, arms and legs crossed. "If I had told you the truth, that I wanted to drop out and cook professionally, then what? You'd have pressured me to stay in school. 'Get your degree first. Then you can do anything you want.'" She minced her voice and wagged her head on this last part, in what Lindsay supposed was meant to be an imitation of them. Of her.

And yeah, that was pretty much what she would have said. But she wasn't wrong.

"You want me to be like Chelsea, and I'm not," Haley continued.

"No, no, young lady. Don't go there. We have never played favorites." At least, she thought they hadn't. "Much as we love Chelsea, one of her is plenty."

Ignored long enough, Ms. Wriggles hopped on the bench, made a circle, and settled down.

"Halo." Scott resurrected her childhood nickname. "Honestly, I think we would have understood. We've bucked a few expectations in our day."

"You, sure. But what's more mainstream than being a lawyer?"

God, Lindsay thought. Smack in the middle of mother–daughter drama. *I have never wanted to trade one of them for a boy, but right now, for half an hour . . .*

"Not fair," Scott said. "Your mother was the first person in her family to finish college. Your grandfather was a welder and your grandmother a school secretary. Going to law school was a big deal."

"Okay, but it's not like being an artist."

"Your father's career proves our point," Lindsay said. "His parents knew making a living as an artist would be hard and convinced him to add an education degree. He taught for years until he made his name as an artist."

"He couldn't wait to quit teaching," Haley fired back. "I don't want to wait until I'm fifty to do what I want."

Lindsay threw up her hands. That was so not the point. Although she did want her kid to follow her dreams, as she herself had not. Not fully. She slid off the bench and padded past Haley to the kitchen and the coffee pot. "Did you never think one of us might walk into the café and see you?"

"I'm a cook, not a server. You wouldn't have seen me."

"Detective Donovan saw you. You had to have known somebody would tell us at some point." She set her hot cup on the morning paper, unopened at half past two. How could they work their way out of this? She scooped up the orange tabby and sat, the soft, warm fur in her arms a comfort.

But being pissy wasn't going to solve the problem.

"Okay, so. I think you can understand why we're angry," she continued. Haley rubbed her arms, eyes wary. "And hurt that you didn't trust us enough to tell us what you were feeling. The question is, what next?"

Haley dropped her keys on the counter. She grabbed a mug, filled it, and plopped onto the empty chair.

"I want to go to cooking school," she said. "Next fall. My boss will help me get in."

Cooking school. Lindsay stared at her daughter. "Cooking school? That's what the fancy soups and souffles are about?"

"Trying to butter us up?" Scott said, but it wasn't funny.

Well, yeah, it was. She pressed her lips together, holding back a laugh as her eyes met her husband's.

Cooking school. It hadn't been the plan. But it was the nature of plans to change. Not part of Newton's Laws, but just as immutable.

And besides, they had to eat.

SATURDAY
March 5, 2016
Portland

"Relax." Ginger reached across the round two-top in the Heathman Hotel bar, fingertips grazing the back of Carrie's hand. "I'm buying."

Carrie fidgeted against the smooth chocolate leather of her chair. She'd seen the price of a martini. "No, it's not that. It's just—"

After the late nights of research and the long days of planting, it was finally time. While her fingers untangled roots and patted dirt into place, her mind had muddled over the details she'd worked out—the whole crazy mess revealed by Baba's box and her online discoveries. Their family tree, scarred and twisted.

How did you tell somebody all that? She turned her attention back to the bar menu. Portland had gone kinda crazy in recent years, too hip for her and her budget. Ginger never said much about her New York life, but it was easy to picture her in shiny places like this.

Places Carrie had never been. Places her sister had wanted to show her, but she'd always said no, preferring to stay home. How dumb was that? A mix of shame and loneliness welled up inside of her, and she swallowed the tears before they could reach her eyes.

"You ready, sis?" Ginger said, and Carrie glanced up with a start. A tiny sapphire glinted in the waitress's nose. Ali had a rhinestone, and when Carrie asked if it hurt when she blew her nose, her daughter's answer had been a roll of the eyes.

"Asher would adore the brass bulldog out front," Carrie said after they'd ordered. "Although why the dog is wearing the same ruffled coat and hat as the doorman, you have to wonder."

"Carrie." Ginger laid her hand on the table, palm down. "I owe you an apology." She paused, eyes locked on Carrie's, and swallowed. "I spent the day with Ali and Asher. We went to the zoo. I get it now."

Carrie's throat shut in a spasm that released as quickly as it had come on. "I can't imagine the horrors you've seen. Women and children dying from poverty and war. I push that out of my mind because I'd rather picture you in the safe, pretty places."

"I let what I've seen influence me. I acted like Asher's illness is no big deal because he can be treated. Even though he can't be cured, and his life will never be . . ." Ginger stopped herself.

"Normal. Pain-free. It's okay. I'm not afraid of the words. But I am afraid of how he'll suffer. And it's getting worse."

"It was brutal of me, and I'm sorry. If you want me to help with the research and go through genetic testing, I'm willing."

Carrie pressed her fist against her mouth. It was what she'd wanted, but now . . . "The testing might not be necessary. I might be sorry I started digging up the past."

Ginger's eyes flashed, nearly turquoise in this light. "What? Tell me."

Worse than being at odds with her sister was having to tell her the truth. Or what she knew of it. Did Ginger need to know?

Yes. Carrie had built her life around protecting people, as Baba had protected them, but she was done with secrets. The secrets had hurt them both too much.

"After the birthday party, I dove into our family tree. I've worked on it every night this week. I found all kinds of cool details about our mother's family—stuff I never knew. But Dad's side was harder." She hadn't stopped thinking of Tony as *their* dad yet.

"West is a common name. You okay?"

Carrie gripped the glass with both hands. "When Baba died, I didn't have time to sort through everything. The nuns helped me pack her house. They gave me a box of papers and photographs. I stashed it in the basement and pretty much forgot it."

"I should have been here to help. I'm sorry."

"No, it's not that. I don't think either of us would have understood until I started working out the genealogy."

"You're scaring me, sis. Get to the point."

"I'm saying we aren't who we thought we were. Our family name isn't West. Dad didn't die in Vietnam. He's serving a life sentence in the Montana State Prison. For murder." Carrie leaned forward, hating what she had to say next. "Ginge, I am so sorry. There's more. He isn't *our* dad. He's mine, but yours . . ."

"What are you talking about? Are you saying we don't have the same father?"

"I don't have any legal proof. It's mostly conjecture, based on timing and photographs, and a stack of papers Baba kept. Do you remember Father Leary?"

Ginger stiffened, her blue eyes wide, her skin pale. In that moment, she looked to Carrie exactly as the priest had when they last saw him, that day in the Grotto more than thirty years ago.

She reached inside the collar of her gray cashmere turtleneck and pulled out a thin gold chain. Caught the medal between her thumb and forefinger.

"So, this? St. Christopher, patron saint of children and travelers. The priest—the *priest*—who gave me this was my *father*?"

Carrie bit her lower lip and nodded.

Ginger jerked the chain hard and it broke. In one fluid motion, she threw the medal on the table and stood.

It was impossible to say what happened first, the wine splashing the air between them or the clink of a glass striking the surface. Carrie glanced from the sapphire-studded waitress to the glass, miraculously unbroken, rocking slowly back and forth across the table.

"Oh my gosh, I am so sorry," Sapphire sputtered.

"Not your fault," Carrie began as Ginger rushed from the room. Carrie's heart was pounding from the sudden crash, her normally unflappable sister's reaction, the whole chaotic situation she had caused.

No, you didn't, she told herself as her breath slowed and Sapphire picked up the glass. Another woman appeared with a damp rag. No wine had landed on Carrie, and Ginger's cosmo sat on the table, undisturbed.

"I'll get you another glass right away," Sapphire said. "Your oysters will be right out. Is she okay?"

"I don't know," Carrie said, "but it has nothing to do with you. I promise."

The photos. Carrie snatched up her bag and rummaged inside. The photos were safe and dry, thank goodness.

She glanced around. No one was staring. Just an accident, excitement over.

Should she go after Ginger? No, let her be. She'd come back for her bag, hanging from the back of her chair, if nothing else.

Sapphire brought a fresh glass of wine, along with a fresh apology. Three sips later, Ginger returned.

"Okay, I'm an idiot. Apparently, a bastard idiot. Does that make me a bitch? Don't answer," she said as she sat, then reached for her drink. "Damn, that's good."

They stared at each other for a long moment, then started laughing. When Sapphire delivered their appetizer, they were drunk with the giggles. Ginger tried to apologize, but the waitress brushed it off.

"Okay," Ginger said, after she'd slurped down two oysters and eaten a chunk of crusty rye bread soaked in the buttery sauce. "Tell me the rest."

Carrie wiped her mouth, then showed her sister the photos and told her about the name change, the prison record, and everything she'd found.

"Woijowski? That means you're half Serb, half Polish. And I'm half Serb, half Irish."

"All the downtrodden peoples of Europe in one unhappy family," Carrie said.

Ginger drained her drink. "Are you done? I'm done."

She tossed a wad of cash on the table. Her fingers hesitated just a moment before picking up the medal.

"Lovely evening for a walk, ladies," the red-coated doorman said as he held the door, the brass dog standing guard.

They walked in silence. When they reached the corner, Carrie glanced at Ginger. Tears streamed down her sister's freckled cheeks.

"Don't tell me you already knew?"

"No–o-o, yes. Kinda. I knew . . ." Ginger puffed her cheeks, then blew out a breath. The light turned and they stepped off the curb. "First, there's my face."

"I love your face!"

"Yeah, but it isn't anything like yours. You look like Baba and Mom. You're all built the same, except for your height. You're gorgeous, like a young Gloria Steinem, with those big brown eyes and great hair, the cheekbones carved from stone."

"What was in that drink of yours?"

"Seriously, sis." They reached the sidewalk on the other side of the street. "You have no idea how well you clean up."

Carrie snorted. The black leggings, olive green sweater, and brown knee-high boots were one of maybe two decent outfits in her closet. Her tan raincoat was years old.

"But it's more than that," Ginger continued. "I was about ten, trying to scrub off my freckles. Baba laughed and said I got them from my father and couldn't do a thing about it, and then, it was like she realized what she'd said and clammed up."

"I never knew," Carrie said. They kept walking.

"Do you remember that day in the church in Billings?" Ginger asked. "Right before we moved out here. I was hiding up front, and you were standing in the doorway."

In a day, a week, of surprises, little Ginger might have said could have surprised Carrie more.

"You remember that?"

Ginger nodded, her profile reflected in the shop windows. No one would peg them for sisters. Shared paternity or not, though, that's what they were.

"Father Mike—Father Leary—was talking with two men," Ginger said. "One young, one old. At least, he seemed old. Probably not much older than Father. 'We know about the girl,' they said. I couldn't figure out why they cared that I'd lost my jump rope. I loved it. I practically slept with it, but I'd lost it and went looking. It wasn't until years later that I realized they weren't talking about me playing in the church. They were talking about something else entirely."

"That's what made you wonder about our dad? I'm not making the connection."

"No reason you should. I didn't start to wonder about him until I got my passport, when I was nineteen, before the field trip to El Salvador. I needed a copy of my birth certificate. Baba said she didn't have one."

"She did," Carrie said. "I found it in her papers."

"She probably hoped I'd let it drop, but I got a copy from the state. There's no father listed. At first, I thought because Dad wasn't there, the nurses left it blank. But the more I thought about it . . ."

"You connected it to Father Leary and the incident in the church? I still don't see—"

"They were talking about me, Carrie. I was 'the girl.' Later, I decided those men thought Father Leary knew who my biological father was—maybe it was the older man, and he wanted it kept secret. I never imagined . . ."

"You thought Mom had an affair." Carrie couldn't believe what they were saying. "You were right." Even if she hadn't known who with, Ginger had been right. And she'd never said a word.

"But why did they care? Who were they?"

"I have no idea," Carrie said. "Between the sunlight and the shadows, I couldn't see their faces. I certainly didn't know them."

They reached the end of the block. Ginger stopped. "Dad—your dad—my God, Carrie, what happened?"

"I don't know the details yet. He was in and out of jail for years," Carrie replied. "Now I think that's why we moved so much when I was little. So Mom could stay close to him. But at some point, she had enough. She changed our name and tried to start over."

"And fell in love with another man. Oh, sis. Who could blame her, though? If he and Dad—Tony—were old friends, then she must have known Father Mike all her life, too."

"She made up the story about Dad being killed in the war so we would have an explanation that made him a hero, not a killer."

"And Baba kept up the facade, so we wouldn't learn the truth." Ginger leaned against a cast iron lamppost, the twin glass lanterns above the curlicues casting a pinky-blue LED glow. "They lied to us."

"They did it out of love." A wave of compassion for her mother flooded through Carrie, a woman dealt a rotten hand but determined to play it the best she could so her girls could have a better life. Carrie understood, and she forgave. Tina and Baba Irene had been driven by the same kind of love that drove her. A love that encompassed everything and everyone. Asher. The girls.

And Ginger. *Oh, Ginger.*

"They thought they were doing the right thing" was all she could manage.

"Did they? Sometimes I wonder," Ginger said. "We're all driven by forces we can't identify. Gremlins in our brains. We keep following the path we started out on, never asking if it's still the right path."

"What are you talking about?"

"You are a rock, Carrie. Me . . ." Her hair glinted in the light from the streetlamp. "I started running ages ago, and I kept running. I send you presents, and I visit, but I never let you know I'm coming. I don't even stay at your house. It's like if I did, I'd see how empty my life is."

"Ginger, stop that. You are amazing. You are brilliant." The warmth that had enveloped her a moment ago evaporated. *What was happening?*

"I knew this guy in Rio, a doctor who ran the medical aid office. 'Look around,' he said one night. 'Why are we here? We're all rootless Americans running from the past.'"

"Maybe you started by running away," Carrie said. "But you ran to something. And it all served a purpose. You and your pictures help people."

"We're sisters, raised together, but we grew up differently. I never had parents, not really. Just ideas of them. Now I don't even have those."

"You had Baba. You have me," Carrie said, gripping her sister by the arm. "You are never getting rid of me."

Ginger stared at her, the blue eyes blank. Then she snapped her head, as if shaking away all the doubt. "Thank God for that, Carrie. Thank God for you."

They hugged, a long slow hug that Carrie didn't want to end. Finally, they pulled apart.

"Oh God," Ginger said. "My father's a priest. Yours is in prison. What a fucking mess."

Carrie took a long breath, grateful for the cool air in her hot lungs. "Let's get one thing straight. I meant what I said. You are the bravest, most determined woman I have ever known, standing up for people who have nothing. Getting assignments no one wanted to give a woman, let alone a cute, petite, young woman. And you have never abandoned me."

Two days ago, she wouldn't have said that. Two days ago, she'd been convinced that her beloved younger sister thought Carrie's life and home beneath her.

Now she understood. Ginger came to visit because she craved connection, but stayed in a hotel because she felt like an interloper. Thought she didn't belong.

Thought loving family meant losing them.

"You said he's still alive. Your father," Ginger said, her voice quiet and controlled. "You have to go see him."

"I can't afford the ticket. Or the time away—I've got jobs scheduled all week. *You* should go. See *your* father. I found him in the Diocesan directory. He's still at St. Pat's." It had been late, and she'd been falling asleep, her eyes bleary, but that name had stood out. *After all these years . . .*

The color had begun to return to Ginger's face, but now it receded. "No. No, I can't. I don't know anybody there—I barely remember the place."

"Then don't go right away. Come stay with me for a while."

"Besides, I've got to get back to work. I've got an assignment in Athens."

"After all this, Ginger, don't lie to me." She'd seen it on the website the other night, when she pulled up Ginger's official portrait. "The charity you've been working for is doing a big push to resettle the refugees camped on the Turkish border. You may be going to Athens, but then you'll go to Istanbul, and from there, you'll wiggle your way back to Aleppo, you and your cameras. I just wish you'd told me."

"I didn't want you to worry."

"Oh, for Chrissake, Ginger. I worry more when you don't tell me what you're doing."

Ginger caught her lip between her teeth and shook her head slowly. "Humans. We spend so much time trying to protect ourselves and each other. Half the time, we make it worse."

"That's the truth."

"I almost told you the other night, but the party was so much fun, I didn't want to spoil it." One side of Ginger's face rose in a wry expression. "I saw you with Ali and Asher, and I was so damned *mad* that you all have to go through this. And jealous. Because you had Mom and Dad, and now you have your own family."

"You're part of it, Ginge. Always."

Ginger looped an arm through Carrie's, and they headed toward the hotel. "I'll buy your ticket to Montana. You can do more family research, to answer the questions Asher's doctors are asking. We'll get to the bottom of this, sis. We'll get to the truth."

Carrie tightened her grip on her sister's arm, rummaging in her brain for the old saying.

"The truth will set you free. If it doesn't kill you first."

SUNDAY
March 6, 2016
Billings

L indsay hadn't bothered trying to keep her mind on Mass. Sometimes she envied those who found comfort in religion. She'd long ago converted her devotion to ritual to the secular world: lighting a candle in the evening. Creating tiny altars of special objects. And when the girls were young, serving breakfast on special days on the red plate with white script reading "You are special" on the rim.

A tricky balance, staying involved in your kid's life without hovering. Without acting like you knew best, even when you were convinced that you did.

Haley had cooked for them last night, a stupendous *beouf bourgignon*. Over dinner, they'd asked questions about the schools she had her eye on—no surprise, they were considerably pricier than MSU-B. The tuition money would go back in the bank, for now. Scott and Lindsay had trouble letting go of the degree idea, Haley countering that cooking schools taught business plans and management—it wasn't just about the perfect hollandaise.

It had not been a comfortable evening, but Lindsay felt sure they'd ultimately find a solution. Were they being manipulated? Or simply being forced to do what they'd always said they wanted to do—raise kids who could make their own decisions. That was the point, after all.

But Haley's deception still rankled. She had mishandled the situation badly, and they needed an apology. More than that, Lindsay wanted to be sure that Haley learned from the experience.

On an after-dinner walk around the neighborhood, she and Scott agreed you needed to be light on your feet when dealing with almost-grown children, ready for a change in plans. Sometimes it seemed like life was one big change in plans. The air was biting, a cold front blowing in, but it felt good to move.

Two pages into *The Paris Wife* for book club, the whirlwind caught up with her, and she fell asleep on the couch. Haley's car had been gone when she got up this morning, and Ms. Wriggles was curled on a cushion in the breakfast nook, so she figured Haley had left for work early, despite the wet spring snow that fell overnight.

Father Coletta finished the closing prayer, and Lindsay steered her mother through the glass Year of Mercy doors to the slick front steps, keeping one hand on her elbow while Pat gripped the railing.

"Springtime in Montana!" a chirpy voice called, and Lindsay turned to see Jana on the step behind her. "Don't see you here very often, Linds. Hello, Pat."

It always surprised her that others her age remained devoted to the Church. Jana had taken over running the holiday food basket program when it became too much for Pat, and attended Mass at least once during the week and every Sunday.

After a brief chat, Lindsay tucked Pat safely in the Prius and drove to the café on Tenth.

"This used to be a grocery store," Pat said, as if she didn't say the same thing every time.

The morning crew had cleared a wide swath, foot-high piles of snow lining the path. Lindsay watched her mother anxiously. Pat might walk slowly these days, but her gait was steady, her footsteps sure in her fur-trimmed black snow boots.

Lindsay tried not to scan the place for her daughter as they followed a young man with a chestnut bun and skinny black pants to a round, wood-topped table near the window. He helped her mother with her coat and the chair, and Lindsay thanked him as she seated herself.

"Is Haley Breck working today?"

The host's eyes lit up. "You bet. She's on crepes and waffles this morning. I highly recommend them."

"Ahh. Thanks." Culinary training and a paycheck might not be all that attracted Haley to this job.

They ordered—toast and two eggs over easy for Pat, the crepes for Lindsay—and settled in with their coffee. Coffee was another part of Lindsay's ritual. She breathed in the sacred aroma. Gazed around the café, the old brick now painted white, the pine floors gleaming. Had anyone else in the Sunday morning crowd biked here as a kid for an ice cream bar or to pick up something her mother needed for dinner? Not likely.

And every table and seat at the counter was full.

"This coffee's too strong," her mother said. "Why do they always make it so strong?"

"It's Italian roast. Very popular."

"Well, I think it's too strong."

Families. "Mom, do you remember Father Leary? He was at St. Pat's and taught at the high school. Twice, I think."

"Of course I do. I'm not senile."

Lindsay stopped herself from rolling her eyes. "They've reopened the investigation into his murder."

"Such a loss. So many of the priests and nuns from your childhood left their vocations, you know."

"Well, he didn't *leave*. He—"

"I know. I know. Two separate thoughts. He loved talking with the children on the playground when he walked through and after he said the school mass on Friday mornings. He had a way with them."

A shiver gripped Lindsay's spine. "Mom, you don't think . . . I mean, the child abuse that happened back then? I'm not suggesting Father Leary was involved, but—"

"No, I don't think that's why Father Leary was killed. In my day, discipline was harsh in some of the Catholic schools. Corporal punishment, it's called. I never experienced it, but your father did. That's why he distanced himself from the church. Times were different then—'*Spare the rod and spoil the child.*' Society evolves, thank God. In some ways, at least." Pat paused. "Is there something you want to tell me?"

"What? Oh no. God, no." Lindsay set her cup in the saucer. "I wasn't aware of anything like that at the time."

Pat nodded. "Shameful, is all I can say."

"And yet, you believe. You go to church every Sunday, rain or shine."

As a school secretary, her mother had perfected the gaze that kept stray children in line, and she used it now. "I might doubt man—and woman—from time to time, Lindsay. But I never doubt God."

She made it sound so simple.

"The massive exodus of priests and nuns in the late sixties, early seventies put a heavy burden on those who stayed, like Father Leary," Pat continued. "Thank God—quite literally—for the Irish priests and nuns who filled in the gaps."

"Ha. Like Sister Claire, the bane of every upper-level girl in the high school." The nun had long retired before her own girls got to high school, but washing their PE uniforms had always reminded her of the locker room. But while some of the abuse allegations that had surfaced in recent years were against nuns, she'd never heard a whisper of sexual abuse by Claire. Or any other nun she'd known. Sometimes a creepy stare is just a creepy stare.

"Well, she wasn't Irish. Not from Ireland anyway," Pat said. "From New York."

"I know. Two separate thoughts, like you said. What was she doing here anyway? If she wasn't one of the regular nuns or the Irish missionary sisters."

"Claire was Stu Kennedy's sister-in-law. You didn't know that?"

Her parents' lawyer, long retired. "How could I know? You never told me."

Pat ignored that. "She came out here after his wife, her sister, died, so he could have family close by to help with all those kids. It's called a compassionate reassignment. Her order back east made the request, the diocese approved, the school made room for her, and that was that."

So simple. There'd been what, six Kennedy kids? All younger than she was, so no reason to have made the connection. Hadn't she seen Claire talking with one of the boys once, seeming almost nice? The day of the locker room incident. The day everything changed.

She took another sip of coffee. Fortification. "Mom, do you remember a woman who kept house for the priests? 1981–82, my senior year. She wasn't here very long. She was raising two grand-daughters, one in my class and one quite a bit younger."

Pat squinted, thinking. "Ye-e-s, now that you mention it. What was her name? She came here with Father Leary, from Miles City, I think. I had the impression she was a relative of his. We waived the grade school tuition. I presume the high school made a similar arrangement."

"They were relatives? Of Father Leary?"

"Maybe not. I don't remember."

"Here we go—two gorgeous breakfasts for two gorgeous women." Their server slid two hot plates onto the table and stepped back, hands together as if he were about to applaud himself.

No sooner had he waltzed away when a dark cloud in a black apron swooped in.

"So now you're checking on me, Mom?" Haley said, two red spots high on her cheeks.

"No, but could you blame me if I were?"

Haley spoke through clenched teeth. "I thought you understood. This is what I want to do with my life."

"And it looks delicious," Lindsay said, gesturing at the white plate of perfectly rolled crepes, stuffed with eggs and cheese and drizzled with hollandaise, roasted herbed potatoes on the side.

"Sorry, Gram," Haley said, leaning down to kiss Pat's cheek. "I know you did your best with her."

"As she's done with you," Pat replied. Haley let out an exasperated sound and marched back to the kitchen.

Lindsay waited until her daughter had disappeared from sight. "Good one, Mom."

"I have my moments." If it hadn't been such a cliché, Lindsay would have said her mother's eyes twinkled as they picked up their forks. The food was as tasty as it looked, and they ate in silence.

"Not to keep coming back to it," Lindsay said a few minutes later. "But what did you hear when Father Leary died? Any theories on what happened? Or who?"

"It was all talk," Pat said. "I never paid any attention. This one said he ran off with a parishioner. That one said he heard something he shouldn't have in the confessional. For some, it was an excuse to resurrect that old anti-Catholic nastiness."

"Like what?"

"Oh, nothing worth repeating. Nothing like the old days, when my parents were children, when the KKK burned crosses in the front yards of Catholic families."

"In Billings? The KKK? I thought they targeted Blacks and Jews."

"Catholics, too. Do you remember Miss Moran? The elderly woman I used to visit? You went with me a time or two." Pat picked up a slice of toast.

"In the pink fairy-tale house on Clark? She had a glass candy jar filled with foil-wrapped toffees. And a butler's pantry."

"Her father built that house. It was nearly done when the Klan left a burning cross in the front yard. It was a miracle the whole neighborhood didn't go up in flames. They came after the Steneruds, too, because of the booze."

"Wow. I never heard any of that." Lindsay leaned toward her mother and dropped her voice. "Are you saying Father Leary's murder may have been a hate crime?"

"Not that I ever heard, no." Pat reached for the black wool peacoat hung on the back of her chair and pulled a tissue out of the pocket. "But people get desperate when they feel threatened."

A little while later, Lindsay parked the Prius in front of her mother's condo. Her brother and sister advocated for a move to a senior community or "independent living." They flew in from Denver and

Dallas every few months and saw the changes—the slower steps, the longer gap between question and response. She saw her mother at least twice a week. In the first few minutes, she'd feel impatient, wondering if the woman wasn't starting to lose it. But then, as today, Pat would prove herself as sharp of mind and tongue as ever.

Lindsay opened her mother's car door and held out a hand.

"I'm all right, dear," Pat said. She looped her red handbag over her wrist. "You don't need to walk me inside. Haley is a good girl. She'll make it work."

"I hope you're right. Cooking for a living seems like a hard choice."

Pat planted her feet squarely on the driveway, ready to push herself up. "Your father and I came from families that accepted our lots. 'Don't make waves.' 'Don't ask for much and you won't be disappointed.' We didn't know how to teach you kids to fight for what you wanted, but with you, we didn't need to. You just knew." She raised her face. "And I think your daughter does, too. She got her guts from you."

Not how it felt. But then, that was one of life's essential mysteries, wasn't it, how differently two people could see the same events, or experience the same relationship?

She kissed her mother's cheek. "Thanks, Mom."

MONDAY
March 7, 2016

"Thank you again for telling me you saw my daughter last week," Lindsay said as she walked with Detective Donovan to the police station interview room. "We probably sound like terrible parents, not knowing our kid dropped out of school to bake cakes."

"Not at all." He stepped aside and gestured for her to enter.

"Turns out she has a mind of her own." Lindsay gave him a wry smile. "Wonder where she gets that? She didn't think we'd approve, and I suppose she's right. But like all parents, we want her to use her talents in a way that will make her happy."

As if you could ever guarantee that.

After Sunday mass and breakfast with her mom, she and Scott had taken their cross-country skis down to the Yellowstone, hoping for one last glide on the trails before the snow melted. The giant cottonwoods stood like sculptures on the riverbank, snow glistening in the crooks of their branches. At one point, they stopped to watch the bald eagles fishing and counted seventeen.

On their way back to the car, they saw a young couple skiing with a toddler in a pull-behind carrier, and Scott gave her one of those warm looks she cherished, full of shared memories and pride.

When they got home, they found two pieces of coconut cake on the kitchen table with a note signed "H."

"If this is her apology," Scott said a few minutes later, his mouth full, "we should fight with her more often."

Lindsay had swatted him with the kitchen towel.

"You were right about the coconut cake," she told Donovan now. "I had no idea she could bake like that."

"I'm almost sorry I know." Donovan sat. "What did you want to see me about?"

She dropped her coat and bag on a chair. "My mother mentioned a woman she thought was a relative of Father Leary's."

"We're on the same track, then. Though Bill and Anna Leary lived in England until he retired a few years ago, and now he's gone."

"Who? No," Lindsay said. "Who's Anna Leary?"

"The widow of Mike Leary's older brother. I hoped she or her son might recall names of old friends, snippets of his life before the priesthood. They both remembered one name. You might know him—Jerzy Simonich."

"Jerzy? Yeah, sure. It was his daughter who was killed—I told you about her last Friday. Mary Ellen Simonich. I wonder why they mentioned him." Lindsay took a seat. "We went all through school together, but the Simoniches moved to a bigger house up under the Rims before we started high school. She got kinda snooty after that."

"And the brother you had a crush on was Andy. I've met him." Donovan sat, the curve of his lips and the glint in his eyes telling her he didn't think much of Andy Simonich.

"He married another girl we hung out with, Jana Stenerud. They split up ages ago. She was in the car when it crashed, but she recovered. I see her fairly often—just finished some legal work for her family. They own the Rainbow."

"I know the place. I gather it has a notorious past."

"Not according to Jana. If you listen to her, there's never been a lick of trouble. Granny made hooch for fun." Lindsay smiled. "Truthfully, they do run a pretty clean operation. Jana's easy to tease—she's so serious."

"You were telling me about Jerzy Simonich," Donovan prompted.

"Property developer, commercial construction." Though that wasn't all. "Tried his hand at historic preservation, but he hated all the regulations. He likes to think big."

"You don't trust him."

"I wouldn't say that, but he's the kind of man who always thinks he should come out on top. 'Course, he usually does."

She'd heard rumors that Jerzy won lucrative construction contracts by deliberate interference, bribing subcontractors so he could put in the low bid and make up for it with a bit of extra on the side. Other rumors said he bought off the right people, but she had her doubts—the city building officials all seemed too honest. Now that she was working with a legitimate buyer for the old theater, she was doubly glad she'd turned Jerzy down years ago when he'd tried to hire her to help him buy the place—she'd never believed he'd see the project through. And she'd been right.

Maybe Mary Ellen wouldn't have grown out of that mean streak. Maybe she'd inherited it from Jerzy. Maybe that was what gave him his edge in business.

Andy didn't have good instincts or meanness. He just had poor judgment. Truth was, he'd never been trusted enough to develop good judgment.

But she couldn't prove any of her suspicions about Jerzy, so she'd kept her mouth shut.

"If there's anyone else around who knew Father Leary in the old days, Jerzy can tell you," she said. "He's the guy—there's one in every crowd, at least in small towns—who keeps track of everybody."

"I went to a Catholic boys' school. I know exactly the guy you mean," Donovan said. "Now, about the woman your mother knew."

Which brought them back to the reason she'd come in.

Lindsay drew the plastic sheet protector out of her bag and laid it on the table.

The detective looked at the photo and the blank back. Raised his eyes to hers.

"I haven't been completely up front with you." Years ago, she had staked her career and all her ambitions on the belief that a lawyer's touchstone was honesty. If Donovan was a stickler for the rules, or if he decided that her holding out had cost him a chance to solve the case, he could call the prosecutor and his pal at the *Gazette*. The state bar would get wind, and they could take her license.

She took a deep breath, then exhaled slowly. "When Trevor Morris brought me the wallet he found, this picture was inside."

If the wallet turned out to be evidence in Father Leary's murder—which it almost surely was—Donovan could charge her with tampering.

She was guilty.

And if the photograph led to his killer, her excuses would sway no one.

"At the time, I knew only that I had seen the girl before. I could not have told you her name—I had no idea." She shoved her chair away from the table and stood. "But memory is a funny thing."

She gripped the metal chair back and told him about walking over to the church with Carrie that long-ago afternoon. "Must have been strange enough to start a new school senior year. But then to leave almost as soon as you came, without a word? I have to admit, I didn't notice a lot over the next few days—that was the weekend Mary Ellen was killed. My whole class was a mess. But Carrie and I clicked. If she'd told me they weren't going to be here long, I'd have remembered."

"And the little girl?" Donovan gave the photograph a nod.

"Her sister. Ginger—from her hair, I assume. Carrie adored her. What happened to their parents, I don't know, but they lived with their grandmother, the priests' new housekeeper. Carrie wanted me to meet them. On the way, she showed me the house they lived in." She yanked the chair closer and perched on the edge, facing the detective. "Brian, it's the house Trevor Morris bought. Where Father Leary's wallet was found."

"In the boxes left in the basement, before they moved it."

She nodded. "Carrie introduced me to her grandmother. She called her Baba, Serbian for grandma. We went outside to get her sister, but we didn't see her, so Carrie went into the church. Not five minutes later, she came rushing out the side door, heading for the rectory, dragging Ginger by the arm. I'm guessing she was eight or nine. About the same age as in that picture."

"Go on."

"Carrie told me—I don't remember precisely what she said. But it was obvious something had happened. Then Father Leary came out and saw me. I'd never heard him speak so harshly. All he said was go home, but underneath the words . . ."

After a long moment, she continued. "This was fourteen years before his murder. There is not one single reason to believe there is any connection."

"But you do."

"Mike Leary was a good priest. He was kind and funny, and he knew how to talk to kids. Imagine a dozen seventeen-year-olds gathered around a table not much bigger than this. We talked with him about our dreams and ambitions. About making the right choices. Ethical dilemmas, marriage, sex, money. For a priest to talk to boys and girls, together, about those things? He was fearless." Or so it had seemed. "But that day on the sidewalk between the church and the rectory, he was terrified."

"I've been through that file every way from Sunday," Donovan said. "And I don't remember seeing the names Carrie or Ginger. Although Ginger could be a nickname. Any idea what their last name was?"

"North? Or West—I can't remember. I didn't remember the grandmother's name until my mother said it. My mother was the grade school secretary for eons, and she remembers everyone. She said they came from Miles City with Father Leary, and she thought they were relatives. The grandmother's name was Irene Danich."

Donovan's eyes went wide. "Be right back," he said, and left the room.

What was up? What can of worms had she opened? But before she could do much more than worry, he was back. He laid a sheet of paper in front of her.

"This is everyone who worked at St. Pat's with Father Leary. I wondered why this woman only stayed a few weeks. Father Coletta has no idea. No one I've talked with does."

He pointed one finger at the name of the short-term house-keeper. *Irene Danich.*

"But that was 1981," Lindsay said. "If they were related to Leary, the picture in his wallet is no big deal—a photo of a young niece or cousin. Perfectly normal." She paused, trying to remember. "Father Leary was our religion teacher. Even if Carrie never said they were related, somebody would have known. Nobody could have kept that secret."

"I drove up to Red Lodge this week," Donovan said. "The current priest took me out to see Anna Leary, the sister-in-law. She actually mentioned Tina Danich, but as a friend of Mike's, not as a relative. In the cemetery, there was an arch-topped monument"—he drew the shape in the air with one finger—"with the name Michael Danich. 'Big Mike.' Blank space for another name—his wife, I presume."

"Irene?"

"There was another marker close by. Might have been part of the same family plot. It's hard to tell sometimes in those old cemeteries."

He pulled out his phone and scrolled through his photos. "Yep, here it is. 'Cristina West. 1946 to 1978.'"

"She died young. Their daughter, you suppose? Carrie and Ginger's mother?"

"I'll get our support specialist on it. She's a research whiz."

But Lindsay pulled her phone out and dialed the Carbon County Clerk and Recorder. "The deputy clerk's an old college friend. And I went to law school with her husband."

She dug a pad out of her bag and started asking questions, scribbling notes, the phone on speaker so Donovan could follow.

"Michael Danich, born in Red Lodge, 1917; died in 1962. Cause of death, heart failure. Married Irene Petrovich in 1940. No death certificate on file for her." She glanced at the detective as she repeated the names and dates, then let the woman continue. "Right. That doesn't mean she's alive—only that she didn't die in Carbon

County. We know she isn't buried there. Thanks, no—I'll get some-one else to check state records. What about Cristina Danich West. C-r-i—no 'H.'"

Pen poised, she listened. "Born 1946, died 1978." Made another note. "Do you have a marriage record for her?"

The only sound was a clicking keyboard as the woman searched. "Curious that Mike and Irene waited so long to have a child. Unless he was off in the war," Lindsay said to Donovan, and then her friend's voice came back on the line. She put the phone to her ear to make sure she got all the details. "Yeah, I'm here. Say that again?"

She could hardly believe the response. "Any birth records for that same last name, say 1962 or later?" She waited while the woman changed screens, then scribbled another note.

"Hey, a million thanks. I owe you lunch."

She punched off the phone and laid it on the table. "You are not going to believe this. Cristina Danich married a local boy. Not West. Anthony Woijowski."

"You're shitting me."

She read from her notes. "One child, Carolina Faith, born January 10, 1964, in Red Lodge. No record of another child, at least not born there. How Carolina Woijowski became Carrie West—I'm sure now it was West—I have no idea."

"What year did you graduate?" Donovan asked. "I'll see what school records we can dig up. We've got full access to the state data-bases, for that name change and Ginger's place of birth."

"Nineteen eighty-two. But we don't know Ginger's real name, or whether she was born West or Woijowski."

"I'd change a handle like that, too. But given what we know about Tony W's criminal record, Tina may have had other reasons."

"Starting over, most likely." Lindsay flexed her fingers, stiff from holding the phone. "Ginger West. Why does that name sound familiar?"

"On TV?" Donovan said.

"Oh my gosh. That's it." She grabbed her phone again, punching and scrolling. "Here she is." She showed him the photograph of a petite woman with strawberry blond curls that fell to her shoulders. In the next photo, the hair was pulled back, a smattering of freckles across the cheeks visible under a tan earned in the sun and wind. Deep lines in the forehead and fine wrinkles around the eyes gave the sense of a life spent outdoors. A serious life, although some photos showed an impish smile.

Lindsay held the phone next to the decades-old school photo. Traces of the girl were clearly visible in the face of the woman.

She clicked, then squinted at the tiny screen. "American news photographer, known for searing images of women and children in refugee camps in Bosnia and Serbia, according to Wikipedia. Quoting, 'After being injured in a shelling in Homs, Syria, in 2012, while on assignment for a news network, West turned her talents to the world of NGOs'—nongovernmental organizations," she translated for Donovan—"'capturing unforgettable images of the suffering caused by the Syrian civil war. West makes her home base in New York.'"

"Anything about her family?"

"No, but I'm sure you can dig that up." She reached for her bag and dropped the phone in. "I've got to run. Meeting with the zoning administrator. Then the monthly lunch date with my high school pals, and it's city council night. About that picture . . ."

"Technically, you withheld evidence that could be material to an ongoing kidnapping and homicide investigation. I have to tell my lieutenant."

Her throat went dry, but she held his gaze. "I wanted to believe in Father Leary. The picture—the picture terrified me. It made me afraid that everything I'd thought about him was wrong. That everything he'd meant to me, everything he'd done for me . . ." She couldn't voice the fear that he'd been an abuser, but knew she didn't need to. "I hope you understand."

"I do," Donovan said. "We wouldn't have reopened the investigation at all without the wallet, and the delay hasn't cost us any leads. But I can't make promises."

That was all she could ask. The risk of her actions becoming a matter of legal discipline wasn't going to keep her up at night. She trusted Donovan to make the best case in her defense to his bosses. "Thanks."

He waved his fingers as if sweeping the issue away. "You remember anything more about Carrie and Irene or the incident outside the church, you let me know. As soon as I've read up on Mr. W, I think a trip to Deer Lodge is in order."

"It's a grim place."

"We're in a grim business. Wouldn't have it any other way, would we?"

She stood and slipped into her coat. This wasn't her business, any of it. But a part of her wished it was.

TUESDAY
June 15, 2004

The Billings Gazette—Bones discovered Saturday north of Billings could be linked to the 1995 disappearance of Father Michael Leary, then co-pastor of St. Patrick's Co-Cathedral in Billings.

The gruesome find occurred when a horse stumbled over an exposed tree root at the base of a sandstone outcropping, leading the rider to dismount. The rider spotted what appeared to be a femur emerging from a rift in the rocks and contacted authorities.

The bones have been sent to the Montana State Crime Lab in Missoula for further testing and determination of cause of death, according to Billings Police Department detective Roy Small, who led the initial investigation. "Thanks to Father Leary's brothers," Small said, "we now have DNA samples, and I'm optimistic that we'll be able to positively identify the remains as his."

No clothing was found, although search crews did locate a strip of leather, possibly a belt, near the bones. Small refused to say whether any other evidence was found at the scene.

A search of *Gazette* articles and police reports reveals no other persons reported missing in the area, which is characterized by deep ravines and sandstone cliffs, grasses, sage brush, and scrub pines.

Leary was summoned by phone in the early hours of October 10, 1995, to administer last rites. According to a statement given by Father James Coletta, who took the call, the caller specifically requested Father Leary's assistance.

The priest was last seen at an all-night service station in the Heights shortly after 3 a.m. According to police reports, the attendant stated that Leary said he had been instructed to call the dying woman's family when he reached the station. A few minutes later, another vehicle arrived. Leary, wearing a dark coat over dark pants, spoke to the driver, then left, following the other vehicle, possibly a dark, late-model pickup.

When Leary did not return to the rectory the next day, he was reported missing. No deaths of women residing in the vicinity, at home or in area hospitals, were reported.

Leary's black 1987 Buick Century was found several weeks later in an unused shed on a ranch west of US 87, about 10 miles north of the city limits. It had been wiped clean of fingerprints. Police report that no link was ever found between the priest and anyone connected with the ranch.

On Christmas Eve of that year, Leary's sacramental bag was discovered underneath straw in a nativity scene on the altar of St. Patrick's.

According to Small, police have investigated several leads over the years, but no suspects have been publicly identified.

MONDAY
March 7, 2016

Why had she let Ginger book her a window seat? From the air, it looked to Carrie like there was nothing between Portland and Billings but mountains, range after range of snow-topped mountains. Stunning, yes, but the plane had bounced on the currents like the kites above the Pacific when they took Asher to Cannon Beach last summer.

Now as they banked for descent, the tilting horizon made her insides go queasy.

"It's only air," she muttered, but the bumpy ride wasn't all that was making her nervous.

Fifty-two years old, and this was her first flight alone. She and Todd took the girls to Disneyland once, and another year they'd all flown to Hawaii with his family for Christmas. That was when she and Todd had decided, walking on the beach and licking macadamia nut ice cream cones, that they would separate and divorce in June, after Ali graduated. But he hadn't waited, telling her on Valentine's Day—Valentine's Day!—that he was moving out. What Todd didn't say was that he'd met another woman, fifteen years younger, and was moving in with her. The relationship hadn't lasted, but there was no going back. Two years later, he'd remarried, and now they were all one big modern family—blended, mended, and extended.

She'd long blamed the unresolved tensions for turning Ali rebellious, leading her to skip college and move in with Jamal. But now she thought Ali was just one of those women who'd been ready for motherhood young.

Last year, Ginger had invited Carrie to meet up in Paris for a week, between photo assignments, but Asher had been starting a new treatment regime and Ali had needed her help.

And now, Asher was the reason for this trip. If finding even a tiny detail in the family medical history that might help him meant traveling alone to a place she had sworn she would never go back to, then that's what she would do.

But now there was another reason. Finding their fathers and learning more about their mother from the men who had loved her.

The woman seated next to her leaned closer to peer out the window. "Isn't the valley gorgeous? I see the river and the Rims, and I know I'm where I belong."

The city was lush and green, nestled between the Rimrocks and the river, covered by a dense canopy of trees. Further east were the badlands and the small towns they'd lived in when she was young. Her mother had hated that country, pining for the mountains and woods surrounding the town where she was born. She'd never gotten to go back. Not alive anyway.

But then, Tina had never gotten much of what she wanted in life.

The wheels touched down, and Carrie's heart nearly leaped out of her throat. She'd been so focused on the view that she'd forgotten the airport sat on top of the Rims.

"Enjoy your visit," her seatmate said. Carrie thanked her with a weak smile.

At the last minute, she'd been able to borrow a decent black roll-aboard from Ellie next door, sparing her the indignity of dragging the pink Barbie suitcase Ali had left in the basement through the airport. Ellie was watching Tux the cat, too.

On the sidewalk outside, she blinked against the harsh sunlight. After so many years in the Northwest, she'd forgotten how big Montana's skies really were.

With the efficiency of the experienced traveler, Ginger had reserved a rental car and a room at the Dude Rancher Inn downtown. Weeping brick outside, pine paneling inside. Leather furniture, fringed pillows, and sun-bleached steer skulls adorned the lobby. She checked in and found her room, thematically correct with brands burned into the headboard.

To unpack or not? She laid the Ziploc with her toothpaste and shampoo on the bathroom counter. Ginger had left the return date open, so Carrie could spend as much time here as she needed.

She sat in the driver's seat of the bright blue Honda and pulled up Google Maps on her phone. The street numbering was crazy—North 29th and South 29th were two ends of the same street, but Fourth Avenue North and Fourth Avenue South were a mile apart.

"You can do this," she muttered.

"What was that?" Siri asked. "I did not understand."

Nothing looked familiar. Despite that, and her queasy stomach, she only turned down a one-way street the wrong way twice before finding the place she was searching for.

St. Patrick's Co-Cathedral was smaller than she remembered. Everything from childhood was.

Until Ginger mentioned that afternoon in the church, Carrie had done her best to push it out of her mind. For the last two days, she hadn't been able to forget it. Her new classmate, the girl who'd stood up to the horrid nun in PE, had walked home with her, and she'd gone into the church to find Ginger. Instead, she'd seen the two men talking to Father Mike in the vestibule.

"We know about the girl."

At the time, she'd simply thought they'd known Ginger was hiding under a pew in the entry, listening in. Now, she thought Ginger was probably right. Baba and Father Leary had decided they needed to leave because someone knew the priest was Ginger's father and had threatened to use that knowledge against him.

But why?

Did their theory even make sense?

All the way here, she had prepared herself for the possibility that Father Leary would tell her she was wrong, he had never been involved with her mother, he wasn't Ginger's father. That he knew nothing about her family that would help her find a cure for Asher.

But she had not been prepared for the feelings that overcame her now. Of grief.

Of guilt over the defiance that had become her trademark after the move, the resentment that boiled over far too often, despite knowing that Baba didn't deserve her insolence. Baba had made a good home for them in Oregon, where they'd gone to decent schools and lived in a decent home, surrounded by decent, caring people. How had Carrie not understood that her grandmother, like their mother before that, had been trying to protect them?

From her mother's shame? From her father's anger?

From what, Baba? From what?

Ginger had checked the weather report and insisted she pack a warm coat and boots, but they weren't enough to thaw the chill inside her.

The streets had been plowed, the sidewalks and steps around the church shoveled. The skies were blue.

She climbed the steps to the rectory and raised a hand to the bell.

The door was answered not by a housekeeper, as she'd expected, but by a priest. A man with dark brown eyes and hair so white it must have been nearly black in his youth.

"I—I was hoping to catch Father Leary."

"I'm sorry, my dear. He's away."

Oh God. She'd come all this way, gone to all this trouble.

"When do you expect him back?"

"Not for a week or more. I'm Father Coletta, pastor of St. Patrick's. Is there some way I can help you?"

His eyes and voice were so kind that she desperately wished he could. "No, I . . . Father Leary was a friend of my parents. They all grew up together. They're gone now, but there are things I want to ask him."

"Oh, good heavens." Father Coletta held the door wider, with a manner that made it impossible not to step inside. "I'm afraid there's been a mistake. Come in, come in."

She followed him down the hall, past the small sitting room. Though black appliances had replaced the harvest gold she remembered, the kitchen looked the same. It still smelled of old house mingled with lemon Pledge and what? A hint of incense—it was Easter season.

And pepperoni and oregano. The telltale box sat on the counter near the back door.

"Do sit, dear. Call me Father Jim." He reached for an electric tea kettle sitting near the sink. "Tell me your name."

"Carrie Matheson. I've just flown in from Portland." She unbuttoned her coat but kept it on, though the kitchen was not cold. A plate with a slice of pizza sat on the round drop-leaf table. She'd interrupted his lunch.

"Ohh, Portland. Do you know the Grotto? So peaceful. A blessing for the community. Black or green, sugar or milk?"

"Uh, green, please, and no, thank you."

He set a mug in front of her and took his seat, pushing his half-eaten lunch to the side. "Curses on the Irish for their common names. Our Father Michael Leary is much too young to have known your parents as children. Not yet forty."

"Oh." The cup stopped halfway to her mouth. "I saw his name on your website, and I thought . . ."

"We should post pictures," the priest said apologetically. "We are far behind the times. I am sorry for your trouble."

Carrie cradled the cup and glanced around. "The place hasn't changed much since my grandmother worked here. She kept house for Father Leary and the Monsignor. I can't remember his name. O something."

"Monsignor O'Shea? That's been a good while." Father Jim dumped sugar into his black tea. "What was your grandmother's name?"

"Irene Danich."

The priest's face froze.

"Father? What's wrong? And where is Father Mike?"

"It's a long story, my dear, and I'll tell you what I know. But first, allow me to make a phone call."

* * *

Detective Brian Donovan wasn't sure what was stranger—following Father Coletta down the hall to his office for the second time in three days or finding himself facing the very woman he and Lindsay Keller had talked about just this morning.

He could hear his old FTO, back in Boston, saying, "You think that's strange, kid? You ain't seen strange yet."

"God works in mysterious ways," Coletta had said on the phone, half serious. But Donovan wasn't sure God's hands were the only ones at play here.

"I told her about Father Leary's passing and that we'd noticed her grandmother's name on a list of former employees you asked me to review," the priest said now as he led the way. "But I said nothing about the investigation. Or the wallet."

"Thanks, Father. I've learned a few things since we talked on Saturday," Donovan said, thinking of the photograph in his pocket, the pieces he and Lindsay Keller had put together this morning, and the details he'd dug up since then. "I hope she can fill in a few blanks."

"And I hope you can ease her mind and heart." They reached the priest's office, and Father Coletta made introductions.

Carrie Matheson clutched the mug in her hands like a man overboard gripped a lifeline. Strong features, determined eyes. She'd tied her dark blond hair back, a loose tendril curling against a broad cheekbone. Attractive—and anxious.

She searched for a place to set her cup on the desk, saw none, and shifted it to her left hand as she stood and held out her right. Red knuckles. A firm grip. A woman who worked with her hands.

Donovan refused the offer of coffee or tea. "Then I'll leave you two alone," the priest said, and closed the door. Donovan picked up the second client chair and turned it so he could face the woman.

"Carrie Matheson. You were Carrie West when you lived in Billings for six weeks in 1981. You and your sister, Virginia, better known as Ginger, lived with your grandmother, Irene Danich. You started at the Catholic high school, then withdrew in mid-September. You did not reenroll in one of the public schools."

She stiffened, her eyes darkening. "How do you know all that? Why do you care who I am?"

"Your mother's name was Tina, short for Cristina. Your father is Anthony Woijowski. Better known as Tony W."

"Why are you digging around in my family? I came to Billings to find out—" She broke off, her breath shallow and quick.

"That's what I'd like to know," he said, softening his tone. "Why you came to Billings now, after all these years."

She stared out the window. He knew she wasn't seeing the bare branches of the cottonwood trees or the backside of the buildings in the next block. She was seeing this place the way it had been thirty-five years ago. She was seeing the tangle of memories and questions that had brought her here.

"Because of my grandson," she said, facing him squarely, which was not at all what Brian Donovan had expected. "Asher is four. He has a genetic condition, a form of cystic fibrosis. It's a terrible disease. It creates mucous in the lungs, like having the worst cold of your life, twenty-four seven. Basically, he's been strangling to death since he was born."

Totally not what he'd expected. He let her continue.

"At the moment, it can only be treated. But researchers are working on a cure. There's a clinical trial. I need to know everything I can about my family's genetic history to give him a chance."

"I'm so sorry. How did your search bring you to St. Pat's?"

She leveled her gaze at him, her square jaw steady. "I've answered your questions. Now you answer mine. Why are you investigating my family? What happened to Father Leary? How did he die? Father Jim implied a crime but said he'd prefer you give me the details. Is my father—Tony Woijowski, I don't even know how to say it—is he involved?"

She was asking all the right questions. "On October 10, 1995, Father Leary was summoned during the night to give last rites to a dying woman, who may or may not have existed. Whoever called him shot him and hid his body in a ravine. It's been more than twenty years, and we have no leads."

One hand flew to her mouth, as if to stop the cries of shock. Her eyes turned wide and round, her skin ashen.

"In a cold case, we start at the beginning. We reinterview everyone. We know your grandmother worked for Father Leary in Miles City. They must have been quite close for her to bring you and your sister here when he was transferred to Billings."

"He and my mother were old friends." She spoke slowly, carefully, and Donovan reminded himself to be patient. "My mother died when I was fourteen, and my grandmother wanted my sister and me to be close to him because we had no other family. She thought it would be good for us to live in a bigger town."

"Yet, you didn't stay in Billings long. Did you move to Portland from here?"

She nodded.

"Was Father Leary an old friend of your father's, too?"

"Yes. They all grew up together in Red Lodge. My parents were childhood sweethearts." Her voice trembled. Her world was badly shaken, and he was going to shake it even more. "I—I can't believe he's gone."

"You thought he might have information about your family, to help you research, for your grandson?"

"Yes, and"—she paused to wipe away a tear—"he was such a kind and gentle man. I can't believe he was murdered. But why are you involved now, after all these years?"

"A new piece of evidence surfaced last week. Father Leary's wallet was found in a box left behind in an old house. It contained his driver's license and a St. Christopher medal." He slipped the photo, still in its plastic sleeve, out of his jacket pocket and laid it on the priest's desk. "And this."

She drew in a sharp breath. Her fingers reached out, stroking the edge of the photo.

"My sister." Her eyes grew damp. "He carried it all those years?"

"It was one of the few personal items we found."

"But you knew that was Ginger before you showed it to me."

"We did. Another witness recognized her."

Silent, she studied him.

"So where do my sister and I fit into the puzzle?" she finally asked. "My grandmother died in 1994."

"Sorry to hear that. She sounds like a remarkable woman. At this point, we aren't sure of all the connections."

She reached into her bag, then laid a photo on the desk next to Ginger's school picture. "My parents on their wedding day." She snapped down the next, as if dealing cards. Not, Donovan thought, to get the upper hand or even the score. Laying her cards on the table. "And them with me as a baby."

"Your mother was stunning."

"Thank you. This is her mother, Irene Danich."

"Ahh," he said. "Where you both got your looks."

Two more photos. "My sister and me, as kids, and the two of us last week at my grandson's birthday party."

"On a pirate ship." He smiled.

"You've heard the term 'redheaded stepchild'? I never thought of my sister that way, even though her features and coloring are nothing like mine, or the rest of the family's." She dealt out two more photos, one an official shot of the photographer Ginger West, the photo he and Lindsay Keller had seen online. Then an older photo of a couple holding a baby.

Not a couple. Or were they? Father Leary wasn't wearing his Roman collar, but Donovan had no trouble recognizing him.

And no trouble seeing the resemblance between him and Ginger.

Everyone he'd talked to had raved about Leary, what a good priest he'd been. Would they have said otherwise if they'd seen this photo?

"You think he's Ginger's father." He picked up the photo. Was it a clue to the priest's death, this sign of a secret life? "When did you figure this out?"

"Last week, while I was working on a family tree. I don't have many photos from my childhood—I chalked it up to moving around so much. But now I know it was because of the lies. They say it's easier to keep track of lies when you keep them simple, and having to explain difficult facts to two young girls could never be simple."

"What do you know about your father and Mike Leary?" He laid the photo back on the table.

"I know my father didn't kill him. He's been in prison since 1973 for killing someone else, as I also just discovered. My mother had already changed our name, before Ginger was born—I found the records in a box of my grandmother's papers, and found the prison records online. He was incarcerated when my sister was conceived. We were told he was killed in the service. But he's alive, isn't he?" Carrie's voice cracked with emotion, with loss and anger and resentment.

"Yes."

"I went digging in the past to see if my grandson's illness ran in the family. I did not expect"—she gestured at the photos—"any of this."

She stood and began to pace. A lock of hair caught on the collar of her maroon sweater, but she didn't seem to notice.

"The man I thought was long dead is alive," she continued. "The man I thought alive is long dead. Now I have to tell my sister her father is gone."

"She didn't come with you?"

"She's headed to the Middle East tomorrow morning. My sister defines herself by her work. I suppose we all do, to some extent—I've got two hundred rose bushes being delivered this week."

"That's some garden."

"Gardens are my job," she said. "Like yours is tracking down criminals. Who do you think killed him? Father Leary."

"I wish I knew. Bones aren't very talkative."

"You're sure they're his?"

"Yes. We have a DNA match with his brothers."

"Brothers? There's DNA? So we can prove whether he was Ginger's father."

"Not sure how that works legally, but it may be possible. The brothers are gone, but they left children and grandchildren. I've seen pictures. There is a resemblance." He exhaled. "But that won't help your quest, will it? They aren't related to your grandson."

She sank into the chair.

Donovan pondered how much to tell her. She'd come in search of her biological history and found herself in the middle of an unsolved mystery. She wasn't a relative of the victim, but her sister probably was. When to tell her that Leary had planned to testify at her father's parole hearing, but had been killed days earlier?

Killed, he was beginning to believe, to keep him from getting there.

Not now, he decided as silent sobs wracked her.

Not right now.

* * *

Twenty minutes later, Carrie and Donovan walked into a small restaurant on the edge of downtown. Surprisingly hip and surprisingly full for one o'clock on a Monday.

She followed the hostess past a table full of women, and one raised a hand to Donovan. Carrie slid onto the bench and looked around. High ceilings and brick walls, hung with giant oil paintings that drew her, though she couldn't say why or what they were supposed to be. They went with the music, all modern and alternative.

She hadn't spent much time around cops. But she'd seen enough true crime on TV to know that murder cases were often filled with twists and turns. Like this one.

They ordered, and she tried to listen as he told her about moving out here from Boston for his wife's job teaching art at the college, but her attention kept straying to the table of five women, obviously old friends. Two dressed like Ginger, with a stylish, professional air of confidence. One looked like she'd thrown on jeans and a rumpled

T-shirt to meet "the girls," but no one seemed to mind. Even though they were all about her age, they behaved like girls, hugging, touching. Laughing, interrupting, listening intently.

What would it be like to be friends for decades, through everything, instead of always on the outside looking in? She couldn't take her eyes off them.

Donovan was speaking to her. She smiled weakly, flustered and apologetic.

"I was asking if this was your first visit back to Billings."

"My first trip back to Montana," she said. "It's changed." She glanced at the other table again, then reached for her iced tea.

A moment later, one of the women approached, a stylish brunette in a navy skirt and a white blouse, a red paisley scarf around her throat.

"Detective, I appreciate your understanding this morning. Sorry I had to dash out so quickly," she said to Donovan, then spoke to Carrie. "Pardon the interruption. I don't believe we've met. I'm Lindsay Keller."

This was the girl. The one who'd walked home with her after school that fateful day, the only one who hadn't treated her like a thistle in a rose bed.

"Actually, I think we have." Carrie took the offered hand. "Carrie Matheson. We met a long time ago, when I was Carrie West."

Recognition struck, and Lindsay sat next to Donovan, aiming her words at him. "Did you know she was in town?"

"Is this some kind of setup?" Carrie said. "Our meeting at the church? Coming here?"

"Coincidence. Father Coletta would call it Divine Providence," Donovan said. He turned to Lindsay. "Though I admit, I picked this place for lunch because I called your office and your secretary told me where you'd be."

"Did you tell her about the picture?" Lindsay demanded.

Donovan nodded.

"Hey, Linds. I got your lunch," the T-shirted woman called. "Consider it your bonus."

262

"Thanks, Jana."

Jana? Carrie glanced over at the woman, but she'd turned her back and begun to pull on her coat.

"Wasn't she in our class? Senior year at the Catholic high school."

"Yeah. Jana Stadler. Jana Stenerud Simonich Stadler. She runs the Rainbow Bar, down the street."

"The Steneruds owned the house we lived in," Carrie said.

Lindsay and Donovan stared at her. Before she could ask why, a woman with a strong profile and long black hair shot with gray hugged Lindsay from behind. "You'll work it out with Haley, I know. Call me if you need to talk."

"Thanks, Charlene. I will."

Carrie watched the woman leave. "Another classmate?"

"Charlene Old Horn. She teaches at our old high school— Montana history and Native American studies."

Charlene Old Horn. "That was the day—the nun in PE. What was her name? She said something awful to Charlene, and you talked back to her. Scared us all."

"Scared myself. My big mouth."

She hadn't acted scared. "There was another girl, one who didn't like me."

"Mary Ellen Simonich. She was going through a phase." A shadow crossed Lindsay's face. "Unfortunately, she never got a chance to grow out of it. You may not remember what happened— you may not have known."

Before Carrie could ask what had happened, Lindsay turned to Donovan. "She could be right. Somebody in the parish owned that house. It could have been the Steneruds, though they must have sold it."

"We'll check it out," he said.

"Your grandmother was Father Leary's housekeeper, right?" Lindsay asked her. "But then you left. Your whole family left, as suddenly as you'd come. Or at least that's how it seemed."

"That's how it was," Carrie said. "We moved to Portland. I flew in this morning."

"So you heard about the wallet. I'm surprised the discovery made the news out there. But why come back here, after all this time?"

"No. I didn't know anything about the murder or the wallet until the detective told me. I came"—she had trusted the girl thirty-five years ago, and she trusted the woman now—"I came because my grandson is ill, and I need to know more about my family."

"I'm so sorry," Lindsay said. "My mother thought you might be relatives of Father Leary. Is that why he had your sister's picture in his wallet?"

"No. Yeah. How did—" The waiter brought their lunch and Carrie sat back, her head spinning. When the waiter left, she spoke. "You're the one who found the wallet."

"Indirectly, yes. My mother thought you were related because you came to Billings with Leary, and assistant pastors don't usually bring their own housekeepers. But for family, arrangements can be made."

For family. That was exactly it. Carrie picked up her fork but didn't eat.

"Lindsay," Donovan said. "The day you met Carrie's grandmother, Mrs. Danich, Carrie and her sister saw two men in the church vestibule, talking with Father Leary. The girls didn't hear the details, but they got the impression of a threat. You saw Father Leary come out the side door alone. Do you have any idea who he might have been talking to?"

Carrie held her breath, waiting for this smart, bold girl—this smart, bold *woman*—to solve the problem, to name names.

But slowly, Lindsay shook her head.

* * *

Donovan dropped Carrie Matheson off at her rental car, parked in front of the church, then headed for the station. Who were the men who'd confronted Leary in the church vestibule in 1981? How could the incident be related to his murder fourteen years later? It was the oddest episode he'd uncovered yet in the priest's life, and anything out of the ordinary bore closer inspection.

"*We know about the girl,*" one of the men had said. Despite the sisters' conclusion, he wasn't convinced that they'd meant Ginger West. A priest who taught high school, a reference to a girl—you had to consider all the possibilities.

Outside the station, he parked, then leaned back in the seat. He hadn't had a chance to talk with Lindsay Keller privately after lunch. She'd only been with the County Attorney's Office a couple of years, but she was a local girl. If she'd ever heard any talk connecting Leary to the child abuse scandals in the church, she'd have told him when she handed over the photo from the wallet.

Wouldn't she?

Did the sisters' speculation about Leary and the late Tina West fall into the category of sex abuse? The big church scandal involved kids—mostly boys—and pedophile priests, but there were incidents with adults, too. Abuse of power took many forms.

But a sexual relationship wasn't abuse if it was truly consensual. The friendship Carrie described—regular visits and dinners, small gifts, helping Tina finding a new job or a rental—could be interpreted either way. A priest taking advantage of a prison widow, or a friendship between two adults who'd known each other since childhood developing into something deeper?

He thought back to the photo of Tina and Leary with baby Ginger. Nothing in their posture, nothing in their facial expressions, suggested any conflict or coercion. It was the perfect picture of a loving family.

But a relationship didn't have to be a crime to spark a scandal, even after all these years.

He had to probe with care.

He tapped the steering wheel rhythmically with the side of his hand. First, talk to the boss. She'd be wicked mad if he ruffled high-flying feathers without letting her in on his plan.

"You're saying we need to reconsider the possibility that Leary was messing around where he shouldn't have been, and someone took matters into their own hands," Lieutenant Hansen said a few minutes later. They were in her office, the door closed. "Wasn't that thoroughly investigated at the time of his disappearance?"

"Yeah, it was." Donovan rested his elbows on his knees. "I cross-referenced our files, and we've got nothing on him. But a lot of victims didn't come forward until recently."

"And no lawyer would let a client accuse a dead man if they suspected a revenge killing," she said. "As I understand attorney–client privilege, lawyers can only report information they learn in confidence if it indicates a present danger to an identifiable person. They can't reveal anything that might implicate their clients in a crime already committed."

Donovan made a circle with his finger, counterclockwise. "I'm thinking the other way around. We need to take another look at what the church knew. Did they identify him as an abuser? Is he one of the guys they moved to avoid suspicion? Other dioceses have been forced to disclose the name of every priest identified or even accused of sexual abuse. That hasn't happened here—a lawsuit's been filed, but no names have been disclosed yet. But there's gotta be a way to find out what they know."

Hansen pondered that. "Call the plaintiffs' lawyers and see if they'll tell you anything. Then make a courtesy call to the bishop. Let him know we've reopened the murder investigation. One of his flock—you know the drill. Was he in charge then?"

"The bishop? No, he's new—couple of years. The predecessors are all dead."

"Make it routine. You're following up on the new evidence, keeping him in the loop." She moved her hand through the air like a gentle wave. "Gauge his response. Then ask for Leary's personnel file. We have an old copy, but they update those things. Go slow, see if you hit a nerve."

She laid her hands flat on her desk. "Now, on another matter. County attorney got a call from a lawyer representing our parking garage scumbag. Who is apparently awake, but not willing to talk to us. Lawyer wants to press charges against the woman who attacked him without provocation, blah blah blah."

"What the hell?" Donovan said, indignation stabbing him like a knife in the gut. "All the evidence—"

"I know, I know." Hansen held up a hand to cut him off, then pointed her finger. "Hopefully, it's just a starting point, an opening move. The best thing we can do is give the prosecutor a clean file. Make no assumptions. Keep your language neutral. Use last names—until this is wrapped up, we don't label anyone the vic or the assailant. He's got history, right? Nail down the details and show how this attack fits the pattern."

No sweat. Add "peace in the Middle East" to his list, and he'd wrap it all up by shift change.

*   *   *

Carrie aimed the Honda north out of Billings, with no plan and no destination. Just driving. All that space.

All those memories.

If she were back home in Portland, she'd be yanking out weeds or stalking the garden paths with clippers in hand. But she had nothing to do here except ruminate, double-digging her thoughts, plowing up the past.

She pulled over by a highway sign reading "ROUNDUP—22," and got out, shading her eyes with her hand. The land wasn't as ugly or as empty as she remembered. Almost pretty, in some ways. Stretched out, the color palette subdued. It wasn't the land's fault that she'd felt lost here as a kid, dragged around from one town to the next. Feeling that though their mother loved her daughters, they were never enough for her.

Now, with the secrets in the open, she finally understood why Tina had always been on the move. Running from Tony's troubles, running to Mike Leary.

Her stomach growled. After the craziness of seeing Lindsay Keller again, she'd barely touched her lunch. The detective had manipulated her, arranging the accidentally on purpose meeting to see how she responded.

But she was grateful. He was helping her reconnect with her history, with the places that had shaped her without her knowledge. And that was what she had wanted.

She headed back into town and grabbed a taco and a Coke. Spent the rest of the afternoon cruising. She drove past the high school, the baseball field, the college. Drove west on a street lined with giant cottonwoods, past tidy schools and parks that made her ache for Asher. Detoured up a few narrow lanes that dead-ended at the base of the Rims, the houses pleasant and well kept, the yards drinking in the sunshine, ready for spring.

So much of this city she'd never gotten to know.

After battling both Siri and downtown's one-way streets, she tucked the rental car behind the motel. She was exhausted, but from emotion and adrenaline, not work, making a nap seem as unlikely as it would be welcome.

One foot inside the lobby, her heart nearly stopped. That small frame, that red hair. The woman turned.

"*Ginger?*"

Her sister held out her arms.

"I thought you'd be in New York by now. On your way to God knows where."

"And miss all this? I've never been to a dude ranch before."

They hugged, then sat on a brown leather couch. "It isn't actually a dude ranch, as you've noticed, although you can buy a package deal to ride the range if you want."

Ginger shuddered.

"What?" Carrie said. "You've been all over the world. You've ridden donkeys and llamas and camels. But riding the prairie on a horse gives you the willies?"

"No, no. I love horses. Give me cockroaches and tarantulas any day. Just keep the snakes."

Carrie smiled and shook her head. "Seriously, Ginge, what changed your mind?"

"You've always looked after me. And you're here as much for me as for you. I can't let you do this all alone."

"But Athens. Syria. Your story—"

"It can wait. But the truth about our lives can't wait any longer. We need to face this together, sis. You and me."

Carrie swallowed past the lump in her throat and squeezed her baby sister's hand.

"You and me."

* * *

"Your decision to approve the plan we've laid out," Lindsay told the City Council, her hands resting on the laminate-topped oak podium, "will allow the purchasers of this historic theater to provide complete technical stage and audience services and promote the facility to a greater number of users. It's almost unheard of for a city this size to boast two theaters capable of presenting major events. You all know how well the Alberta Bair is doing, largely because of the investments you've made in it over the years. Adding a second historic theater downtown will bring in even more people. And they won't just see a play or hear a concert. They'll eat, drink, shop, and stay downtown. That's the point of urban renewal financing—leveraging tax dollars for the good of the community. What goes around comes around."

"Thank you, Ms. Keller," the mayor said. "You've answered all my questions. Anyone else?"

The financing proposal for the century-old Babcock Theater had been in the works for months, winding its way through staff review and committee meetings before reaching the council. There'd been last-minute questions about the collateral for the loan, but they'd ironed out the details earlier today. Lindsay had adored watching movies and magic shows in the Babcock as a kid, rocking in the red velvet seats and popping Junior Mints. It was a gracious building, ornate but intimate, and she was convinced the community would benefit from its full restoration. And equally convinced that without help, it would remain stuck in a cycle of renovations begun by previous owners and left largely unfinished. Her client had grown up in Billings, too, and loved the venerable space as much as she did. But though he'd built a career in entertainment management and understood the needs of the building, his pockets were only so deep.

"What I don't understand," said a citizen who attended nearly every council meeting and opposed almost every measure, "is why anybody would buy an old heap of bricks if they couldn't afford to do the work themselves."

"Few people can," Lindsay replied. "What we're asking for is a loan, at a good but competitive rate. This is not a boondoggle at tax-payer expense."

So it went until the public comment period closed and council members moved on to discussion. Lindsay sat at the front table next to her client, her left shoulder stiff, her features tired from holding a pleasant expression. But this wasn't a moment to unwittingly lapse into resting bitch face.

This morning, she'd skirted around Detective Donovan's suggestion that she didn't trust Jerzy Simonich. He was right; she didn't, though she'd have had trouble saying why. Years ago, Jerzy had wanted her help buying the old theater, flattering her that no one else around had the know-how to do the deal. Her knowledge of the public financing system and his ability to turn a buck, he'd said, were a match made in heaven.

She hadn't liked the glint in his eye. She'd told him no. He'd found another lawyer who persuaded the city to back the purchase. Two years later, with little to show for the public money, he'd put the holding company into bankruptcy and put the theater on the auction block. The city and his subs all lost money, but she'd always assumed Jerzy made a profit. Jana, who kept her finger on the Simonich pulse for the sake of her sons, had as much as said so today at lunch, when Lindsay mentioned tonight's meeting.

When she walked away from the prosecutor's office and a job she loved, she'd vowed to create a career she controlled, one that did some tangible good in the world. It had taken her a while, until they moved home and she set up her own practice. But she'd kept that promise.

All afternoon, as she worked on the last-minute details, an unanswered question had lingered in the back of her mind. What was Jerzy Simonich's tie to Father Leary?

Leary had seemed like such a—what was the word? Not a simple man. Wrong connotations. *Transparent.* That was it. A modern word for a concept we shouldn't need, like "organic food."

But if Carrie Matheson was right about her sister's paternity, then Leary had been hiding a big secret all along.

The mystery of his death kept coming back to the triad: Leary, Jerzy, and Tony W. She thought back to the aborted parole hearing in 1995. Jerzy and Andy had been there. What had Andy said? Not that his dad knew Tony, but that he knew the victim's family. A local farmer, killed out west, in a murder staged to look like an accident.

Jerzy Simonich was courtly and cunning, sly and successful. And always right in the thick of things.

She vaguely remembered Mary Ellen talking about an uncle who'd died as a young man. Had Leary known him, too? Hadn't he mentioned something in class about losing a friend in his youth? No, not in class. It was when he came into the bookstore a few weeks before graduation. She'd never made the connection.

But there had to be one. Did the detective know?

The gavel ended the discussion period, bringing her attention back to the present, and the mayor called the vote. She could feel the nervous tension radiating from her client.

Then the vote was over, and they'd succeeded. The financing had been approved. She and the city staff had been through this process before; they'd wrap up the paperwork in no time.

In the hallway, her client pumped his fist. "I have pictured myself owning that theater since I was ten years old. I've been plotting how to get it for a decade. Now we can finish this project and do it right."

"You're the right man for the job," she said.

"You, too. The right woman, I mean. No other lawyer would have fought so hard to get me through this maze."

She let out a long, slow breath. This work really did make a difference.

"The show will go on," he continued, and rubbed his hands together.

"But will you sell Junior Mints at the concession stand?"

"For you, Lindsay Keller, free Junior Mints for life."

*   *   *

Donovan skimmed his to-do list on the cold case. His wife said the only way she could manage teaching, making art, and raising kids was to remember that just because she *could* add a project to her list didn't mean she *had* to.

Unfortunately, he couldn't say the same of police work.

He popped the lid on the curry from the Thai restaurant around the corner, and the steamy red sauce blasted him in the face. He grabbed a chunk with his chopsticks, letting the hot, slathery rice cool in his mouth before swallowing. Damn, it was good.

Working a cold case was always tough, but even harder in a small department. He couldn't spend all his time on one investigation. He didn't get a team of detectives and officers to run down every detail, like in a fresh case. Cold cases had to be tucked between other assignments.

Which was why he sat here, after hours, surrounded by takeout and notebooks from the original investigation. Both kids were in the school play, and Beth was taking them to rehearsal. He had to pick them up at nine.

He pried open the second container to let the egg rolls cool a bit.

This case had grabbed him from the start. Because of the priest, yes. The grace of God and all that.

Though where had grace gotten Father Leary?

He dipped an egg roll in lime chili sauce. Took a bite, catching a drip before it hit his notepad.

The support specialist had promised him a history of the little house in a day or two. Identifying former owners was easy, but he wanted the tenants' names, too, which took more digging. If the wallet had been a trophy, why hide it in the basement and leave it there? Or had someone found it and tossed it in a box, someone unconnected to Leary? Nothing else in the box had any clear link to him. They'd picked up the other crates from the contractor's shop; plowing through them was next on his list.

Maybe the wallet hadn't been taken on purpose. Maybe it had fallen out of Leary's pocket in a struggle. Or maybe he'd left it in his car—sitting on a wallet could be a literal pain in the butt. But why take it? Not to slow the cops from identifying the car—the plates had been left on, the registration in the glove box. *Amateurs.*

Donovan smeared his half-eaten egg roll in sauce. Whoever killed Leary had wanted him to be killed and forgotten. To suffer, die alone, and not be found.

Why? If not for something he had done—like molestation—then for something he'd heard in the confessional? Donovan bit into the eggroll. That was supposed to be secret. Sacred. Were the words related? He didn't remember enough Latin to know.

Leary had been willing to break the sacred vow of chastity. Had he also been willing to expose a penitent's confession?

Donovan reached for the curry. If he was right, the killer had believed Leary meant to disclose details seen or heard or pieced together. What details? And who would they harm?

That brought him back to the known associates. He licked a finger.

Coletta had taken the phone call, but that broken arm had put him on the priestly equivalent of light duty. Monsignor O'Shea, now deceased, had been asleep, and he'd had no firsthand knowledge of the summons or Leary's departure. Small and his team had corroborated it all and detailed the file.

Besides, the caller had asked for Leary.

The call had come from a pay phone outside a casino in the Heights, the same number Leary had called from the garage. The casino had been closed, and they hadn't found anyone who'd witnessed someone using the phone or waiting nearby. Fingerprinting had turned up zip.

The other priests in town had been vetted at the time, and nothing useful learned. No grudges or animosity uncovered. Donovan hadn't had a chance to reinterview those still living, or the then-housekeeper, a Mrs. Kuehn. Later this week, if the criminally minded citizenry didn't act up.

The list of high school faculty and staff was long, as was the list of ushers, servers, and Altar Society women who'd been in the church on the Christmas Eve when Coletta found Leary's sacrament bag.

Heck, half the children in the parish had been on the altar that night.

Then there were the parishioners. Small's crew had interviewed dozens, concentrating on those who were most active or who had seen Leary in the days before his disappearance. No serious conflicts with Leary had surfaced. No one reported anything unusual. No one had thought him upset or distracted.

Donovan crossed the office to the window and stared out at North 27th. By day, a busy street, officially a state highway, but quiet now. He watched a northbound semi roll to a stop at the corner.

The truck made him think of Tony W. The man might have gotten away with murder if a curious trucker hadn't seen his car half hidden in the brush and scribbled down the plate number. Tony had been in prison at the time of Leary's murder, but while that cleared him of direct involvement, he might know something. Like who else knew Leary's secrets—the affair with Tony's wife, and the baby.

Though if Donovan had been Tony, he might have wanted to put out a hit on the priest. Not much of a theory, but not impossible.

Back at his desk, Donovan pushed the lists aside and reached for the files he'd managed to gather. He set the alarm on his phone for fifteen minutes before he needed to be at the grade school door, and for the next hour, pored over the past.

Tony W had a bad record, no question. But it was all petty shit, even the felonies. The kind of guy who'd be involved in drugs and drug-related robberies today. Who might have a girlfriend and a kid or two he couldn't take care of, and convinced himself that crime was the only way. But crime only made a down-on-your-luck life worse.

Like a few guys he'd known in the old neighborhood. The guy he might have become if he hadn't met Beth and realized he could choose between his crowd or making a better life with her.

Talk about the grace of God.

The more Donovan read, the itchier he got. Too many unanswered questions. Questions nobody had asked about Tony W. Like what had triggered a pissant crook's jump to murder. Why was he out in western Montana? Why had he targeted Robert Ziegler? Woijowski had bounced around the state doing construction and driving short haul, but there was no indication he'd ever lived in Billings or had any connection to the man. The trucker who had ID'd Woijowski's car—that was mighty convenient, wasn't it?

He was beginning to wonder whether Tony W had been as much the victim of a setup as Ziegler.

But why?

Despite what veteran cops told puzzled rookies in bad movies, Donovan knew motive mattered. It wasn't an element of the crime, like intent, and you didn't have to prove it to the jury. But thinking about the *why* helped you focus your investigation. Once you identified a suspect, motive helped you anticipate what they might do next.

Motive didn't mean psychobabble mumbo jumbo excuses about a bad childhood. Not a whining *Why, oh why?*, but *What was he thinking?* Literally: What was he thinking?

Nothing in Tony Woijowski's file gave Donovan even a hint of an answer.

He rummaged in his desk drawer for a spoon and scooped up the last of the curried rice, now cold and a tad gummy. Almost time to get the kids. Motive was the big unanswered question in Leary's murder, too. The killing hadn't been random or for financial gain. The kidnapping was part of the plan.

That meant they were after a reasonably intelligent killer. One capable of making and carrying out a plan that involved deception and physical strength, and an accomplice, witting or not. But an amateur. Amateurs were often wracked by guilt.

Guilt gave an investigator leverage. It made keeping secrets harder, although Leary's killers had kept their secrets a long time.

That implied a relationship of trust or necessity. Trust, based on mutual need. And mutual need for silence.

When the body was discovered, Small had kept one detail back. Donovan had kept it quiet, too. He studied the picture of Leary's wrist bones, crossed behind his back and wrapped with wire. Galvanized, fourteen gauge. Sturdy stuff.

For the first time, it struck him.

The wire wasn't just meant to impede the priest's mobility. It was a sign and a symbol.

Handcuffs.

* * *

Lindsay tucked a bare foot beneath on her on the couch, the burgundy chenille soft and warm. Outside, the slivery moon perched on the chimney of the house across the street. The day had been clear and bright, and the new snow was nearly gone.

Scott took his favorite seat, an oak-and-leather rocker scavenged from a lodge where he'd once worked.

"She had no idea Leary was dead?" he asked. "He'd be what, seventy, seventy-two, and she didn't think to check?"

"She saw Father Michael Leary listed on the church website and never imagined that it might be a different man. The name is so common and the murder so old—nearly twenty-one years—that you've gotta google a long way down to find it. She wanted to see him, yes, but her main reason for coming here is tracing family history, so she can figure out the genetic link to her grandson's illness. She isn't aware of any living relatives besides her daughters and her sister, so she's heading up to Red Lodge tomorrow to see what she can dig up." Lindsay set her phone on the coffee table. "She wants me to go with her."

"You should go." Haley stood in the doorway. "That would be a hard thing to do by yourself, and you're good at asking questions."

"I didn't hear you come down."

When the girls were teenagers, Lindsay had been pleased that they seemed to enjoy hanging out with their parents, unlike some of their friends. Which was part of why the recent push–pull had been so upsetting. Was it finally easing?

Haley scooped Ms. Wriggles off the wingback chair and sat, the cat in her lap. The tabby arched her back at the affront, then nestled into her girl's embrace.

"How'd it go at the City Council?" Haley asked.

"Good." Lindsay sipped her tea. "They approved the loan. My client thinks he can have the new sound equipment in place by early summer and start booking shows any day now."

"Two historic theaters in a town this size. That's a real coup," Scott said.

"Cross your fingers," Lindsay said. "We've been down this road before."

"Why are you worried, Mom? You got what you wanted, as usual. Of course the council was skeptical—that theater restoration's been botched so many times—but you stand up, you persuade them that this time it's for real, and they say, 'How much money do you need, Ms. Keller?'"

"Well, it wasn't quite that easy," Lindsay replied, uncertain whether she was being complimented or challenged.

But Haley was on a roll. "The Steneruds were fighting over boxes of old photos, and you got them to sit down and pass the whiskey bottle and they all sang 'Kumbaya.'"

"Okay." Lindsay straightened her leg and stretched it. "But that wasn't really about the boxes or the money. It was about Rose's feeling that their father had always favored Pete, and when it came to business, he did—Pete was his only son. But we found something Rose wanted that Pete was willing to give up, and we put the deal back together."

Give and take. Never easy, always critical.

She changed the subject. "Your boss says you're the best young baker she's seen in years."

"That cake convinced me," Scott said.

"Thanks," Haley replied, but a hint of wariness had crept into her voice.

"Cooking professionally is a tough business. It takes more than good cake to succeed, and I want you to be fully prepared in ways

I never was." Lindsay set her now-cool tea on the table. "Let me tell you a story. About my own choices. And failures."

She told her daughter about landing her dream job as a prosecutor, then losing it. About feeling dogged by the knowledge that a man spent years in prison because she'd lost her nerve. About finding—creating—other work she loved, but never shaking the sense of failure.

"Mom, that's nuts. You didn't screw up. Your boss was crooked, and you couldn't expose him without violating legal ethics and tainting yourself." Haley leaned forward, one hand on the cat's striped back. "You fixed it as soon as you could."

"Don't make me into some whistleblower hero. The point is, I was passionate about criminal law, and because of a situation I couldn't control, my passion got derailed. I was able to find something else I believed in just as much." And she did, she realized. She believed in keeping the community spirit alive, one old building at a time, as much as any other work she'd ever done. "But only because I had the tools. I—we—want you to have the tools—the education—because life throws curveballs all the time. We want you to do what you love, but we also want you to be able to change direction if you need to."

"*When* you need to," Scott added. "It's part of life."

Haley tightened her grip on the cat, her lower lip protruding. After a long moment, she met Lindsay's gaze. "I get that, Mom, I do. Though I do think you're kind of a hero, even if you don't."

How could she respond to that except to smile in thanks?

Haley slid the cat off her lap and stood. "Bedtime. It's a good thing I love baking, because I don't love getting up at three in the morning."

She kissed Scott's cheek, then leaned in to hug Lindsay. Her arms were strong and warm, and the embrace was the sweetest thing Lindsay had felt in a long time. Sweeter even than coconut cake.

"Text your friend, Mom. Go to Red Lodge with her."

Moments later, the sound of her daughter's footsteps on the stairs behind her, Lindsay reached for her phone.

TUESDAY
March 8, 2016

Lindsay parked and dashed across the street to the Dude Rancher. In the coffee shop, Carrie sat at a four-top, listening to the petite redhead seated across from her.

"Good morning, Carrie. And you must be Ginger." She held out her hand, and the redhead rose to take it. "Welcome to Billings."

"She showed up last night," Carrie said. "Completely took me by surprise." The waitress filled a third cup and set the pot on the table, ready to take their orders.

"Wouldn't life be dull if our friends and families didn't keep surprising us?" Lindsay sat and picked up the menu.

* * *

Donovan was grateful for the strong coffee as he waited for his call to be shuffled to the right person at the state prison.

"No guarantees," the assistant warden said when he finally came on the line. "He isn't known for talking."

"It's a nice day for a drive," Donovan replied.

"What's your visit about, you don't mind my asking?"

"His daughter." Half the truth anyway.

But before he left, he needed to read another file. A dusty file from 1981.

* * *

Carrie wanted to say the road to Red Lodge looked familiar. But it didn't.

She'd let Ginger sit in front. The back seat provided the touch of isolation she craved right now. Her own little bubble of memory, filled with blanks.

They crossed the Yellowstone at Laurel and drove southwest. This was farm and ranch country. Most places were neat and tidy, newborn calves lying next to their mothers in pastures close to the barns. But at one junky spread, old tractors and other farm equipment littered the yard. A white semitrailer with a round red and green "Consolidated Freightways" logo stood beside a tiny house, badly in need of paint.

"*Cornflake,*" her father's voice whispered in her memory.

"I hope I did the right thing," Lindsay was saying, "telling her about my own great big screwup and agreeing to help her with culinary school the same as we would have with college. It's so hard to tell."

Ginger touched her arm. "That sounds just right."

"Screwups are part of being a parent," Carrie said, hoping she'd heard the conversation right. "The hardest part is admitting them. Are these the Beartooth Mountains? Mom loved them."

"Red Lodge is a cute town. Scott had some pieces in a gallery show last summer, and we came up for the opening. Stayed overnight at the Pollard, built in the 1890s."

"Is that the hotel where a guest robbed the bank across the street while other guests watched, and he turned out to be the Sundance Kid?" Ginger asked. "I did some reading last night."

"That's the story. It might even be true."

They drove into town, passing blocks of older homes, patches of snow clinging to the small front yards. *Must be the elevation,* Carrie decided, heart pounding as she peered out the window. Lindsay turned off the main street.

"This should be the block," Ginger said, glancing at the list of addresses Carrie had scribbled on her notepad. Had that just been last week? "But I don't see the number."

Lindsay stopped in front of a duplex. "It's gotta be this lot. I bet when the house was torn down and the duplex built, they created two new house numbers in place of the old one."

Two doors, one red and one blue, opened onto a shared front porch. A metal chair salvaged from an old ski lift hung between the doors. In one driveway, a couple loaded skis onto a roof rack. It was cute, Carrie thought, but disappointing. The house where Father Leary grew up was gone. She reached over the back of the seat to squeeze Ginger's shoulder.

On the next street, in the middle of the block, stood the tidy bungalow where Mike and Irene Danich had lived for the twenty-two years of their marriage. Tina's childhood home. Lindsay parked and they all got out and stood on the sidewalk.

"Kinda like your house, sis, with the gables and the white trim. Look, roses." Ginger pointed to a curved garden bed that wound around the front of the house, beneath a wide porch. Telltale canes stuck up like thorny fingers reaching for the sun.

They walked up the street, searching for Anton and Zofie's house.

"It was on this side, I'm sure," Carrie said, her footsteps slowing. Near the end of the block, she stopped in front of a small cottage painted pale yellow.

"This is it," she said. "It looks so . . ."

"Ordinary," Ginger supplied.

Exactly. A double stroller sat on the small porch. A calico cat eyed them from a window, her tail flicking the curtain. Not what you expected of a killer's childhood home. That was the problem, though, wasn't it? You wanted to think killers came from predict-able backgrounds—broken homes, in every sense of the outdated phrase—so you could avoid them. So you could console yourself that they didn't live on your street or go to school with your kids. That your kid would never be one of them.

That your father wasn't one of them.

Despite the heavy sweater under her coat, Carrie shivered.

"I've seen enough," she said, and as they turned to head down the street, in a narrow bed beside the house, she spotted the dried stalks of last year's hollyhocks.

*　*　*

Donovan reached for his coffee. Stone-cold. He made a fresh pot, pondering. The 1981 fatality on Black Otter Trail, the narrow road that curved sharply along the top of the Rims, had no clear connection to Father Leary's murder, but he'd hoped it might help him understand Jerzy Simonich.

Three kids, booze, a fast car, and a bad road. A teenage girl driving a Camaro down a steep, winding road while her brother and another girl squeezed into the passenger seat.

Was that what had happened? Mary Ellen's blood alcohol content had been through the roof. A seventeen-year-old girl at that level should have passed out. Jana Stenerud—who later married and divorced Andy Simonich—also had a level above the limit. But Andy's blood alcohol had barely showed a beer or two.

Would a sober nineteen-year-old have let a dead-drunk sister drive so he could feel up her drunk girlfriend? Not likely. Andy Simonich may not have inherited his father's ambition or his sister's brains, but he wasn't a complete idiot.

Then there were the injuries. Donovan plucked a car from the prop collection. Drew a line down the middle of a sheet of paper. Consulted the sketch on the crash report that showed where the Camaro left the road and where it landed. It was an old-style form, with tiny check boxes for info like injuries and seatbelts, but they kept a laminated code sheet in the office. He dug it out and deciphered the details. Double-checked what it said about who'd been sitting where.

"If the car left the road here, and flipped once—"

"Talking to yourself, Boston Boy? First sign of senility," another detective said as he walked in.

"Look at this, will you?" Donovan pried up the two prongs on the manila file folder and lifted out the crash report. Typed, the once-white paper crisp around the edges. "Sports car flips on Black Otter, lands on its roof, hits a boulder and stops. Good thing, or it could have kept going right off the cliff."

"Geez-*us*." The other detective set the file in his hand on his desk and reached for the report. "Anybody killed?"

"They should have all been killed. One girl was ejected. She died at the scene. The two survivors got cuts and scrapes, although the girl broke a leg. The only logical explanation is that the two survivors were wearing seatbelts." Donovan punched the air with a finger. "Picture this: sober guy in the driver's seat, belted. Drunk girlfriend in the passenger seat. He belts her in. Where's he put the second girl, his sister?"

The other detective perched on the corner of a desk, ankle on his knee, report dangling from one hand as he watched Donovan act it out.

"Simonich puts his sister in the back seat," Donovan said. "No belt, barely any room. Techs found stains on the upholstery. Not blood. Vomit, maybe."

"Simonich? The developer's kid, runs the mall?" The other man frowned. "Andy. Spends most of his time on the golf course the old man built south of town. She"—he glanced down at the report— "Mary Ellen, could not have been driving. Not a stick shift, not with that BAC. Plus, look where she ended up, spread eagle on top of a whiskey bottle."

The two men studied the diagram. They reread the narrative, passing the pages back and forth.

"They lied. He was driving. He was speeding, or he got distracted by the girlfriend, and wrecked the car. They blamed the dead girl," Donovan said. "Is that why the old man can't stand the sight of his own son, even after all these years?"

"They were coming from a kegger out past the airport," the other detective read. "Sheriff's deputies quizzed the other kids at the party, but nobody remembered seeing who was driving when the Camaro left. No eyewitnesses to the crash. You read the rest of the notes? Nobody tumble to the inconsistencies?"

Donovan flipped through the file. "Crash happened on a Friday. Log says case referred to the prosecutor for review on Monday, but I don't see any response."

"Monday? Look at the date on this page. What's the date on that one?"

Donovan checked the date, frowned, checked again. The accident had occurred on September 18. The first page of the report was dated September 22; the last page, September 28, nearly a week later. The typeface looked different. And the report wasn't signed.

"You thinking what I'm thinking?"

"I read the narrative," Donovan said slowly. "There's not the slightest hint that anybody thought the kids might be lying."

"So who phonied the report? Prosecutor's office? File comes back without any charges, nobody ever touches it again. No one would ever notice that somebody substituted a false page for the real one."

"But why? Because the prosecutor didn't want to throw a kid in jail for killing his sister, or because he was bought off?" Jerzy Simonich had lost one kid. Had he applied pressure to avoid losing the other, so his son wouldn't be haunted by what he'd done? Donovan couldn't blame the man for his feelings. But his actions were fair game.

"Who was county attorney then?" he asked, but the other man shook his head. Google would be a rabbit hole, and he didn't want to call the current county attorney's office and raise suspicions. Roy Small would know, but Donovan didn't want to pester a man with a dying wife. He grabbed his phone and texted Lindsay Keller.

* * *

They got to the Carbon County Historical Society in Red Lodge moments before it closed for a midmorning coffee break.

"There's a bear paw at the bakery with my name on it," the woman in charge said, her coat on, but she set her purse and keys on the counter and listened to their questions. "There are still

Petroviches in town. Distant cousins, I imagine. The Daniches are gone, though. Tina was a couple of years ahead of me. Always nice to the younger kids. Your father was older—I didn't really know him," she said to Carrie. Disapproval was written all over her face.

"Is the Woijowski family still around?" Carrie asked.

"Not to my knowledge. We do have an extensive archive of county records, old photos, family records, even letters and diaries. You're welcome to make an appointment to search through them yourselves. Or we can do the work for a reasonable fee."

Carrie nodded. A poster on the counter announced an upcoming exhibit on early twentieth-century women rodeo performers.

"Carbon County history is quite colorful," the woman said, following her gaze. "Ranching and rodeo life, as you see, and the timber industry and, later, recreation. But mining put the town on the map. Have you heard of our Festival of Nations?"

"We used to bring the girls," Lindsay said. "They learned Irish dance steps and ate *lefse*."

"Red Lodge had diversity before anyone knew what the word meant," the woman replied.

Carrie asked if she remembered any of Tina's friends.

"No. Except Mike Leary, God rest his soul. I don't believe in curses, but you have to wonder. If Mike hadn't gone into the priesthood and Tina hadn't married Tony—but that's what girls did in those days." The woman picked up her bag. "Now, if you ladies want to come back later . . ."

"Yes, of course." Lindsay laid a business card on the counter. "Sorry to keep you. Where did Ginger go?"

Carrie spotted her sister in front of a large glass case in the corridor.

"Our donor display," the woman said. "Can't have a museum without donors, and we wouldn't be much of a historical society if we didn't acknowledge our own history."

A few minutes later, as they were getting out of the car at the cemetery, Lindsay's phone buzzed. She scanned the text, her brow furrowed, then thumbed a quick response.

"Problem at work?" Carrie asked.

"No, just a strange question. Why would Detective Donovan want the name of the county attorney from 1981?"

"Why ask you? Do you even know?"

"Probably because I worked there for a few years," Lindsay replied. "Later, but for the same guy. Stan LeMoyne. Pretty sure he's dead." She shoved the phone into her pocket and closed the door. But it was clear to Carrie that the detective's question troubled her.

The snow had melted along the paths and on most of the head-stones, though white patches dotted the ground between.

"Ever since we lived at the abbey outside Portland," Ginger said, "I've found cemeteries peaceful places. Burial customs worldwide are fascinating."

Carrie wrapped her arms around herself. How had Baba described Montana? A place of perfect emptiness and freedom. She'd dismissed that as absence making the heart not merely fonder, but blind. Now, though, with the snow-covered mountains above and the valley stretched out below, she caught a glimpse of what Baba had meant.

They found the Petrovich plots, and the Daniches. Ginger and Carrie knelt at their mother's grave. Irene had never brought them here, though Carrie suspected she might have visited alone. *We work so hard to save other people from pain,* she thought, *only to make it worse.*

She caught up with Lindsay at the Simonich plot.

"By the dates, those must be Jerzy's parents," Lindsay said. She pointed to a single stone beside it. "And Ed. The uncle who died young."

"What about Mary Ellen?" Carrie asked. She plucked a faded pink daisy out of a mound of snow and stuffed it in her pocket. "God, I hate plastic flowers."

"She's buried in Billings," Lindsay said, walking on. "There are the Learys, including that baby sister Donovan mentioned. Appalling how many children died young, even in the 1940s."

"I tried searching causes of death online," Carrie said, "but the records weren't detailed enough."

"We should have asked our friend at the Historical Society," Lindsay said.

"Ha. Like she'd have let you keep her from that bear paw one more minute," Ginger said.

"You'll understand," Lindsay replied, "once you've eaten one."

On their way back to the car, Carrie tried to picture her mother and grandmother growing up here. If the woman at the Historical Society was right about attitudes toward pregnant teenagers—and she'd been frank, not mean—it wasn't hard to understand why her parents had left. And if Tony's criminal record was local knowledge, why Tina had not come back.

She understood, and yet she wanted to lie down in the snow and cry. For herself, for her parents, and Baba and Ginger and Father Leary. For everyone who'd had a part of them slowly worn away by secrets.

Ginger enveloped her from behind. "Bear paw, bear paw," she chanted, and the chill that gripped Carrie's gut began to thaw.

Back in the Prius, Lindsay punched the heater on "High" and turned to face Ginger. "You sure you want to do this? When I called after breakfast, I didn't say you might be related. I said you two are visiting, you just learned of his death, and you want to offer your condolences."

Ginger nodded and Carrie settled back, grateful for this new-old friend.

Bill Leary the son was as friendly as his wife and Anna, his mother. When Meg brought out coffee and a tray of bear paws, and the visitors burst into laughter and told the story, the Learys laughed, too. Carrie had trouble taking her eyes off Bill. He was Father Mike's nephew, roughly her age but already retired from some obviously successful career, and he was a clone of the man. Did he have any idea, as he sat at the round oak kitchen table telling strangers stories about his family, how alike he and Ginger were? Even the way they rested their hands on the table.

"My father always said his mother was determined that one of her boys become a priest, and she settled on Mike because he was the youngest," Bill said.

"Like in Jane Austen," Lindsay said. "The oldest ran the family estate, the second went into the navy, and the third took the collar."

Anna laid a hand on her son's arm. "That was your father's way of saying he was happy he met me. And happy to bring a blonde into this family of redheads." She smiled at Ginger, who raked a hand through her own red hair, and Carrie wondered if the old woman had guessed at the family tie no one mentioned.

"It seemed like a genuine vocation," Lindsay continued. "From what I saw as a teenager. Lots of priests and nuns left in the seventies and eighties. But he stayed."

"It was his calling," Bill said. "Even if his mother had a hand in it. He was a good priest."

It was easy for him to stay, Carrie thought. Father Leary hadn't needed to abandon his vocation to get what he wanted. He got to serve God and screw her mother.

But that wasn't fair. She suspected that both Mike and Tina had loved Tony, in their own ways. Tina had run, but she'd never divorced Tony. Instead, she'd explained his absence with a lie about his death.

Maybe Mike had wanted to marry her, to leave the priesthood and live an honest life, and she'd refused.

They would never know.

"Forgive me for asking," Lindsay said, "but did the brothers have any theories about Father Leary's death?"

"Like I told the detective," Anna said, "no. But tell them about the letters."

A lock of sandy hair fell across Bill's forehead. "This morning, after you called, I remembered that we had some of Uncle Mike's letters. I hauled them out and read through them. He sent Dad a birthday card that arrived in England after his disappearance, and he said he was going to make things right. What he meant, I have no idea. Curious, though."

Carrie glanced at Lindsay, but the lawyer showed no reaction. Tina was dead by then. Had he been referring to her father's parole hearing?

"Did you tell Detective Donovan about that?" Lindsay asked.

"No. Should I?" Bill's brow creased, his voice concerned. "You're not saying you think that has anything to do with his death?"

"No, but it's curious." Lindsay glanced around. "What a lovely home you have—my husband would envy those high ceilings. And that view."

On their way out a few minutes later, Carrie watched as Ginger lingered by a table full of framed family photos, then picked one up.

"You have a beautiful family," Ginger told their hosts. "And some talented photographers."

But Carrie saw that the picture that caught her eye was not of a child or grandchild. It was a black-and-white snapshot, taken in front of the house they'd seen this morning, of a small, fair woman surrounded by three beaming sons. Mike, Bill, and Frank with the late Mrs. Leary, a dead ringer for the granddaughter she had never known.

* * *

You never knew what to expect when you saw a man in prison, especially a man you only knew from his record. Some were beaten down, diminished. Others thrived in the male jungle.

Tony W appeared to be a reasonably well-adjusted man for one sentenced to live his life by rules others set, in a place he couldn't leave.

He's at peace, Donovan thought, studying the weathered face across from him. Early seventies, tall, fit, neither too thin nor too muscled. His gaze was steady, but not challenging. Dress him in regular clothes, drop him in the real world, and you'd never guess what he'd done.

"You act like you think I have a choice in the matter," Tony said after Donovan explained why he'd come to see a man sentenced to life before Donovan was born.

"See, now, I disagree. I do think you have a choice," Donovan said, and a flicker of surprise crossed Tony's face. Then another emotion replaced it, and the man's voice grew harder.

"I suppose you're going to say all I have to do is raise my hand, and the parole board will tell me I'm a free man. You don't know nothin' about my life."

"Oh, I'm not naive. It won't be that simple. But I think I've finally figured out who you've been protecting, and why."

The text from Lindsay Keller had been the clincher. He'd called Lieutenant Hansen and filled her in, and she'd promised they'd run down the history of Tony W's victim and the mall property ASAP. Was Donovan confident enough that they'd confirm his suspicions to go ahead with the interview, she'd asked. He was.

"I killed a man. I laid in wait, I ran him off the road, and when he didn't drown, I made sure he was dead." Tony's words were almost defiant, desperate, as if he needed Donovan to take this no further, to let him suffer as he deserved. But at the same time, there was a longing in his voice, an ache. A hope.

"Yeah." Donovan stuck his finger in his ear and twisted it. "But what's been bugging me is the question nobody ever asked. *Why* did you do it?"

Tony's cuffed hands rested calmly on the heavy square table. "Because I'm a no-count loser."

Worth probing, if he were psychologizing the man. *Is that what your parents told you? Your teachers, your wife, the cops?*

Your buddy the priest?

No, not the priest. He'd known the truth.

"I think you killed to protect someone. Not from Robert Ziegler. Oh, he was a threat, all right." Donovan stood. "But not to you. You never met Robert Ziegler. You never lived in the same town or went to the same church. You weren't in the farm business. I don't imagine you ever heard of him until you got a call from an old friend, asking you to solve a problem."

"Your imagination's been working overtime, Detective."

"Doesn't take much imagination to see that you are one of those men—and I'm one, too—who will do anything to protect the people they love."

Eyes hooded, Tony lifted his chin, though whether in challenge or wariness, Donovan couldn't tell.

"In fact, looks to me like all three of you were like that," he continued. "You, Mike, and Jerzy. Do you know you have grandchildren? Two girls in their twenties. I've met your daughter, Carrie. Spitting image of your wife. You know Tina's gone, don't you? Cancer."

Tony nodded, pain on his face.

"Beautiful women," Donovan continued. "A beautiful family. And you have a great-grandson."

Tony's shoulder twitched. Trying not to fidget. To betray his interest and give the cop the upper hand. *Good.* Unsettling the man was good. Goad him into talking. Into telling the rest of the story.

"What I think you need to do"—Donovan leaned in, making the point while making it clear he could walk out of here and never look back—"is tell the truth. You killed Robert Ziegler to keep Jerzy Simonich quiet. To keep him from destroying your family. And your best friend."

"I did that." Tony spoke too quickly. "I destroyed them with all the stupid shit I did. I've got to pay the price."

"Now we're back to where we started, you thinking this is all out of your hands." Donovan straightened. "You were a petty crook, the kind that's easy to catch. A dime a dozen." Like the one in the hospital back in Billings, who Donovan intended to keep out of the business of attacking women in parking garages for good. "I don't know why you thought that was easier than honest work, but none of it would have landed you here for life. You had a wife you adored, a baby girl, and a good buddy priest to pray for you. But on one of your stays inside, your wife and your buddy got close. Too close, and another baby girl came along. You did the math, and you knew."

Tony W kept his face blank, his mouth shut.

"But here's how I know you aren't the asshole you want everybody to think you are. You didn't say a thing. Oh, you might have talked to Tina and had a few harsh words for your old pal, Mike. But you could have filed for divorce on the grounds of infidelity. You could have screamed out loud to the whole world that she cheated on you." Donovan raised a finger. "And one note to the bishop, and Father Michael Leary would have been transferred to the end of the earth where he'd never catch another glimpse of Tina or the girls."

They'd watched *Spotlight* again over the weekend, he and Beth, and he had no doubt the church had operated the same way all across the country. Keeping its scandals under wraps, making quiet payoffs when it had to. The code of silence worked because the people who knew what had happened were too afraid to admit it. Donovan had wanted to believe—because he was a cop, damn it—that if word of a priest screwing around with a parishioner and fathering a child dropped into the lap of the newspaper editor or the chief of police, they'd expose the man for a liar and a hypocrite. But he'd come around to Beth's point of view, that the media and the police wouldn't get outraged by private behavior that didn't break any laws. Man's laws anyway—God's laws were another story. Especially when naming the priest would have exposed the woman and children. So the silence kept the flock ignorant and the priest safe.

But that didn't mean one well-placed man with harmful intent and personal knowledge couldn't destroy both the priest's reputation and the woman's. A campaign of whispers would have been as damaging as any news report. Maybe more.

Tony raised his cuffed hands to his chest, rubbing the palms and heels together.

"Jerzy blamed you for his brother's death," Donovan said. "All those years ago in a mountain lake. He got his revenge by slowly destroying the two of you. He knew your secrets, and he used the fear of scandal to force you to kill for him. To force Leary to keep quiet and keep you both away from the woman you loved."

This next bit was the sketchy part of his theory, though he was sure the property records search would back him up. "You did what Jerzy asked you to do, so he could get what he wanted. You killed Ziegler so Jerzy could snap up that farmland, build his mall, and save himself from financial ruin. So Tina and the girls would not have to live in fear. Jerzy took the money and the power, and you took the blame."

"But—but Mike," Tony sputtered, then went silent.

"What I haven't figured out is how Mike knew Jerzy's role in the murder. Jerzy sure didn't tell him. Did you? Or did he work it out himself? He intended to testify at your parole hearing in 1995, and I think he meant to expose Jerzy. He couldn't exonerate you, but he could claim that you'd acted under extreme pressure. You didn't want him to talk, did you? You went to prison to protect him and your family, and he was about to risk exposing it all."

"He said it was time. Tina was gone, the girls were grown. I was only hurting myself."

"And him."

"He said he deserved his pain and loneliness." Tony bit his lower lip. "He said I'd sacrificed myself long enough. But I knew Jerzy would never let it happen."

"You knew Mike wouldn't get here alive."

"All I ever wanted was to protect my family. I could never manage to do it the way other men did, with jobs and houses and staying put. Maybe that was Jerzy's doing, too. I don't know. So I did it the only way I knew how."

"You even protected Ginger, who wasn't yours."

"I couldn't let a child of Tina's suffer for what we did." Tony's eyes filled with anguish. "Mike and I, we both loved Tina from the time we first saw her as kids. Hell, you would have, too. She had a heart big as the sky. We weren't either of us good enough for her."

And though Detective Brian Donovan would never understand why Tony had done what he did, he understood that.

* * *

Trust Ginger to notice the photograph.

This past week had been a whirlwind set in motion by old photographs.

They drove out of Red Lodge in silence. Carrie stared out the window, barely noticing the view. They'd learned so much because of the photographs. Ginger knew now who her father was, and she knew his family. In some small town they'd lived in, a nun had told Carrie's class that everyone had a twin somewhere in the world, someone who looked just like them with the same name and family and even the same kind of dog or cat. Whether the woman meant to impress upon them the vastness of the world or make them feel insignificant in God's mighty hands, Carrie had never known.

But she had never believed it. And even though that nun might chalk Ginger's resemblance to the Leary clan up to divine plan, Carrie didn't believe it now. Put the pictures and the facts together, and it was plain as the nose on your face.

And yet she was no closer to finding the truth for Asher than she'd been last week on the deck of a pirate ship.

Everything she thought she knew had changed since then.

No, not everything. She still knew she had to follow this trail, no matter where it led.

"I'm not going to say anything," Ginger said from the front seat.

"What?" Carrie leaned forward. "About what?"

"About Father Leary being my father. I'm not going to ask Detective Donovan to give me the DNA tests, and I'm not going to visit the Learys again. Sooner or later, they'll wonder about me, and I don't want to destroy their memories of him. It won't do anyone any good."

"But—but what he did was wrong." The moment the words were out, she regretted them. If Leary and their mother hadn't broken their vows, there would have been no Ginger. "I'm sorry, Ginge. I didn't mean—"

"No, I know. I never felt unloved. Mom and Baba saw to that. I did believe I didn't get to have a home and family like everyone else, but I never felt unloved." Ginger twisted in her seat, facing Carrie. "After you told me your theory about Father Leary, I did some research. There are support groups for children of priests, lawsuits, settlements. But I don't see the point. They're both dead. I almost understand what they did, with Dad—Tony—in and out of jail. Leary was her rock. They loved each other, didn't they?"

"Yeah. I don't know the whole story, or why he didn't leave the priesthood for her. But yeah, I do believe they loved each other."

Ginger's face changed and she settled back in her seat, eyes forward. Carrie knew that expression. *Decision made.*

She exhaled, relieved.

"Wait. That's why your grandmother moved you, isn't it?" Lindsay said. "So you two wouldn't figure out that Leary was Ginger's father. But the men in the church knew. And somehow, for some reason, that put you two in danger."

"What?" Carrie stretched forward.

"At lunch yesterday, Carrie, you told Donovan that the man talking to Leary in the church vestibule said, 'We know about the girl,' and you were sure he meant Ginger, but you didn't know why. Donovan pointed out that he could have meant anyone. But with everything else you've learned, now you think he knew Leary was Ginger's father."

"Right, right. But—oh my god. That's it." Carrie felt gut-punched. "Baba and Father Mike and Monsignor talked about it in the kitchen, but I couldn't hear the whole conversation. I was so mad, as soon as they said we were moving again, I never asked why. I didn't think they'd tell me."

"It makes sense, doesn't it?" Lindsay pressed. "Whoever that man was, he was threatening to expose the truth. But what if it was more than that? What if he was threatening you?"

"We need to go back to the Historical Society," Ginger said.

"We're ten miles out of town," Lindsay said.

"We have to go back."

Twenty minutes later, they parked in front of the old brick building. Ginger was already inside when Carrie and Lindsay caught up with her, standing in front of the display of photographs and memorabilia from the museum's history.

"It's him." She pointed to a color studio portrait from the 1980s of a smiling man in a camel hair coat.

"Our biggest benefactor," the woman at the desk, the same woman they'd met this morning, called out. "He purchased this building and gifted it to the museum."

"Are you sure, sis?" Carrie said as she read the name below the photograph.

"Holy shit," Lindsay said.

WEDNESDAY
March 9, 2016
Billings

To think this house used to seem so glamorous, so ritzy, way back when, Lindsay thought as she raised the brass knocker on the Simoniches' dark-paneled front door. Nice enough, but dated. Almost—the word Ginger had used yesterday for the house in Red Lodge popped into her mind—almost *ordinary*.

Jerzy opened the door, his eyes watery and bloodshot.

"Hello, Jerzy. It's been a long time." He had looked so powerful once, tall and imposing. He'd looked that way to Carrie in the church vestibule. And he'd looked that way to her when she'd refused to be his lawyer, wondering as she did whether he intended to make sure she regretted turning him down.

Now, he looked like a broken old man. But she wasn't going to let that fool her.

"Why are you here, Lindsay?"

"I've known you since I was a little girl. You were our neighbor, my best friend's father."

"Why are you here?" he repeated.

"Because I learned a few things yesterday that I can't keep to myself. But I thought you deserved to know before I go to the police."

His expression darkened. Had she made a mistake?

"Because of Mary Ellen," she said.

"Come in," he replied.

* * *

Brian Donovan studied the house from his unmarked car. Lindsay Keller had said the Simoniches moved to "the snooty house" before the girls started high school. Tucked beneath the Rims near the college, this street may have seemed snooty then to a fourteen-year-old who resented her friend's big talk. But not now. These days, the status-conscious lived on top of the Rims, where their wealth was visible for miles, or west of town, with acreage and killer views.

Down the street, backup officers were in place. Though spring was officially two weeks away, grass was greening where the weekend snow had given it a good dousing. Dated landscaping—sprawling junipers at the foundation, a cluster of yucca around the mailbox. He was surprised to see a white Prius in the driveway. He'd pegged the Simoniches for Cadillacs.

An older woman whose sleek silver hair brushed the collar of her white silk blouse answered the door, her knuckles swollen, her fingertips a dark metallic red. He showed his badge, and she paled. "My husband is in his study."

Jerzy Simonich stood with difficulty when Donovan appeared in the doorway, his eyes red rimmed. The fine lines that ran from the corners of his eyes to his jaw had become ruts, the wrinkles around his chin crevasses. The aquiline nose appeared fragile, like one of the sandstone rocks clinging to the Rims, that had been there forever and could break off any moment.

His face was a map of agony and struggle.

"Thank you, Barbara," Simonich said.

Donovan noticed a flicker of irritation in the woman's eyes. He also noticed that she didn't completely close the door.

And he noticed another woman standing near the window.

"Ms. Keller," he said. "I suppose I shouldn't be surprised to see you."

She crossed the space between them, hand extended, her expression determined. Not the worried face of the woman who'd brought him the priest's wallet, or the guilt-ridden face of the woman mourning the long-dead.

"You were next on my list this morning, Detective, though I had a few things to tell Jerzy first," she said. "Maybe we should all sit." She gestured to the pair of brass-studded leather chairs in front of the desk.

Jerzy Simonich's office—his study, as his wife had called it—wore a decorator's hand. All dark wood and leather, an Oriental rug. Bronzes of bucking horses, oil paintings of a West that never existed. A tall wooden gun case. The dossier the department had hastily assembled on Simonich listed a furniture store, sold a few years back, as one of his many business ventures. Sell someone land, build them a house, send them to another business you owned to furnish it. Very handy.

"What brings you here, Detective?" Lindsay asked once they were all seated, and Donovan realized she'd just played the room, evening the power dynamic by putting all three of them at the same level.

"Why don't you go first?" he said. "Since you wanted to talk to us both."

He watched the old man's face as the lawyer described what she'd learned, with help from the West sisters, about Jerzy's threats to expose Mike Leary as Ginger West's father and create a scandal that would have destroyed the fragile Tina and tainted her daughters. Barely a flicker of acknowledgment on Jerzy's stony face, despite the terrible facts laid out one after the other. No wonder he'd been such a formidable businessman, a formidable opponent and father.

It made sense, once the pieces clicked together. But he knew that broken vows were only part of the leverage Jerzy Simonich had held over Leary and Tony. And over Tina, whom they'd both loved.

Maybe Jerzy had loved her a little, too.

"There's more, but it can wait. Your turn, Detective," Lindsay said, and Donovan had just an instant to decide whether letting her stay would make a difference. She would be shocked—her bond with this family ran deep, and what he had to say was going to change much of what she thought she knew about them, and about her own life.

But she was going to find out sometime. If she stayed, if she heard the details firsthand and witnessed Simonich's reaction, her anger and her sense of betrayal could make her a powerful ally.

Donovan glanced over her shoulder at the bookshelves. Montana history and sports biographies. A handful of golf trophies. More family photos.

He turned his attention to Jerzy Simonich. "I see you like to read. I've been doing a lot of reading myself lately. Old case files."

Simonich reached for a cut crystal water glass.

"Carbon County sent me what they had on your brother's death," Donovan continued, aware of Lindsay Keller's eyes on him. "A real tragedy."

"Broke my mother's heart." Simonich's eyes darkened, and his lips pressed together. "She died a year later."

"My condolences. Then to lose your daughter in another tragic accident. I can't imagine your grief." He really couldn't.

The old man did not reply.

"When we spoke the other day at the mall about Father Leary's murder, I got the impression you didn't know him well. Was I mistaken?" Christ, the man had to have known Donovan would figure out that he and Leary had gone way back.

"Our paths crossed here and there. As I told you."

"I take it your brother converted." Donovan gestured toward the St. Christopher medal in the shadow box behind the desk. "In fact, it's your brother I want to talk about. I spotted Mike Leary's name in the report on his death."

Simonich grew still, his knuckles white against the water glass.

"And that of another man, one we've just been talking about."

The old man set the glass on his desk and grasped one hand with the other. After a long moment, he spoke. "Tony. Tony Woijowski."

He said it the same way Tony W had. The way Carrie Matheson had guessed, the sound of her birth name lingering in a lost memory. "Mike and Tony were both there when your brother died. Years

299

later, when Tony W was up for parole, you and Mike were both listed as witnesses. That must have been hard."

A nerve in the man's left cheek twitched, the only sign he was listening.

"That must have been hard," Donovan repeated. "Testifying against an old friend."

"I never testified."

"No, that's right. You didn't. Neither of you did. Mike disappeared earlier that week, and when he didn't surface, Tony withdrew his request for parole. I suppose he thought he didn't stand a chance, with you against him and Mike gone."

"I don't know what Tony thought. Brutal animal like him." Simonich rubbed an ache in his neck.

"He thought he was helping you. But we'll come back to that. I also read the file on your daughter's accident. Your children's accident, I should say. I sympathize, I've got a boy and a girl myself. You were lucky—you could have lost them both." He paused, waiting for Simonich's reaction. None came.

"I'm a little confused about what happened, though," he continued. "Why don't you tell me?"

"Pretty simple. People thought I spoiled my daughter, buying her that car. Maybe they were right. Mary Ellen always drove too fast. She lost control and the car flipped. She was killed. The Stenerud girl was injured, but she recovered. Andy was unharmed, thank God."

He heard a sharp intake of breath from the woman next to him. It was about to get worse. He could have insisted she leave and allow him to conduct an official police interview in private.

But it was time. Past time.

"That's what I thought, until I tried to work it out." He pulled a Matchbox Camaro out of his pocket, scavenged last night from a box in his son's closet, and set it on the smooth, dust-free desktop. "She's speeding down Black Otter and gets distracted. Or the front right tire catches the edge of the road—I understand it wasn't well maintained back then—and she goes off the edge. The car flips and lands on its roof." He turned the car upside down. "Makes sense that the driver would fly out and the other two would be trapped inside, like the report says. But that's not what happened, is it?"

Simonich stared at him, stony-faced.

"I think your son was driving. Went off the road right up there, didn't he?" Donovan saw Lindsay's hand fly to her mouth as he pointed out the window to the Rimrocks, the base of the cliff not thirty feet away. "I think he panicked, understandably. He climbed down the rocks—I hear he was quite the athlete back then—and came to you for help. You called your friend, the prosecutor. Now, Stan LeMoyne wasn't above making things turn out the way he wanted." As Lindsay Keller's story about the case that had driven her out of the prosecutor's office had demonstrated. "The three of you worked out this scenario, which had the added bonus of keeping LeMoyne out of the embarrassing position of prosecuting the son of a major campaign donor for vehicular homicide. Andy wasn't drunk, so he'd have been spared the maximum sentence. But you'd have done anything to keep him out of prison, wouldn't you? After all, you'd seen how prison changed your old pal, Tony."

Simonich reached for his water glass. His hand shook.

Donovan glanced at Lindsay Keller.

"What else?" she demanded. "Tell us the rest." His gamble had paid off. She was on his side.

"The wild card was Jana Stenerud," he said. "She'd had a lot to drink, according to the kids at the party and her blood test at the hospital. How much she might remember was anybody's guess. Is that why Andy married her, to keep her quiet? Nothing bonds a couple like a secret neither of them can risk telling."

"She couldn't have known," Lindsay blurted out. "Not Jana."

He reached for the toy car. "What convinced me—and I'll confess, I didn't tumble to this right away—but here's the problem. The pages in the report were created at different times. When LeMoyne doctored the file, he didn't replace all the originals. Your daughter wasn't thrown from the car, as the report indicates. She was trapped in the back seat, and that's consistent with her injuries, which were mainly internal. No head injury, none of the broken bones you'd expect if she'd been ejected. Your son pulled her out, then staged the scene. I am sorry to be so blunt, especially with your wife listening at the door. Please come in, Mrs. Simonich."

He stood as she entered, one hand over her mouth. He led her to his chair.

"I don't believe you knew any of this, and I'm sorry you had to learn it this way."

"Jerzy, is it true? He can't be telling the truth."

Donovan watched Barbara Simonich search her husband's face for the answer. If the old man moved a muscle, he couldn't see it, but they'd been married fifty-plus years, and it was clear from the way her shoulders collapsed that she saw what Donovan didn't.

Lindsay Keller reached over and took her hand.

"I'll leave it to the county attorney to decide what charges to bring against you and Andy," Donovan continued. "It was a long time ago. The law's changed a lot since then. And you were trying to protect your son, which could be a mitigating factor. You must have breathed a sigh of relief when LeMoyne died. What I'm more concerned about now is the death of Mike Leary." He turned back to Mrs. Simonich, still clutching Lindsay's hand. "Again, ma'am, I do apologize for springing all this on you. That was not my intention. Nor on you, Lindsay, but you've figured out quite a bit already."

Lindsay nodded. She claimed to hate the courtroom, but she'd mustered a good courtroom face.

Barbara Simonich stifled a sob. Lindsay rummaged in her pink leather bag and found a pack of tissues. The older woman took the pack but didn't open it.

Jerzy Simonich's eyes flicked to the shadow box. "Mike was in the wrong place at the wrong time." He'd recovered his usual certainty. "Druggies, thinking they could score some cash."

"I've got a different theory," Donovan said. "That it was all a setup. It was smart. And it was brutal. You've heard the term *modus operandi*? It means how a criminal acts. When two cases bear a lot of similarities, you have to ask if they might be related. That's what

I'm seeing: two cases where a man was lured out of his way, into a remote area where his car and body might never be found.

"Now, there are differences between this case and the other one I've been reading about, but the most striking similarity is that the man who wanted these two men dead likes to use other people as weapons. Get them to do his dirty work. And it worked, because he had leverage."

"You watch too many crime shows, Detective," Simonich said.

"You know what they say—truth is stranger than fiction." Donovan folded his arms. "As I said, I have a son, too. He's a good kid. He's not as bright as his younger sister, and he knows it. It pains him—we see that, but we try to make sure he never feels like he doesn't measure up. That must have been hard on Andy. He's what, fifty-four or -five, and you still hold the purse strings. You've skipped right over him, giving his sons the responsibility that should have been his. But of course, the real leverage you hold is that you know what really happened up on Black Otter."

Simonich gripped the arms of his leather chair. "I think I've heard enough, Detective."

In his jacket pocket, Donovan's phone buzzed. He read the lieutenant's message and tucked the phone away. "Now, I didn't have a great relationship with my dad, but this takes the cake. And it's got to have crushed Andy, to realize you would use him that way. It's how you used Tony, too. But Mike—well, you never could get Mike to go along, could you?"

"Detective Donovan," Barbara Simonich said. "Surely you don't believe my husband had anything to do with Father Leary's death."

"Indirectly, ma'am, I'm sorry to say I do." Knowing this was all going to destroy her made him hate Jerzy Simonich a little. He turned back to the man behind the big desk. "That's the second element of *modus operandi* at work here. You used your leverage to get others to do your dirty work. We dug up the *Gazette* archives from 1973, looked at some court filings. You were on the verge of bankruptcy, but you had a plan. And an enemy. Robert Ziegler."

Jerzy Simonich raised his chin, his eyelids heavy as he glared at Donovan. And Lindsay Keller glared at Simonich.

"He was outspoken, and people were listening. You set up a scheme to lure him down that lonely stretch of highway out west. You got Tony to stage an accident that would kill Ziegler so you could buy up his land. It was your ticket out of trouble after your business nearly failed. His widow was left with nothing but four kids and a farm she couldn't run. She hated to sell—she knew her husband had been determined to draw the line against development and keep that stretch of the valley in agriculture. But when you came swooping in with loads of cash, what else could she do?"

"Robert Ziegler was a fool, tilting at windmills. Thinking he could stop progress."

"Thinking he could stop you. But you kept your distance. You sent Tony instead."

"My mistake, not realizing Tony wasn't smart enough to not get caught."

"Jerzy!" Barbara's voice rose. "You're not saying he's right, with this crazy talk of murder?"

"Classic case of two birds and one stone," Donovan said. "You silenced Ziegler and bought his land, and you ruined Tony and Mike. As Lindsay said, you knew Tony's wife had an affair, and you knew who with. You knew he was acknowledging a daughter who wasn't his, and that he would do anything to keep the secret."

"That was only part of it."

"Yes. The other part was your brother, Ed. That brings us back to Mike Leary, whom you never stopped blaming. You made Mike and Tony your prisoners." He turned to Barbara, her expression a mix of anger and confusion. "Mrs. Simonich, you might not want to hear this."

Her silver hair swung as she shook her head. "I'm not leaving this room until I understand exactly what happened."

"All right. That text—"

"I—I taught him to swim," Jerzy Simonich said, his voice burdened with guilt. "I taught all of them, and I showed them the perfect rock for jumping into the lake."

"Jerzy." Barbara leaned forward, stretching out a hand. "It wasn't your fault. Ed's death wasn't your fault."

Donovan glanced at Lindsay Keller, following the conversation intently. She did not appear surprised.

"It was," Jerzy said. "They were playing a game I'd taught them. Throwing objects into the lake and diving for them. Tying each other's hands or feet, so they had to escape underwater."

A fact the Carbon County sheriff had never disclosed to anyone but the family, who had a copy of the full report. Jerzy's guilt was as strong a driver as his anger at the other two boys.

Donovan picked up the shadow box, the box that held Ed's St. Christopher medal. Jerzy had made a point, when they talked at the mall, about not being confirmed in the Catholic Church. That he was Orthodox. To keep Donovan from connecting him to Leary? But Tony W had told him that Ed had converted and been confirmed with his buddies, and the three boys had all gotten medals for confirmation. That explained the one in Leary's wallet, and why he had given young Ginger a medal, too.

"The text I just got was from my lieutenant," he said. "She and a team have taken your son into custody. He'll be charged later today with kidnapping and deliberate homicide in the death of Father Michael Leary."

"No!" Jerzy and Barbara spoke at once. Lindsay looked shocked but said nothing.

After a long, long moment, Jerzy spoke. "I killed Mike. Andy had nothing to do with it."

Donovan leaned against a bookcase, resting his elbow on a shelf. "Walk me through it."

"It was easy." Simonich raised one shoulder. "Mike was a sucker for late-night calls. Made him feel wanted. So when I called, he came."

He was shooting in the dark. He didn't know the caller had been a woman. "Go on."

"I met him at a gas station out in the Heights. We drove north into the scrub off the Roundup Road, in his car. I shot him and I dumped the body. Rolled him off the edge of the rocks into a gully. Then I stashed the car. Hiked back to my truck. I was quite fit in those days."

That much anyone could have pieced together from the newspaper stories.

"How'd you know where to stash the car?"

"I'd been looking at some property out there for a golf course, and I remembered that hay shed. I figured I'd get the car moved before the snow fell, but we had an early storm and the rancher needed the hay."

Half plausible, but the research team had found the real link. "You shoot him in his car or where you left him?"

Donovan watched the other man weigh the odds of one answer or the other.

"Don't remember," Simonich finally said. "After all this time."

"How'd you get him from the car to the rocks?"

Simonich raised his head, fear in his eyes. Donovan had his answer. The man did not know another detail never reported, a detail not learned until the body was found nineteen years later: that the priest's hands had been bound with baling wire, likely from a roll found in the shed where his car was hidden.

"Nice try, Jerzy. After all these years of manipulating your son, you finally give him a break and try to take the blame for the murder he committed."

Barbara let out a soft cry.

Lindsay was right about Jerzy Simonich threatening Mike Leary in the church vestibule way back in 1981. When two girls misunderstood what they heard and saw. The priest had understood, and so had Irene Danich.

But neither she nor the West sisters had given any thought to the other man, the younger man.

"Andy knew the whole story, didn't he? He'd read the file you have on Ed's death. He was there, in the church vestibule. He knew you needed to stop Mike from testifying at Tony's parole hearing, and why. Pretty sad, thinking he could kill his way back into your good graces."

That was the last question he would get to ask the old man today. Years of granite-hard anger eroded and gave way as Jerzy Simonich's shoulders drooped, and his big white head bowed.

* * *

"I should be furious with you, Detective, for springing all that on me at the Simonich house this morning," Lindsay Keller said. They were standing in the reception area of her office. No sign of her secretary, Carla, so Donovan doubted there was much chance of the cup of coffee he desperately wanted. "But I'm the one who insisted on staying."

"I wouldn't blame you," he replied. "I'd be angry, too."

The phone rang. "Figures," Lindsay said. "Carla takes a late lunch, and the phone goes crazy. Let me check this call." She stepped behind the reception desk and glanced at the machine. Read the caller ID and frowned.

"Why's she calling?" she muttered, then raised her head and gestured toward her office. "Let's have a seat."

Like the woman herself, the space was warm and welcoming with its redbrick walls and wood floors, the original features of the historic building accented by modern touches. A world apart from Jerzy Simonich's study. No pretense here.

She slipped behind her well-worn oak desk. "Is Andy talking?"

"I'm hoping you can add a few details before we interview him."

"I still can't believe it. How the hell did Andy Simonich ever grow enough balls to kill someone? To protect his father. Because Mike Leary intended to blow the whistle at the parole hearing and reveal that Tony killed a man on Jerzy's behalf, even though Tony always refused to say so."

"You remember I told you that when Leary turned up missing, Small and his team searched his office at the rectory? They found an envelope from the parole board in the trash, but no letter."

"Right. They always send a letter, to victims, the family, and anyone who's requested notice. We know Leary got it, because he planned to testify. So where did it go?"

"I suspect Andy took it," he said, "along with Leary's appointment book, although how, I don't know."

"Ahh. I might know the answer. Jana told me they'd been seeing Father Leary for marital counseling right before he died. Andy must have seen the letter—maybe his father got one, too—and made up an excuse to get back in the office later. Forgot his coat, dropped his keys. Maybe Leary had written notes on it, for his own testimony."

"Good guess. Without that letter, Small and his team had no reason to suspect a link between the hearing and Leary's disappearance."

Lindsay put her elbows on the desk and cradled her face in her hands. "So Andy removed the threat to his father. Paying him back for helping him out the night Mary Ellen died."

"Although, of course, Jerzy was protecting himself as much as Andy when he got LeMoyne to doctor the original crash report."

"They replaced the original with a false report that put Mary Ellen in the driver's seat, and they really thought no one would ever find out?"

Ballsy, but it had worked. "No one did, from 1981 to now." If anyone ever glanced at the file again—and why would they?—they wouldn't have given the conclusions a second thought, unless they looked closely. How many other times had LeMoyne suppressed inconvenient evidence? They might never know.

Lindsay lowered her hands into prayer position, fingers touching her lips. "Did Leary know? About the false report."

"I was hoping you could tell me." Whether the knowledge came from the confessional or somewhere else, it would have been one more reason the priest had to die. Both father and son were the kind of men who viewed knowledge as power that could be used against them.

"No idea. Jerzy was a self-made man. He grew up with nothing and did everything to succeed."

"Still, pretty cold-blooded to order a hit to gain control of a piece of property." Not that he meant to play devil's advocate. Simonich was as guilty as the day is long.

She leaned back, arms wrapped across her chest. A family photo sat on the credenza behind her. "He went from a being a man who dug ditches and nearly lost his equipment in foreclosure to running a company that controls most of the major construction projects in the state, all because of his gamble on that mall."

A trail of violence, triggered by greed—for money, yes, but also for revenge. "You had something else you wanted to tell me, after you told us what you'd learned about Leary and Tina."

"Yes, but you were ahead of me there, too." Her lips curved, not quite a smile. "Or we were on the same track. It was about Ed Simonich. I always knew Mary Ellen had an uncle who died young, but nothing else. We saw his gravestone in the cemetery in Red Lodge."

Donovan nodded and she continued.

"I'd forgotten all about this until I saw the graves. Spring of senior year, Father Leary came into the bookstore in the mall where I worked. It was a few weeks before graduation, and I was a mess over Mary Ellen. He told me he understood because he'd lost a friend when he was a kid, and always blamed himself. He was talking about Ed."

"Ed goofing around with his buddies, Mike and Tony, who couldn't save him," Donovan confirmed. The drowning was why, when Jerzy arranged for Tony to kill Ziegler, he chose a mountain lake. That was another reason Donovan had known Jerzy hadn't killed Mike Leary. Up in the sagey lands that had been the Steneruds' pioneer homestead, there was not one drop of water.

"Oh gosh," she said. "Andy was there, in the mall. I walked up just as he was leaving. Father Leary said, 'You'll be in my prayers,' or something like that. Maybe he did know that Andy was driving when Mary Ellen was killed."

"Priests say that all the time."

"Not Father Leary. Not unless there was a good reason." She tightened her lips and shook her head. "I wonder, though. How much did Jerzy really blame the other boys, and how much was he blaming them to ease his own guilt, for teaching them the dare-and-dive game? Forcing Tony to drown another man, on purpose, cost him what he loved most—his family and his freedom. Making Father Leary pay was easier. Jerzy knew how he suffered for his betrayal of Tony. But when you came calling, Jerzy tried to protect Andy by taking the blame for Father Leary's murder. He must have been torn up inside—"

"You're giving the man credit for a conscience," Donovan interrupted. "He figured out years ago that Andy killed Leary, and he lived in fear that the truth would come out. Not for Andy. For himself. Because then it would all unravel."

"Oh, Andy," she said softly. "Poor, dumb Andy."

Donovan let the silence linger, as she reconciled what she knew now with what she'd long believed about her old friends. He heard the front door open, heard a woman's footsteps cross the small entry. Carla returning from lunch, no doubt. But they were almost done. He'd have to grab that cup of coffee on his way to the jail.

He'd thought he'd feel good, solving the coldest case in the county. But that had been pride and ego talking, eager to boost his cop cred. In the end, it was another sad case of bad choices and lives gone wrong. Like the parking garage asshole. Tony had said Donovan didn't know anything about his life. But he did. He knew the difference between him and the criminals he put away was not the opportunities they'd had, but the choices they made.

"One more thing," Donovan said when Lindsay raised her head and met his gaze. "I have good news, too. Prosecutor wasn't happy that you held back that photo, but they aren't going to do anything about it. Because you've been so instrumental in solving the case."

"*To thee we come, before thee we stand, sinful and sorrowful,*'" Lindsay said.

The words struck a distant bell in Donovan's memory.

"We had this PE teacher who made us say the Memorare before every class," Lindsay continued. "Like rote recitation would save us. I prefer to think that we can be compassionate and still seek justice."

"Jerzy gave himself away," Donovan said, "because he thought he knew all the details. But he didn't know about the baling wire on Leary's wrists or that the caller was a woman."

"Oh," Lindsay said, her voice thin and hollow. "Oh no. Carrie thought the Steneruds owned that house when she lived in it. My guess, Andy sold it years ago, when he and Jana were still married and he was managing the family property. Told her he got rid of everything, but he left those boxes. I can't say for sure, but it fits. The Steneruds never throw anything away. You open the rest of those crates, and I bet you'll find the letter and appointment book."

"We'll get right on it," Donovan replied. Maybe they could find the gun, too.

"You guessed, didn't you? That Jana made the call that summoned Father Leary," she said. "The shed where Father Leary's car was stashed, that was on her family's old homestead, wasn't it? Though I know they don't own that property anymore. We used to go out there, she and Mary Ellen and I. That's how Andy knew about it. The hooch shed."

He nodded. This was the part he hadn't wanted to tell her. "We picked Jana up a little while ago."

"Did Andy trick her? Lie to her? She must have found the wallet in his rig and figured out what happened."

The wallet again. The touch DNA test might prove who'd handled the wallet, but if he wanted to know the truth, he'd have to get Jana to talk.

"That's why she called me," Lindsay continued. "Right when you walked in. I figured she wanted me to represent Andy. But no."

"She wants you to represent her."

"Anything she did, she did for her husband. Her family. If she made the call to Father Leary, she honestly believed a woman was in need. When she found the evidence, she must have been horrified. But she is loyal to the core."

Oh, what people do, Donovan thought, *and tell themselves it's out of love.*

311

THURSDAY
March 10, 2016

Lindsay read the name on her electronic calendar, puzzled. Most of her clients were people she'd worked with before or referrals from other lawyers.

"Carla, my ten o'clock. Your note says, 'a family matter.' What's that about?"

"I told her you don't do family law, but she said no, it wasn't that. She was quite insistent."

Potential clients often balked at sharing details with a secretary. "Hmm. Okay." *Not my family,* she prayed. *Not more Haley stuff.*

An hour later, she heard the door open and a woman ask for her. Ten minutes early. She swept the documents she was working on into a file and headed to the reception area.

"Thank you. Coffee would be lovely, black, but I'll keep my coat," the woman replied to Carla's questions. She held out her hand to Lindsay. "I'm Paula Vaughn. So good to meet you."

"Lindsay Keller. My pleasure. Come on in."

Settled, Lindsay asked how she could be of help.

"It's hard to explain," Paula Vaughn said. Lindsay put her at about sixty, with a broad face and ash-blond hair cut short. Full-figured, in black pants and a gray tunic with a soft cowl neck, and a silver pin in the shape of a heart, engraved with the word "Mom." "I

BLIND FAITH

live in the West End, but my family has roots in Red Lodge, and I've been doing research at the Historical Society."

Lindsay nodded, encouraging her to go on.

"The archivist heard from one of the volunteers that you stopped in this week, asking about the Petrovich family." She paused, and Lindsay nodded again. "I'm a Vukovich by birth, but my great-grandmother was a Petrovich. I've been working on the family tree for ages, but I've never come across you or any Kellers. Unless that's a married name?" She didn't wait for Lindsay this time, instead rushing on. "I'd be so thrilled to meet another cousin, no matter how many times removed."

"It's not me, I'm afraid," Lindsay said, sorry to disappoint this eager, friendly woman. "You're looking for the women I was with. Their grandmother was a Petrovich."

Paula reached into her black tote, bringing out an iPad. "Can you tell me their names? I've got the tree right here. There aren't many of us."

"The grandmother was Irene," Lindsay said. "By chance was your family plagued by childhood illness or deaths?"

The woman's face told her the answer. Lindsay waited as Carla entered with two cups, then left, closing the door.

"This may sound intrusive," Lindsay said, leaning forward, "and I apologize, but are you familiar with the lung disease cystic fibrosis?"

Paula's hand flew to her chest. "How do you . . .?"

Lindsay explained Carrie's search, Paula's expression growing more serious. "My friend came here to find out if there were other relatives and a possible hereditary link. To learn anything that might help her grandson or give researchers another genetic line to study."

It turned out that Paula's older daughter suffered from the disease and, with aggressive treatment, was doing reasonably well. Her son had married a woman without the gene—they'd done all the testing—and their two children were healthy. Her younger daughter was twenty-five and single. "I don't know what she'll do," Paula said. "But I want her to have choices."

313

A lump the size of Yellowstone County swelled in Lindsay's throat.

What every parent wanted for their child. What she and Scott had been telling themselves they wanted for Haley. What Jerzy Simonich had taken from Andy.

Choices.

* * *

The street-front gallery, a block down Montana Avenue from her office, was already hopping when Lindsay arrived. Another project she'd help navigate through the legal minefield. Upstairs, tiny rooms had been opened up into art studios and affordable apartments. The first floor, once home to a junk shop, had the plank floors and high ceilings, the exposed brick and piping, of the classic edge-of-downtown rehab.

She glanced at her watch. Only a few minutes late. Everything had taken twice as long today, her brain working at half speed.

Color dominated the west wall, where Harry Koyama's massive oil portraits of Crow Indians hung next to Kevin Red Star's acrylics. Northern Cheyenne ledger art covered another wall, and on the last wall hung pieces by Native American art students. Student sculptures, pottery, and baskets filled the middle of the room. A giant Crow star quilt hung from a cross beam.

Scott stood with a group of former art faculty colleagues. He excused himself and hurried over. Kissed her cheek. "You look great, babe."

Ah, love, she thought. Still blind after all these years. "Thanks. Did Haley make it?"

"Lindsay, you're here!" Charlene Old Horn's beaded earrings brushed Lindsay's face as they embraced. "How *are* you? When I heard about Andy and Jana, I couldn't believe it."

For the last day and a half, disbelief had been Lindsay's refrain. She'd always suspected Jerzy Simonich of skirting the law, of bribing subs and attempting to buy influence, but this—using his anger and his hunger for revenge against Tony Woijowski and Mike Leary for the tragic but accidental death of his brother more than fifty years ago. Using his knowledge of the complicated web between Tony, Mike, and Tina to intimidate Tony into the worst kind of dirty work. Covering up his son's role in the accident that killed his daughter, her old friend. Sitting on his suspicions that his son had murdered Leary to keep it all quiet.

It was all beyond belief.

Sorting out the details would take weeks. She'd been interviewed at length this afternoon, managing to hold off the tears until she could hide in her office.

Despite Jerzy's last-ditch attempt to take the blame for Father Leary's murder, Andy had admitted that it was his doing. His alone, he'd insisted, and Lindsay prayed that proved true.

Because it was terrible enough to know that Jana had made the call to Father Leary for Andy and that later she'd found the priest's wallet and sacrament bag. Returned the bag to the church, where she felt it belonged. Her sense of order and propriety had kicked in, but nothing could keep her from suffering the past twenty years under the weight of her own suspicions, biting her tongue for the sake of Andy and their sons.

You couldn't make this stuff up.

No wonder Jana had been so rattled that day in the Rainbow when Lindsay tried to ask her about the little house.

"Our old friend," Charlene said, her voice trembling.

Could Lindsay still be a friend to Jana? Did she have that kind of mercy in her? She wasn't sure, not yet. She tucked her arm through Charlene's. "She's going to need friends more than ever. Now, let's drink in this gorgeous exhibit."

They were standing in front of a giant Red Star painting of dancers at the Crow Indian Fair when an arm slipped around her waist.

"Haley." She turned to her daughter, her funny, smart, amazing, talented daughter, and the last of the tensions between them melted away. She gripped Haley's hands and smiled at her black boots and tights, the maroon streak in her hair the same shade as her dress. "Cute. Very cute."

Scott handed her a glass of wine and beamed at them both. Lindsay took a sip, thinking about her own mother, whom she'd taken to see Barbara Simonich that morning. You try hard to avoid the mistakes your parents made, but you forget sometimes what they did right. She hoped her girls remembered what she did right.

Across the room, she spotted Brian Donovan, his arm around his wife. Some of the younger artists in the exhibit were her students. He had to be exhausted, but here he was.

As he'd walked her out of the interview room a few hours ago, she'd seen him rubbing the scar on his arm. He'd noticed. "I shot and killed a man in the line of duty," he'd said, "and got a permanent reminder of how fragile life is."

She'd looked him in the eye, unblinking. "Fragile, and resilient. You're a good cop, Brian Donovan. Let your scars remind you of that, too."

Now she turned back to her husband and daughter. "There's an opening on the parole board. I'm thinking about applying."

"Mom, really? Awesome." Haley flung her hands wide to indicate the reclaimed building, an ideal gathering spot. "But keep doing what you're doing, right?"

Oh, she would. There was more than one way to serve the community.

"You don't need to do that, babe," Scott said quietly. "You don't owe anyone any penance."

"I know. But maybe I owe it to myself."

And maybe, she thought as she watched her husband point out to their daughter how Red Star used color to create contrast between light and dark, that was the only debt that mattered.

FRIDAY
March 11, 2016

Friday was his turn to pick up the kids while his wife spent the day in her studio. Brian Donovan got to the grade school early but didn't pull into the pickup lane. Instead, he circled the block and parked across from St. Patrick's. Raised his eyes to the rose window and the two towers, one crowned with a steeple.

Church had failed his mother. Failed to protect her from his brute of a father, failed to protect her from beatings and disappointment, from growing old far too young. From the consequences of loving a man who didn't honor and cherish and protect those close to him, the way a man was supposed to.

When the law failed to hold someone accountable or, as in the case that led Lindsay Keller to give up her career as a prosecutor, when it held the wrong man accountable, people blamed "the system." Lost faith in the entire institution, from the cop on patrol to the chief of police. He got that. Institutions were supposed to serve and protect people. Rout out the corrupt and right the wrongs.

But people were human. They failed. They wanted what they couldn't have, like Mike Leary wanting Tina Danich, even while he wanted to serve God as a priest.

He, Brian Donovan, just wanted to be a good man. A good father, a good husband, a good cop. He wanted his kids to be happy and his wife to smile at him the way she'd smiled that day when they were sixteen and he'd first spotted her on a Boston sidewalk. He wanted the people of Billings to feel safer because he was on the job. He wanted the woman who'd fought off her attacker in a downtown parking garage to sleep easily. And he wanted his own nightmares, the ones where a dead man came after him, night after night, the blade of a knife glinting in the rain-spattered glow of a streetlight, to stop, once and for all.

You didn't always get what you wanted. As the life and death of Mike Leary made so painfully clear.

A sharp rap on the window interrupted his thoughts. He glanced up, then pushed the button to slide the window down.

"Waiting for me, Detective?" Father Coletta asked. "More questions?"

Oh, he had questions. Lord, did he have questions. Chief among them, whether this devoted servant of God, fresh from rehab, with the bushy brows and the kind eyes, could help him find the answers.

You never knew, as he always told the kids, unless you asked.

SATURDAY
March 12, 2016

The sisters were waiting as Lindsay pulled up in front of the Dude Rancher.

"We spent the afternoon with Paula Vaughn," Carrie said as she slid into the passenger seat. "We're I don't know what degree of cousins, but it's like we've always known each other."

Lindsay laid her hand on Carrie's. "I know the feeling."

The warmth of Carrie's smile said the feeling was mutual.

"She knows more about our family than we do. She's got binders full of medical and genealogical research," Ginger said from the back. "Her daughter has the same form of CF as Asher, though she didn't know about the clinical trial. Whether cystic fibrosis is what plagued the rest of the family, we don't know for sure, but it seems likely."

"It's probably why our grandparents were married six years before our mother was born," Carrie said. "They lost an infant and a toddler, though I doubt they knew why. The disease wasn't even identified until 1938. The death certificates were in Baba's box— thank goodness I brought it with me."

"Baba closed the door on the painful past," Ginger said, "but not completely, thank God."

"What a relief to find the family history that can help you," Lindsay said.

"More than I bargained for," Carrie replied, "but yes. And thank you for helping us."

Lindsay squeezed her hand. "Ginger, when are you headed to the Middle East?"

The sisters exchanged glances over the seat, and Ginger spoke. "I'm taking some time off. Tomorrow we're driving east to Miles City, then circling around to the other towns we lived in. We'll end up back in Red Lodge, to make arrangements to bury Baba next to Big Mike and Mom."

A road trip. Road trips were good for the soul. Maybe she and Haley could take one, to check out cooking schools. "She'd like that, I think," Lindsay said. "Carrie, are you going to go see your father?"

"I haven't decided yet. Donovan says he's actually kind of a nice guy. For a killer." Carrie arched her brows and rolled her eyes. "Now, what's all this mystery? Where are you taking us?"

"Patience, grasshopper." Lindsay put the car in gear and drove to the house on North 24th. Parked out front, not saying a peep. They sat for a long moment, the sisters stunned into silence, before Carrie squeezed Lindsay's hand and the three of them got out. Lindsay stayed on the sidewalk and watched the two sisters make their way to the front porch.

In the week or so since she'd seen the place, Trevor Morris and his crew had finished the roof and siding, removed the construction debris, and begun planting shrubs and laying sod.

And next to the front door, as she'd asked when she called him yesterday, he'd planted a rose.

A shadow passed overhead. Lindsay shaded her eyes with one hand and watched as a red-tailed hawk circled lazily in the sunlit blue sky. Cerulean, the color of promise.

NOTE TO READERS

Readers, it's a thrill to hear from you. Drop me a line at Leslie@LeslieBudewitz.com, connect with me on Facebook at LeslieBudewitzAuthor or LeslieBudewitz and Alicia Beckman, or join my seasonal mailing list for books news and more. (Sign up on my website, www.AliciaBeckman.com or www.LeslieBudewitz .com.) Reader reviews and recommendations are a big boost to authors; if you've enjoyed my books, please tell your friends, in person and online. A book is but marks on paper until you read these pages and make the story yours.

Thank you.

ACKNOWLEDGMENTS

During my senior year of high school in Billings, Montana, I gave a ride to a new girl, dropping her off at a motel on the edge of downtown, where she lived with her grandmother and her little sister. Days later, she was gone. Why and to where, I never knew. This story is one answer.

Although I grew up in Billings and attended its Catholic schools, the characters and events in this book spring wholly from my imagination. To my knowledge, nothing like this ever happened. But it could have. And I hope that's the scary part.

My deep appreciation to Linda and Katie Jacobson and the Pirtz family for allowing me to borrow the Rainbow Bar, run by the same family on Montana Avenue since 1935. And yes, it actually did get its start in bootlegging. What I've done with the place is absolutely not their fault. The Stenerud family is entirely my invention. Like Lindsay, I have fond memories of the Babcock Theater; as far as I know, it is in good hands. I worked in the mall as a teenager shortly after it opened, a few years before Lindsay's time, but the shenanigans surrounding its development are fictitious. Unfortunately, faulty hair analysis did result in at least two wrongful convictions in Montana, although I am not aware of any elected officials playing a role in its misuse.

ACKNOWLEDGMENTS

Forgive me a pair of geographic liberties: in reality, Black Otter Trail is east of the residential area where the Simoniches live. There is no longer a rectory next to St. Patrick's Co-Cathedral, but it made sense to the story to keep it there. The grade school was still in use in 2016, when the modern scenes occur; it has since been closed and replaced by the new consolidated Catholic grade school next to St. Thomas the Apostle Church in the West End, near Donovan's home on the street where I grew up.

Many friends gave me an assist and deserve my thanks: Sandra Schiavon for reading with an eye on our hometown. Mystery writer Angela Sanders for sharing her amazing knowledge of perfume and giving me a new sense of characterization. Bob Marsenich for recollections of a Serbian childhood in a Montana mining town, though not this one. Linden Berry and her visiting writer pals for their ears and encouragement, and lovely evenings on the deck overlooking the Swan River, sharing our work. Debbie Burke, for early brainstorming and later reading. Peter Lengsfelder, for not holding back. And the late Ramona DeFelice Long, for asking questions that made this story better in ways I never could have imagined.

Thanks to Don Maass, Lorin Oberweger, Brenda Windberg, and my classmates at the Breakout Novel Graduate Learning Retreat in April 2019 for pushing me to take what I thought was a finished manuscript to a deeper level.

My agent, John Talbot, worked hard to find this story a home. My editor, Terri Bischoff, championed this manuscript—and me—and for that I will always be grateful. Thanks to the art department at Crooked Lane Books for a stunning cover, and to the rest of the staff for their work bringing this story, which lived only in my head for so long, to the page and into your hands.

And as always, thanks to my husband, Don Beans, for medical advice and all the support a writer could ever hope for.